To Mum
wishing you a very happy
birthday,
love Susan
February 1989

Wave Me Goodbye

Stories of the Second World War

Wave Me Goodbye

Stories of the Second World War

EDITED BY

ANNE BOSTON

Published by VIRAGO PRESS Limited 1988
20-23 Mandela Street, Camden Town, London NW1 0HQ

Collection, Introduction and Notes copyright (c) Anne Boston 1988

British Library Cataloguing in Publication Data
Wave me goodbye : stories of the Second World War.
   1. Short stories in English. Women writers, 1900—. Special subjects.
   World War 2.
   Anthologies
   I. Boston, Anne
   823'.01'08358 [FS]
   ISBN 0-86068-838-0

Typeset by Burns & Smith, Derby.
Printed and bound in Great Britain by Billings and Sons Ltd,
Worcester.

Contents

Acknowledgements

MY THANKS are due first to Elizabeth Berridge and Reginald Moore who kindly let me consult their library of wartime periodicals, pointed the way to many authors and sources, and offered invaluable encouragement. I am also grateful to Nicola Beauman, and to Ian Hamilton, for their helpful suggestions; and to Bridget Fisher, librarian at the University of East Anglia, who managed to call up material from halfway round the world. My thanks go too to Richard Boston, Simon Caulkin, and Alexandra Pringle of Virago Press for their help and advice.

Permission to reproduce the following stories is gratefully acknowledged: 'When The Waters Came' by Rosamond Lehmann from *Penguin New Writing* edited by John Lehmann 1942, and from *The Gipsy's Baby*, first published by Collins 1946, reprinted by permission of The Society of Authors and Miss Rosamond Lehmann; 'Gas Masks' from *Mrs Miniver* by Jan Struther, published by Chatto & Windus 1939, copyright © Jan Struther 1939, reprinted by permission of Curtis Brown Ltd; 'I Was Too Ignorant' by Rosamond Oppersdorff from *New Writing and Daylight* Winter 1942–3 edited by John Lehmann, published by The Hogarth Press; 'Defeat' by Kay Boyle, from *Modern Reading 10* edited by Reginald Moore 1944, reprinted by permission of the Tessa Sayle Literary and Dramatic Agency on behalf of Kay Boyle; 'Goodbye, My Love' by Mollie Panter-Downes, reprinted by permission, © 1941, 1969 the *New Yorker* Magazine, Inc; 'Night in the Front Line' by Molly Lefebure from *Selected Writing II*, edited by Reginald Moore, copyright © Molly Lefebure 1942; 'Miss Anstruther's Letters' by Rose Macaulay, from *London Calling*, edited by Storm Jameson, Harper NY 1942, reprinted by permission of A. D. Peters & Co Ltd; 'Face of My People' by Anna Kavan from *Horizon* 1944, edited by Cyril Connolly, and from *I am Lazarus* by Anna Kavan, published by Peter Owen, London, copyright © Anna Kavan 1945, 1978; 'A Journey' from *Growing Up* by Olivia Manning, published by Heinemann 1948, reprinted by permission of David Higham Associates Ltd; 'Goodbye Balkan Capital' from *Civil to Strangers* by Barbara Pym, published by Macmillan, London and Basingstoke 1988, copyright © Hilary Walton 1988, reprinted by permission of Hilary Walton and Macmillan; 'I Spy a Stranger' by Jean Rhys, from *Penguin Modern Stories I* 1969, reprinted by permission of André Deutsch Ltd; 'Grandma Isn't Playing' from *One Basket* by Edna Ferber, published by Simon & Schuster 1947; 'The Lovely Leave' by Dorothy Parker 1943, from *The Collected Dorothy Parker*, 1973, published by Gerald Duckworth, reprinted by permission of Gerald Duckworth & Co Ltd; 'Mysterious Kôr' from *The Demon Lover* by Elizabeth Bowen, published by Jonathan Cape Ltd 1945, reprinted by permission of the Estate of Elizabeth Bowen; 'Night Engagement' by Margery Sharp from *Lilliput* magazine 1941, reprinted by permission of A. D. Peters & Co Ltd; 'The Bomb' by Pat Frank from *The Strand Magazine* January 1941; 'Sweethearts and Wives' and 'Poor Mary' from *The Museum of Cheats* by Sylvia Townsend Warner, published by Chatto & Windus 1947, reprinted by permission of the Estate of the author and Chatto & Windus; 'The Land Girl' by Diana Gardner from *Horizon* 1940, edited by Cyril Connolly, copyright © Diana Gardner 1940; 'The Sailor's Wife' by Ann Chadwick from *English Story, 6th Series*, edited by Woodrow Wyatt, published by Collins 1945; 'Sunday at Home' from *Me Again* by Stevie Smith, published by Virago Press Ltd 1981, copyright © James MacGibbon 1950; 'The Black Madonna' from *Winter's Tales* by Doris Lessing, published by Macmillan Ltd, copyright © 1957 Doris Lessing reprinted by permission of Jonathan Clowes Ltd, London, on behalf of Doris Lessing; 'The Iconoclasts' from *Innocents* by A. L. Barker, published by The Hogarth Press 1947, copyright © 1947 A. L. Barker, reprinted by permission of the author; 'The Mandoline' from *The Crystal Fountain and Other Stories* by Malachi Whitaker, published by Carcanet Press Ltd 1983; 'According to the Directive' by Inez Holden from *Cornhill Magazine* vol 163, 1947-49; 'Bread and Butter Smith' from *Mum and Mr Armitage* by Beryl Bainbridge, published by Gerald Duckworth 1985, reprinted by permission of Gerald Duckworth & Co Ltd; 'The Maiden' by Jean Stafford from the *New Yorker* 1950 and from *The Collected Stories* published by The Hogarth Press/Chatto & Windus Ltd 1986, copyright © 1950, 1978 by Jean Stafford, reprinted by permission of Russell & Volkening as agents for the author and Chatto & Windus; 'Gravement Endommagé' from *Hester Lilly and Other Stories* by Elizabeth Taylor, published by Peter Davies 1954, reprinted by permission of Virago Press Ltd.

Every effort has been made to trace copyright holders in all copyright material in this book. The editor regrets if there has been any oversight and suggests the publisher is contacted in any such event.

I was guided by two principles in making the selection – principles which weren't always compatible, as it turned out: first, the story's literary qualities, and second, its historical interest. The best short-story writing, of course, is much more than the proverbial 'slice of life'; what turns it into art is the imaginative tension between surface, exterior events and the silent reality beneath; the dramatic insight implicit in the descriptive truth. At the same time, everyday human experience in wartime could be so extraordinary that it hardly needed to be embellished in fiction. Much of the writing was close to the rawness of journalism, and realism was often the most appropriate medium; it suited the urgency of the time. On a purely descriptive level I wanted the stories to cover as many aspects of 'the people's war' as possible. On those grounds, authenticity is given precedence over polished prose, and if a graphic semi-documentary sketch seemed a more truthful response than a highly crafted 'literary' exercise, or added a different aspect to the range of experience, I chose it. Nonetheless I also looked for the widest variety of structure and approach: surreal interior accounts of fantasy and breakdown, popular romance, a black fable against war, a propaganda story written to commission – all have a place. The qualifying factor was that each story had to offer a particularly vivid glimpse into the special circumstances of wartime; not only physical conditions, but above all the territory of feelings, emotions and attitudes.

The fact that this collection could include so many of the finest women writers of their generation – among them several who had rarely, until then, used the short-story form – is itself a by-product of war. Short stories enjoyed an unexpected burst of popularity in wartime, when ordinary life was subject to constant interruption and time was at a premium. Most writers – like everyone else – were involved in war work of some kind, and the extended concentration novelists needed for creating full-length fiction was hard to come by. There were, also, overwhelming difficulties in encompassing events that were too huge and too close to bring into focus: as Elizabeth Bowen wrote, 'These years rebuff the imagination as much by being fragmentary as by being violent.' Short stories and poetry, with their snap-shot immediacy, could capture a single incident in dramatic close-up – Rose Macaulay's 'Miss Anstruther's Letters' is an outstanding example of the wartime story's effectiveness in the hands of a novelist who rarely strayed into the genre.

At the same time, there was a growing audience. In the early stages of the 'phoney war' cinemas and theatres were closed, and with blackout enforcement and the disruption of normal social life people read more, and far more widely, than before. A collection of stories offered instant variety and could be read in short bursts in the endless waiting for All-Clear sirens, on long journeys or stuck in remote parts of the countryside. The lending libraries did record business, Forces libraries were set up for the armed services, and paperbacks and periodicals were in unprecedented demand.

Because of the paper shortage, new magazines were prohibited from May 1940. But the ban did not apply to new publishing companies; some two hundred were set up in 1940 alone, producing dozens of 'little magazines', disguised in the form of anthologies of poems and prose. Paperback series like *Penguin New Writing*, edited by John Lehmann, and the indefatigable Reginald Moore's *Modern Reading, Selected Writing*, and *Bugle Blast* (for the Forces), opened their pages to unknown and amateur writers along with the famous and established. Fiction in the women's magazines tended to follow the convention of romance backed up by a patriotic message, though there were exceptions – the stories and serials in *Woman's Journal*, for instance, contained hardly a single reference to the war throughout 'the duration'. (Fiction from women's magazines didn't survive the final selection process for this anthology, though I kept one romance, Pat Frank's 'five-minute story' 'The Bomb' from *The Strand Magazine*.)

I turned eagerly to *Horizon*, the leading wartime literary journal (and a familiar presence on the family bookshelves) as the first source for this anthology, only to be rebuffed by its editor Cyril Connolly's celebrated denunciation of 'experiences connected with the Blitz, the shopping queues, the home front, deserted wives, deceived husbands, broken homes, dull jobs, bad schools, group squabbles ...' as too close to ordinary life to be worth recording. Apart from revealing Connolly's disenchantment with his own civilian circumstances, his statement shows how easy it was (and is) to dismiss at a stroke virtually every aspect of women's lives as subjects worth writing about, especially the domestic and personal areas where women writers tended to excel. Not surprisingly the two stories from *Horizon* included here – Diana Gardner's land girl disrupting a household like a cuckoo in the nest, and Anna Kavan's powerful impressionistic study of psychological war damage – are each, in different ways, an antithesis of conventional 'women's' themes.

War, of course, had always been a masculine occupation, and from the first line of the *Aeneid* – 'Arms and the man I sing' – to Hemingway's *Men Without Women*, war fiction has been about men in uniform, men in action. The fine anthology edited by Dan Davin, *Short Stories from the Second World War*, is part of this tradition; all but four of the stories are by servicemen like himself, describing the terror, boredom, muddle and exhilaration of the battlefield. Men were brought up to be part of the ritual of war, and some writers accepted it almost as a need: F. J. Salfeld's story 'Fear of Death' begins 'Why did I want to join the Navy and fight? Mostly I wished to test the unknown in myself.'

But even in countries which escaped invasion women were very much participants in this war, and they too deserve a hearing. Total war was a great equaliser: children, the old, and both sexes now took the brunt of slaughter and devastation along with the young men. It's salutary to remember that more British civilians than servicemen lost their lives by enemy action during the first three of its six years. At least now there was none of the terrible ignorance that had divided those at home from the men who fought in the Great War. Even so, despite the shared experience, war writing was still seen as the province of the serviceman: as the poet Keith Douglas put it, 'Whatever changes in the nature of warfare, the battlefield is the simple, central stage of the war; it is there that the interesting things happen.' The only woman represented in Dan Davin's anthology, Elizabeth Bowen, saw her war writing as outside the main tradition; in a postscript to her brilliant wartime collection *The Demon Lover* she distinguishes between *war* stories and *wartime* ones like her own, which 'are, more, studies of climate, war-climate, and of the strange growths it raised'. Her distinction equally applies to most of the stories in this anthology; the war is their environment, if not always their subject. Rosamond Lehmann's 'When the Waters Came' isn't ostensibly 'about' the war at all, yet it hangs like a darkening cloud over this subtle, sensitive account of a child saved from drowning, the violent thaw after the first grim winter bringing not relief but more omens of disaster. In Elizabeth Taylor's 'Gravement Endommagé' the hostilities are over, but the after-effects are felt everywhere, in a marriage mortally damaged by long separation and in the shattered French landscapes the couple are driving through: 'Grass grew over grief, trying to hide collapse, to cover some of the wounds.'

The experience of war was as individual as it was universal, and one dubious advantage for writers was that its 'strange growths' produced any amount of narrative material. So we see an American bystander thrown into nursing injured and dying troops on the Front Line in France, a journalist caught up in the panic as Axis troops move into central Europe; women making bombs, practising air-raid drill, buried by rubble in the Blitz – and saying heartwrenching goodbyes, bringing up children alone, coming to terms with a husband who has turned into a stranger. That said, the stories are no more restricted to 'women's subjects', if they can be labelled as such, than they are to female protagonists: see Doris Lessing's savage impression of neo-Fascism in colonial Africa, the A. L. Barker story of a boy destroyed by his desire to be a war hero, the refugee Kling tortured by memories in Anna Kavan's 'Face of My People'; while at least half a dozen more are seen through the eyes of a male character.

As diverse as they are, almost without exception these stories are concerned with the personal and the particular – which may be more to do with the short story's general dictates than with the fact that they are by women. It's arguable, though, that writing turned more to introspection in wartime, when every aspect of personal life and self-expression was under attack. Given the grossly depersonalising effects of violence and deprivation, fiction was a place of retreat to individual feelings and emotions – conserving, as V. S. Pritchett wrote, 'the human fragments in an iron age when human lives, what I feel and you feel, are considered to be shameful'.

Men who enlisted exchanged the peacetime world of work and family for other loyalties; for most women war meant going on as before, but with all the bulwarks of security that were normally taken for granted removed. No wonder so many of the stories remain stubbornly rooted in the domestic and personal – surrounded by destruction, women had the job of preserving life, of making do, keeping a brave face in front of the children. The absurd discrepancy between their attempts to hold on to ordinary existence while expecting the worst, gas attack and invasion included, is especially strong in the early 'phoney war' stories by

Rosamond Lehmann, Jan Struther and Mollie Panter-Downes. 'One had to laugh', says Mrs Miniver, and the contrast between everyday trivia and catastrophic events elsewhere is a recurring theme. Barbara Pym characteristically makes a poignant comedy out of non-events with faded, sweet-faced Laura dreaming of faraway drama, hemmed in all her life by disapproving relations and now by 'all the rather ludicrous goings-on of a country town that sees nothing of the war'. And Sylvia Townsend Warner has an unerring eye for the oddities and anomalies of hidden lives away from the 'central stage'. I included two of her stories, and was tempted to use more from a whole gallery of wartime character and incident, often wickedly funny and always alive with social insight and humane perception. (Other writers – notably Elizabeth Bowen and Rosamond Lehmann – equally deserve to be represented by more than one story; but space was short, and the consideration that Sylvia Townsend Warner's work is less widely read and less often included in anthologies was among my justifications for making her the exception.)

In the Blitz stories, any semblance of normality is lost and the writing becomes part of the process of intense struggle to stay whole as a person as a matter of survival. Rose Macaulay's story goes straight into the full shock of despair as the inhuman violence of an air raid destroys a woman's home, and in doing so dislodges all her pent-up anguish at the death of her lover. Her past reduced to ashes, she loses even the few pathetic possessions she has salvaged to looters and demolition men, deepening the horror. Under surreal conditions of danger and deprivation, Elizabeth Bowen's characters are dislocated from reality, creating their own worlds in visions of hallucinatory strength. The girl and her lover in 'Mysterious Kôr' have nowhere to stay together for the night; there is, too, the impossible strain of trying to stay detached from the person you love, for fear of what might happen to them. 'Think about people? How can anyone think about people if they've got any heart?' she bursts out. Denied even this emotional anchor, she retreats defiantly into fantasy: 'This war shows we've by no means come to the end. If you can blow whole places out of existence, you can blow whole places into it.' Dreaming, she passes into the 'wide, void, pure streets' of her imaginary city, Kôr.

Cut off from the future and the past, characters escape inward into themselves – sometimes, when conditions become unbearable, into madness. The nightmarish 'I Spy a Stranger' by Jean Rhys, like Anna Kavan's 'Face of My People', shows how the already insecure and alienated could be driven literally out of their minds by the conspiratorial, xenophobic war-climate. 'Inhuman', 'depersonalised', 'the impersonal machine' are the recurring language of paranoia in these two frighteningly convincing accounts of breakdown; they also accurately describe a society implacably geared to war.

The Anna Kavan and Jean Rhys stories express the profoundest alienation from the whole business of war, whatever the cause. To some extent this isolation was common to civilian writers and the 'intelligentsia' of either sex who held to any sort of independent critical stance; there was also a strong pacifist movement before and in the early stages of the war. But for women, brought up outside the masculine war tradition, the alienation could be doubly felt, and much of these writers' bitterest criticism is directed not at the enemy abroad, but at the disembodied system which makes conflagration part of accepted policy. Behind Stevie Smith's unquenchably spirited picture of two women friends crying companionably into their cocoa over 'the evil, and the cruelty, and the scientific use of force, and the evil' while the 'doodle bombs' sail down outside, is an eloquent sub-text of the connections between male chauvinism, religion, science and war. 'The Iconoclasts' by A. L. Barker leaves a horribly memorable after-image of the way war feeds on myths, breeding violence into generations to come.

Only twenty years after the chauvinistic excesses of the First World War, the British exercised a good deal more caution about flag-waving in the second. Initial reluctance to accept its inevitability gave way to general agreement that this one was a necessary evil: Hitler had to be stopped, somehow. But acceptance didn't necessarily mean approval, and the stories by British writers in particular shy away from false heroics; their overriding tone is of scepticism, lack of illusion, the determination to register things honestly and faithfully. Even the frankly patriotic 'Mrs Miniver' stories are careful to avoid the 'licensed lunacy, of boycotting Grimm and Struwwelpeter ... to guard against that was the most important of all the forms of war work which she and other women would have to do.' The Hollywood screen version of *Mrs Miniver* was said to have helped galvanise American public opinion into joining the war – Churchill told Parliament it was worth a flotilla of battleships – but as Mollie Panter-Downes reported with typical understatement in the *New Yorker*, its rampant sentimentality made British audiences 'a trifle warm under the collar'. Ruth, the protagonist in her own story 'Goodbye, My Love', embodies the quintessential mixture of resignation, unspoken patriotism and quiet despair that seems to stand for British Everywoman in wartime.

By the time the Japanese attack on Pearl Harbour had brought in the United States, the British were exhausted by three gruelling years which on the Home Front alone had taken in near-defeat at Dunkirk, the air Battle of Britain and the recurring fury of the Blitz. Beside the self-deprecating irony of the British writing, the American stories by Edna Ferber and Dorothy Parker are full of vitality and conviction. It's doubtful whether any writer this side of the Atlantic could have carried off Edna Ferber's propaganda commission 'Grandma Isn't Playing', written to boost women's part in the war effort, with such bold and sympathetic credibility.

The Edna Ferber story is relatively unusual in making women at work its subject, which might seem surprising at a time when an army of Rosie the Riveters on both sides of the Atlantic found a new independence in war work of all kinds. This could be partly due to an inevitable class bias in these stories; writing was still essentially a middle-class occupation, whatever the democratising effects of the war. Another notable exception is Pat Frank's 'The Bomb', which I included for its fascinating mixture of bomb-making technology with the language of formula romance; conventional 'femininity' still struggling for supremacy in a brave new world of overalls and high explosives. A girl and her boyfriend are almost killed by a German bomb aimed at the munitions factory where she works. Waiting for it to explode, she wonders 'whether the enemy also used liquid oxygen and lignite and carbon. How delicately one must handle it! Woman's work. It took a woman's gentle hands...' Her triumphant conclusion is that their salvation lay in the power (and incompetence) of love.

For the most part, though, women's work surfaces only in asides, incidental to the overriding priorities of interior life and personal allegiances. The war changes everything and nothing; women (when they are honest enough to admit it) still feel left behind, left out while their men go off to the world of 'telegrams

and anger'. Dorothy Parker's irrepressible young wife in 'The
Lovely Leave', who breaks all the rules of stiff-upper-lip decorum
on her husband's brief homecoming, must have expressed the
frustration of thousands of women when she erupts with her own.
First she embarrasses him by being emotional, then she openly,
unforgiveably admits to feeling jealous of his new army loyalties.
'You see,' she said with care, 'you have a whole new life – I have
half an old one. Your life is so far from mine, I don't see how
they're ever going to come back together.'

Like Dorothy Parker, Sylvia Townsend Warner deals deceptively lightly with the chasms of incomprehension between men and
women separated sometimes for years on end. In 'Sweethearts and
Wives', William, coming home on leave from the Navy to a
ramshackle cottage full of women and messy domesticity, can't
help reflecting that 'children on a destroyer would be kept in better
order and cleaned at regular intervals'. The second of her stories,
'Poor Mary', turns the husband-on-leave convention on its head
with a rueful encounter between a conscientious objector husband,
working on the land, visited by his wife, grown plump and military
after four years in the ATS; their wartime marriage, incongruous
from the start, is now more improbable than ever. The role reversal
is completed by Mary's thwarted longing for a heroic martial
destiny, a neat comment on the limitations of women's aspirations
at the time.

'Poor Mary', like the stories from the post-war years, is full of
misunderstandings and doubts and ambiguities, as if the war had
drained the world of certainty or happy endings. The impeccably
constructed story by Jean Stafford, set in post-war Heidelberg,
quietly exposes the barbarism of the victorious New World beside
the monstrous refinements of the Old. Beryl Bainbridge's narrator
has lined his pockets from the war, in 'a good line of business to be
in if you didn't mind being called a racketeer, which I didn't'. The
world is made shabbier, diminished by destruction. Elizabeth
Taylor allows just a hint of hope to her couple contemplating their
wrecked marriage in a battle-ruined French town: 'Oh, from the
most unpromising material, he thought, but he did seem to see
some glimmer ahead, if only of his own patience, his own
perseverance, which appeared in this frame of mind, in this place,
a small demand upon him.'

Elizabeth Bowen suggested that 'all wartime writing is ... resistance writing': interior life putting up its own resistance to the annihilating effects of war. In her own stories, her soaring imagination found its defence in 'resistance fantasies' against the pressures of reality. For other writers, that resistance meant simply registering events as honestly and directly as possible, without embellishing them with sentiment or melodrama or mock heroics. Self-expression could be an act of personal defiance against the weight of a world that seemed to be disintegrating; humour and irony, sympathy and rage continued to assert themselves in the battle for sanity and survival. Comic, stoical, compassionate, angry, subversive, these intensely individual voices bring a human proportion to the outsize events that reverberated round them; they speak for no one but themselves, yet each opens a window on to a hidden landscape of war.

Anne Boston

ROSAMOND LEHMANN

When the Waters Came

VERY long ago, during the first winter of the present war, it was still possible to preserve enough disbelief in the necessity for disaster to waver on with only a few minor additions and subtractions in the old way. The first quota of evacuated children had meant a tough problem for the local ladies; but most of them, including her own, had gone back to London. Nothing very disturbing was likely to happen for the present. One thought, of course, of sailors freezing in unimaginable wastes of water, perhaps to be plunged beneath them between one violent moment and the next; of soldiers numb in the black-and-white nights on sentry duty, crammed, fireless, uncomforted on the floors of empty barns and disused warehouses. In her soft bed, she thought of them with pity – masses of young men, betrayed, helpless, and so much colder, more uncomfortable than human beings should be. But they remained unreal, as objects of pity frequently remain. The war sprawled everywhere inert: like a child too big to get born it would die in the womb and be shovelled underground, disgracefully, as monsters are, and after a while, with returning health and a change of scene, we would forget that we conceived it. Lovers went on looking on the bright side, stitching cosy linings, hopeful of saving and fattening all the private promises. The persisting cold, the catastrophes of British plumbing, took precedence of the war as everybody's topic and experience. It became the political situation. Much worse for the Germans, of course. Transport had broken down, there was no coal in Berlin. They'd crack – quite likely – morale being so low already.

The climax came one morning when the wind changed, the grey sky let out rain instead of snow. Then, within an hour, the wind veered round again to the north, the rain froze as it fell. When she went into the kitchen to order the day's meals, the first of the aesthetic phenomena greeted her. The basket of vegetables had come in folded in a crust of ice. Sprouts, each crinkled knob of green brilliance cased in a clear bell, looked like tiny Victorian paperweights.

The gardener scratched his head.

'Never seen nothink like it in fifty years, Better be careful walking out, 'M. There'll be some broken legs on the 'ill. It's a skating rink. I slipped up a matter of five times coming along. Young Bert's still trying to get up to the sheep at the top. He ain't done it yet.' He chuckled. 'It's a proper pantomime. The old Tabbies'll have to mind their dignities if they steps out today.'

The children ran in with handfuls of things from the garden. Every natural object had become a toy: twigs, stones, blades of grass cased in tubes of ice. They broke up the mounds, and inside were the smooth grooved prints of stems and leaves: a miracle.

Later she put on nailed shoes and walked with difficulty over the snowy field path to the post office. The wind was a steel attack; sharp knobs of ice came whirling off the elms and struck her in the face. She listened by what was once a bush of dogwood, now a glittering sheaf of long ice pipes that jangled and clashed together, giving out a musical ring, hollow, like a ghostly xylophone.

At the post office, the customary group of villagers was gathered, discussing the portents, their slow, toneless, deprecating voices made almost lively by shocked excitement. The sheep in the top field had been found frozen to the ground. Old Mrs Luke had slipped up on her doorstep and broken her thigh. The ambulance sent to take her to hospital had gone backwards into the ditch and overturned. Pigeons were stuck dead by their claws on branches. The peacock at the farm had been brought in sheathed totally in ice: that was the most impressive item.

'I *wish* I'd seen it!'

Stiff in its crystal case, with a gemmed crest, and all the blue iridescence gleaming through: a device for the birthday of the Empress of China.

That night was the end of the world. She heard the branches in the garden snapping and crashing down with a brittle rasp. It seemed as if the inside of the earth with all its roots and foundations had become separated from the outside by an impenetrable bed of iron; so that everything that grew above the surface must inevitably break off like matchwood, crumble and fall down.

Towards dawn the wind dropped and snow began to fall again.

The thaw came in February, not gradually but with violence, overnight. Torrents of brown snow-water poured down from the hills into the valley. By the afternoon, the village street was gone, and in its stead a turbulent flood raced between the cottages. The farm was almost beleagured: water ran through the back door, out the front door. The ducks were cruising under the apple trees in the orchard. Springs bubbled up in the banks and ditches, gushed out among roots and ivy. Wherever you looked, living waters spouted, trickled, leaped with intricate overlapping voices into the dance. Such sound and movement on every hand after so many weeks of silence and paralysis made you feel light-headed, dizzy, as if you, too, must be swept off and dissolved.

'Oh, children! We shall never see the village looking like this again.'

She stood with them at the lower garden gate, by the edge of the main stream. There was nobody in sight.

'Why not?' said John, poking with the toe of his Wellington at the fringe of drifted rubbish. 'We might see it next year. No reason why not if we get the same amount of snow.'

Where were all the other children? Gathered by parents indoors for fear of the water? The cottages looked dumb.

'It's like a village in a fairy story.'

'Is it?' said Jane, colouring deeply. 'Yes, it is.' She looked around, near and far. 'Is it safe?'

'Of course it's safe, mutt,' said her brother, wading in. 'Unless you want to lie down in the middle of it and get drowned.'

'Has anything got drowned, Mummy?'

'No. The cows and horses are all safe indoors. Only all the old dead winter sticks and leaves are going away. Look at them whirling past.'

The water ran so fast and feverish, carrying winter away. The earth off the ploughed fields made a reddish stain in it, like blood, and stalks of last year's dead corn were mixed and tumbled in it. She remembered *The Golden Bough*, the legend of Adonis, from whose blood the spring should blossom; the women carrying pots of dead wheat and barley to the water, flinging them in with his images. Sowing the spring.

The children ran along the top of the bank, following the stream, pulling sticks from the hedge and setting them to sail.

'Let's race them!'

But they were lost almost at once.

'Mummy, will they go to the sea?'

'Perhaps. In time.'

Jane missed her footing and slithered down into the ditch, clutching at John, pulling him after her.

'It's quite safe!' he yelled. 'It only comes half-way up her boots. Can't we wade to the cross-roads and see what happens?'

'Well, be terribly careful. It may get deep suddenly. The gravel must be washing away. Hold her hand.'

She watched them begin to wade slowly down away from her, chattering, laughing to feel the push and pull of the current at their legs.

'It's *icy*, Mummy! It's lovely. Bend down and feel it.'

Moving farther away, they loosed hands and wandered in opposite directions, gathering up the piles of yellow foam-whip airily toppling and bouncing against every obstruction. She saw Jane rub her face in a great handful of it.

Oh, they're beginning to look very far away, with water all round them. It can't be dangerous, I mustn't shout. They were tiny, and separated.

'Stay together!'

She began to run along the bank, seeing what would happen; or causing it to happen. It did happen, a moment before she got there. Jane, rushing forward to seize a branch, went down. Perfectly silent, her astonished face framed in its scarlet bonnet fixed on her brother, her Wellingtons waterlogged, she started to sink, to sway and turn with the current and be carried away.

'How could you ... John, why didn't you? ... No, it wasn't your fault. It was mine. It wasn't anybody's fault. It's all right, Jane! What a joke! Look, I'll wrap you in my fleecy coat, like a little sheep. I'll carry you. We'll hurry home over the field. We'll be in hot baths in ten minutes. I'm wet to my knees, I've got ice stockings – and all of Jane is wet. How much of John is wet?'

'None of me, of course,' said John, pale and bitter. 'Have *I* got to have a bath?'

An adventure, not a disaster, she told herself unhopefully,

stumbling and splashing up towards the garden over the ploughed field, weighed into the earth with the weight of the child, and of her ever more enormous clogged mud-shoes that almost would not move; and with the weight of her own guilt and Jane's and John's, struggling together without words in lugubrious triangular reproach and anxiety.

But by the end of the day it was all right. Disaster had vanished into the boothole with the appalling lumps of mud, into the clothes-basket with sopping bloomers and stockings, down the plug with the last of the mustard-clouded bath water. Jane lay wrapped in blankets by the nursery fire, unchilled, serene and rosy. John toasted the bread and put on his two yodelling records for a celebration. Adventure recollected in tranquillity made them all feel cheerful.

'I thought I was done for that time,' said Jane complacently.

'It'll take more than that to finish you – worse luck,' said John, without venom. 'We haven't had a moment's peace, any of us, since you were born. Tomorrow I'm going to make a raft and see how far I can get.'

'I'm afraid by tomorrow it'll all be dry land again.'

She looked out of the window and saw that the water in the fields had almost disappeared already. After countless white weeks, the landscape lay exposed again in tender greens and browns, caressing the eye, the imagination, with a promise of mysterious blessing. The air was luminous, soft as milk, blooming in the west with pigeon's breast colours. In the garden the last of the snow lay over flower-beds in greyish wreathes and patches. The snowman stood up at the edge of the lawn, a bit crumpled but solid still, smoking his pipe.

What will the spring bring? Shall we be saved?

'But you were wrong about one thing, Mummy,' said Jane, from the sofa. 'You know what you said about ... you know.'

'About what?'

'Go on. Cough it up.'

'About nothing being ... you know,' said Jane with an effort. 'Drowned.'

'Oh dear, was I wrong?'

'Yes, you were wrong. I sor a chicking. At least, I think so.'

JAN STRUTHER

Gas Masks

CLEM had to go and get his gas mask early, on his way to the office, but the rest of them went at half past one, hoping that the lunch hour would be less crowded. It may have been: but even so there was a longish queue. They were quite a large party – Mrs Miniver and Nannie; Judy and Toby; Mrs Adie, the Scots cook, lean as a winter aspen, and Gladys, the new house-parlourmaid: a pretty girl, with complicated hair. Six of them – or seven if you counted Toby's Teddy bear, which seldom left his side, and certainly not if there were any treats about. For to children, even more than to grown-ups (and this is at once a consolation and a danger), any excitement really counts as a treat, even if it is a painful excitement like breaking your arm, or a horrible excitement like seeing a car smash, or a terrifying excitement like playing hide-and-seek in the shrubbery at dusk. Mrs Miniver herself had been nearly grown-up in August 1914, but she remembered vividly how her younger sister had exclaimed with shining eyes, 'I say! I'm in a war!'

But she clung to the belief that this time, at any rate, children of Vin's and Judy's age had been told beforehand what it was all about, had heard both sides, and had discussed it themselves with a touching and astonishing maturity. If the worst came to the worst (it was funny how one still shied away from saying, 'If there's a war,' and fell back on euphemisms) – if the worst came to the worst, these children would at least know that we were fighting against an idea, and not against a nation. Whereas the last generation had been told to run and play in the garden, had been shut out from the grown-ups' worried conclaves: and then quite suddenly had all been plunged into an orgy of licensed lunacy, of boycotting Grimm and Struwwelpeter, of looking askance at their cousins' old Fräulein, and of feeling towards Dachshund puppies the uneasy tenderness of a devout churchwoman dandling her daughter's love-child. But this time those lunacies – or rather, the outlook which bred them – must not be allowed to come into being. To guard against that was the most important of all the forms of war work which she and other women would have to do: there are no tangible gas masks to defend us in wartime against its slow, yellow, drifting corruption of the mind.

The queue wormed itself on a little. They moved out of the bright, noisy street into the sunless corridors of the Town Hall. But at least there were benches to sit on. Judy produced pencils and paper (she was a far-sighted child) and began playing Consequences with Toby. By the time they edged up to the end of the corridor Mr Chamberlain had met Shirley Temple in a Tube lift and Herr Hitler was closeted with Minnie Mouse in an even smaller rendezvous.

When they got into the Town Hall itself they stopped playing. Less than half an hour later they came out again into the sunlit street: but Mrs Miniver felt afterwards that during that half-hour she had said goodbye to something. To the last shreds which lingered in her, perhaps, of the old, false, traditional conception of glory. She carried away with her, as well as a litter of black rubber pigs, a series of detached impressions, like shots in a quick-cut film. Her own right hand with a pen in it, filling up six yellow cards in pleasurable block capitals; Mrs Adie sitting up as straight as a ramrod under the fitter's hands, betraying no signs of the apprehension which Mrs Miniver knew she must be feeling about her false fringe; Gladys's rueful giggle as her elaborate coiffure came out partially wrecked from her ordeal; the look of sudden realization in Judy's eyes just before her face was covered up; the back of Toby's neck, the valley deeper than usual because his muscles were taut with distaste (he had a horror of rubber in any form); a very small child bursting into a wail of dismay on catching sight of its mother disguised in a black snout; the mother's muffled reassurances – 'It's on'y Mum, duck. Look – it's just a mask, like at Guy Fawkes, see?' (*Mea mater mala sus est*. Absurdly, she remembered the Latin catch Vin had told her, which can mean either 'My mother is a bad pig' or 'Run, mother, the pig is eating the apples.')

Finally, in another room, there were the masks themselves,

stacked close, covering the floor like a growth of black fungus. They took what had been ordered for them – four medium size, two small – and filed out into the street.

It was for this, thought Mrs Miniver as they walked towards the car, that one had boiled the milk for their bottles, and washed their hands before lunch, and not let them eat with a spoon which had been dropped on the floor.

Toby said suddenly, with a chuckle, 'We ought to have got one for Teddy.' It would have been almost more bearable if he had said it seriously. But just as they were getting into the car a fat woman went past, with a fatter husband.

'You did look a fright,' she said. 'I'ad to laugh.'

One had to laugh.

ROSAMOND OPPERSDORFF

I Was Too Ignorant

THERE is nothing new or startling in the introduction to this story, yet a word of explanation is needed.

The scene is laid in a Military Camp in Brittany. It begins with the Battle of Flanders, and ends with the Battle of France. The old story of refugees will be omitted. Silence also over the collapse of France. That this, too, is ancient history, does not matter.

I was on this particular and very remote spot because of my husband. I was trapped there because of the war. I had never in my life done any hospital work. I had never had the least desire to. In fact I had always kept away from blood or anything to do with sickness.

There were four hospitals in the camp. These were full almost at once, before the Battle of Flanders was even over. A fifth hospital, known as the G5, was hastily slung together, and in no time this, too, was full. Two hundred and fifty more beds.

It was at this moment, with every hour, for me, dragging in impotent idleness and inside agony, that I offered my services for what they were worth, and was accepted. They had no choice.

For the 250 beds in the G5 there were at first four nurses, not including myself, who could hardly be called a nurse. In the end, when everything went from bad to worse, we were three, including myself.

I have travelled a long way since that first day when I entered G5. I do not think that I was either heroic or brave. On the contrary, I was a coward and wanted to run. But I couldn't run.

Fright is based on ignorance. I hope no one will ever be caught in such ignorance as I was.

*   *   *   *

8.45 a.m. Nanotte is at the main door of the G5 to greet me. I'm to stick to Nanotte. She is my boss.

Eyes stare at the new nurse. There is no escape from those eyes. Can they guess that in spite of the white dress and veil, the new nurse is absolutely ignorant? That the sight of blood, running or coagulated, makes her wince? That pus and sour smells make her sick?

Beds are easy to make. Anyone can make beds. Physical work is an outlet, also a shield. I go at it with a vengeance, but very definitely trying not to look too closely. Coward ... you asked for this, now face it. But no. The eye is like a butterfly, flitting here and there, yet never lighting. And if it lights ... then off again, as far as it can go. More beds. Now a pail of water and some rags. Scrub the shelves and floor. Upstairs for this. Down for that. Up again. Keep going. The first day is over. The first day of sights and smells.

The second day. Already a feeling of rhythm and routine. The long lines of eyes don't bother to stare. Your own eye is less of a butterfly. It lingers here and there, timidly, but with a desire to get acquainted. Nanotte is massaging. Surely I can do that. The swollen ankle and misshapen foot, full of corns and bunions, stinks. I swallow hard, and try to think of something else, as dirt plus ointment rolls off into thin black worms, but I am ashamed of my feelings. I must be inhuman to be such a hot-house flower. Nanotte is 'cupping'. That doesn't look very difficult. Just needs a steady, quick hand. I will try. A thin crust of courage is forming. There is already a bridge, although a shaky one.

The third day. I accompany the doctors and Nanotte from bed to bed, in the three ground floor wards which are in her care. She with her charts, I with my notebook. The notebook is a camouflage behind which I hide. The butterfly is astonishingly brave today. Trying to show off, no doubt, because the doctor is there. A few more pegs are driven into the bridge. Each day brings healing.

One thing leads to another. No. 8, in Ward 2, the Belgian, has a drain from his stomach. The dressing doesn't hold. Yellow ooze leaks out. He asks ... will I change the dressing? Yes ... of course, immediately. But inside ... no, I won't. This is still too much. The smell alone. Flies hover over the spotted sheets. You shoo them off, but back they come, drugged, to the same spots. Nanotte ... No. 8, the peritonitis fellow, must have pads, another bandage. It's quite a mess. I'll get the things. I'll watch ... then I can do it next time. Steady, butterfly.

Please ... may we have clean sheets for 5 and 6? They're absolutely black and stiff with blood. Sorry, they'll have to stay black – and stiff.

Please ... 14 is in great pain. Can I have a pillow to ease his back? A real pillow ... not one of those bolster things. My dear, what do you think this is ... a luxury hospital?

Where are the towels? *Towels*, did you say? There are none. And soap? You'll have to bring your own, we don't supply it. I've told you before ... this is not a luxury place, so stop asking for impossible things.

But *please* ... where can one get tea? The doctor has ordered it for some of the Moroccans. Oh ... tea ... You'll have to run over to the kitchens for that. They're out there (a wave of the arm) ... just beyond H3. (Approximately three city blocks away.)

And from these kitchens, twice a day, the food is brought in, in pails. Great lumpy goulashes and green greasy soups that always look the same and smell the same, and are still more lumpy and revolting by the time they are dumped on to the aluminium dishes that are greasy too.

One day slides into another without much room for thought. The faces beneath the numbers on the cots change, and change again. The Moroccans are now all bunched together in one ward and can keep each other company in their semi-convalescence. They sit cross-legged on the beds, playing cards, jabbering in their own language, sometimes chanting weird nostalgic tunes. They use their beds like tents. Amazing what one finds in them. All sorts of hidden food reserves to nibble on at odd hours. Bits of half-chewed cheese, biscuits, coloured candies, a square of mangey chocolate tediously wrapped up in newspaper, a broken comb, a piece of mirror.

We can't get Allah up. We can't do anything with Allah. He has his own ideas. He lies all day long with the covers pulled over his head, and his dirty yellow feet protruding well beyond the bed.

Ali Ben Hassam can be dismissed tomorrow, for convalescent leave. But Ben Ali doesn't want to go. His friends are all here ... why should he go away? Next morning, just before the doctor's round, he starts moaning and groaning, and develops a terrible pain in his stomach. It works. The doctor orders tea only, but under the cover of the sheets he stuffs all that his comrades have stolen for him ... a meal in itself. The next day at the appointed hour the terrible pain has shifted mysteriously to his head, and is accompanied by frenzied dirges to Allah (the real Allah, of course). The doctor smiles. The third day he is sternly ordered out. The last I saw of Ali Ben Hassam was his back, and the sad droop and pinched look of his shoulder blades as he trudged down the road, quite alone ... and very far from his native land.

Several weeks have passed, and we get our first breathing spell. Many of the men are up. Some of the beds are empty.

We have time now for flowers. Each ward has its bunch of daisies, long-stemmed buttercups or foxgloves. In the late afternoons, we go with our sewing things and repair tears on blood-stained uniforms that smell strongly of sweat. These are the gracious tasks. Flowers always bring cheers and thanks. Magazines too, even though they are torn and smudged. The only two puzzles are put together, pulled apart, put together again and again. But it is our sitting there with our sewing that the men love the most.

Reliving this first period, which at the time I thought such a terrible trial and so full of heartaches over the hopelessness of the conditions, I realize now that it was mere child's play, and in view of what followed, it was just an initiation.

For suddenly, our few days of respite were at an end. Orders came through to make ready. A new lot were on the way.

Midnight past. Still waiting for the ambulances. They were due at ten. It has been a long day, and a hard one, with so many beds to shift around, and everything to make ready. Now the place is quiet. In the wards the men doze fitfully. Subconsciously, they too are waiting. Our new blackout shades throw rings of pale sickly light on the concrete floor. We talk in hushed voices with the doctors and orderlies, smoking innumerable cigarettes and taking turns to sit on the two wooden benches in the entrance.

Here they come ... the first ambulance ... second, third, tenth, seventeenth. How many are there? One by one the men are lifted out and the stretchers laid on the floor. The entrance is filled. The corridors too ... The ghastly, unbelievable suffering. The cries. The groans. The distorted, dilated eyes. No words can describe this scene, nor will any amount of time ever efface it from my memory. Six in the morning. We have just left G5. No question of sleep.

Even if one wanted to, one couldn't. Besides, we must be back in a few hours.

I have had a bath. That is to say, I have sat cross-legged in my rubber tub, and poured a pitcher of lukewarm water over me. There is no running water where I live. The lack of rain has dried the wells, and we are limited to two small pitchers a day. This is uncomfortable enough at any time, but in the heat, and today of all days, it is a calamity. Water can wash away so many things.

Eight-thirty. I linger over coffee. Pour a second cup. Light a second cigarette. I've got to go back up there. No use thinking that something will happen to save me. Nothing will. I really am a coward. Now I know it for sure. Slowly, very slowly ... up the hill, to G5.

One look over the wards is enough. Enough to make one want to run. The further away the better.

I don't know much about a dying man, but No.19 is going to die. Can't call for Nanotte, she's been transferred to the sterilization room. I'll get the Polish nurse, who has the last three wards on the ground floor. Mustn't run. Must walk. No one has told me this, but I'm sure. The others mustn't know what's happening, mustn't sense my panic. The Polish nurse also says he's dying. We must get him out of the ward. We must have a doctor's permission to move him. The doctors are operating. Can I open the door ... and just go in? Every moment counts. I open the door, step inside, close it quickly. Help. What are they doing to this one. Another leg I guess, but I can't quite see. He is surrounded. The basins are full of blood. The heat and stench are nauseating. Strangely enough, the butterfly doesn't turn a hair. The doctor has seen me at last, but he is still intent. Finally: well, what is it? Doctor, No.19 in Ward 1, the man with the leg off at the hip, is dying. Will you give me permission to get him out of the ward? Yes – go ahead – I'll come up when I can. But he never came. There was nothing he could have done, and he knew it.

Upstairs, in a little bedroom, with windows tightly closed, Charvet, the Infirmier Major, who was a soldier and not a doctor, and myself, waited and watched No.19 struggle to die. It took about an hour, and I was foolish enough to think all the time that, in spite of everything, I could *will* him to live.

And a few moments later, the blood donors arrived. If they had come sooner ... but no use thinking that now. There are others. Six more in my wards who need transfusions. Remember: walk, don't run.

That night, after more than twenty-six hours on duty, I slept. But even in sleep, the nightmare didn't let me go. My dying fellow was with me all the time, squashing May-bugs between his fingers, and calling for Jeanette. Next morning, the same heavy feeling of dread. With faltering steps, faltering heart, and precious little courage ... back to G5.

Since Nanotte's desertion, I'm all alone. Alone in the same three wards (sixty beds in all), and because these wards are nearest to the air-raid shelters, all the worst wounded are there. No one to tell me anything now, neither how nor what nor why. All I know is that the doctors rely on me to keep cool and clear.

Charts and temperatures come first, of course. I had done these with Nanotte, but never alone. Then, the washing, which alone is also a job. And all the time, through everything, a traffic of stretchers going to and coming from the dressing-room, all in prescribed order. And ... those beds which for a time are empty, to make over quickly. And then always be there when the poor devil is brought back, usually with undried tears on his cheeks. From another list, others who must be X-rayed, and sent to another building altogether. Luckily I do not have to go into the dressing room often ... but one can't help hearing.

This way, stretcher-bearers. Easy now ... legs first ... and by inches, the rest of the body. Be careful going out the door, I tell you. Too late. They've bumped him. Brutes. And on the top of everything, they have the nerve to grumble.

No.15 is twenty years old, and has hardly more than a torso left to him. No.8 is amputated below the knees, and his two stumps stick up in the air. No.16 is much older. He was a stretcher-bearer. He has lost one arm, and has a bad bullet wound in the other shoulder. And so on.

Listen to them talk, only three days later ... and know what kept me going and why I didn't run away.

15 (the legless fellow) has decided to be a ballet dancer – no, a tight-rope walker. 16 (without an arm) is going in for boxing. 8 (also amputated) thinks that a bit of ski-ing would do him a world of good. 11 and 9 (each lacking a foot) pipe up, and decide that tap dancing will be their cup of tea. And so on. Jokes of this sort are

tossed back and forth across the wards, and we all laugh. Pity is the one thing which one cannot offer.

No.7 is finally beginning to register, and take note of his surroundings. He had lost his speech and senses, and has been lying there for five days in an open-eyed gaze, which was getting us all down, who by now were prone to chatter.

Speaking of washing: it takes days of hard scrubbing to get the blood off their hands, and it's almost impossible to get it out of their nails, so deeply is it lodged. Hair is matted and clotted with it.

Some of the old ones are still with me, including Allah, who has turned into an angel. 'Bonjour La Ma Sœur. Allah très sage. La Ma Sœur beaucoup à faire. Allah aide La Ma Sœur.' He fetches water, carries things, is always hanging around to do odd jobs, and trots off with a beaming face, full of importance to do them. The same with Napoleon, the Corsican, and Buddah, the Indo-Chinaman.

In the outside world, so mixed up with ours, the air is full of goodbyes. The Poles are off, singing as usual. Belgians and French are coming in. There is confusion in the camp. The other night the French Battalion of Tanks had moved up to the Front. All day they have thundered past, shaking the bowels of the earth, powdering the dust to smaller and ever smaller atoms. The Commanding Officer was our friend, and many others, so we went down to the next junction to see them off. The tanks were strung with branches of laurel and yellow gorse. All the men were singing. One would have thought that they were off to the Battle of Flowers at Nice. The evening sky was cloudless. The singing went zig-zagging off into the night, and we were left, at least I was, remembering the men at G5, with an unwanted and silly choke caught somewhere in my throat.

Thank God for work. I go back to G5 after supper, and in the mornings rise earlier, hardly able to wait, for I am only happy when I am there. In between times, I bathe my feet and swollen ankles with the water left over in my hot water bottle – a little trick I've devised, a way of cheating, to get more water, for we are down to one small pitcher a day now. The heat is terrific.

I have found a refuge of quiet. It is a miniature valley beyond the refuse dump back of the café. The wheat is up to my waist. Cherry trees come bursting over the top, like giant old-fashioned bouquets. There are daisies too, very white, and swaying slightly in the moonlight.

Five hundred more wounded have just come in. I do not know where they will be put. But this is no business of mine. All my beds are full.

You from G5, where are you today? You who called me l'Ange Rose ... how could I have deserted you as I did? Walked out five minutes before the Germans walked in? You who had no one, who were powerless to move, what did you think and feel that morning of 18 June? Did Nanotte go, as she promised me to do, from bed to bed (this was the only thing I had time to arrange), telling you each in turn that I was forced to leave, that my husband, who was a Pole, had come back at the last minute – dropped mysteriously from the blue – and taken me away, that I had no choice? By now, you have understood no doubt ... and perhaps you have forgiven me. But will you ever, ever know what this cost me? Or how much I loved you ... all your queer mutilated shapes which I know by heart, but which frightened me so much at first?

More than a year has passed since then, yet time and distance do not take you from me. Wherever you are, believe me, I am still with you. And may God forgive me that I wasn't even capable of treating your bed-sores, which were wounds in themselves, open and festering. *I was too ignorant.*

KAY BOYLE

Defeat

TOWARDS the end of June that year and through July, there was a sort of uncertain pause, an undetermined suspension that might properly be called neither an armistice nor a peace, and it lasted until the men began coming back from where they were. They came at intervals, trickling down from the north in twos or threes, or even one by one, some of them prisoners who had escaped and others merely a part of that individual retreat in which the sole destination was home. They had exchanged their uniforms for something else as they came along – corduroys, or workmen's blue, or whatever people might have given them in secret to get away in – bearded, singularly and shabbily outfitted men getting down from a bus or off a train without so much as a knapsack in their hands and all with the same bewildered, scarcely discrepant story to tell. Once they had reached the precincts of familiarity, they stood there a moment where the vehicle had left them, maybe trying to button the jacket that didn't fit them or set the neck or shoulders right, like men who have been waiting in a courtroom and have finally heard their names called and stand up to take the oath and mount the witness stand. You could see them getting the words ready – revising the very quality of truth – and the look in their eyes, and then someone coming out of the post office or crossing the station square in the heat would recognize them and go towards them with a hand out, and the testimony would begin.

They had found their way back from different places, by different means, some on bicycle, some by bus, some over the mountains on foot, coming home to the Alpes-Maritimes from Rennes, or from Clermont-Ferrand, or from Lyons, or from any part of France, and looking as incongruous to modern defeat as survivors of the Confederate Army might have looked, transplanted to this year and place (with their spurs still on and their soft-brimmed, dust-whitened hats), limping wanly back, half dazed and not yet having managed to get the story of what happened straight. Only, this time, they were the men of that tragically unarmed and undirected force which had been the French Army once but was no longer, returning to what orators might call reconstruction but which they knew could never be the same.

Wherever they came from, they had identical evidence to give: that the German ranks had advanced bareheaded, in short-sleeved summer shirts – young blond-haired men with their arms linked, row on row, and their trousers immaculately creased, having slept all night in hotel beds and their stomachs full, advancing singing and falling singing before the puny coughing of the French machine-guns. That is, the first line of them might fall, and part of the second, possibly, but never more, for just then the French ammunition would suddenly expire and the bright-haired blond demi-gods would march on singing across their dead. Then would follow all the glittering display: the rust-proof tanks and guns, the chromium electric kitchens, the crematoriums. Legends or truth, the stories became indistinguishable in the mouths of the Frenchmen who returned – that the Germans were dressed as if for tennis that summer, with nothing but a tune to carry in their heads, while the French crawled out from under lorries where they'd slept maybe for every night for a week, going to meet them like crippled, encumbered miners emerging from the pit of a warfare fifty years interred with thirty-five kilos of kit and a change of shoes and a tin helmet left over from 1914 breaking them in two as they met the brilliantly nickelled Nazi dawn. They said their superiors were the first to run; they said their ammunition had been sabotaged; they said the ambulances had been transformed into accommodations for the officers' lady friends; they said *Nous avons été vendus* or *On nous a vendu* over and over, until you could have made a popular song of it – the words and the music of defeat. After their testimony was given, some of them added (not the young but those who had fought before) in grave, part-embittered, part vainglorious voices, 'I'm ashamed to be a Frenchman' or 'I'm ashamed of being French today,' and then gravely took their places with the others.

There was one man, though, who didn't say any of these things,

probably because he had something else on his mind. He was a
dark, short, rather gracefully made man, not thirty yet, with hot,
handsome eyes and a cleft chin. Even when he came back without
his uniform and without the victory, a certain air of responsibility,
or authority, remained because he had been the chauffeur of the
mail bus before the war. He didn't sit talking in the bistro about
what he had seen and where he had been, but he got the black
beard off his face as quickly as he could, and bought a pair of new
shoes, and went back to work in stubborn-lipped, youthful, almost
violent pride. Except one night he did tell the story; he told it only
once, about two months after he got back, and not to his own
people or the people of the village but, as if by chance, to two
commercial travellers for rival fruit-juice firms who were just
beginning to circulate again from town to town in the Unoccupied
Zone. They sat at the Café Central together, the three of them,
drinking wine, talking about the anachronism of horse-and-mule-
drawn cannon in Flanders and the beasts running amok under the
enemy planes, and saying how they had all believed that the French
line was going to hold somewhere, that it wasn't going to break.

'At first we thought it would hold at the Oise,' one of the
travelling men said. 'We kept on retreating, saying the new front
must be at the Oise, and believing it too, and then when we
dropped below the Oise, we kept saying it would hold at the
Marne, and believing it, and then we thought it would be the Seine,
and even when we were south of Paris we kept on believing about
some kind of a line holding the Loire ...'

'I still don't know why we stopped retreating,' said the other
commercial traveller. He sat looking soberly at his glass. 'We can't
talk about the Italians any more. I still don't see why we didn't
retreat right down to Senegal. I don't see what stopped us,' he said.
Then the quiet-mouthed little bus-driver began telling them about
what had happened to him on the fourteenth of July.

He had been told, he said, that in some of the cities the enemy
hadn't taken or had withdrawn from, processions formed on the
fourteenth and passed through the streets in silence, the flagstaffs
they carried draped with black and their heads bowed. In some of
the villages, the mayor, dressed in mourning, laid a wreath on the
monument to the last war's dead while the peasants kneeled about
him in the square.

'I was in Pontcharra on the fourteenth,' said one of the

travelling salesmen, 'and when the mayor put the wreath down and
the bugle called out like that for the dead, all the peasants
uncovered themselves, but the military didn't even stand at
attention.'

'By that time none of the privates were saluting their officers in
the street anywhere you went,' said the other salesman, but the
bus-driver didn't pay any attention to what they said. He went on
telling them that he'd been taken prisoner near Rennes on the
seventeenth of June, and that there he saw the tracts the Boche
planes had showered down the week before. The tracts said,
'Frenchmen, prepare your coffins! Frenchwomen, get out your
ball dresses! We're going to dance the soles off your shoes on the
fourteenth of July!' He told the commercial travellers exactly what
use they made of the tracts in the public places there. He was more
than three weeks in the prison camp, he said, and on the night of
the twelfth of July he and a copain made their escape. They went in
uniform, on borrowed bicycles. They kept to the main road all
night, wheeling along as free and unmolested in the dark as two
young men cycling home from a dance, with their hearts light, and
the stars out over them, and the night air mild. At dawn they took
to the side roads, and towards eight o'clock of the new day they
saw a house standing alone, a little in advance of the village that
lay ahead.

'We'll ask there,' the bus-driver had said, and they pushed their
cycles in off the road and laid them down behind a tree. The house,
they could see then, was the schoolhouse, with a sign for 'Filles'
over one door and for 'Garçons' over the other. The copain said
there would be nobody there, but the bus-driver had seen a woman
come over to the window and look at them, and he walked up to
the door.

The desks were empty because of what had happened and the
time of year but the bus-driver said he knew it must have been the
schoolmistress who was standing in the middle of the room
between the benches, a young woman with fair, wavy hair, eyeing
them fearlessly and even sharply as they came. The bus-driver and
his copain said good morning, and they saw at once the lengths of
three-coloured stuff in her hands and the work she had been doing.
They looked around them and saw four French flags clustered in
each corner of the classroom and great loops of bunting that were
draped along three sides of the room. The first thing the bus-driver

thought was that she ought to be warned, she ought to be told, and then, when he looked at her face again, he knew she knew as much as or more than they.

'You ought to keep the door locked,' he had said, and the schoolmistress looked at him almost in contempt.

'I don't care who comes in,' she said, and she went on folding the bunting into the lengths she wanted to cut it to drape across the farthest wall.

'So the village is occupied?' the bus-driver said.

'Yes,' she said, but she began cutting the tricolour bunting.

'There's one thing,' said the copain, looking a little bleakly at the two others. 'If you give yourself up, at least you don't get shot.'

The schoolmistress had put her scissors down and said to the bus-driver, 'You'll have to get rid of your uniforms before there's any chance of your getting through.' She glanced around the classroom as though the demands of action had suddenly made it strange to her. 'Take them off and put them in the cupboard there,' she had said, 'and cover yourselves with this stuff while you wait,' and she heaped the blue, white and red lengths upon the desks. 'In case they might come in,' she said. She took her hat and filet off the hook as she said, 'I'll come back with other clothes for you.'

'If there would be any way of getting something to eat,' the bus-driver had said, and because he asked this, the tide of courage seemed to rise even higher in her.

'Yes,' she said, 'I'll bring back food for you.'

'And a bottle of pinard,' said the copain, but he didn't say it very loud.

When she was gone, they took their uniforms off and wrapped the bunting around themselves, doing it for her and modesty's sake, and then they sat down at the first form's desks, swathed to their beards in red, white and blue. Even if the Boches had walked into the schoolroom then, there probably wasn't any military regulation made to deal with what they would have found, the bus-driver had said to his copain – just two Frenchmen in their underwear sitting quietly inside the colours of their country's flag. But whether he said the other thing to the teacher as soon as she brought the bread and sausage and wine and the scraps of other men's clothing back, he didn't know. Sometimes, when he thought of it afterwards, he wasn't quite sure he had ever got the actual words out, but then he remembered the look on her face as she stood by the tree where the bicycles had lain and watched them pedalling towards the village just ahead, and he knew he must have said it. He knew he must have wiped the sausage grease and the wine off his mouth with the back of his hand and said 'A country isn't defeated so long as its women aren't' or 'until its women are' or 'as long as the women of a country aren't defeated, it doesn't matter if its army is' – something like that, perhaps saying it just before they shook hands with her and cycled away.

That was the morning of the thirteenth, and the bus-driver told how they rode all day in the heat, two what-might-have-been peasants cycling slowly hour after hour across the hushed, summery, sunny land. The war was over for them, for this country the war was over; there was no sound or look of it in the meadows or the trees or grain. The war was finished, but the farmhouse they stopped at that evening would not take them in.

'Have you got your bread tickets with you?' the peasant said, and even the white-haired sows behind his legs eyed them narrowly with greed.

'We're prisoners escaped. We've got a bit of money,' the bus-driver said. 'We'll pay for our soup, and maybe you'll let us sleep in the loft.'

'And when the Boches come in for the milk they'll shoot me and the family for having taken you in!' the peasant said, and the bus-driver stood looking at him bitterly a moment before he began to swear. When he had called the man the names he wanted to, he said, 'Look here, we were soldiers – perhaps you haven't got that yet? We haven't been demobilized; we were taken prisoner, we escaped. We were fighting a little war up there.'

'If you'd fought it better, the Boches wouldn't have got this far,' the peasant said. He said it in cunning and triumph, and then he closed the door.

They slept the night at the next farm (the bus-driver told the commercial travellers), eating soup and bread and drinking red wine in the kitchen, and when they had paid for it they were shown up to the loft. But they were not offered the side on which the hay lay; the farmer was thinking of next winter and he told them they could lie down just as well on the boards. They slept heavily and well, and it was very light when they woke in the morning, and so that day, the day of the fourteenth, they did not get far. By six that night they were only another hundred kilometres on, and then the copain's tyre went flat. But a little town stood just ahead and they pushed their bicycles towards it through the summer evening, and down its wide, treeless street. They hadn't seen the uniform yet, but they knew the Germans must be there. Even on the square in the heart of town they saw no sign, but still there was that unnatural quiet, that familiar uneasiness on the air, so they pushed their wheels through the open doors of a big garage, past the dry and padlocked petrol pumps, and stood them up against the inside wall. There, in the garage's half-security and semi-dark, they looked around them; twenty or more cars stood one beside the other, halted as if forever because of the lack of fluid to flow through their veins. Overhead the glass panes of the roof were still painted blue; the military and staff cars parked in the shadowy silence still bore their green-and-khaki camouflage. The war was over, everything had stopped, and out beyond the wide-open automobile doorway they saw the dance platform that had been erected in the square, and the dark, leafy branches twined on its upright beams and balustrade, and the idle people standing looking. There were no flags up, only this rather dismal atmosphere of preparation, and it was then the bus-driver and his copain had remembered it was the fourteenth.

'It's a national holiday and we haven't had a drink yet,' the copain said. He stood there in the garage with his hands in the pockets of the trousers that didn't belong to him, staring bleakly out across the square. Even when two German soldiers who were putting electric wiring up in the dance pavilion came into view, his face did not alter. He simply went on saying, 'We haven't had the apéritif all day.'

The bus-driver took a packet of cigarettes out of his jacket pocket and put one savagely on his lip. As he lit it, he looked in hot, bitter virulence out to where the Germans were hanging strings of bulbs among the fresh, dark leaves.

' "Frenchmen, prepare your coffins!" ' he had said, and then he gave a laugh. 'They've made only one mistake so far, just one,' he said, and as he talked the cigarette jerked up and down in fury on his lip. 'They've got the dance-floor and the decorations all right, and they've probably got the music and maybe the refreshments too. So far so good,' he said. 'But they haven't got the partners. That's what's going to be funny. That's what's going to be really funny.'

The bus-driver sat there in the Café Central telling it to the two commercial travellers, perhaps because he had had more to drink than usual, telling them the story, or perhaps because it had been weighing long enough heavy on his heart. He told them about the dinner the garage owner gave him and his copain: civet and fried potatoes and salad and four kinds of cheese and armagnac with the coffee. He said they could scarcely get it all down and that then their host opened a bottle of champagne for them. That's the kind of man the garage owner was. And during the dinner or afterwards, with the wine inside of him, it seems the bus-driver had said it again. He had said something about as long as the women of a nation weren't defeated the rest of it didn't matter, and just as he said it the music struck up in the dance pavilion outside.

The place the garage owner offered them for the night was just above the garage itself, a sort of storeroom, with three windows overlooking the square. First he repaired the copain's tyre for him, and behind him on the wall as he worked they read the newspaper cutting he had pinned up, perhaps in some spirit of derision. It exhorted all Frenchmen to accept quietly and without protest the new regulations concerning the circulation of private and public vehicles.

'Without protest!' the garage owner had said, taking the dripping red tube out of the basin of water and pinching the leak between his finger and thumb. 'I'll have to close this place up, and they ask me to do it without protest.' He stood rubbing sandpaper gently around where the imperceptible hole in the rubber was. 'We weren't ready for war and yet we declared it just the same,' he said, 'and now we've asked for peace and we aren't ready for that, either.' When he had finished with the tyre he showed them up the stairs.

'I'll keep the light off,' he said, 'in case it might give them the idea of coming up and having a look,' but there was no need for any light, for the illumination of the dance pavilion in the square shone in through the windows and lit the rows of storage batteries and the cases of spare parts and spark plugs. From outside, they heard the music playing – the exact waltz time and the quick, entirely martial version of swing.

'Somebody ought to tell them they're wasting their time,' the bus-driver had said, jerking one shoulder towards the windows. He could have burst out laughing at the sight of them, he explained, some with white gloves on even, waiting out there, to the strains of music for what wasn't going to come.

The garage owner shook out the potato sacks of waste on the floor and gave them the sacks to lie down on, and then he took one look out of the window at the square and grinned and said good night and went downstairs. The copain was tired and he lay down at once on the soft rags on the floor and drew a blanket up over him, but the bus-driver had stood a while at one side of the window, watching the thing below. A little group of townspeople was standing around the platform where the variously coloured lights hung, and the band was playing in one corner of the pavilion underneath the leaves. No one was dancing, but the German soldiers were hanging around in expectation, some standing on the steps of the platform and some leaning on the garnished rails.

'For a while there wasn't a woman anywhere,' the bus-driver told the commercial travellers. 'There was this crowd of people from the town, perhaps thirty or forty of them looking on, and maybe some others further back in the dark where you couldn't see them, but that was all,' and then he stopped talking.

'And then what happened?' said one of the travelling men after a moment, and the bus-driver sat looking in silence at his glass.

'They had a big, long table spread out with things to eat on it,' he said in a minute, and he didn't look up. 'They had fruit tarts, it looked like, and sweet chocolate, and bottles of lemonade and beer. They had as much as you wanted of everything,' he said. 'And perhaps once you got near enough to start eating and drinking, then the other thing just followed naturally afterwards – or that's the way I worked it out,' he said. 'Or maybe, if you've had a dress a long time that you wanted to wear and you hadn't had the chance of putting it on and showing it off because the men were away – I mean if you were a woman. I worked it out that maybe the time comes when you want to put it on so badly that you put it on just the same whatever's happened, or maybe, if you're one kind of a woman, any kind of a uniform looks all right to you after a certain time. The music was good, it was first class,' he said, but he didn't look up. 'And here was all this food spread out and the corks popping off the bottles, and the lads in uniform, great big fellows, handing out chocolates to all the girls ...'

The three of them sat at the table without talking for a while after the bus-driver's voice had ceased, and then one of the travelling men said, 'Well, that was just one town.'

'Yes, that was just one town,' said the bus-driver, and when he picked up his glass to drink, something as crazy as tears was standing in his eyes.

MOLLIE PANTER-DOWNES

Goodbye, My Love

ADRIAN'S mother welcomed them as though this were just an ordinary visit, with nothing particular about it. They found her, as they had found her so many times before, working in the big herbaceous border facing the sea, crouching girlishly with a frail little green plant in the palm of one earthy hand. She greeted them abstractedly, pushing back her wispy grey hair with the back of the hand that held the trowel and leaving a smudge. While they talked, Ruth looked at the border, which Adrian had built for his mother on a ledge of the cliff garden, facing it with a paved path beside which the rosemary and the seeded mulleins sprang. Even now, in late autumn, with the sea mist hanging in drops on the spiders' webs that festooned the last red-hot pokers, it was beautiful. Sometimes Ruth wondered if the cold woman, her mother-in-law, didn't express some secret frustration in these savage reds and yellows, these sullen purples, which she caused to gush out of the warm Cornish earth.

Ruth was grateful now for the lack of outward emotion which had so often chilled her. When Mrs Vyner asked Adrian, as they walked back to the house, 'Which day do you go?' she might have been asking about some weekend visit he was going to make. He said 'Wednesday', and she repeated 'Wednesday' in a vague voice, her attention wandering to a bough of japonica which the wind had loosened from the wall they were passing. She sat down on the porch to unlace her shocking old gardening boots.

'I suppose you don't know where you're going to be sent,' she said. 'I know it has to be very secret nowadays, because of the submarines.'

'I think it's Syria,' Adrian said. 'From the stuff we're taking, I'm pretty certain.'

'You can't be sure,' Mrs Vyner said. 'There's a Mrs Mason who's come to live at the Cross Glens. You know, Adrian, where old Colonel Fox used to live. Well, Captain Mason went off with a topee and shorts, poor man, and the next thing she heard was that he was sitting up on a fiord in Iceland. It's all done to put the spies on the wrong track. I'll point Mrs Mason out to you in church tomorrow.'

Later, when the Rector came in, he made more of an occasion of it than his wife had. He gave Ruth a heartier kiss than usual. 'It's good of you to think of the old people when you've got so little time left,' he said. Ruth disliked the phrase 'so little time left'. Suddenly she was inordinately conscious of time. The house was full of it, ticking between simpering shepherdesses on the mantelpiece, grumbling out of the tall mahogany case in the hall, nervously stuttering against Adrian's wrist. The church clock, just across the rectory garden, struck every quarter. Ruth thought, 'Four days, and one of them nearly gone.'

After dinner the Rector got out *The Times* atlas and pored over it with Adrian, while Mrs Vyner sat knitting a sock and talking about the garden and the village. The Rector's broad thumb, tracing the possible course that a convoy would take out into the Atlantic, swooped down upon the Cape. He and Adrian sounded quiet and contented, as though they were plotting a fishing holiday.

Ruth and her mother-in-law sat knitting a little apart, chatting in low voices.

'The black spot has been dreadful on the roses this year,' Mrs Vyner said. 'Really dreadful. What do you plan to do after he's gone?'

'I shall get a job,' Ruth said. 'I thought I might go into one of the services. Shorthand and typing ought to be useful. Anyway, I'm going to do something.'

'That's sensible,' Mrs Vyner said. 'After all, you'll be perfectly free, won't you? It isn't as though you have any ties.'

'No, I've got no ties at all,' Ruth said.

When they were undressing in the big, chilly guest room, she said to Adrian, 'Somehow, now that you're going I wish we'd had a child. You know, the Sonnets and all that – "And nothing 'gainst Time's scythe can make defence, Save breed, to brave him when he takes thee hence." '

'I'm not sorry,' Adrian said. 'This way I shan't be missing anything. When I get back we'll have the fun of kids together.'

'Yes, we will,' Ruth said, raising her voice slightly, as though she were talking to someone behind him. 'How long do you think the war's going to last?' she asked, picking up her hairbrush.

'Darling! As though it matters a damn what I think. I don't know – maybe another couple of years or so.'

'Some people say it will be over next spring.'

'Some people talk a hell of a lot of nonsense,' he said.

The bed was a big, old-fashioned double, its mattress divided into two gentle troughs where successive generations of guests had lain. Ruth got in and pulled the covers up to her chin. She watched Adrian moving around the room. 'They were an awful long time demobilizing people after the last war, weren't they?' she said. 'Maybe the firm would make a special application for you, or whatever they do. After all, they'll be terribly anxious to get you back. Mr Hobday told me himself that he didn't know how they were going to get on without you.'

'Oh, they'll manage,' Adrian said.

At intervals all through the night, Ruth kept waking up and listening to the sea. She pictured it running up the jagged inlets of the long, cruel coast, along which she and Adrian had often sailed in his little boat. He was asleep, breathing softly and lightly, his face close to her shoulder. She lay thinking this way until it began to get light and the birds started shouting in Mrs Vyner's wild garden.

They went to church next morning, walking through the gate in the yew hedge into the bleak little churchyard. The congregation that had come to hear the Rector preach was small and badly dressed, for the parish was thinly populated and poor. It was easy, without Mrs Vyner's whisper, to identify the more prosperous Mrs Mason, tweedy in a front pew, with a plain little girl on either side. Captain Mason had at least provided her with two defences 'gainst Time's scythe, hideous though they were in their spectacles and with gold bands round their teeth, before he took himself off to his Icelandic fiords. Ruth looked across the aisle at Mrs Mason, who was cheerfully singing the Te Deum. 'I'll get used to it, too,' she thought. The only other representative of the local gentry in church was Major Collingwood, who read the lessons in a voice beautifully husky with Irish whiskey and buttonholed Adrian afterwards in the porch. 'Well, my boy! Just off, I hear,' he said. 'Going East, I suppose? No, no, don't tell me - mustn't ask, mustn't ask. Well, it looks like a big showdown there this winter. Hitler's going to try and break through. Yes, we've got to be prepared for heavy fighting, heavy fighting.'

'The old fool,' Ruth thought. She walked away and began reading some of the inscriptions on the crosses of local grey stone at the heads of the few green mounds in the churchyard. Most of the men were fishermen who had been drowned in winter storms along the coast. 'John Tregarthen, who lost his life off Black Point, 10 December 1897,' she read. 'Samuel Cotter, drowned in the wreck of the Lady May, 25 January 1902.'

Adrian came up and took her arm. 'Hungry?' he asked. She shook her head, and he saw that there were tears in her eyes. 'Damn that old idiot!' he said. 'Darling, it's going to be a quiet winter. What do you bet? We'll be stuck in some bloody desert, eating our heads off with boredom. We're going to be forgotten men, forgotten by Hitler, forgotten by the General Staff, forgotten by - '

'It's all right,' she said.

Mrs Vyner came up, fastening her shabby fur round her long, thin neck, and the three of them walked back into the rectory garden.

Next day, Ruth and Adrian went back to London. That night they went out with friends and had plenty to drink. Ruth was able to sleep that night. The next evening, their last, they dined quietly in the flat. She had cooked the things he liked best, but neither of them had much appetite. At last they gave up trying. The one clock in the flat went on sucking time, like an endless string of macaroni, into its bright, vacant face. Every clock in London seemed to crash out the quarters outside their drawn curtains. When the telephone rang as they sat over their coffee, Adrian got up to answer it as though he were glad of the interruption. It turned out to be a man who used to be in love with Ruth and who had been out of England for some time. Adrian had always disliked him, but he sounded very cordial now. Afterwards he said, 'I'm glad Mike has turned up again. I want you to go out with him. That's why I said to him just now, "When I'm gone I'd take it as a personal favour if you'd give Ruth a ring now and then and take her out and give her a good time." '

'I don't want to go out with Mike,' she said.

'Please do,' he said. 'It will make me feel better to think of you looking pretty, out dancing and enjoying yourself.'

The following morning there was plenty to do - breakfast, a taxi, last-minute things. Meeting at some moment in the bustling, efficient nightmare, Adrian said, 'I don't suppose I'll be able to wire you, but I'll give someone a letter to post from the port after we sail,' and Ruth said, 'That will be fine.' She felt cold and frightened and a little sick, as though this were the morning fixed for a major operation. She wasn't going to the station, so they said goodbye in the hall, a tiny cupboard built for a man to hang his hat in, for a woman to read a telephone message in - not for heroic partings.

'Well, take care of yourself,' Adrian said. 'Don't forget what we said last night. If the bombings start again, you go down to Cornwall, you go anywhere. Anyway, you get out of here. Promise? Otherwise I won't be able to keep my mind on this war.'

'I promise,' Ruth said, smiling. Language was inadequate, after all. One used the same words for a parting which might be for years, which might end in death, as one did for an overnight business trip. She put her arms tightly round him and said, 'Goodbye, my love.'

'Darling,' he said. 'I can't begin to tell you - '

'Don't,' she said. 'Don't.'

The door shut, and presently Ruth heard the taxi driving away. She went back into the living room, sat down, and looked at the breakfast things. Adrian's cup was still half full of coffee, a cigarette stubbed out in the wet saucer. The cigarette seemed to have acquired a significance, to be the kind of relic which in another age would have been put carefully away in a little box with the toenail parings of a dead man, the hair clippings of a dead woman.

The next two days were bad. Ruth felt that the major operation had come off but that she still had not come round from the anaesthetic. She pottered about the flat, went for a walk, bought some things she wanted, dropped in at a movie and a concert. Time now seemed to have receded, to be an enormous empty room which she must furnish, like any other aimless woman, with celluloid shadows of other people's happiness, with music that worked one up for nothing. An hour or so after Adrian left, she put through a call to Cornwall. 'Adrian's gone,' she said, and across the bad line, across a rival conversation between two men who were trying to arrange a board meeting, she heard her mother-in-law's calm, tired voice saying, 'Yes, it's Wednesday, isn't it? I knew he was going on Wednesday.' As she hung up the receiver, she suddenly remembered a French governess out of her childhood who used to rage, weeping with anger, 'Oh, you British, you British!' Her friends rang her up with careful, planned kindness. Their stock opening was 'Has he gone? Oh, you poor darling! But aren't you terribly relieved it's over?' and then they would date her up for a dinner or a theatre. Their manner was caressing but sprightly, as though she were a stretcher case who mustn't be allowed to know that she was suffering from shock. She slept very badly and had terrible dreams, into which the sea always seemed to come. She went to sleep picturing the blacked-out ship creeping out cautiously into the dark sea. The girl who washed her hair had once told her that her brother had been torpedoed off Norway and that he had been rescued, covered with oil from the explosion. In one of Ruth's dreams Adrian was struggling in a sea of oil while Mrs Vyner, watching from her cliff garden, said 'Yes, it's Wednesday, isn't it? I knew he was going to drown on Wednesday.'

On the third day, Ruth woke up feeling different. It was a queer feeling, exhausted but peaceful, as though her temperature had fallen for the first time after days of high fever. The end of something had been reached, the limit of some capacity for suffering. Nothing would be quite as bad again. She thought, 'After all, there are thousands of women going through what I'm going through, and they don't make a fuss.' She got up and dressed, with particular care, because she planned to go round to one of the women's recruiting stations today and find out about a job. It would be important to make a good impression at the first interview. Afterwards she would write a funny letter about it to Adrian, she thought. Although it would probably be months before any mail caught up with him, she would write tonight and tell him not to worry, that she had finished making a fuss and was being sensible, like all the other women in England – like Mrs Mason, the jolly woman in tweeds singing away at the Te Deum as though there were still something to be thankful about.

She was out all day, and when she put her latchkey in the door she was humming. As she took off her hat, the telephone rang, and she went to it, still humming, and said 'Hello?' Adrian's voice said 'Darling?' and her knees went weak. She sat down suddenly, while his voice raced on, sounding excited and a bit blurred, as though he had had two or three drinks. 'I'm at the station, I'll be right round. Got to the port, but something went wrong. We all waited, then the message came through that it was cancelled. I wasn't allowed to phone you.'

'Cancelled?' she said stupidly. 'You're not going?'

'Not for another week,' he said. 'Maybe ten days. God, what luck. I'm going out to find a taxi. Darling, don't move until I get there.'

Ruth heard the click as he hung up, and she hung up slowly, too. For a moment she sat quite still. The clock on the table beside her sounded deafening again, beginning to mark off the ten days at the end of which terror was the red light at the end of the tunnel. Then her face became drawn and, putting her hands over it, she burst into tears.

Night in the Front Line

"ALF A MO, 'Itler, 'alf a mo,' said Mrs Minnow as the remains of her former staircase descended upon her, burying her in a welter of wood, dust and plaster.

She struggled and groped in the darkness, her one thought to find the attaché case of valuables which she had placed handy when she had retired under the stairs for refuge at the commencement of the raid. As she groped she talked.

'Wot the b— 'ell. I've been bombed that's wot. Well, nothing like it. Where'd I put that case? Well I'll be blowed. 'Ere it is, just where I thought.' And clutching the case tightly she heaved, scrambled and fought her way out from the debris surrounding her, and stumbling over many unexpected and unseen obstacles for several desperate moments, found herself in the brick-littered street.

'I been bombed that's wot,' said Mrs Minnow once again. 'Lucky I'm not 'urt and lucky I was under them stairs.'

'You all right, ma?' said a man's voice. It was the warden. Mrs Minnow staunchly replied yes. He told her to wait a tick and disappeared again. Mrs Minnow, recovered from her first shock, was now able to take stock of the world about her. It was a very confused world. The night was furiously bloodstained by the blazing docks and quivering in the echoing blasphemy of the guns. Great flashes of searing gunfire rick-racked across the sky and the exploding shells burst there like burning and passionate kisses. Below this vast dome of sound and fury seethed a human clamour; shouting, crying, screaming, traffic hooting and ambulance bells clanging, footsteps racing in the dark; people colliding, searching, cursing, dying.

Mrs Minnow was most intensely aware of another sound which

grew closer every minute ... a steady, belly-thumping, rhythmic, slow, low throb, gaining upon the ear till it was directly overhead, beating the world out; then three long streaks of sound, like the tearing of three long strips of silk, and Mrs Minnow was crouching beside what had been left of her front doorstep, with the world rumbling, tumbling around her again. Another warden helped her up and she dusted herself down. She tried to say something appropriate to his kindness and the occasion, but only managed to gasp, 'Getting a bit too much if you ask me.'

'You all right?' asked the warden.

'Yes,' said Mrs Minnow.

'All right, you trot along to the school, they'll take care of you there. Mind the 'ose pipes.'

Clutching her case Mrs Minnow started to grope her way to the school. The pavements were littered with debris and hose pipes snaked across them. Now and then she was obliged to make detours. She overtook Mr and Mrs East, also bound for the school. Mrs East was weeping bitterly. Mr East carried the canary and wore his old straw hat.

''Ouse is gone,' he said laconically. 'Direct 'it on Mason's. All killed they say. Three little kids there.'

'It's a bloody shame to leave kids in this,' said Mrs Minnow. ''Ell it is, proper 'ell. Blimey, 'ere comes Jerry again.'

'Oh, never mind 'im,' said Mr East with superb scorn. 'Where was you, in the Anderson?'

'No, under the stairs. The others all went along to the Landers' Anderson ... I say I 'ope they're all right ... no, I was under the stairs. I'd took a look at the fire and didn't like the look of things so I went under the stairs. Always reckoned safe in the last war stairs was ...'

'Bombs is different this war,' said Mr East. 'Where's old Jim?'

'Down at the docks 'elping put out the fire.'

'All that nice furniture gone and the nice new clock wot our Jack give us,' wailed Mrs East. 'Oh, lemme die, lemme die.'

'Now 'old on, Liza,' said Mr East. 'Cheer up, Liza. We're nearly there now. Oughta be glad you're alive you ought. Downright ungrateful that's wot you are.'

They came to the school. The big hall was crowded with people, most of them lying upon rugs and mattresses on the floor. The lights had gone out and lamps were being used. Somebody gave

Mrs Minnow a cup of hot tea and a biscuit. She sat on a canvas stool drinking the tea and nibbling the biscuit.

'Don't think much of that biscuit,' she remarked presently to a small woman beside her. 'Government oughter be able to give us a better biscuit 'n that.'

'My Joey's gone,' said the small woman, in a monotonous voice. 'I've lost my Joey.'

'What 'appened, duck?' asked Mrs Minnow kindly.

'My Joey's gone,' said the small woman again. 'I've lost my Joey.'

'Nutty,' observed the stout lady on Mrs Minnow's right.

'You oughta go to 'ospital,' said Mrs Minnow to Joey's mother. 'Ain't there nobody to take care of 'er proper?' she asked.

She'll be orright. We'll all be orright in the morning or else we'll be bleeding well dead.'

Mrs Minnow finished her biscuit and went in search of Mrs East. She was still weeping and did not respond to Mrs Minnow's kindly attentions. 'Blooming downpour,' said Mrs Minnow, a trifle disgusted. 'Blimey, I'll be glad to get outa this. Wot's the good of crying over spilt milk.' She felt cold and weary. The hall was packed with people and she found a place on the floor in the corridor. A women with two small boys gave her a blanket to wrap up in.

'We was in a shelter,' she told Mrs Minnow. ''Ad our blankets there and our clothes.' She indicated the bulging pillow-cases her children rested their heads upon. 'Blasted bomb dropped near the shelter. We was about the only ones to get out all right.'

'Musta been a nasty shock.'

'Not 'alf,' said the mother. She didn't say much more, but looked nervously at her children now and again. Mrs Minnow saw her extend a furtive hand and run it over the smallest child's slumbering body.

They lay there. It was chilly and dark. Around them the murmuring of many voices, sounds of broken weeping and low moaning. Heavy raucous snores. Again and again the engines of German planes thumping and circling overhead, the screaming of falling bombs, dull shattering explosions ... Mrs Minnow's heart pounding in pulpy dread as she pressed her stout person as flat as possible against the hard unyielding floor as if she would burrow a shallow hole there and in it hide.

Presently, through sheer exhaustion, she slept. Her sleep was thick, murky and blotched with the dust of debris and the smoke of fire. She would suddenly start awake, to find her stomach cold and sick and her hip-bone sticking sharply into the floor. Then she would mutter, sigh heavily, and sleep again.

In the early hours of the morning she was once more flung awake, her head splintering into many little pieces, her brain ripped into fragments by the agonized shrieking of many persons. Something stifling was pressing her down, there was a vast roaring and the sliding shaking of buildings collapsing.

Her first instinct was to lie quite still, while the floor seemingly tilted and retilted beneath her. Then it steadied. Something warm trickled down her left leg. A woman's voice yelled in agony. 'Get me out! Get me out!'

Mrs Minnow began to heave and struggle. She rose and fell in the debris like an ooze-embedded prehistoric monster reincarnating. More plaster, more dust, more splintering wood. After long suffocating moments of kicking and clawing, panting and groaning, a hand seized her shoulder and a rough voice said, ''Old on ma, we've got you.'

She emerged. She noticed, without realizing the full meaning of her escape, that a great lump of stone had fallen a few feet from her. Beside her, beneath broken rafter and rubbish, something moaned and moved. Her shivering mind recalled her case. She cried, 'My case, my case,' and tried to stoop to search for it in the dust and muck at her feet, but somebody took hold of her and led her into the playground. She sat on some stone steps. She felt inside her blouse where she had pinned her purse and old-age pension book and they were still there. She held her hands close to her face ... inspected them ... they were black with grime. She pulled up her torn skirt and looked at her leg, it bore a slight cut.

She sat very still. The guns thundered and exhorted; she paid them no heed. Then a picture flashed before her eyes, a sound cut her ears: the mother of the two little boys, following a man carrying one of them. She uttered strange shrill cries. Her face was white and open like a window when the curtains blow through. Her hands drooped in front of her, lacerated and bloodstained from her wild efforts to dig out her children.

Mrs Minnow recoiled. Then she got up. She was going to clear out of this. She was going to find a nice deep shelter and stay there till it was all over. Get away. Hide and get right away from it all. Her brain sagged as though the elastic had gone from an old pair of knickers. She mooched across the playground, down the street. She narrowly escaped being knocked over by an ambulance.

A policeman stopped her. 'Where are you going, mother?'

'A shelter,' said Mrs Minnow. 'I wanta shelter. A deep shelter.'

The policeman took her to a shelter; he was a kind man. Mrs Minnow descended into that humid atmosphere and there, huddled on a bench below ground, inert and motionless, she waited for the morning. When the All Clear sounded she ascended into the desolate, smoking, reeking wasteland which had been her world and was now a dark pile of ruins. She thought only of getting out of the place and going to her sister in Chingford. She felt dimly that first she should look for her old man, though what would be the good? However, she made her way towards the docks, but was stopped by a police barricade. She was told they were still putting out the fire. She turned to go back home, but remembered home was no more, and reaching the end of her street one glance told her it was of no use to stop there. She said to a warden she knew, 'If my Jim comes 'ome tell 'im I've gone to Elsie's at Chingford.'

The warden said he would.

She was given a lift on a coster's pony-cart to Bow Road. Here the coster met his brother's wife who was evacuating with his own family to Ilford, and as there was not enough room on the cart for them all Mrs Minnow was put down on the pavement, expressing her thanks and saying she hoped they would all meet again in better times. Then she walked on, along Bow Road to Stratford.

On either side walked people like herself; some wheeling their salvaged belongings in prams, others pushing little hand carts such as children play with in the streets, others carrying cases or stuffed pillow-cases, others just like Mrs Minnow with only themselves rescued from the bombs.

Along the roadway streamed a constant procession of little carts, cars, lorries, vans, conveying escaping families with their hastily snatched belongings; some had even managed to bring away bedding and furniture. Buses also passed, packed with paper-faced children.

A young woman carrying a baby and followed by a girl of ten and a little boy, struggling to bear between them a bulging old case, approached Mrs Minnow and asked, 'Got a pram?'

'No,' said Mrs Minnow.

'Know anybody 'oo 'as?'

'No.'

'This case is bleeding 'eavy,' said the young woman plaintively.

Mrs Minnow shook her head and walked on. She felt as though her feet would drop off and decided to hitch-hike, so she stopped on the kerb edge and raised a forlorn thumb to a passing lorry. It did not stop.

'Blooming 'ard-'earted unchristian be'aviour,' said Mrs Minnow bitterly, turning to a young woman waiting at the nearby bus stop. The buses and trolley-buses were few and far between, and when they came they were filled to overflowing. Mrs Minnow tried boarding one or two but retired defeated. Suddenly she wanted to talk. To talk and go on talking. She turned once more to the young woman and recited her woes in a blank abandoned monologue.

'Bombed twice I been. Once in me own 'ouse ... then in the school. School full of people ... nearly all killed. Oh, terrible it's been, terrible. But I'm getting out of it, going to me sister's at Chingford. Couldn't bear another night I couldn't, drive me mad. Wouldn't go through that again not for a 'undred pounds. All night at it they was. Never stopped. All me 'ome gone. Not much I 'ad, but it was me little all. Everythink gone. Look at me. Look at the sight I am! Look at me 'ands! No water to wash 'em with. No light. No gas. Nothink left to me but me purse and pension book. Nothink. My God, what a blooming awful world it is.'

The young woman leapt at a passing bus and was borne away arguing violently with the exasperated conductor. Mrs Minnow stared vacantly after her, muttered 'My God,' once more, then slowly turned to continue her journey to Chingford.

Another lorry approached. She hailed it dispiritedly, it drew up. It was carrying coals. The driver thrust out a blackened face.

'Give us a lift, mate,' said Mrs Minnow.

The driver hesitated. Then he opened the door of his driving-cabin. 'All right, ma,' he said. ''Oist yerself up now. 'Ere, give us yer 'and.'

ROSE MACAULAY

Miss Anstruther's Letters

MISS Anstruther, whose life had been cut in two on the night of 10 May 1941, so that she now felt herself a ghost, without attachments or habitation, neither of which she any longer desired, sat alone in the bed-sitting-room she had taken, a small room, littered with the grimy, broken and useless objects which she had salvaged from the burnt-out ruin round the corner. It was one of the many burnt-out ruins of that wild night when high explosives and incendiaries had rained on London and the water had run short: it was now a gaunt and roofless tomb, a pile of ashes and rubble and burnt, smashed beams. Where the floors of twelve flats had been, there was empty space. Miss Anstruther had for the first few days climbed up to what had been her flat, on what had been the third floor, swarming up pendent fragments of beams and broken girders, searching and scrabbling among ashes and rubble, but not finding what she sought, only here a pot, there a pan, sheltered from destruction by an overhanging slant of ceiling. Her marmalade for May had been there, and a little sugar and tea; the demolition men got the sugar and tea, but did not care for marmalade, so Miss Anstruther got that. She did not know what else went into those bulging dungaree pockets, and did not really care, for she knew it would not be the thing she sought, for which even demolition men would have no use; the flames, which take anything, useless or not, had taken these, taken them and destroyed them like a ravaging mouse or an idiot child.

After a few days the police had stopped Miss Anstruther from climbing up to her flat any more, since the building was scheduled as dangerous. She did not much mind; she knew by then that what she looked for was gone for good. It was not among the massed debris on the basement floor, where piles of burnt, soaked and blackened fragments had fallen through four floors to lie in indistinguishable anonymity together. The tenant of the basement flat spent her days there, sorting and burrowing among the chaotic mass that had invaded her home from the dwellings of her co-tenants above. There were masses of paper, charred and black and damp, which had been books. Sometimes the basement tenant would call out to Miss Anstruther, 'Here's a book. That'll be yours, Miss Anstruther'; for it was believed in Mortimer House that most of the books contained in it were Miss Anstruther's, Miss Anstruther being something of a bookworm. But none of the books were any use now, merely drifts of burnt pages. Most of the pages were loose and scattered about the rubbish-heaps; Miss Anstruther picked up one here and there and made out some words. 'Yes,' she would agree. 'Yes, that was one of mine.' The basement tenant, digging bravely away for her motoring trophies, said, 'Is it one you wrote?' 'I don't think so,' said Miss Anstruther. 'I don't think I can have ...' She did not really know what she might not have written, in that burnt-out past when she had sat and written this and that on the third floor, looking out on green gardens; but she did not think it could have been this, which was a page from Urquhart's translation of Rabelais. 'Have you lost *all* your own?' the basement tenant asked, thinking about her motoring cups, and how she must get at them before the demolition men did, for they were silver. 'Everything,' Miss Anstruther answered. 'Everything. They don't matter.' 'I hope you had no precious manuscripts,' said the kind tenant. 'Books you were writing, and that.' 'Yes,' said Miss Anstruther, digging about among the rubble heaps. 'Oh yes. They're gone. They don't matter ...'

She went on digging till twilight came. She was grimed from head to foot; her only clothes were ruined; she stood knee-deep in drifts of burnt rubbish that had been carpets, beds, curtains, furniture, pictures, and books; the smoke that smouldered up from them made her cry and cough. What she looked for was not there; it was ashes, it was no more. She had not rescued it while she could, she had forgotten it, and now it was ashes. All but one torn, burnt corner of note-paper, which she picked up out of a battered saucepan belonging to the basement tenant. It was niggled over with close small writing, the only words left of the thousands of words in that hand that she looked for. She put it in her note-case and went on looking till dark; then she went back to her bed-sitting-room, which she filled each night with dirt and sorrow and a few blackened cups.

She knew at last that it was no use to look any more, so she went to bed and lay open-eyed through the short summer nights. She hoped each night that there would be another raid, which should save her the trouble of going on living. But it seemed that the Luftwaffe had, for the moment, done; each morning came, the day broke, and, like a revenant, Miss Anstruther still haunted her ruins, where now the demolition men were at work, digging and sorting and pocketing as they worked.

'I watch them close,' said a policeman standing by. 'I always hope I'll catch them at it. But they sneak into dark corners and stuff their pockets before you can look round.'

'They didn't ought,' said the widow of the publican who had kept the little smashed pub on the corner, 'they didn't ought to let them have those big pockets, it's not right. Poor people like us, who've lost all we had, to have what's left taken off of us by *them* … it's not right.'

The policeman agreed that it was not right, but they were that crafty, he couldn't catch them at it.

Each night, as Miss Anstruther lay awake in her strange, littered, unhomely room, she lived again the blazing night that had cut her life in two. It had begun like other nights, with the wailing siren followed by the crashing guns, the rushing hiss of incendiaries over London, and the whining, howling pitching of bombs out of the sky onto the fire-lit city. A wild, blazing hell of a night. Miss Anstruther, whom bombs made restless, had gone down once or twice to the street door to look at the glowing furnace of London and exchange comments with the caretaker on the ground floor and with the two basement tenants, then she had sat on the stairs, listening to the demon noise. Crashes shook Mortimer House, which was tall and slim and Edwardian, and swayed like a reed in the wind to near bombing. Miss Anstruther understood that this was a good sign, a sign that Mortimer House, unlike the characters ascribed to clients by fortune-tellers, would bend but not break. So she was quite surprised and shocked when, after a series of three close-at-hand screams and crashes, the fourth exploded, a giant earthquake, against Mortimer House, and sent its whole front crashing down. Miss Anstruther, dazed and bruised from the

hurtle of bricks and plaster flung at her head, and choked with
dust, hurried down the stairs, which were still there. The wall on
the street was a pile of smoking, rumbling rubble, the Gothic
respectability of Mortimer House one with Nineveh and Tyre and
with the little public across the street. The ground-floor flats, the
hall and the street outside, were scrambled and beaten into a
common devastation of smashed masonry and dust. The little
caretaker was tugging at his large wife, who was struck
unconscious and jammed to the knees in bricks. The basement
tenant, who had rushed up with her stirrup pump, began to tug
too, so did Miss Anstruther. Policemen pushed in through the
mess, rescue men and a warden followed, all was in train for
rescue, as Miss Anstruther had so often seen it in her ambulance-
driving.

'What about the flats above?' they called. 'Anyone in them?'

Only two of the flats above had been occupied, Miss
Anstruther's at the back. Mrs Cavendish's at the front. The
rescuers rushed upstairs to investigate the fate of Mrs Cavendish.

'Why the devil,' enquired the police, 'wasn't everyone downstairs?' But the caretaker's wife, who had been downstairs, was
unconscious and jammed, while Miss Anstruther, who had been
upstairs, was neither.

They hauled out the caretaker's wife, and carried her to a
waiting ambulance.

'Everyone out of the building!' shouted the police. 'Everyone
out!'

Miss Anstruther asked why.

The police said there were to be no bloody whys, everyone out,
the bloody gas pipe's burst and they're throwing down fire, the
whole thing may go up in a bonfire before you can turn round.

A bonfire! Miss Anstruther thought, if that's so I must go up
and save some things. She rushed up the stairs, while the rescue
men were in Mrs Cavendish's flat. Inside her own blasted and
twisted door, her flat lay waiting for death. God, muttered Miss
Anstruther, what shall I save? She caught up a suitcase, and
furiously piled books into it – Herodotus, *Mathematical Magick*,
some of the twenty volumes of *Purchas his Pilgrimes*, the eight
little volumes of Walpole's letters, *Trivia, Curiosities of Literature*,
the six volumes of Boswell, then, as the suitcase would not shut,
she turned out Boswell and substituted a china cow, a tiny walnut

shell with tiny Mexicans behind glass, a box with a mechanical bird that jumped out and sang, and a fountain pen. No use bothering with the big books or the pictures. Slinging the suitcase across her back, she caught up her portable wireless set and her typewriter, loped downstairs, placed her salvage on the piled wreckage at what had been the street door, and started up the stairs again. As she reached the first floor, there was a burst and a hissing, a huge *pst-pst*, and a rush of flame leaped over Mortimer House as the burst gas caught and sprang to heaven, another fiery rose bursting into bloom to join that pandemonic red garden of night. Two rescue men, carrying Mrs Cavendish downstairs, met Miss Anstruther and pushed her back.

'Clear out. Can't get up there again, it'll go up any minute.'

It was at this moment that Miss Anstruther remembered the thing she wanted most, the thing she had forgotten while she gathered up things she wanted less.

She cried, 'I must go up again. I must get something out. There's time.'

'Not a bloody second,' one of them shouted at her, and pushed her back.

She fought him. 'Let me go, oh let me go. I tell you I'm going up once more.'

On the landing above, a wall of flame leaped crackling to the ceiling.

'Go up be damned. Want to go through that?'

They pulled her down with them to the ground floor. She ran out into the street, shouting for a ladder. Oh God, where are the fire engines? A hundred fires, the water given out in some places, engines helpless. Everywhere buildings burning, museums, churches, hospitals, great shops, houses, blocks of flats, north, south, east, west and centre. Such a raid never was. Miss Anstruther heeded none of it; with hell blazing and crashing round her, all she thought was, I must get my letters. Oh dear God, my letters. She pushed again into the inferno, but again she was dragged back. 'No one to go in there,' said the police, for all human life was by now extricated. No one to go in, and Miss Anstruther's flat left to be consumed in the spreading storm of fire, which was to leave no wrack behind. Everything was doomed – furniture, books, pictures, china, clothes, manuscripts, silver, everything: all she thought of was the desk crammed with letters that should have been the first thing she saved. What had she saved instead? Her wireless, her typewriter, a suitcase full of books; looking round, she saw that all three had gone from where she had put them down. Perhaps they were in the safe keeping of the police, more likely in the wholly unsafe keeping of some rescue-squad man or private looter. Miss Anstruther cared little. She sat down on the wreckage of the road, sick and shaking, wholly bereft.

The bombers departed, their job well done. Dawn came, dim and ashy, in a pall of smoke. The little burial garden was like a garden in a Vesuvian village, grey in its ash coat. The air choked with fine drifts of cinders. Mortimer House still burned, for no one had put it out. A grimy warden with a note-book asked Miss Anstruther, have you anywhere to go?

'No,' she said, 'I shall stay here.'

'Better go to a rest centre,' said the warden, wearily doing his job, not caring where anyone went, wondering what had happened in North Ealing, where he lived.

Miss Anstruther stayed, watching the red ruin smouldering low. Sometime, she thought, it will be cool enough to go into.

There followed the haunted, desperate days of search which found nothing. Since silver and furniture had been wholly consumed, what hope for letters? There was no charred sliver of the old locked rosewood desk which had held them. The burning words were burnt, the lines, running small and close and neat down the page, difficult to decipher, with the o's and a's never closed at the top, had run into a flaming void and would never be deciphered more. Miss Anstruther tried to recall them, as she sat in the alien room; shutting her eyes, she tried to see again the phrases that, once you had made them out, lit the page like stars. There had been many hundreds of letters, spread over twenty-two years. Last year their writer had died; the letters were all that Miss Anstruther had left of him; she had not yet re-read them; she had been waiting till she could do so without the devastation of unendurable weeping. They had lain there, a solace waiting for her when she could take it. Had she taken it, she could have recalled them better now. As it was, her memory held disjointed phrases, could not piece them together. Light of my eyes. You are the sun and the moon and the stars to me. When I think of you life becomes music, poetry, beauty, and I am more than myself. It is what lovers have found in all the ages, and no one has ever found before. The sun flickering

through the beeches on your hair. And so on. As each phrase came
back to her, it jabbed at her heart like a twisting bayonet. He
would run over a list of places they had seen together, in the secret
stolen travels of twenty years. The balcony where they dined at the
Foix inn, leaning over the green river, eating trout just caught in it.
The little wild strawberries at Andorra la Vieja, the mountain pass
that ran down to it from Ax, the winding road down into Seo
d'Urgel and Spain. Lerida, Zaragoza, little mountain-towns in the
Pyrenees, Jaca, Saint Jean Pied-du-Port, the little harbour of
Collioure, with its painted boats, morning coffee out of red cups at
Villefranche, tramping about France in a hot July; truffles in the
place at Perigueux, the stream that rushed steeply down the village
street at Florac, the frogs croaking in the hills about it, the gorges
of the Tarn, Rodez with its spacious *place* and plane trees, the little
walled town of Cordes with the inn courtyard a jumble of
sculptures, altar-pieces from churches, and ornaments from
châteaux; Lisieux, with ancient crazy-floored inn, huge four-
poster, and preposterous little saint (before the grandiose white
temple in her honour had arisen on the hill outside the town),
villages in the Haute-Savoie, jumbled among mountain rocks over
brawling streams, the motor bus over the Alps down into Susa and
Italy. Walking over the Amberley downs, along the Dorset coast
from Corfe to Lyme on two hot May days, with a night at
Chideock between, sauntering in Buckinghamshire beech-woods,
boating off Bucklers Hard, climbing Dunkery Beacon to Porlock,
driving on a June afternoon over Kirkdale pass ... Baedeker
starred places because we ought to see them, he wrote, I star them
because we saw them together, and those stars light them up for
ever ... Of this kind had been many of the letters that had been for
the last year all Miss Anstruther had left, except memory, of two-
and-twenty years. There had been other letters about books, books
he was reading, books she was writing; others about plans, politics,
health, the weather, himself, herself, anything. I could have saved
them, she kept thinking; I had the chance; but I saved a typewriter
and a wireless set and some books and a walnut shell and a china
cow, and even they are gone. So she would cry and cry, till tears
blunted at last for the time the sharp edge of grief, leaving only a
dull lassitude, an end of being. Sometimes she would take out and
look at the charred corner of paper which was now all she had of
her lover; all that was legible of it was a line and a half of close

small writing, the o's and a's open at the top. It had been written twenty-one years ago, and it said, 'Leave it at that. I know now that you don't care twopence; if you did you would' ... The words, each time she looked at them, seemed to darken and obliterate a little more of the twenty years that had followed them, the years of the letters and the starred places and all they had had together. You don't care twopence, he seemed to say still; if you had cared twopence, you would have saved my letters, not your wireless and your typewriter and your china cow, least of all those little walnut Mexicans, which you know I never liked. Leave it at that.

Oh, if instead of these words she had found light of my eyes, or I think of the balcony at Foix, she thought she could have gone on living. As it is, thought Miss Anstruther, as it is I can't. Oh my darling, I did care twopence, I did.

So each night she cried herself to sleep, and woke to drag through another empty summer's day.

Later, she took another flat. Life assembled itself about her again; kind friends gave her books; she bought another typewriter, another wireless set, and ruined herself with getting necessary furniture, for which she would get no financial help until after the war. She noticed little of all this that she did, and saw no real reason for doing any of it. She was alone with a past devoured by fire and a charred scrap of paper which said you don't care twopence, and then a blank, a great interruption, an end. She had failed in caring once, twenty years ago, and failed again now, and the twenty years between were a drift of grey ashes that once were fire, and she a drifting ghost too. She had to leave it at that.

ANNA KAVAN

Face of My People

BEFORE they took over the big house and turned it into a psychiatric hospital, the room must have been somebody's boudoir. It was upstairs, quite a small room, with a painted ceiling of cupids and flowers and doves, the walls divided by plaster mouldings to simulate pillars and wreaths, and the panels between the mouldings sky blue. It was a frivolous little room. The name Dr Pope looked like a mistake on the door and so did the furniture, which was not at all frivolous but ugly and utilitarian, the big office desk, the rather ominous high, hard thing that was neither a bed nor a couch.

Dr Pope did not look at all frivolous either. He was about forty, tall, straight, muscular, with a large, impersonal, hairless, tidy face, rather alarmingly alert and determined-looking. He did not look in the least like a holy father, or, for that matter, like any sort of father. If one thought of him in terms of the family he was more like an efficient and intolerant elder brother who would have no patience with the weaknesses of younger siblings.

Dr Pope came into his room after lunch, walking fast as he always did, and shut the door after him. He did not look at the painted ceiling or out of the open window through which came sunshine and the pleasant rustle of trees. Although the day was warm he wore a thick dark double-breasted suit and did not seem hot in it. He sat down at once at the desk.

There was a pile of coloured folders in front of him. He took the top folder from the pile and opened it and began reading the typed case notes inside. He read carefully, with the easy concentration of an untroubled singlemindedness. Occasionally, if any point required consideration, he looked up from the page and stared reflectively at the blue wall over the desk where he had fastened with drawing pins a number of tables and charts. These pauses for reflection never lasted more than a few seconds; he made his decisions quickly and they were final. He went on steadily reading, holding his fountain pen and sometimes making a note on the typescript in firm, small, legible handwriting.

Presently there was a knock and he called out, 'Come in.'

'Will you sign this pass, please, for Sergeant Hunter?' a nurse said, coming up to the desk.

She put a yellow slip on the desk and the doctor said, 'Oh, yes,' and signed it impatiently, and she picked it up and put a little sheaf of handwritten pages in its place and he, starting to read through these new papers with the impatience gone from his manner, said, 'Ah, the ward reports,' in a different voice that sounded interested and eager.

The nurse stood looking over his shoulder at the writing, most of which was her own.

'Excellent. Excellent,' Dr Pope said after a while. He glanced up at the waiting nurse and smiled at her. She was his best nurse, he had trained her himself in his own methods, and the result was entirely satisfactory. She was an invaluable and trustworthy assistant who understood what he was trying to do, approved of his technique, and cooperated intelligently. 'Really excellent work,' he repeated, smiling.

She smiled back, and for a moment the identical look of gratification on the two faces gave them a curious resemblance to one another, almost as if they were near-relatives, although they were not really alike at all.

'Yes,' she said. 'We're certainly getting results now. The general morale in the wards has improved enormously.' Then her face became serious again and she said, 'If only we could get ward six into line.'

The smile simultaneously disappeared from the doctor's face and a look that was more characteristic appeared there; a look of impatience and irritation. He turned the pages in front of him and reread one of them and the irritated expression became fixed.

'Yes, I see. Ward six again. I suppose it's that fellow Williams making a nuisance of himself as usual.'

'It's impossible to do anything with him.' The nurse's cool voice contained annoyance behind its coolness. 'He's a bad type, I'm afraid. Obstructive and stubborn. Unfortunately some of the youngsters and the less stable men are apt to be influenced by his talk. He's always stirring up discontent in the ward.'

'These confounded trouble-makers are a menace to our whole work,' Dr Pope said. 'Rebellious undesirables. I think friend Williams will have to be got rid of.' He pulled a scribbling-pad across the desk and wrote the name Williams on it, pressing more heavily on the pen than he usually did so that the strokes of the letters came very black. He underlined the name with deliberation and drew a circle round it and pushed the pad back to its place and asked in a brisker tone:

'Anyone else in six giving trouble?'

'I've been rather worried about Kling the last day or two.'

'Kling? What's he been up to?'

'He seems very depressed, Doctor.'

'You think his condition's deteriorating?'

'Well, he seems to be getting more depersonalized and generally inaccessible. There's no knowing what's in his head. It's not the language difficulty, either: his English is perfectly good. But he's hardly spoken a word since that day he was put in the gardening squad and got so upset.'

'Oh yes; the gardening incident. Odd getting such a violent reaction there. It should give one a lead if there were time to go into it. But there isn't, of course. That's the worst of dealing with large numbers of patients as we are.' A shade of regret on the doctor's face faded out as he said to the nurse still standing beside him:

'You see far more of Kling than I do. What's your own opinion of him?'

'I think, personally, that he's got something on his mind. Something he won't talk about.'

'Make him talk, then. That's your job.'

'I've tried, of course. But it's no good. Perhaps he's afraid to talk. He's shut up like an oyster.'

'Oysters can be opened,' the doctor said. He twisted his chair round and smiled directly up at the good nurse he had trained. He was very pleased with her and with himself. In spite of troublesome individuals like Williams and Kling the work of the hospital was going extremely well. 'Provided, naturally, that one has the right implement with which to open them.'

He got up and stood with his back to the window which, to be in keeping with the room's decoration, should have had satin curtains but instead was framed in dusty black-out material. He had his hands in his trouser pockets and he was still smiling as he went on:

'We might try a little forcible opening on oyster Kling.'

The nurse nodded and made a sound of agreement and prepared to go, holding the signed pass in her hand.

'Lovely day, isn't it?' she remarked on her way, in order not to end the interview too abruptly.

Dr Pope glanced into the sunshine and turned his back on it again.

'I'll be glad when the summer's over,' he said. 'Everyone's efficiency level drops in this sort of weather. Give me the cold days when we're all really keen and on our toes.'

The nurse went out and shut the door quietly.

The doctor swung round again in his energetic fashion and opened the window as wide as it would go, looking out over grassy grounds dark with evergreens. On a hard tennis court to the right a circle of patients in shorts clumsily and apathetically threw a football about and he watched them just long enough to observe the bored slackness of their instructor's stance and to note automatically that the man was due for a reprimand. Then he went back to his desk under the smiling loves.

As if he were somehow aware of the doctor's censorious eye, the instructor outside just then straightened up and shouted with perfunctory disgust, 'You there, Kling, or whatever your name is; wake up, for Christ's sake, can't you?'

The man who had not been ready when the ball was thrown to him, who had, in fact, altogether forgotten why he was supposed to be standing there on the hot reddish plane marked with arbitrary white lines, looked first at the instructor before bending down to the ball which had bounced off his leg and was slowly spinning on the gritty surface in front of him. He picked up the big ball and held it in both hands as though he did not know what to do with it, as though he could conceive of no possible connection between himself and this hard spherical object. Then, after a moment, he tossed it towards the man standing next to him in the ring, not more than two yards away, and at once forgot it again, and nothing remained of the incident in his mind except the uneasy resentment that always came now when anyone called out to him.

For many months he had been called Kling, that being the first syllable and not the whole of his name, which was too difficult for these tongues trained in a different pronunciation. To start with, he had not minded the abbreviation, had even felt pleased because, like a nickname, it seemed to admit him to comradeship with the others. But now, for a long time, he had resented it. They've taken everything from me, even my name, he thought sometimes when the sullen misery settled on him. By 'they' he did not mean the men of another race with whom he shared sleeping room and food and daily routine, or any particular individuals, but just the impersonal machine that had caught and mauled him and dragged him away from the two small lakes and the mountains where his home was, far off to this flat country across the sea.

And then there was that other reason why the sound of the short syllable was disturbing.

The game, if it could be called that, came to an end and the patients slowly dispersed. There was a little free time left before tea. Some of the men walked back to the hospital, others lighted cigarettes and stood talking in groups, several lay full length on the grass or dawdled where ilexes spread heavy mats of shade.

Kling sat down by himself on the top of a little bank. He was young, very big and broad, very well-built if you didn't mind that depth of chest, dark, his hair wiry like a black dog's, arms muscled for labour, his eyes only slightly decentred. He did not look ill at all, he looked enormously strong, only his movements were all rather stiff and slow, there was a marked unnatural rigidity about the upper part of his torso because of the lately healed wound and because of that heavy thing he carried inside him.

The bank was in full sunshine. Kling sat there sweating, dark stains spreading on his singlet, under the arms, sharp grasses pricking his powerful, bare, hairy legs, his breast stony feeling, waiting for time to pass. He was not consciously waiting. His apathy was so profound that it was not far removed from unconsciousness. A breeze blew and the tall grass rippled gently but he did not know. He did not know that the sun shone. His head was bent and the only movements about him were his slow breaths and the slowly widening stains on the singlet. His chest was hot and wet, and gloom ached in the rocky weight the black stone weighed under his breastbone, and his big blackish eyes, dilated with gloom, stared straight ahead, only blinking when the sun-dazzle hurt, and sweat stood in the deep horizontal lines on his forehead.

While he sat there a row of patients with gardening tools, spades, rakes, hoes, on their shoulders came near. They walked in single file in charge of a man walking alongside, himself in hospital clothes, but with stripes on his sleeve. Kling watched them coming. All of him that still lived, resentment, gloom, misery, and all his clouded confusion, slowly tightened towards alarm. He could see the polished edges of spades shining and he shuddered, all his consciousness gathering into fear because of the danger signals coming towards him across the grass. As he watched, his breathing quickened to heave his chest up and down, and, as the gardening squad reached the foot of the bank, he made a clumsy scramble and stood up.

Standing, he heard the clink of metal, and saw a shiny surface flash in the sun. The next moment he was running; stumbling stiffly, grappling the weight inside him, running from the men with the spades.

He heard the *Kling!* of his name being shouted, and again a second clattering *kling!* and, running, heard the spade kling-clink on the stone, he seemed to be holding it now, grasping the handle that slipped painfully in his wet hands, levering the blade under the huge ugly stone and straining finally as another frantic *kling!* came from the spade, and the toppling, heavy, leaden bulk of the stone fell and the old, mutilated face was hidden beneath, and Kling, stopping at the door of ward six where he had run, choking with strangled breath, while two men passing gazed at him in surprise, felt the dead mass of stone crushing his own breast.

He went into the ward and lay down on his bed and closed his eyes against the drops of sweat which trickled into the ends of his eyes. Then for a time there was nothing but the soreness of breath struggling against the stone.

This was what he had known a long while, ever since the truck had been blown thirty feet down into a ravine and he had seen the falling stone and felt it strike, felt it smash bone, tearing through muscle, sinew and vein to lodge itself immovably in his breast. Ever since then the stone had been there inside him, and at first it had seemed a small stone, just a dead spot, a sort of numbness under the breastbone. He had told the MO* about it and the MO had laughed, saying there was no stone or possibility of a stone, and after than he had not spoken of it again; never once. But from

* Medical Officer

the start he had been very uneasy, oppressed by the stone and by
the heaviness that could come from it suddenly to drive away
laughter and talk. He had tried not to think of the stone, but it had
grown heavier and heavier until he could not think of anything
else, until it crushed everything else, and he could only carry it by
making a very great effort. That was not so bad really because with
the weight of the stone crushing him he was nothing, and that was
not painful or frightening, it was just a waiting and that was
nothing as well. But sometimes, perhaps at the moment of going to
sleep, the dead weight lifted a little and then there were all the
uncovered faces, the stone and the digging, and the old man would
come back.

And so he lay very still on the bed, waiting for the deadness to
overlay him, lying there in the knowledge that, if the dead-weight
of the stone lifted to let him breathe, the old man would come.

Strange how it was always this one who came and never one of
the others.

The stone weight was lifting now and Kling, who had dozed a
little while after his breath had stopped struggling, woke suddenly,
frightened by the return of the bloody-faced man lying in brown
leaves with hairs growing out of his nostrils and a torn shirt
fluttering.

That was his father who had lain dead in the room beside the
Blue Lake. No, not that man. When he thought of his home he
couldn't see any faces, only the jagged line of the mountains like
broken egg-shell against the sky; and the two lakes, the Blue Lake
and the lake shaped like a harp. That, and sometimes the inn with
the acid wine of the district greenish in thick glasses, the swarming
trout in the small tank on the wall, crowded sleek fish-bodies,
slithering past the glass. But no faces ever. The stone blocked out
all the home faces.

When he thought of the war it was always the digging he thought
of because, seeing him so strong and used to work with a spade,
they had put him on that job from the beginning; and then there
were faces, wrecked or fearful or quiet or obscene faces, far too
many of them; how he had laboured and toiled till his saliva ran
sour, desperate to hide the faces away from the brutal light.

How many faces had he covered with earth and stones? There
surely were thousands; and always thousands more waiting: and he
all the time digging demented, always the compulsive urge in him

like a frenzy, to hide the ruined faces away. And sometimes he remembered that officer in charge of the burying party, the one who joked and sang all the time, he must have been a bit cracked really, boozed or something; but they had dug and shovelled till their hands were raw and blistered and hardly noticed the pain because of his Hey! Hi! Ho! and the jolly loud voice that he had.

There had been no singing that afternoon in the gully where the corpses, boys' and old men's among them, sprawled in the withered oak leaves between the rocks. Only haste then and the bitter taste in the mouth and the aching lungs, hacking the stony ground that was hard like iron to the weak bite of the spade, and the sky grey and muggy and flat and quiet. In the end someone had shouted and the others all started running back to the truck; and he had run too, and just then he had seen the old man lying flat on his back with blood congealing all down one side of his shattered face and the dry leaves gummed and blackening the blood.

Kling was looking now at this object that the stone had rolled aside to reveal. There was no stone weighting him any more as he watched the object, feeling the bed shake under him as he shook and the muscles twitching in his forearms and thighs.

Then, watching the object while his heart pounded, he saw the hairs sprouting at his father's nostrils as he lay dead on the wooden bed that was like a wagon without wheels, he saw a movement detach itself from this man in the gully, or perhaps it was the torn shirt which flapped in the wind, only there was no wind, and he did not stop to investigate but, knowing only the obsessional urge to hide at all costs that which ought not to be exposed to the level light, hoisted his spade and shoved and battered and fought the top-heavy rock until he heard a grinding crash and knew the torn face bashed out of sight, shapeless – smashed and hidden under the stone: and was it the same stone that burst his own chest and sank its black, dead heaviness in his heart?

The weight fell again now so that there was no more pain or fright and the bed did not shake; there was only the waiting that was nothingness really, and the men in blue talking and moving about the ward.

That was all that he knew, sweat slowly drying as he lay on the bed, and the old man mercifully buried by the stone. The others took no notice of Kling, nor he of them, and he heard their talk and did not know that he heard until a woman's voice cut through sharp. 'Williams, and the rest of you, why are you hanging about in the ward?' He turned his head then to the nurse who had just come in, she was speaking to him, too, 'Kling, you're to go to Dr Pope after tea. You'd better get up and make yourself decent,' and he saw her flat, cold eyes linger on him as she went out of the door.

'Get up and make yourself decent,' the man called Williams said. 'That's no way to talk to a fellow who's sick.'

Kling said nothing but looked up at him, waiting.

'To hell with them,' Williams said. 'To hell with the whole set-up. Bloody racket to get sick men back into the army. Cannon-fodder, that's all they care about. Taking advantage of poor mugs like us. Pep talks. Pills to pep you up. Dope to make you talk. Putting chaps to sleep and giving them electric shocks and Christ knows what. Lot of bloody guinea pigs, that's what we are. Bloody, isn't it?'

Kling was staring at him with blank eyes.

'Look at Kling here,' Williams said. 'Any fool can see he's as sick as hell. Why can't they leave him in peace? Why should he go back into their bloody army? This isn't his country anyway. Why should he fight for it?'

From the far reaches of his non-being Kling looked at the faces round him. They were all looking at him but they had no meaning. Williams had no meaning any more than the others. But he heard Williams go on.

'Damned Gestapo methods. Spying and snooping around listening to talk. Bitches of nurses. Why the hell do we stand for it?'

A bell was ringing and the patients started to move out of the ward. Kling, staring up, saw the meaningless shapes of their faces receding from him. He looked at Williams who was still there and Williams looked back at him, smiling, and said, 'Coming to tea, chum?' And in the words Kling half recognized something forgotten and long-lost, and some corresponding thing in him which had died long ago almost revived itself; but the stone was too heavy for that resurrection, and he could not know that what he wanted to do was to smile.

'So long, then, if you're stopping here,' Williams said. He pulled a packet of Weights out of his pocket and put a cigarette on the bed beside Kling's hand, which did not move. 'Don't let that bastard of a doctor put anything over you,' Kling heard Williams, walking towards the door, call back to him as he went.

Kling did not smoke the cigarette, or pick it up even; but after a time rose, and with those stiff motions which seemed to be rehearsing some exercise not well remembered, washed, dressed himself in shirt and blue trousers, combed his thick hair, and went along corridors to the door upon which was fastened the doctor's name.

There was a bench outside the door, and he sat down on it, waiting. The passage was dark because the windows had been coated with black paint for the black-out. Nothing moved in the long, dark, silent passage at the end of which Kling sat alone on the bench. He sat there bending forward, his hands clasped between his knees, his red tie dangling, his eyes fixed on the ground. He did not wonder what would happen behind the door. He waited without speculation or awareness, of waiting. It was all the same to him, outside or here or in the ward, he did not notice, it made no difference to his waiting.

A nurse opened the door and called him and he got up and stepped forward, and, looking past her along the wall of the corridor, thought: how many stones are there in this place; so many faces and stones: and lost the thought before it meant anything, and went into the room.

'I want you to lie on the couch,' Dr Pope told him. 'We're going to give you a shot of something that will make you feel a bit sleepy. Quite a pleasant feeling. It won't hurt at all.'

Obedient, null, with that unnatural stiffness, Kling laid himself down.

Lying on the high couch he looked at the exuberant ceiling without surprise. The flowers and the crowding cherubic faces did not seem any more strange to him than anything else. The ceiling did not concern him any more than the doctor concerned him. Nothing concerned him except the heaviness in his breast. He waited, looking at the doctor as if he had never seen him before, the nurse busy with swab and spirit and tourniquet, and he felt far off on his arm the tourniquet tightening, the bursting pressure of flesh against tightening fabric, and then the small sharp sting as the needle entered the vein.

'Just try to relax,' the doctor said, watching, while the fluid in the hypodermic went down, the blank waiting face with wide-open extremely dilated eyes.

He smiled his professional smile of encouragement and looked from the face at the chest and the massive shoulders bulked rigid under the white shirt that they stretched tight, at the clenched strong hands, the rough blue cloth strained on the tensed thigh, the stiffly upthrust boots not neatly laced, and back to the blank face again. He noticed on the face how the deep tan of the outdoor years was starting to turn yellowish as it slowly faded inside hospital walls.

'Well, how do you feel now?' he asked, smiling, of the man who stared up at him without answering.

'I want you to talk, Kling,' he said. 'I want you to tell me what's worrying you.'

Kling, his patient, looked away from him and up at the ceiling.

'What is it you've got on your mind?' asked the doctor.

Kling stared upwards without speaking, and now his limbs started twitching a little.

'You'll feel better after you've talked,' Dr Pope said.

The nurse finished the long injection and withdrew the syringe adroitly. A single drop of blood oozed from the pierced vein and she dabbed a shred of cotton wool onto it and silently carried her paraphernalia into the background and stood watching.

'You've got to tell me what's making you miserable,' the doctor said, speaking loud. He bent down and put his hand on Kling's shoulder and said loudly and very distinctly, close to his ear, 'You are very miserable, aren't you?'

Kling looked at him with his wide, black, lost animal's eyes and felt the hand on his shoulder. His shoulder twitched and something inside him seemed to be loosening, he felt sick in his stomach, and a sleepy strangeness was coming up at him out of nowhere, turning him tired, or sick.

'Why are you miserable?' he heard the question. 'Something happened to you, didn't it? Something you can't forget. What was that thing?'

Kling saw the doctor standing far too close, bending down almost on top of him. The hand that had hold of his shoulder gripped hard like a trap, the distorted face looked monstrous, foreshortened and suspended beneath painted faces, the eyes glaring, the threat of the mouth opening and shutting. Kling groaned, turning his head from one side to the other to escape from the eyes, but the eyes would not let him go. He felt the strangeness of sleep or sickness or death moving up on him, and then something gave way in his chest, the stone shifted, and sleep came forward to the foot of the couch, and he groaned again, louder, clutching his chest, crumpling the shirt and the red tie over his breastbone.

'Was it something bad that was done to you?' he heard the doctor's voice shout in his ear.

He felt himself turning and twisting on the hard bed, twisting away from the eyes and the voice and the gripping hand that was shaking him now. He shut his eyes to escape, but a salt prick of tears or sweat forced them open, he did not know where he was or what was happening to him, and he was afraid. He was very frightened with the strange sleep so near him, he wanted to call for help, it was hard for him to keep silent. But somewhere in the midst of fear existed the thought, they've taken everything; let them not take my silence. And the queer thing was that Williams was somehow a part of this, his smile, the cigarette, and what he had spoken.

'Was it something bad that *you* did?' Kling heard.

He did not feel the hand that was shaking his shoulder. He only felt his face wet, and on the other side of sleep a voice kept on moaning while another voice shouted. But he could not listen because, just then, the stone moved quite away from his breast and sleep came up and laid its languid head on his breast in place of the stone.

He tried to look at the strange sleep, to know it, but it had no form, it simply rested sluggishly on him, like gas, and all he could see above was a cloud of faces, the entire earth was no graveyard great enough for so many, nor was there room to remember a smile or a cigarette or a voice any more.

The old man was there and had been for some time, not sprawled in leaves now but standing, bent forward, listening; and Kling knew that this time something must pass between them, there was something which must be said by him, in extenuation, or in entreaty, to which the old man must reply: though what it was that had to be said, or what words would be found to express it, did not appear yet.

The old man bent over him and blood dripped onto his face and he could not move because of what lay on his breast, and when the old man saw he could not move he bent lower still and Kling could see the tufts of bristly hairs in his father's nostrils. He knew he would have to speak soon, and, staring wildly, with the old man's face almost on his, he could see the side of the face that was only a bloodied hole and he heard a sudden frantic gasp and gush of words in his own language, and that was all he heard because at that moment sleep reached up and covered over his face.

Dr Pope and the nurse had both seen that Kling was going to start talking. The doctor had seen it coming for about half a minute and waited intently. The nurse looked expectant. When the first sounds came both of them had moved forward at once and the doctor had bent lower over his patient, but now they stepped back from the couch.

'I was afraid that might happen,' Dr Pope said in his irritable voice. 'Damned annoying. I suppose there's no one in the place who could translate?'

'I'm afraid not,' the nurse said.

'Exasperating,' the doctor said. 'So we can't get anything out of him after all.'

'I'm afraid not,' the nurse said again.

'Most frustrating and disappointing,' said Dr Pope. 'Oh, well, it's no good trying to work on him now.'

OLIVIA MANNING

A Journey

MARY Martin, setting out to report the Hungarian occupation of Transylvania*, believed that journalists were magically immune from danger. Another woman, a journalist, had asked her to go to Cluj, while she herself remained to see how things went in Bucharest. 'I wouldn't do anything for her if I were you,' said one of the newspaper men in the Athenee Palace bar. 'It's pretty risky and you'll get no thanks.' Mary's husband, an oil engineer, was even less enthusiastic. 'The plane service has stopped. You'll have to go by train. It'll be a grim journey.' But she had made up her mind to go and it was too late to start the process of altering it.

The train was crowded. The peasants stood tightly packed in the corridors gazing out with their solemn faces at the wildly-moving crowds on the platforms. They would stand so, gazing for hours as though they saw no difference between stations and the varying countryside. Mary found a seat in the restaurant-car. Here the sun poured through hotly on to dishevelled business men sleeping with their heads on the tables among crumbs and spilt wine. The train stood another two hours before moving out. As the shadows slid across the tables and things began to shake and rattle, the men roused themselves. The majority of them were Hungarian. Mary could not understand what they said, but from the malicious pleasure of their tone and gestures she guessed they were imagining the discomfort of the Rumanians running from Cluj.

The sun slowly moved off the tables. The atmosphere remained stifling. It was heavy with tobacco smoke. They were soon off the Bucharest plain where the oil derricks stood in hundreds, spidery in the hard light, and climbing the foothills into the mountains. At the first skiing village Mary took a walk on the platform. Outside the air sang past her face with a startling freshness. Among the

* To appease Germany, Rumania was forced to cede territory to the Soviet Union, Bulgaria and Hungary. Transylvania, including Cluj, was annexed by Rumania's old enemy Hungary in August 1940.

dark peaked pines that covered the hills were trees already turning yellow, patching the green like lion-skins. She had to get back inside the train, where the heat carried up from the summer-hot capital was stupefying.

More people crowded into the carriage at every station, but the restaurant-car, where no one dared enter who could not pay for a meal, remained half-empty. Twilight fell. At stations faces came against the window, seemed to stick a moment as though blown there like leaves, and then whisked away again. Dinner was served; meat that a few months before would have been thrown back at the waiters, was accepted without comment. Everyone knew the best meat now had to go as a bribe to Germany.

By dark they were on the great Transylvanian plateau. The train was very late. The men fell asleep one by one, collars undone, coats off, hair tousled. Mary began to feel anxious about arriving so late. She had wired a hotel, but received no reply. She did not know if a room were booked for her or not. She knew only one person in Cluj – an English governess whom she had met once in Bucharest. Now that the carriage was quiet she could hear two Rumanian Jews talking in half-whispers at the table behind her. They were, she gathered, going to settle some business in Cluj before the barrier of a new frontier came down. One was apparently of Austrian origin; the other from the Bukhovina. One of them said: 'Much use it is now, a Rumanian passport.' The other said: 'The sooner one changes it, the better.'

At last some time in the middle of the night they reached Cluj. The station was deserted and glossy-looking in the meagre electric light. Half a dozen soldiers with rifles stood at the station entrance. Some of the businessmen forced their way out first, as though in a panic. Outside, Mary realized their eagerness had been to get one of the half-dozen rickety horse-carriages that had been waiting for the train. There were no taxis. All petrol had been requisitioned by the Rumanian army, so the Hungarians could get none of it. Mary changed her suitcase into her right hand and set out to walk the two miles from the station to the main square. A line of lights in frosted globes stretched down the centre of the road. People hurried darkly on the pavements as though to get out of sight, to get under cover.

A dim light came from the hotel in the square. Some people were leaving as Mary entered. The clerk shook his head at her before she spoke. She was near to tears from anxiety and tiredness.

'But I sent a wire,' she said.

'We have had many wires. There is not a bed to be found in the town.'

She sat down on her suitcase as though broken at the waist. After some moments, she said in a small voice: 'Can you suggest anything?'

'Shall I telephone the British consul for you?'

'It's too late. He'd be asleep.'

'No matter,' said the clerk. 'It is his business. But if you prefer I could telephone the sanatorium. They don't like it – but perhaps as a concession for a young foreign lady.' He dialled a number and Mary, as though through the haze of a drug, listened to one side of a conversation in German. 'They agree,' said the clerk. 'Now if you will come to the door I will show you the road you must take. I regret I cannot come with you.'

He refused to accept any reward and Mary, startled, said: 'You must be a Saxon.'

'I'm a German. I come from Coblenz. Good night.'

She found the sanatorium at last. An elderly night nurse opened the door and put out a hand as though she needed to be helped in. She followed the nurse down a white passage lit with red buttons. The door of one of the rooms opened and another nurse hurried out. From within came the sound of a deep, harsh voice rambling in Hungarian. There was, Mary felt, something peculiarly horrible about delirium in a foreign language.

'He is very ill,' said the nurse. 'Dying, we fear.'

Mary could still hear the man's voice in the distance as she sat down on her iron bedstead with its thin, sterilized covers. A temperature chart hung on the wall. Dimly lit, in one corner of the room, stood a chromium-plated surgical machine of some sort. A little black-shaded reading-lamp lit the pillow. She thought of her own bed that she shared with her kindly, comfortable husband and wondered why she had ever come here.

Next morning her mood had changed. The strange town was full of the movement of a break-up. There was a tenseness and suspicion in the atmosphere. The shop windows had their shutters up against riots. Some were shut, others had their doors half open on the chance of somebody at such a time giving thought to purchase of furniture, shoes and books. Women crowded round the grocery stores asking one another when life would be organized again and bread, milk and meat reappear for sale. Only the large café on the square, that baked its own rolls, was open. A waiter stood at the door holding the handle and only opening for those whose faces he knew. Curiosity persuaded him to let Mary in. When she had eaten her rolls and drunk a pint of strong, sweet coffee, she felt life regaining its charm. Through the large café window, in the centre of the square, stood the cathedral, new and uninteresting, rebuilt after fire. Around the cathedral went the traffic – the only petrol-driven vehicles were the military cars filled with the dressy, anxious, little Rumanian officers. Everything else – carriages, motor-cars, tractors, buses, carts –was being pulled by men or horses. They were laden with Rumanian goods being hastily got out of the way of the coming Hungarians. Mary had nothing definite to do – only wander around and notice things and get people talking. She wanted first to find the English governess, Ellie Cox, who might be able to tell her a great deal.

The Hungarian Jewish family with which Ellie had worked were delighted when Mary telephoned. One female voice after another came to the telephone and chatted delightedly in English – but Ellie was not there. No, she had not gone to Bucharest. She had married. She had married a Hungarian, a doctor, and now lived at the hotel in the square with her husband. Mary, making excuses to the family that would have had her come to luncheon, went to the hotel in the square. The German clerk was not on duty, but another told her that the English lady had gone out. They were sure she had gone to visit her new flat, which was in Strada Romano. Mary found the flat – one floor of an enormous eighteenth-century Hungarian mansion. Ellie was measuring the windows in the main room. She gave a friendly squeal when she saw Mary.

'You lucky woman,' said Mary at the door.

Ellie's eyes followed Mary's round the big white room. 'Not what you'd call homey,' she said. 'Not what I'd have chosen myself.'

'It's wonderful. We've had to live in such awful places. We'd have given anything to find a place like this.'

'My hubby found it.'

They stood together by one of the big windows watching the flight of the Rumanians. A farm motor-tractor went past laden with bedding and pulled by an old horse. Ellie gave a giggle.

'Look at that,' she said. 'You can't help laughing – but it's an awful nuisance all this happening just now when we want to get our flat ready. We've got a lot of stuff waiting to come here and we can't get a furniture van for love nor money.'

'It doesn't worry you – the idea of being left alone here in the centre of Europe?'

'Well, I won't be exactly alone. I've got my husband. And the people I used to work for are ever so decent.'

'Are there any other English people here?'

'Only the consul. He's a nice little chap. He's been ever so kind and he told me to keep my British passport in case I want to leave – but why should I? I'm all right here. But he'll have to go soon. You know, we'll probably have the Germans here.'

'I see the shops are boarded up.'

'Oh it's been awful. Shocking, it's been. Crowds rushing about the streets and fighting and throwing stones. It really wasn't safe to go out. What's the good of their behaving like that? And of course the Rumanian army – army! I ask you! – just stood and grinned. Anybody could take anything for all they cared. Then the Germans said they'd come in to restore order and that pulled them up with a jerk. They got busy taking the stuff out before someone stopped them. And it's all Hungarian stuff, too – all left after the last war. Yesterday they dismantled the telephone exchange.'

'Can't I telephone Bucharest?'

'Doubt it.' Ellie started laughing again as another ridiculous conveyance went past. She was a tall, large-boned, blonde girl. Her face was very English. Mary suddenly felt a deep affection for her.

'What made you come here in the first place?' she asked her. 'It's such a long way from home.'

'I don't quite know. I was doing some classes at the Polytechnic, just for fun, and these people wrote wanting a young lady who'd go and live with them and teach them all English. The letter was put up on the board and I read it. I didn't give it a thought. My friend Addie Clay said just for a joke: "Why don't you go, Ellie, you're always wanting to see the world." "What, me!" I said, "out in the wilds. Not likely." Then I began to think about it and it began to get me – and here I am.'

'The English are like that,' said Mary, thinking of a memorial she had seen in the English port where she had been born – erected to ships' crews, to ordinary Englishmen who might have stayed comfortably at home and instead had gone to the ends of the earth to die of yellow fever or cholera or at the hands of enemies about whom they knew nothing.

There were footsteps echoing up the empty stairway. A handsome, middle-aged man entered the room. Ellie's confidential seriousness of manner dissolved into playfulness.

'What do you think of my hubby?' she asked.

'Perhaps he can give me the latest news,' said Mary.

'News,' the Hungarian looked her up and down, and laughed. 'What about? The fashion in hats?'

Ellie put on a severe look: 'Don't you be so silly. You always think women can't understand anything. Mary's come here for a newspaper. She's a reporter.'

The Hungarian became serious, as was required of him. He had been taking lessons from Ellie and spoke English with a stiff precision. The latest news was that Manu, the Transylvanian leader, had arrived – but he had arrived too late. Two days before, when the riots were at their height, the peasants had held the post office for a short time and had telephoned Manu in Bucharest: 'Come and save us from the Germans,' they begged. He had answered: 'Don't be foolish. Go back to your work and I will come later.' For a day they had hung round the station expecting him by every train. What a welcome he would have received! What a hero he would have been! But now, enthusiasm had died; the riots were suppressed. There had been no one at his house when he arrived by car, and no one had cared. A small crowd had gathered outside when his arrival became known and he had gone out and said: 'Have patience. Now we can do nothing, but our time will come. I return now to Bucharest to work for our cause.' Then he had gone inside to pack his goods.

'I'll have to go,' said Mary. 'I must try and see Manu. Perhaps I can send a telegram.'

'It will be delayed for days,' said Ellie's husband.

She walked through the bare-looking, comfortless town to the post office that was still the centre of activity. It was crowded; the telephone boxes were being dismantled and the Rumanian police were holding back groups of indignant Hungarians. Mary waved her British passport and was allowed to enter. Inside people were fighting for telegraph forms. She struggled through to the counter and asked how long it would take a telegram to get to Bucharest. 'Two, three, four days,' said the clerk. She decided to go back with her news that night.

She hurried to police headquarters to report her entry into the town and to get permission to leave it. All doors lay wide open and men hurried past her too busy to notice her. She wandered in and out of empty rooms and up to the iron gallery running round the central court yard. Here the police were throwing down bundles of papers to the lorries below. Furniture, typewriters, the glass from the windows, the handles from the doors, the radiators, the shutters were all stacked up awaiting transport. Only the shell of a building remained.

A clerk leaning against a doorway patted Mary on the shoulder. 'This time it does not matter,' he said. 'Everyone is coming and going without permits.'

Mary set out to find Manu's house. None of the carriages would leave the centre of the town, so she walked to the outskirts to which she had been directed. The town thinned out quickly into the rich, flat countryside. Manu's house looked to her like the setting for a Russian play. It stood back in its garden, square and naked-looking with a small porch flanked by nineteenth-century stone nymphs. The door of the house lay open. Within the wide hallway the furniture was covered with sheets, and crowded around it were ornaments, mirrors, oil paintings in heavy oval frames, and suitcases. Two busy young men were in the old-fashioned depths of the house. Mary called to them. They gazed at her without understanding. 'Manu,' she insisted. 'Journal Londres.' They grasped it at last and one sped up the great curve of the staircase. At once Manu appeared on the upper landing, made a little gesture of pleasure as though Mary were an old friend, and fixing her with a steady glare of pleasure, surprise and questioning, descended the long flight of stairs with the competent grace of an actor. At the bottom he flung out a hand, then hurrying to her, took hers and held it.

'Journal? London?' he enquired eagerly.

'Yes,' Mary nodded.

'Ah!' he smiled with great charm.

Mary knew only that he was notable in Bucharest as the one, the only, honest Rumanian politician. He was a short, sturdy, middle-aged man with a long nose and a bright, empty stare. He wore an outdoor cape and carried a wide-brimmed hat which he put on as he stepped into the air.

'Do you speak French or English?' asked Mary.

No, he spoke only Rumanian, Hungarian and German. And

she? Only French and a little Rumanian. They looked at one another, silenced, but smiling. Mary watched a large, silvery butterfly that had settled on his shoulder. A smell of apples came from the trees.

'What now?' she asked in Rumanian.

Ah! He lifted a hand and replied rapidly: 'We must have patience. Now we can do nothing, but our time will come. I return now to Bucharest to work for our cause.' She nodded her recognition of the sentence. He took her hand again and patted it, then bowed very low over it. She went down the flight of steps from the porch and looked back. He took off his hat and waved it a little towards her. His smile was brilliant.

She was relieved the interview was safely over, but she felt a little dazzled, as though she had come for a moment within the aura of a distinguished actor.

The Istanbul Express was said to be arriving at Cluj at eight o'clock. She went down to the station in the afternoon to get her ticket stamped. The offices, waiting-rooms and buffets were all shut and padlocked. A telephone was ringing urgently within. She found an official who told her that the Istanbul Express would not stop there that evening because it had been besieged the evening before. She said she would come to the station nevertheless, and asked him to stamp her ticket. He took it, stared at it as though he did not know what it was, then pushed it back into her hand and walked away.

Under the brilliant sunlight stood half a dozen trucks laden with rich furniture. In one truck was a gilded French suite upholstered in red satin. There was nothing else but the naked rails, the grit heaps and the shut, dusty, dispirited-looking station. The peasants who had been cleared off the station lay in heaps around the square outside.

Back in the town Mary saw Ellie rushing towards her: 'What a life!' Ellie cried and rushed past, beaming and excited by something. At Cook's Agency Mary found that not only was the train expected to stop at Cluj, but an extra wagon-lit was being put on. People were snatching over each other's shoulders to get berths. Mary got the last and feeling like someone who has just taken out an insurance policy against life, faced the rest of the day. She found a large bookshop modelled on German lines. Inside she discovered it was kept by the family that had employed Ellie. The mother questioned her when she was leaving and how? Who was looking after her? Who would take her to the station? She said she supposed she would go alone.

'Ah!' she said. 'We would take you were we not forced to an engagement tonight. But I will give you this boy,' she called to a small messenger-boy, 'he will carry the trunk.'

'But I can carry it; it is only a light suitcase.'

'No, he will take it. He can go now and get it for you and when you come he will be waiting for you.'

This kindness lessened a little for Mary the star of anxiety that was burning in her solar plexus.

By twilight crowds of incipient rioters had collected again, but they had no leader. Manu had left Cluj and now people did not know what they wanted. They moved about in shadowy groups, rushing suddenly this way and that in pursuit of a rumour. They seemed harmless. No one took much notice of them. A tremendous rose-and-violet sunset stretched up from behind the cathedral. Clouds were flung in semicircles as though by a sower. The streets were fading in a misty, greenish light through which groups of youths drifted out of side-streets and round corners and were lost in the distance. The lorries were still dragging past with their loads of furniture. The Hungarians were gathered on the pavements to watch the flight of the Rumanians. Sometimes a military car went past at important speed, hooting unceasingly. Only a few street lamps were coming on. The electricity plant was being disabled. People were saying that the water was cut off. Some of the grocery shops had opened and women were queuing outside them. A Rumanian aeroplane sped at an angle round the square a few feet above the house-tops.

Mary had arranged to see Ellie at the hotel and found her sitting crocheting in a comfortless little private sitting-room; her husband was lying down in the bedroom beyond.

'Did you hear the latest?' she asked. 'No water and they're drawing water from the old well. Not very nice, I don't think. Not very safe.'

At that moment there was a rapid knock on the door. A man entered without waiting to be called and asked for Ellie's husband. Ellie motioned him into the inner room. The two men began talking furiously while Ellie's husband put on his outdoor shoes.

'Did you ever!' said Ellie, with a shocked, excited gasp.

'What is the matter?' asked Mary.

'Those Rumanians! They're taking away all the instruments and things from the hospital. And in 1918, when it was handed over – everything was there complete to the last needle. My hubby says the doctors stood like soldiers and handed over everything complete to the last needle ... There! You don't understand, do you? He's just saying that they're taking the beds and bedding from under the patients; they're even taking the chromium handles off the doors ... My hubby says perhaps if all the doctors go and reason with them, it may shame them. What a hope!'

The two men hurried out. Ellie clicked her tongue as the door shut and started a new row of her crochet. She was about thirty, but looked much younger.

Mary said: 'I wonder how long it will be before we meet again? It looks as though we may have to make a getaway soon.'

'Yes,' Ellie shook her head over her work. 'Things don't look too good. It's all right for me now, being married to a Hungarian – but it's awful for you being cut off from England like this. Where will you go?'

'We don't know. Perhaps we can get to Egypt.'

'Bit of a journey.'

'Yes.' Mary could only think of Ellie left alone here in all her Englishness as the English retreated out of Europe. 'Where is your family?'

'Highgate. My pop's got a shop there. I've written them that I'm married and won't be leaving like the other people. The consul put it in the bag for me. Very decent he's been. I hope they won't worry about me. They'll know I'll be all right.'

It was time for Mary to go to the station.

'I wish I could go with you. But I've got my in-laws coming to dinner. They're nice old things, but they don't know a word of English.'

'You've been very kind.' There was a strong sympathy between them there in the foreign hotel-room in the centre of Europe as the time came to separate.

'I haven't got my Hungarian passport yet,' said Ellie. 'They don't half make a fuss about giving you one.'

'They won't touch you – a young woman alone here. If you were a man ...' Mary, thinking of her husband, caught her breath and said quickly: 'We must get away soon.'

Ellie said nothing for a moment, then: 'You're English. That means a lot.'

'After France fell, they made us realize it meant a lot less.'

Ellie came down to the hotel door. The bat-black plane was still swooping above the square. The little boy with the suitcase was waiting for Mary. She set out with him down the long, wide road to the station. There were crowds of other people carrying bags and parcels. Mary, half in panic, began hurrying and the small boy, changing the bag from one hand to the other, manfully hurried too. When she wanted to take a turn in carrying the bag he would not give it up. In the distance there was a dark wavering movement of people packed round the station. She began to feel sick with apprehension. At the third-class entrance the peasants were fighting to get in.

Rumanians and Jews were moving steadily through the first and second-class entrances. The half-lit station was a desolate place in spite of the crowds. The peasants were settling down prepared for a long wait. Some were cooking their messes of maize over spirit-stoves. They remembered the cruelty with which they had driven out the Hungarians and they were not waiting to give them revenge. The parents-in-law of some who had married into the enemy were trying to persuade them to remain, but their instincts advised them more soundly. Groups of women were weeping together. Furniture heaped across the platform formed a barricade over which people climbed to get from one end to the other.

Mary tried to make enquiries of a porter. She spoke in Rumanian, then French. He brushed past her roughly, saying: 'Speak Hungarian.' She spoke to one of the Rumanians in the crowd. He told her they were all expecting the express, which had now been signalled two hours late. It should be in at ten. She found some seats among the heaped furniture and settled down like the peasants to wait. She tried to persuade the small boy who had carried the bag to go home to bed, but he refused. She gave him a hundred lei piece, thinking he might then go more willingly, but he remained. Every few moments he opened his small, dirty hand, took a glimpse at the coin, then quickly closed his fingers over it. Suddenly, amazingly, a train came in. It was a wooden, third-class local train. The peasants flung themselves to their feet and ran madly, from carriage to carriage. The doors were locked. They climbed in through the glassless windows hauling one another up by arms and legs until the carriages were choked. Then they climbed on to the roof. While some were still only half in and half on, the train suddenly moved out. Bunches of people fell off like lice. Others ran along the line yelling madly. From one of the bridges came the crackle of rifle fire. The peasants panicked back to the platform and huddled against the wall.

It was now half past ten. Mary again tried to persuade the boy to go. He shook his head. She showed him by pantomime that he should be asleep – he smiled with a thin, tired cynicism.

Some time after eleven a second local train came in. The peasants rushed at it. A few minutes later there was the sound of another train coming in on the line behind. People shouted to one another that this was the express, but for some moments they stood uncertainly, expecting the local train to move away. Then someone shouted that the express was leaving. People began to run to the end of the platform to get round the local train to the rail behind. Mary ran too, and the small boy who would not give up the suitcase came after her. When they rounded the engine of the local train they were in complete darkness. Tripping over slag-heaps and rails they got into the space between the two trains. The doors of the express were locked. People climbed up the steps and thumped on the windows, but no one attempted to open for them. The express engine had been uncoupled. Suddenly it spurted forward. Mary and the boy threw themselves back against the local train and felt the heat of the passing engine. She caught the boy's hand and ran round to the other side of the express carriages. At the end there was an open door from which a light fell across the line. She ran madly for it and leapt up the steps. The boy handed up her bag and, as she took it, the train moved, pulling away his hand, and she did not see him again.

She was, she found, at the kitchen door of the restaurant-car. Trembling, nearly sobbing, she leant for some moments staring into the kitchen, stunned as though she had come in out of a storm. Inside, the cook, a remote, dark little man, was sharpening his knives. He was absorbed, as though by a work of creation. When he glanced at her she gave him a smile that was almost affectionate. Gentle and humble with relief at her escape, she asked if she could pass through to the dining-car. He made way for her at once. Inside the car the tables were occupied, mostly by men, dissociated like the whole train from the chaos outside. In a few moments

Mary had adjusted herself and was as dissociated as they. The train shunted back to the station. She lifted the blind and glanced out at the faces lifted a moment to the patch of light. There was a sound of shots, some cries and a heavy pelting of feet. The train started again. A stone struck the window glass and she lifted the blind. People were running beside the train, waving their hands, shouting unheard, trying to jump on the steps to the kitchen door. As the train gathered speed they fell back one by one. A waiter started serving the third dinner.

Goodbye Balkan Capital

THE six o'clock news blared out, crowding the already overcrowded little drawing room with all the horrors of total war in 1941. The photographs on the piano shook with the noise. The Archdeacon's face, or as much of it as was not concealed in his bush of beard, seemed to express distaste at the vulgarity of it all. Mrs Arling looked as she had in life, meek and resigned. Thirty years of her husband's thundering sermons had hardened her to loud voices and violent opinions. And anyway, all this that was happening was no concern of theirs. They had both died in the 1920s, when Hitler was writing *Mein Kampf*, and the Archdeacon, also a disappointed man, had turned to preparing a collected edition of his sermons as a consolation for a vacant Bishopric which he had failed to get.

The Misses Arling, accustomed to these horrors, sat quietly listening. Janet, the elder sister, was knitting a khaki sock. A cigarette jutted from her square face, and she held her head thrust up to avoid getting the smoke into her eyes. Her fingers went on mechanically with the knit two, purl two ribbing. There would be no need to look until she started to turn the heel.

Laura Arling was arranging some polyanthus in a bowl. She was dim and faded, with a face that might once have been pretty in her distant Edwardian youth. It was an unfashionable face, but somehow nostalgic and restful in a world so full of brutality and death. If anyone troubled to look at her they might say that she had a sweet expression, if, indeed, that phrase is ever used seriously now.

She had spread a sheet of *The Times* on the round mahogany table, and the flowers, crimson, purple, yellow and creamy white, were scattered all over the Deaths column, so that as Laura picked up a flower her eyes would light on a death and then go all down the column, looking fearfully for the words 'by enemy action'. She wished Janet wouldn't have the wireless quite so loud. It must be because of her deafness, although she would never admit it. The words seemed to lose all their meaning when they were blared out like this. It reminded Laura of the police car which had come round on that dreadful September evening, telling them to get ready for five hundred evacuee children who had arrived at the station. Laura smiled as she remembered the sad little procession dragging through the garden gate, labels tied to their coats, haversacks and gas masks trailing on the ground. Janet had been so splendid. She had sent them all to the lavatory, which was just what they wanted, if only one had been able to think of it, for after that they had cheered up and rushed shouting about the garden until it was time for bed. It seemed such a long time since those first days of the war. The children had all gone back after a month or two and the house had seemed unnaturally quiet until April, May and June, when the distorted voice of the wireless had flung so many terrible pieces of news at them, that now, a year later, it seemed hardly possible that they had survived it all and were still here.

Now it was the Balkans, the *Drang nach Osten*, Janet said, and she always knew about things like that. At the beginning of the war she had got a translation of *Mein Kampf* out of Boots. Of course, as everyone said, the Balkans didn't seem quite so bad. They were further away, for one thing, and after the collapse of France one no longer had the same high hopes of other people. Also, it was mildly comforting to feel that the Germans were going in the opposite direction. Now after the usual War of Nerves, German troops had begun to enter another Balkan Capital. But this time it seemed more real and important. Laura stopped arranging the polyanthus and listened. This was *his* Balkan Capital, her dear Crispin's. He was First Secretary at the Legation there, and they were saying that the British diplomats were ready to leave at any moment.

'You can't trust these Balkan people. No guts,' said Janet, brushing a wedge of ash off her knitting. She got up and turned the wireless off with a snap.

Laura did not protest. She was remembering Crispin at a Commemoration Ball in Oxford, when she was eighteen and he twenty-one. They had danced together an improper number of times, having somehow got separated from the decorously chaperoned party in which they had started the evening, and at six o'clock, when the dance was over, they had gone on the river in a punt and had breakfast. It had been like a dream, walking down the Banbury Road in the early morning sunshine, wearing her white satin ball gown and holding Crispin's hand. Even Aunt Edith's anger and her threat to Tell the Archdeacon had failed to terrify her, because she was remembering Crispin's kisses and the beautiful things he had said. It had been their first and last meeting, for she had never seen him again after that morning. She supposed that she must have been a little unhappy at parting, she must surely have longed for letters which never came, but her memory did not help her here. It had kept only the happiness, enshrined in all its detail like those Victorian paperweights which show a design of flowers under glass, and which are now sought again, in days when Victorian objects are comforting relics of a period when the upper middle classes lived pleasant, peaceful lives, and wars were fought decently in foreign countries by soldiers with heavy drooping moustaches. Laura had never loved anyone else, not even in the last war, when officers used to come to supper on Sunday nights, and her poor mother had dared to hope that it might not be too late even then. Crispin had gone into the Diplomatic Service after leaving Oxford and it had been quite easy to get news of him. Laura had been able to imagine him in Madrid, in Washington, in Peking, in Buenos Aires, and now in this stormy Balkan Capital, where he had been First Secretary for several years. Indeed, she was expecting that he might be made Ambassador or Minister somewhere, although she feared that there must be a lot of unemployment among diplomats, with the Germans occupying so many countries.

Laura's imagination and *Harmsworth's Encyclopaedia* had helped to give her quite a vivid picture of the town where Crispin now lived. She could see its fine modern buildings, the streets all glass and steel and concrete skyscrapers, with brilliant neon lighting flashing out foreign words into the darkness, and the fine Art Gallery and Museum were as familiar to her as if she had really trudged round them on a wet afternoon. The British Legation was in the old part of the town, near to the famous Botanical Gardens. Laura often thought of Crispin walking there on fine spring mornings, perhaps sitting on a seat reading official documents, with lilacs, azaleas, and later, scarlet and yellow cannas making a fitting background for his dark good looks. For she could not think of him as fat or bald, the brightness of his hazel eyes dimmed or hidden behind spectacles, his voice querulous and his fingers, gnarled with rheumatism, tapping irritably on his desk. Devouring Time might blunt the Lion's paws; these things could happen to other people, but not to Crispin.

'I've got a WVS* meeting tonight,' said Janet brusquely. 'We're going to divide the town into districts and get somebody to canvass each street.'

'What for?' asked Laura vaguely.

'Pig swill,' said Janet briefly. 'There's still far too much food being wasted, especially among the poorer classes.'

Laura studied her sister dispassionately. She was so formidable in her green uniform, or splendid, that was what one really meant, what everyone said. She was like the Archdeacon, firm as a rock, much more efficient than poor Laura, who took after their mother and was dreamy and introspective. Perhaps it's because I haven't got a proper uniform, thought Laura, who, as a member of the ARP† Casualty Service, had only a badge and an armlet. Uniform made such a difference, even to women.

The next day the news was worse. The perfidious Balkan State had signed the Axis Pact, the British Legation was leaving, and there was a talk on the wireless about what happens when diplomatic relations are broken off. Laura now imagined Crispin in his shirt sleeves, burning the code books, stuffing bulky secret documents into the central heating furnace, a lock of dark hair falling over one eye. She was sure he would be doing something really important, for he had always seemed so fine and exciting to Laura, shut in then by the Archdeacon and North Oxford aunts in Edwardian England, and now by Janet and all the rather ludicrous goings-on of a country town that sees nothing of the war.

> In the Balkans, in the dangerous places,
> Where the diplomats have handsome faces ...

she thought, as she walked along with her shopping basket. But that wasn't right at all. It was the Highlands and the country places, and Highlands brought her back to porridge and oatmeal. Lord Woolton had said that we must make more use of oatmeal.

* Women's Voluntary Service   † Air Raid Precautions

Janet had got some recipes from the WVS and they were going to have savoury oatmeal for supper tonight.

One couldn't honestly say that it was very nice, but it was filling and made one feel virtuous and patriotic, especially when eggs or something out of a tin would have been so much more tasty. But Janet had banned all tin opening and the eggs were being pickled for next winter, when they would be scarce, or *difficult*, that was the word she had used.

They had just finished supper when the siren went. Laura's stomach always turned over when she heard the wailing, although this was the fifteenth time this year, according to her diary. Still, it was eerie when it went at night, and one never knew for certain that the planes were just passing over on their way to Liverpool. Sometimes they sounded as if they were right over the house, and, as the Head Warden had said, not without a certain professional relish, two or three well placed HE bombs could practically wipe out their small town.

'What a good thing you've had supper,' said Janet, splendidly practical as always. 'I should change out of that good skirt if I were you.'

Janet ought really to have been the one to go out, thought Laura, but she had resigned from ARP after a disagreement with the Head of the Women's Section. It had started with an argument about some oilcloth and had gone on from strength to strength, until they now cut each other in the street. And so it was Laura, always a little flustered on these occasions, who had to collect her things and hurry out to the First Aid Post.

She came downstairs carrying her gas mask and a neat little suitcase, in which she had packed her knitting, *Pride and Prejudice*, some biscuits, and a precious bar of milk chocolate. On her head she wore a tin hat, painted pale grey and beautiful in its newness. They had been given out at the practice that evening, but Laura had hidden hers in her room, wanting to surprise Janet with it the next time she had to go out.

Janet seemed rather annoyed when she saw it. It made Laura look quite important and professional. 'I should think it must be very heavy,' she said grudgingly. 'I'll leave a thermos of tea for you, though I suppose you'll get some there.'

'Well, expect me when you see me, dear,' said Laura, her voice trembling a little with excitement. Going out like this and not

* High Explosive

knowing when she would return always made her feel rather grand, almost noble, as if she were setting out on a secret and dangerous mission. The tin hat made a difference, too. One felt much more *splendid* in a tin hat. It was almost a uniform.

Laura went out and switched on her torch, being careful to direct the beam downwards. The bulb was swathed in tissue paper and tied as on a pot of jam, so that she wanted to write on it 'Raspberry 1911', as their mother used to. After a while her eyes got used to the darkness, and she could see that it was a lovely night with stars and a crescent moon. The planes were still going over, a sinister purring sound somewhere up there among the stars. Laura hurried on. Her tin hat was loose and heavy on her head, making it feel like a flower on a broken stalk.

'Liverpool again,' said a calm, melancholy voice behind her. She recognized the shape of a woman she knew.

'Yes, I'm afraid it must be. It's so terrible,' said Laura helplessly, wishing there were something adequate one could say. But there was nothing. It was of no consolation to the bombed that the eyes of women in safe places should fill with tears when they spoke of them. Tears, idle tears were of no use to anyone, not even to oneself. This oppressive sorrow could not be washed away in the selfish indulgence of a good cry.

At the First Aid Post everything was jolly and bustling. Stretcher bearers and First Aid parties in dark blue boiler suits were filling water bottles and collecting blankets. Women were hurrying to and fro carrying large bottles, dressings and instruments. An efficient girl was at the telephone and the doctor, stout and reassuring, was hanging his coat on a peg and looking forward to a game of bridge later on. Everything was ready for the casualties that might be brought in.

Laura put on her overall. It was of stiff blue cotton, voluminous and reaching to her ankles. It had full, short sleeves, a neat collar and ARP embroidered on the bosom in scarlet letters. She got out her knitting and sat down on the bed with the nurse and the friend she had walked up with.

At first they were all very jolly and talkative. These nocturnal meetings were a social occasion enjoyed by everybody. The most unlikely people were gathered together, people who would otherwise never have known each other, bound as they were by the rigid social conventions of a small country town. Conversation was

animated and ranged over many topics, horrible stories of raid
damage, fine imaginative rumours, titbits about the private lives of
the Nazi leaders gleaned from the Sunday papers, local gossip and
grumblings about ARP organization. Time passed quickly, an
hour, two hours. The throb of enemy planes was drowned with
voices until everything was quiet, except for the chatter and the
welcome hissing of the Primus from another room. When this
sound was heard everybody began to get out their little tins of
biscuits, rare blocks of chocolate were broken up and shared, like
the Early Christians, Laura thought, having all things in common.
At last somebody came round with cups of tea on a tray and thick
triangular slices of bread and margarine, with a smear of fish paste
on each. No banquet was ever more enjoyed than this informal
meal at one o'clock in the morning. Whatever would poor Father
and Mother have thought of this gathering? Laura wondered.
Perhaps it was a good thing that they had not been spared to see it.
Laura had always thought that the shock of a Labour Government
in office had hastened the Archdeacon's end.

After the meal everyone settled into lethargy. Conversation died
down to a few stray remarks. The doctor's voice was heard saying,
'Double five hearts,' and there was a hum of voices from the
decontamination room. The women knitted rather grimly, and the
men, already tired after a day's work, dozed and smoked. The
room was very hot and people were seen dimly through a haze.
Laura thought longingly of rivers, pools and willows, of her own
linen sheets, or plunging one's face under water when swimming,
even of the inside of a gas mask, with its cool rubbery smell and
tiny space of unbreathed air.

They had turned the light out now and the room was in
darkness, except for the glowing ends of cigarettes and a Dietz
lantern which flickered on the table. The scene would have made a
good subject for a modern painter; there was nothing in Dali and
the Surrealists more odd than this reality, the smoky room
crowded with silent men and women, lying or sitting on beds,
chairs or the floor, some covered with dark army blankets, others
with coats, one or two faces with mouths a little open, defenceless
in sleep, one man, surprisingly, for it was very hot, clasping a stone
hot-water bottle with 'HM Govt' stamped on the end. As still life
garnishings there were the tables covered with dressings, bottles
and instruments, with all that their presence implied, long metal

Thomas splints lying on top of a cupboard, heavy wooden walking sticks and crutches crowded into a corner. In a hundred years' time this might be a problem picture. What were these people doing and why?

Laura sat bolt upright, leaning against the wall. She closed her smarting eyes and tried to sleep. But she found herself thinking about Crispin in the Balkans, wondering what he was doing at this minute. He was probably lying down in a comfortable sleeper in a special diplomatic train, like the luxurious Nord or Orient Expresses, which glide silently into stations at night, their dark windows shuttered, conveying their rich sleeping passengers with the least possible disturbance across a sleeping Europe. But Europe was never sleeping, and now less than ever. Things happened in these hours when human vitality was at its lowest ebb; bombers rained death between one and four in the morning, troops crossed the frontiers at dawn. Crispin was probably awake too, looking through important documents, perhaps even dictating to a secretary, while the great train, diplomatically immune from the inconveniences of *Zoll* and *Douane*, carried him eastwards to Moscow or Istanbul, further and further away from his Legation. Laura saw it as a large suburban house, built in continental wedding-cake style, a magnolia tree, impersonal in its beauty, in bud in the garden, and inside all the desolation of a house whose occupants have had to leave it in a hurry. Drawers open and empty, out-of-date foreign newspapers on the floor, dead flowers in the vases, dust on the rococo furniture and the massive square stoves, their pretty majolica tiles cold now and stuffed with the dead ashes of the code books and secret documents. The keys had been left with the kind, homely American Ambassador, who had promised to keep an eye on the things that couldn't be taken away, like the valuable paintings and the stuffed eagle shot by the Minister on a hunting tour in the mountains, just as if they were going to the seaside for their summer holidays and would be back in a month. But it was 'Goodbye Balkan Capital!' and the train was rushing through the darkness to deposit its important passengers, blinking like ruffled owls in the early morning sunshine, on the platform of some other foreign capital, where Great Britain still had a representative to greet them. And then, after a cup of tea, so to speak, they would be pushed on to another train or boat, always on the move like refugees, except that they had their own country waiting for them at the end of the journey, houses in Mayfair or Belgravia and loving friends to welcome them, servants to put cool, clean sheets on their beds ...

A beautiful note sounded through the room, piercing and silvery as the music of the spheres must sound. It was the All Clear. In a surprisingly short time the blanket-covered shapes became human and active, everything was put away and they walked out into the sharp, cold air, their voices and footsteps ringing through the empty streets. They were all much jollier and noisier than they normally would have been, because they were up at such an odd hour of the morning and they felt the glow of virtue which comes from duty done. There had been no bombs and no casualties but they had been standing by. They had missed their night's rest so that if anything *had* happened they would have been there to deal with it.

Laura let herself into the house very quietly. She went into the drawing room and sat by the dead fire, drinking the tea that Janet had left for her. It wasn't very hot and had that tinny taste peculiar to thermos tea, but Janet would be hurt if she left it. It did not occur to Laura that she could pour it away.

It was an exquisite pleasure to turn over in the cool sheets and stretch her tired limbs. She remembered some lines from Sir Philip Sidney:

> Take thou of me smooth pillows, sweetest bed,
> A chamber deaf of noise and blind of light,
> A rosy garland and a weary head ...

It was as if she had never really been tired before.

Outside the first birds began to sing. It would soon be dawn. How thrilling one's first sight of Moscow must be, Laura thought. All those curiously shaped domes and towers, the Kremlin, Lenin embalmed ...

Eventually, as Laura gathered from much anxious listening to the news, the Legation staff did arrive in Moscow. They were to take the Trans-Siberian railway back to England. This journey was so great and so amazing that even Laura could hardly conceive what it would be like. A journey to the moon would have been easier to imagine. She studied her atlas carefully, but it was all too vague to be real except for the ending, the eventual safe arrival in England on a sunny day in June, July or August – she had no idea how long it would take – with the plane trees in the squares in full, dusty leaf. She wondered whether Crispin had a house in London and where it was. She hoped that it had not been bombed, and even began the futile occupation of studying the addresses of people in *The Times* killed 'by enemy action' to see what parts of London might be supposed to be in ruins.

It was while she was doing this one day that she came across it, *his* obituary among the long, impersonal list. She read it through mechanically, attracted by the name Crispin, without at first realizing that it was anybody she knew. He had died at the house of his sister Lady Hinge, in a village in Oxfordshire. It didn't say anything else, but Laura discovered a small paragraph about him on one of the inner pages. 'Since leaving Oxford,' it said, 'he had been in the Diplomatic Service, retiring from it in 1936.' Five years ago! Laura was annoyed to think that she had missed that information, if, indeed, it had ever been mentioned anwhere. The paragraph ended with three dry words. 'He was unmarried.' Laura had somehow thought that he would not be married. Her reading and imagination had given her a picture of diplomats which did not include wives, although she had not been so unworldly as to suppose that there could not be substitutes which were just as good. And at the back of her mind there may have been a hope that he would one day come back to England and the romantic first meeting would happen all over again.

When she had recovered from the first shock Laura found herself grieving not so much for his death, as that could make no practical difference to her, but for the picture she had had of him. The remembrance of her wonderful imaginings about his journey made her feel foolish and a little desolate, when all the time he had been perfectly safe in an Oxfordshire village, his life as dull as hers. He might even have been an Air Raid Warden. She paused, considering this possibility for Crispin with amusement and dismay.

She cut out the notice with her embroidery scissors. It was sad to think that the only tangible souvenir she had of Crispin was the bald announcement of his death. And yet her memory had a great deal. She found it hard to look forward to the future and a New Social Order, when there had been so much happiness in the past, the bad old days, as she had heard them called. Surely *they* (by whom she usually meant people like Mr Herbert Morrison and Mr Ernest Bevin) would leave her that, her Victorian paperweight, with its bright and simple design of flowers? Perhaps she had already been punished for her self-indulgent dreaming by her disillusionment about Crispin. No dramatic 'Goodbye Balkan Capital!' but a quiet death in a safe part of England. It was even possible that *her* end might be more violent and exciting than his.

Why, she thought, when the siren went that evening, I might get killed by a bomb! And yet that would not be right. It was always Crispin who had had the dramatic adventures, and after all these years Laura did not want it to be any different. In life or in death people are very much what we like to think them. Laura knew that she might search in vain in the Oxfordshire churchyard among the new graves with their sodden wreaths to find Crispin's. But it would be easy in the Balkans, in the dangerous places. There would always be something of him there.

JEAN RHYS

I Spy a Stranger

'THE downright rudeness I had to put up with,' Mrs Hudson said,
'long before there was any cause for it. And the inquisitiveness!
She hadn't been here a week before they started making remarks
about her, poor Laura. And I had to consider Ricky, hadn't I?
They said wasn't his job at the RAF Station supposed to be so
very hush-hush, and that he oughtn't to be allowed –'

While her sister talked Mrs Trant looked out of the window at
the two rose beds in the front garden. They reassured her. They
reminded her of last summer, of any day in any summer. They
made her feel that all the frightening changes were not happening
or, if they were happening, that they didn't really matter. The roses
were small, flame-coloured, growing four or five on the same
stalk, each with a bud ready to replace it. Every time an army lorry
passed they shivered. They started shivering before you could see
the lorry or even hear it, she noticed. But they were strong;
hardened by the east coast wind, they looked as if they would last
for ever. Against the blue sky they were a fierce, defiant colour, a
dazzling colour. When she shut her eyes she could still see them as
plainly as if they were photographed on her eyelids.

'They didn't stop at nasty remarks either,' said Mrs Hudson.
'Listen to this:

People in this town are not such fools as you think and unless you get rid
of that crazy old foreigner, that witch of Prague, who *you say* is a
relative, steps will be taken which you will not like. This is a friendly
warning but a good many of us are keeping an eye on her and if you
allow her to stay ...

This time next year ...

You'll be all very much the worse for wear.

'That was the first,' she said. 'But afterwards – my dear, really! You think who, in a small place like this, who?'

'I might give a guess.'

'Ah, but that's the worst of it. Once start that and there's no end. It's surprising how few can be trusted. Here's a beauty. Written on quite expensive paper too.'

' "A Gun for the Old Girls ..." A gun for the old girls?' Mrs Trant repeated. 'What's that mean?'

'There's a drawing on the other side.'

'*Well*!'

'Yes. When that came Ricky said "I can't have her any longer. You must tell her so." '

'But why on earth didn't you let me know what was going on? Malvern isn't the other end of the world. Why were you so vague?'

'Because it *was* vague. It was vague at first. And Ricky said "Take no notice of it. Keep quiet and it'll all blow over. And don't go and write a lot of gossip to anybody, because you never know what happens to letters these days. I could tell you a thing or two that would surprise you." So I said "What next? This is a free country, isn't it?" And he said there wasn't much free nowadays except a third-class ticket to Kingdom Come. And what could you have done about it? You couldn't have had her to stay. Why, Tom detests her. No. I thought the best thing was to advise her to go back to London.'

And hadn't she tried to be as nice as possible and speak as kindly as she could?

'Laura,' she had said, 'I hate to tell you, but Ricky and I think it best that you should leave here, because there's such a lot of chatter going on and it really isn't fair on him. The Blitz is over now, and there are all these divan rooms that are advertised round Holland Park or the Finchley Road way. You could be quite comfortable. And you can often find such good little restaurants close by. Don't you remember the one we went to? The food was wonderful. The one where the menu was in English on one side and Continental on the other?'

'What do you mean by Continental?'

'Well, I mean Continental – German, if you like.'

'Of course you mean German. This Anglo-German love-hate affair!' she had said. 'You might call it the most sinister love affair of all time, and you wouldn't be far wrong ...!'

'She could be very irritating,' Mrs Hudson continued. 'She went on about London. "I daresay, Laura," I said, "I daresay. But London's a big place and, whatever its disadvantages, it has one advantage – there are lots of people. Anybody odd isn't so conspicuous, especially nowadays. And if you don't like the idea of London, why not try Norwich or Colchester or Ipswich? But I shouldn't stay on here." She asked me why. "Why?" I said – I was a bit vexed with her pretending as much as all that, she must have known – "Because somebody has started a lot of nasty talk. They've found out that you lived abroad a long time and that when you had to leave – Central Europe, you went to France. They say you only came home when you were forced to, and they're suspicious. Considering everything, you can't blame them, can you?" "No," she said, "it's one of the horrible games they're allowed to play to take their minds off the real horror." That's the sort of thing she used to come out with. I told her straight, "I'm sorry, but it's no use thinking you can ignore public opinion, because you can't." "Do you wish me to leave at once?" she said, "or can I have a few days to pack?" Her face had gone so thin. My dear, it's dreadful to see somebody's face go thin while you're watching. Of course, I assured her she could have all the time she wanted to pack. If it hadn't been for Ricky I'd never have asked her to go, in spite of that hound Fluting.'

'Oh Lord,' said Mrs Trant, 'Was Fluting mixed up in it?'

'Was he? Was he not? But it was her own fault. She got people against her. She behaved so unwisely. That quarrel with Fluting need never have happened. You see, my dear, he was dining here and he said some of the WAAFs* up at the Station smelt. And he was sarcastic about their laundry allowance. "Pah!" he said. Just like that – "Pah!" *Most* uncalled for, I thought, especially from a man in his position. However, what can you do? Smile and change the subject – that's all you can do. But she flew at him. She said, "Sir, they smell; you stink." He couldn't believe his ears. "I *beg* your pardon?" – you know that voice of his. She said "Inverted commas". He gave her *such* a look. I thought "You've made an enemy, my girl".'

'I call that very tactless – and badly behaved too.'

'Yes, but tactless and badly behaved on both sides, you must admit, I told her "It's better not to answer to them. Believe me, it's a mistake." But she thought she knew better. It was one silly thing

* Women's Auxiliary Air Force

like that after another, making enemies all over the place ... And she brooded, she worried,' said Mrs Hudson. 'She worried so dreadfully about the war.'

'Who doesn't?'

'Yes, but this was different. You'd have thought she was personally responsible for the whole thing. She had all sorts of cracky ideas about why it started and what it meant.'

'Trying to empty the sea with a tin cup,' Mrs Trant said sadly.

'Yes, just like that. "It's too complicated," I said to her one day when she was holding forth, "for you to talk about the why and wherefore." But she had these cracky ideas, or they'd been put into her head, and she wanted to try to prove them. That's why she started this book. There was no harm in it; I'm sure there was no real harm in it.'

'This is the first I've heard about a book,' said Mrs Trant. 'What book?'

Mrs Hudson sighed. 'It's so difficult to explain ... You remember all those letters she used to write, trying to find out what had happened to her friends? Through the Red Cross and Cook's and via Lisbon, and goodness knows what?'

'After all, it was very natural.'

'Oh yes. But suddenly she stopped. She never had any news. I used to wonder how she could go on, week after week and month after month, poor Laura. But it was curious how *suddenly* she gave up hope. It was then that she changed. She got this odd expression and she got very silent. And when Ricky tried to laugh her out of it she wouldn't answer him. One day when he made a joke about the Gestapo getting her sweetheart she went so white I thought she'd faint. Then she took to staying in her room for hours on end and he didn't like it. "The old girl's got no sense of humour at all, has she?" he said. "And she's not very sociable. What on earth does she do with herself?" "She's probably reading," I said. Because she used to take in lots of papers – dailies and weeklies and so on – and she *hung* about the bookshops and the library, and twice she sent up to London for books. "She was always the brainy one of her family." "Brainy?" he said. "That's one word for it." I used to get so annoyed with him. After all she paid for the room and board and the gas meter's a shilling in the slot. I didn't see that it was anybody's business if she wanted to stay up there. "If you dislike her so much, it's all to the good, isn't it?" I said. But that was the funny thing - he disliked her, but he couldn't let her alone. "Why doesn't she do this, and why doesn't she do that?" And I'd tell him "Give her time, Ricky. She's more unhappy than she lets on. After all, she'd made a life for herself and it wasn't her fault it went to pieces. Give her a chance." But he'd got his knife into her. "Why should she plant herself on us? Are you the only cousin she's got? And if she's seen fit to plant herself on us, why can't she behave like other people?" I told him she hadn't planted herself on us - I invited her. But I thought I'd better drop a hint that was the way he felt. And there she was, my dear, surrounded by a lot of papers, cutting paragraphs out and pasting them into an exercise-book. I asked what she was doing and if I could have a look. "Oh, I don't think it will interest you," she said. Of course, that was the thing that, when the row came, they had most against her. Here it is - the police brought it back. Ricky said I must destroy it, but I wanted to show it to you first.'

Mrs Trant thought, 'First those horrible anonymous letters, now a ridiculous exercise-book!' She said, 'I don't understand all this.'

'It's what I told you - headlines and articles and advertisements and reports of cases in court and jokes. There are a lot of jokes. Look.'

The exercise-book began with what seemed to be a collection of newspaper cuttings, but the last pages were in Laura's handwriting, clear enough at first, gradually becoming more erratic, the lines slanting upwards, downwards, the letters too large or too small.

'It was only to pass the time away,' Mrs Hudson said. 'There was no harm in it.'

'No, I suppose not.'

Mrs Trant turned to the handwriting at the end.

She said, 'The top part of this page has been torn out. Who did that?'

'I don't know. The police, perhaps. It seems they had a good laugh when they read it. That must have been one of the funniest bits.'

Mrs Trant said 'A forlorn hope? What forlorn hope?'

... a forlorn hope. First impressions - and second?

An unforgiving sky. A mechanical quality about everything and everybody which I found frightening. When I bought a ticket for the Tube, got on to a bus, went into a shop, I felt like a cog in a machine in contact with others, not like one human being associating with other human beings. The feeling that I had been drawn into a mechanism which intended to destroy me became an obsession.

I was convinced that coming back to England was the worst thing I could have done, that almost anything else would have been preferable. I was sure that some evil fate was in store for me and longed violently to escape. But I was as powerless as a useless, worn-out or badly-fitting cog. I told myself that if I left London I should get rid of this obsession – it was much more horrible than it sounds – so I wrote to the only person whose address I still had, my cousin Marion Hudson, hoping that she would be able to tell me of some place in the country where I could stay for a while. She answered offering me a room in her house. This was at the end of what they called the 'phoney war' ...

'But she seems to be writing to somebody,' said Mrs Trant. 'Who?'

'I've no idea. She didn't tell me much about herself.' Mrs Hudson added, 'I was pleased to have her. She paid well and she was good about helping me in the house, too. Yes, I was quite pleased to have her – at first.'

... the 'phoney war', which was not to last much longer. After I realized I was not going to get answers to my letters the nightmare finally settled on me. I was too miserable to bear the comments on what had happened in Europe – they were like slaps in the face.

I could not stop myself from answering back, saying that there was another side to the eternal question of who let down who, and when. This always ended in a quarrel, if you can call trying to knock a wall down by throwing yourself against it, a quarrel. I knew I was being unwise, so I tried to protect myself by silence, by avoiding everybody as much as possible. I read a great deal, took long walks, did all the things you do when you are shamming dead.

You know how you can be haunted by words, phrases, whole conversations sometimes? Well, I began to be haunted by those endless, futile arguments we used to have when we all knew the worst was coming to the worst. The world dominated by Nordics, German version –what a catastrophe. But if it were dominated by Anglo-Saxons, wouldn't that be a catastrophe too? Then, of course, England and the English. Here everybody, especially Blanca, would become acrimonious. 'Their extraordinary attitude to women.' 'They're all mad.' 'That's why.' And so on. Blanca's voice, her face, the things she used to say haunted me. When I had finished a book I would imagine her sharp criticisms. 'What do you think of that? Isn't it unbelievable? What did I tell you? Who was right?' All these things I could hear her saying.

And I began to feel that she wasn't so far wrong. There is something strange about the attitude to women as women. Not the dislike (or fear). That isn't strange of course. But it's all so completely taken for granted, and surely that is strange. It has settled down and become an atmosphere, or, if you like, a climate, and no one questions it, least of all the women themselves. There is *no* opposition. The effects are criticized, for some of the effects are hardly advertisements for the system, the cause is seldom mentioned, and then very gingerly. The few mild ambiguous protests usually come from men. Most of the women seem to be carefully trained to revenge any unhappiness they feel on each other, or on children – or on any individual man who happens to be at a disadvantage. In dealing with men as a whole, a streak of subservience, of servility, usually appears, something cold, calculating, lacking in imagination.

But no one can go against the spirit of a country with impunity, and propaganda from the cradle to the grave can do a lot.

I amused myself by making a collection of this propaganda, sometimes it is obvious, sometimes sly and oblique, but it's constant, it goes on all the time. 'For Blanca.' This is one way they do it, not the most subtle or powerful way of course.

Titles of books to be written ten years hence, or twenty, or forty, or a hundred: *Woman an Obstacle to the Insect Civilization? The Standardization of Woman, The Mechanization of Woman, Misogyny* - well, call it Misogyny - *Misogyny and British Humour* will write itself. (But why pick on England, Blanca? It's no worse than some of the others.) *Misogyny and War, the Misery of Woman and the Evil in Men or the Great Revenge that Makes all other Revenges Look Silly.* My titles go all the way from the sublime to the ridiculous.

I could have made my collection as long as I liked; there is any amount of material. But why take the trouble? It's only throwing myself against the wall again. You will never read this, I shall not escape.

Mrs Trant, who had been frowning at the words *Misogyny and War*, exclaimed indignantly 'Couldn't she find something else to occupy her mind – now, of all times?

'Do you know,' said Mrs Hudson, 'there are moments – don't laugh – when I see what she meant? All very exaggerated, of course.'

'Nonsense,' Mrs Trant repeated, examining sketches of sharp-nosed faces in the margins of the last few pages.

I am very unpopular in this damned town – they leave me in no doubt about that. A fantastic story about me has gone the rounds and they have swallowed every word of it. They will believe anything, except the truth.

Sometimes people loiter in the street and gape up at this house. The plane tree outside my window has been lopped and they can look straight into my room, or I think they can. So I keep the curtains drawn and usually read and write in a very bad light. I suppose this accounts for my fits of giddiness.

Why do people so expert in mental torture pretend blandly that it doesn't exist? Some of their glib explanations and excuses are very familiar. I often think there are many parallels to be drawn between –

Here the sentence broke off. Mrs Trant shook her head and shut the exercise-book. 'What a stifling afternoon!' she said. 'Too much light, don't you think?'

She glanced at the roses again and decided that their colour was trying. The brilliant, cloudless sky did that. It made them unfamiliar, therefore menacing, therefore, of course, unreal.

'It's all very well to say that nobody liked Laura,' she thought. 'Judy liked her.'

Judy was her youngest daughter and the prettiest. But too moody, too fanciful and self-willed. She had stood up to her father about Laura. It had been amusing at the time, but now she wasn't so sure – a girl ought to play safe, ought to go with the tide, it was a bad sign when a girl liked unpopular people. She imagined Judy growing up to be unhappy and felt weak at the knees, then suddenly angry.

She must have said 'Judy' aloud, because Mrs Hudson remarked 'You worry too much about Judy, She's all right – she's tough.'

'She's *not* tough,' thought Mrs Trant. 'She's the very reverse of tough, you sterile old fool.'

She moved her chair so that she could not see the rose beds and said 'Well, if you told Ricky about these hallucinations, I don't wonder there was a row.'

'I never told him.'

'Well, why was there all this trouble? Did she seem crazy? Did she look crazy?'

'No, not exactly. Only a very strained expression. I don't know why they made such a dead-set at her. Her *gift* for making enemies, I suppose.'

'Fluting?'

'Not only Fluting. She was so careless.'

– Careless! Leaving the wretched book lying about, and that daily woman I had spread a rumour that she was trying to pass information on to the enemy. She got on the wrong side of everybody – everybody –

'You know old Mr Roberts next door – well, she quarrelled with him. You can't imagine why. Because his dog is called Brontë, and he kicks it – well, pretends to kick it. "Here's Emily Brontë or my pet aversion," he says, and then he pretends to kick it. It's only a joke. But Ricky's right; she has no sense of humour. One day they had a shouting match over the fence. "Really, Laura," I told her, "You're making a fool of yourself. What have you got against *him*? He's a dear old man." She gave me such a strange look. "I don't know how you can breathe after a lifetime of this," she said ...

'Well, things did go very wrong, and after the anonymous letters came, Ricky said I must get rid of her."When is she going?" he would say, and I would tell him "One day next week." But the next week came and she didn't go, and the week after that and she didn't go ...'

– I should have insisted on her leaving, I see that now. But somehow I couldn't. And it wasn't the three guineas a week she paid. I said two, but she said it wasn't enough. Three she gave me, and goodness knows it's nice to have a little money in your pocket without asking for it. Mind you, I wouldn't say that Ricky is a mean man, but he likes you to ask; and at my age I oughtn't to have to ask for every shilling I spend, I do think. But it wasn't that. It went right against the grain to turn her out when she was looking so ill. Seven stone ten she weighed when she left. Even the assistant in the chemist's shop looked surprised.

Then the day when I was going to give her another hint, she said 'I've started packing'. And all her things were piled on the floor. Such a lot of junk to travel about the world with – books and photographs and old dresses, scarves and all that, and reels of coloured cotton.

A cork with a face drawn on it, a postcard of the Miraculous Virgin in the church of St Julien-le-Pauvre, a china inkstand patterned with violets, a quill pen never used, a ginger jar, a box full of old letters, a fox fur with the lining gone, silk scarves each with a history – the red, the blue, the brown, the purple – the green box I call my jewel case, a small gold key that fits the case (I'm going to lock my heart and throw away the key), the bracelet bought in Florence because it looked like a stained glass window, the ring he gave me, the old flowered workbox with coloured reels of cotton and silk and my really sharp scissors, the leather cigarette case with a photograph inside it ... Last of all, the blue envelope on which he wrote 'Listen, listen', in red chalk ...

'When I told Ricky "She's going, she's packing her things," he said "Thank God. That's the best news I've heard for a long while." But it was the next night that it happened. We were down in the kitchen. The worst raid we've had – and no Laura. I said "Do you think she's asleep?" "How could anybody sleep through this? She'll come when she's ready. I expect the zip in her ruddy siren suit's got stuck," Ricky said, and I had to laugh ... You know, he really was horrid to her. "What's the old girl want to clutter up the bathroom for?" he'd say, and I'd say "Well be fair, Ricky, she must wash, whatever her age is. If she didn't it would only be another grievance against her" ... She had some good clothes when she first came and she used to make the best of herself. "These refugees!" he'd say, "all dressed up and nowhere to go." Then she got that she didn't seem to care a damn what she looked like and he grumbled about that. She aged a lot too. "Ricky," I said, "if you do your best to get people down you can't blame them when they look down, can you?" Sometimes I wonder if she wasn't a bit right – if there isn't a very nasty spirit about.'

'But there always has been,' Mrs Trant said.

'Yes, but it's worse now, much worse ... Well, when the lull came I rushed upstairs. She was smoking and playing the gramophone she'd bought, and as I came in the record stopped and she started it again. "Laura," I said, "*is* this the moment to fool about with *music*? And your black-out's awful." While I was fixing it I heard the warden banging at the door and shouting that we were showing lights. "I thought so," she said. "The Universal Robots have arrived," and something about *RUR*. Then she went to the head of the stairs and called out to the warden "The law? The law! What about the prophets? Why do you always forget them?" In the midst of this the All Clear went. Ricky said to me "That's enough now. She's as mad as a hatter and I won't stand for it a day longer. She *must* get out." I decided not to go to bed at all, but to do my shopping early for once, and as soon as I was in the butcher's I knew it had got round already – I knew it by the way people looked at me. One woman – I couldn't see who –

said "That horrible creature ought to be shot." And somebody else said "Yes, and the ones who back her up ought to be shot too; it's a shame. Shooting's too good for them." I didn't give them any satisfaction, I can tell you. I stood there with my head up, as if I hadn't heard a word. But when I got back here the police were in the house. They'd been waiting for a pretext – not a doubt of that. They said it was about the lights, but they had a warrant and they searched her room. They took the book and all her letters. And at lunch-time Fluting telephoned to Ricky and said there was so much strong feeling in the town that something must be done to get her away at once ... I don't know how I kept so calm. But I look older too, don't you think? Do you wonder? ... After the police left she went upstairs and locked herself into her room and there she stayed. I knocked and called, but not a sound from her. When Fluting telephoned Ricky wanted to break the door down. I've never seen him in such a state – my dear, green with rage. I said No, we'd get Dr Pratt, he'd know what to do.'

'And did Dr Pratt say she was insane? What a terrible thing!'

'No, he didn't, not exactly. She opened the door to him at once and when he came downstairs Ricky talked about getting her certified. "I'll do nothing of the sort," Pratt said. "There's too much of that going on and I don't like it." '

'Pratt's an old-fashioned man, isn't he?'

'Yes, and obstinate as the devil. Try to rush him and he'll go bang the other way. And I got a strong impression that somebody else has been on at him – Fluting, probably. "She's been treated badly," he said, "from all I can hear." "Well," Ricky said, "why can't she go somewhere where she'll be treated better? I don't want her here." Pratt said he knew that the police weren't going to press any charge. "They hadn't any charge to press," I said, "except the light – and goodness knows it was the *merest glimmer*." And he smiled at me. But he told us it was advisable for Laura to leave the town. Wasn't there any friend she could go and stay with, because it would be better for her not to be alone? We said we didn't think there was – I remembered what you told me about Tom – and we all went up to her room. Pratt asked her if she was willing to go to a sanatorium for a rest and she said "Why not?" Ricky shouted at her "You get off to your sanatorium pronto. You ought to have been there long ago." "You're being inhuman," Pratt said. Ricky said "Well, will the bloody old fool keep quiet?" Pratt told him he'd guarantee that.'

'Inhuman,' said Mrs Trant. 'That's the word that keeps coming into my head all the time now – inhuman, inhuman.'

Her sister went on, 'And she was perfectly all right until the last moment. The taxi was waiting and she didn't come down, so I thought we'd better go and fetch her. "Come along, old girl," Ricky said. "It's moving day." He put his hand on her arm and gave her a tug. That was a mistake – he shouldn't have done that. It was when he touched her that she started to scream at the top of her voice. And swear – oh my dear, it was awful. He got nasty, too. He dragged her along and she clung to the banisters and shrieked and cursed. He hit her, and kicked her, and she kept on cursing – oh, I've *never* heard such curses. And I wanted to say "Don't you dare behave like that, either of you," but instead I found I was laughing. And when I looked at his face and her face and heard myself laughing I thought "Something has gone terribly wrong. I believe we're all possessed by the Devil ..." As soon as we got into the garden Ricky let go of her, a bit ashamed of himself, I will say. She stood quietly, looking around, and then – d'you know what? – she started talking about the roses and in quite a natural voice, "How exquisite they are!" "Aren't they?" I said, though I was shaking all over. "They weren't here," she said, "last time I went for a walk." I said, "They come out so quickly, so unexpectedly. Have one for your buttonhole." "No, let them live," she said. "One forgets the roses – always a mistake." She stood there staring at them as if she had never seen roses before and talking away – something about how they couldn't do it, that it wouldn't happen. "Not while there are roses," she said two or three times. Quite crazy, you see, poor Laura, whatever Pratt's opinion was. "The taxi's waiting, dear," I said, and she got in without any fuss at all.'

'Is this the place?' Mrs Trant said.

There was a photograph on the cover of a prospectus showing a large, ugly house with small windows, those on the two top floors barred. The grounds were as forbidding as the house and surrounded by a high wall.

'I don't like this place.'

'What was I to do, my dear? The sanatorium Pratt suggested was far too expensive. She's got hardly any money left, you know.

I had no idea how little she had. What will happen when it's all gone I daren't think. Then Ricky got on to this place near Newcastle. I showed her the prospectus. I asked her if she minded going and she said "No". "You do realize you need a rest, don't you?" I said. "Yes," she said, "I realize that." She can come away if she wants to.'

'Can she, do you think?'

'Well, I suppose she can. I must say the doctor there doesn't seem – I know I ought to go and see her, but I dread it so. I keep on putting it off. Of course, there's a golf links there. Not much of a garden, but a golf links. They can play golf as soon as they are getting better.'

'But does she play golf?' said Mrs Trant.

'Let's hope,' said Mrs Hudson, 'let's hope ...'

EDNA FERBER

Grandma Isn't Playing

SHE should, by now, have been a wrinkled crone with straggling
white hair and a dim eye. Certainly her mother in the Old Country
had been that at forty. Yet here was Anna Krupek, a great-
grandmother at sixty, with half a century of backbreaking work
behind her, her lean hard body straight as a girl's, her abundant
hair just streaked with iron grey, her zest for life undiminished.
The brown eyes were bright and quizzical in the parchment face;
the whole being denoted a core of soundness in a largely worm-
eaten world. Not only did this vital sexagenarian enjoy living; she
had the gift of communicating that enjoyment to others. When,
with enormous gusto, she described a dish she had cooked, a movie
she had seen, a flower that had bloomed in her garden, you
vicariously tasted the flavour of the dish, you marked the picture
for seeing, you smelled the garden blossom.

She never had been pretty, even as a girl in her Old World
peasant finery, bright-hued and coquettish. But there was about
her a sturdy independence, an unexpected sweetness such as you
find in a hardy brown sprig of mignonette.

On first seeing Anna Krupek in her best black, you were plagued
by her resemblance to someone you could not for the moment
recall – someone as plain, sustaining, and unpretentious as a loaf
of homemade bread. Then memory flashed back to those
photographs of that iron woman Letizia Bonaparte, mother of the
ill-starred Emperor – she who, alone of all that foolish family, had
been undeceived and unimpressed by the glittering world around
her.

It wasn't that Anna didn't show her years. She looked sixty – but
a salty sixty, with heart and arteries valiantly pumping blood to the
brain. Her speech still was flavoured with the tang of her native

tongue, though forty-four years had passed since she had crossed the ocean alone to marry Zyg Krupek and live with him in Bridgeport, Connecticut. This linguistic lack was only one of many traits in Anna which irked her daughter-in-law Mae, and rather delighted her grandson, Mart, and her grand-daughter Gloria.

'Heh, Gram, that's double talk,' Mart would say.

Anna's son, Steve, would rather mildly defend his mother from the waspish attacks of his wife, Mae. 'Now, Mae, leave Ma alone. If you don't like the way she does things why'n't you do 'em yourself?'

For Anna Krupek lived in that household and the household lived on Anna, though none of them realized it, least of all she. It was Anna who kept the house spotless; it was Anna who cooked, washed, darned, mended. But then, she had been used to that all her life; she was a dynamo that functioned tirelessly, faithfully, with a minimum of noise and fuss, needing only a drop or two of the oil of human kindness to keep her going.

Mae, the refined, the elegant, perhaps pricked a little by her conscience would say, perversely, 'I wish I had your energy. You never sit still, makes me tired just to watch you rushing around.'

'Inside is only,' Anna would say above the buzz of the vacuum or the whir of the mixer, for Mae's house was equipped with all the gadgets of the luxury-loving American home.

' "Inside is only." Only what, for God's sake! Drives me crazy the way you never finish your sentences. Fifty years in this country and you'd think you landed yesterday. Inside is only what?'

Mildly Anna would elaborate. 'Your legs and arms isn't tired, and back, like is good tired from work. Inside you only is tired because you ain't got like you want. You got a good husband, Steve, you got Mart and Glory, is swell kids, you got a nice house and everything fixed fine, only is like all the time fighting inside yourself you would like big and rich like in the movies. Is foolish.'

'I don't know what you're talking about.'

But she knew well enough. Mae Krupek definitely felt she had married beneath her when she, with generations of thin native blood in her veins, had condescended to Steve Krupek, son of that Bohunk Anna Krupek. Steve had been all right, a nice boy, and earning pretty good money in the Bridgeport General Electric, but everybody knew his mother had supported herself and her children and educated them by doing scrubbing and washing for

Bridgeport's comfortable households. Before her marriage to Steve twenty years ago, Mae had taken the secretarial course in a Bridgeport business school, but she never could learn to spell and her typed letters looked like sheet music. She never kept a job more than a week or two. But she knew what was what; she never had worn white shoes to work; and now her nails were maroon, she pronounced 'and' with two dots over the *a*, her picture even sometimes appeared in the club and society page of the *Bridgeport Post* when there were local drives or community doings or large municipal activities of an inclusive nature. Still, she wasn't a complete fool. Though she thought it would be wonderful to have the house to herself with her husband, Steve, and her son, Mart, and her daughter, Gloria, she knew, did Mae, that her mother-in-law was a pearl of great price when it came to cooking the family meals, doing the family dishes, scrubbing the family floors, all of which tasks are death on maroon nail polish.

But if the second generation, embodied in Anna Krupek's son and his wife, took her for granted or grudgingly accepted her, the third generation, surprisingly enough, seemed to meet her on common ground. Mae had managed to get herself and her husband on the membership roll of a second-rate country club. Mart and Gloria never went near it. Mae and Steve, in the century's twenties and thirties, had dutifully followed the pattern of hip flask and high speed and cheap verbal cynicism. Theirs had been a curious grocer's list vocabulary of rejection: 'Nuts!' 'Applesauce!' 'Banana oil!' 'Boloney!' To the ears of Mart and Gloria this would have sounded as dated and ineffectual as the 'nit', 'rubberneck', 'skiddoo' of a still earlier day.

When Gloria Krupek had been born, almost eighteen years ago, the first thing that struck her family's eye was her resemblance to her Grandmother Krupek. It was fantastic – the little face with its wrinkles and its somewhat anxious look; thin, wiry, independent. The Connecticut neighbours said, 'She's the spit of her grammaw, the way she looks at you. Look, she's trying to set up!'

They had named her Gloria (influence of the movies on Mae), and Anna Krupek had not interfered, though her nice sense of fitness told her that it somehow didn't sound well with Krupek. She thought that a plain name like Sophie or Mary or Anna would have been better. She did not know why.

Perhaps the day and age into which they were born had given

young Mart and Gloria their curiously adult outlook, their healthy
curiosity about the world. The years of the Depression had been
followed by the war years. These two young things never had
known a world other than that. Emotional, economic, and
financial turmoil, all were accepted by them as the normal
background to living. They had been catapulted into chaos and
had adjusted themselves to it. Their parents, Mae and Steve, were
like spoiled, foolish children to them. They were fond of them,
tolerant of them, but not impressed. But the old woman of peasant
stock – hardy, astringent, shrewd, debunked – this one they
understood and respected. They knew the simple story of her early
days – a trite enough story in American annals. They never thought
of it, consciously, but they knew her for a courageous human being
who had faced her fight with life, and fought it. She didn't bore
them as she bored Mae and – sometimes – Steve. Mae and Steve
were impatient and even contemptuous: 'Oh, Ma, you're a pain in
the neck! This isn't the Old Country!'

The Old Country. Anna Krupek never thought of it now, except
when she saw the familiar name in the newspapers. War-torn now,
the peaceful village in which she had been born. Ravaged, blood-
sodden, gruesome. Anna had been fourteen when Zyg Krupek
sailed away to America. She would have married him before he
left, but he had no money for her passage and her parents forbade
his marrying her and leaving her, though he had promised to send
the passage money as soon as he should begin to work in the rich
New World overseas.

'Yes, a fine thing!' they scoffed. 'Marry and off he goes and
that's the last of him. And then you'll be here on our hands with a
baby more likely than not, and who will marry you then!'

They had tried to make her marry Stas after Zyg had gone –
Stas, who was an old man of thirty or more, with a fine farm of his
own and cows and pigs and God knows what all besides, and a silk
dress and gold earrings and a big gold brooch containing a lock of
his first wife's hair – she who had died giving birth to her fifth. It
was the old plot of a trite story, but it wasn't trite to Anna. She had
held out against them in the face of a constant storm of threats and
pleadings. For months she wept until her eyes were slits in her
swollen face, but her tears were shed only in the privacy of her
pillow and quietly, quietly, so that the other seven children should
not hear. And then when she was sixteen and faced with

spinsterhood in that little village from which the young strong men had fled to the golden shores of the New World – then Zyg's letter had come with the passage money. It was like a draught of new life to one dying. Pleadings and remonstrance meant nothing now. The child of sixteen packed her clothes and the linen she herself had woven and she embarked alone on the nightmarish journey.

Conn-ec-ti-cut. Bridgeport, Conn-ec-ti-cut. A place you couldn't say, even. She stepped off the gangplank in New York Harbour in her best dress, very full-skirted and tight-bodiced, with six good petticoats underneath and her bright shawl over her hair and the boots that came up to her shins. And there in the crowd stood a grand young man who looked like Zyg, but older, in a bright-blue suit and a fashionable hat with a brim and a white linen shirt and a blue satin necktie and yellow leather shoes and a gold ring on his finger. When he saw her he looked startled and then his face got red and then for one frightful moment she thought he was about to turn and run through the crowd, away from her. But then he laughed, and as she came toward him his face grew serious and then he took her in his arms and he was Zyg again, he was no longer the startled stranger in the splendid American clothes, he was Zyg again.

Sixteen to sixty. There was nothing startling or even fresh about the story. The Central European peasant girl had joined her sweetheart in America, had married him, had borne four children, all sons, and had settled in a community in which there were many from her own native land, so that she spoke with them, and her English remained bad. She had lived her lifetime, or most of it, an hour's train ride from the dazzling city of New York; she had never seen it, for you could not count that brief moment of her landing when she had been too blinded by love, happiness, bewilderment, weariness, and the effects of three weeks of seasickness in an unspeakable steerage to see or understand anything.

She had been widowed at twenty-six. Then life would have been a really grim business for anyone but a woman of Anna Krupek's iron determination. Strong, young, bred to physical labour, with centuries of toiling ancestors in her bones and blood and muscles, she had turned scrubwoman, washerwoman, cleaning woman, emergency cook for as many Bridgeport families as her day would allow. She had fed her four, she had clothed them, sent them to school; they had turned out well, not a black sheep among the lot of them. Sig, the first-born, had settled in the West and Tony had followed him and both had married. Anna had never seen their children, her grandchildren. She had thought to see them next year and next year and next, but she never had. Andy had a farm in Nebraska. None of these three of peasant farm stock had found the rocky soil of New England to their liking. Only Steve, of the four, had stayed in Bridgeport and had married there.

It was Mae who had stopped the scrubbing and the washing and the cooking and cleaning by the day.

'She's got to stop it, I tell you, Steve Krupek! It isn't fair to the children having a washwoman for a grandmother. When Gloria grows up and marries –'

'Oh, now, listen! She's five years old!'

'What of it! She won't stay five forever. She'll be going to school and everything and the other girls won't have anything to do with her.'

'Well, if they're stinkers like that I don't care if they don't.'

'You don't know what you're talking about. I know, I tell you. And I just won't have people saying that my children's grandmother is a common washwoman!'

'Just take that back, will you!'

'All right then. Washwoman. An elegant washwoman.'

'I can't support two households, not the way things are now.'

'What about those brothers of yours?'

'They're having a tough time, crops and prices and weather and all. You only have to read the papers. Fifty dollars every three months for her would look big to them. Me too, for that matter.'

So it was that Anna Krupek had come to live with her son Steve, and her daughter-in-law Mae, and her grandchildren Martin and Gloria, in the neat white house with the bright-blue shutters and the garage attached and the four trim tall cedars and the single red maple in the front yard. It was then situated on a new street in what had been a subdivision of the sprawling smoke-etched factory town; but the town had crept up on them. It still was a neat street of comfortable six or seven-room houses with a garage for every house and a car for every garage. Lawn mowers whirred, radios whanged, vacuums buzzed, telephones rang, beef roast or chicken or loin of pork scented the Sunday noontime air.

Anna Krupek's group of Bridgeport households had been stricken at her abandoning them. 'What'll we do without you,

Anna! The washing! The cleaning! Your cakes! Who'll iron my net curtains?'

'You get somebody all right.'

'Not like you, Anna.'

'Maybe I come and help for fun sometime, I don't say nothing to my folks.'

But she never did. Mae wouldn't have it. Besides, there was enough to keep Anna busy the whole day through in the house on Wilson Street. Hers was the little room off the kitchen in which Mae had fondly hoped to have a maid installed when Steve's income should soar to meet her ambitions. The maid never had materialized, but the room was a bright, neat little box, and after Anna's green thumb had worked its magic in the back yard, the hollyhocks and delphiniums and dahlias looked in at her window.

Anna Krupek had made this adjustment as she had all her life surmounted adverse or unfamiliar circumstance. She missed her independence, but she loved the proximity of her grandchildren. When, in the beginning, it had been explained to her that a grandmother who went out to clean by the day was not considered a social asset in Mae's set she had turned bewildered eyes on her son Steve.

'All my life I work.' She looked down at her gnarled brown hands, veinous, big-knuckled. She looked at them as you would look at two faithful friends who have served you a lifetime. 'I worked you and the boys should have everything nice, school and nice shoes and good to eat so you grow big, like your pa wanted.' It was not said in reproach. It was a simple statement of fact uttered in bewilderment.

'I know, Ma. I know.' Steve was shamefaced. 'You been swell. It's only that Mae thinks – we think you've worked hard enough all your life and now you ought to take it easy.'

'I got no money to take it easy.' This, too, was not said in reproach. The truth only, spoken by a realist.

Then Mae took matters in hand. The children of the people you scrub and wash for ... same school as Gloria and Martin ... it isn't fair to them ... won't want to play with a washwoman's grandchildren ...

Anna turned and looked at her son, and his eyes dropped and a sick feeling gripped him at the pit of his stomach. A little silence beat in the room. Hammered. Pounded. Then Anna Krupek's hands that had been fists of defiance opened, palms up, on her knees in a gesture of acceptance.

'I don't want I should do anything would hurt Glory or Mart. I guess things is different. I been so used to work all the time, but maybe I like to play like a lady now.'

'Sure, Ma. Sure!' Steve, hearty and jocular so that the hurt look might vanish from her eyes.

She had five dollars each month from one of the four sons, turn and turn about, and usually ten dollars from each of them at Christmastime. Her wants were few. Her neat starched gingham dresses in the house, her black for best, a bus into Bridgeport's Main Street for a little shopping and an occasional motion picture. Ten cents for an ice-cream cone for Glory; a quarter surreptitiously slipped to Mart for one of his mechanical contraptions.

For a time, in her late forties and early fifties, she had felt very shaky and queer; there were times when she could scarcely get through a day's work. But that passed and then a new strength had seemed to flow back into her body; it was almost as if she were young again. There seemed little enough that she could do with this new energy. The housework had become routine, the rooms shone, the meals were hot and punctual, the flowers bloomed in the garden, she even planted some vegetables each year because she loved to tend them and to pluck the succulent leaves and roots and pods.

A shining car in the garage – two, in fact, if you counted the rackety, snorting vehicle that Mart had contrived out of such parts and pieces as he could collect from derelict and seemingly dead motors of ancient vintage. Overstuffed furniture in the living room. A radio that looked like a book-case. Silk stockings so taken for granted that Gloria never had heard of anything else. Movies. They never walked. They jumped into the car to go down to the corner to get a loaf of bread, to buy a pack of cigarettes at the neighbourhood drugstore.

Anna should have been content and happy, but she was uneasy. Here was more of luxury than she and her compatriots had ever dreamed of in the days of the Central European village, even when they had talked of the wonders of the golden New World. Something was missing, something was wrong. She began to be fussy, she was overneat, the two women bickered increasingly. But there was Mart and there was Gloria. Anna drank new life and new meaning in life from the wellspring of their youth and vitality.

Mart, from his fourteenth year, had lived a mysterious life of his own in a world made up of mechanical things that inhabited a corner of the cellar. He was nearly twenty now. Bolts, nuts, screws, rods, struts, engines, fuselages, jigs, tanks, wings, presses, drills, filled his life, made up his vocabulary. Food scarcely interested him except as fuel. He stoked absentmindedly and oftenest alone and at odd hours, his face turned away from his plate as he read the latest magazine on mechanics. His boyish incisive voice would be heard from the cellar depths.

'I can't come up now. I'm busy. Put it on a plate somewhere, will you, Gram?'

'Everything gets cold.'

'Naw.' When he emerged an hour later, grease-stained and sooty-faced, there was his food, neatly covered over and somehow miraculously hot and succulent, awaiting him.

'Is good?'

'Huh? Oh. Yeah. Swell.' His eyes on the book, his mouth full, his legs wound round the chair rungs. But, finished, he would carry his plate to the kitchen sink and scrape it neatly and even make as though to wash it.

'Go away. I do that.'

'I might as well learn kitchen police right now.'

Suddenly he would grab her, he would twist his lean frame into the latest jitterbug contortions, he would whirl her yelping through space. He would set her down carefully, soberly, and disappear into the cellar workshop, where a single bulb lighted the metal-strewn bench.

Breathless, enchanted, she would screech down the cellar stairs, 'Crazy fool! I tell your pa!'

'Madam, close that door. Visitors not allowed in private office of aviation experts.'

Gloria, going on eighteen, was a modern streamlined version of her grandmother; the firm chin, the clear-eyed look, the mouth that curled up a little at the corners. Usually her dark hair hung softly to her shoulders, but sometimes, busy at some task, she slicked it away from her face and then the resemblance between the old and the young was startling. In shorts or slacks, uncorseted, bare-legged, sandalled, Gloria moved with the freedom of a winged thing.

'Skinny is all the go now,' Anna Krupek would say, her fond

eyes following the girl. 'Your age I used to cry I was so thin. Zyg, your grampaw, he made fun; he said I was like a chicken, scrawny. It was then stylish to be fat. Now girls got legs like boys, thinner even, and on top too.'

The two were like the upper and lower halves of a wholesome bread sandwich, and between them was Mae Krupek of the middle generation, a limp lettuce leaf spiked with factory mayonnaise, serving only to bind the two together.

There were plans of great elegance for Gloria. Mae wanted her to attend a private school after she had finished at the high school. 'Well, I guess I could swing it,' Steve said, 'if she wants it. I didn't know there was a place in Bridgeport where –'

'Not Bridgeport,' Mae interrupted, and trying to make it sound casual. 'There's a lovely girls' school in Boston, near Harvard; that Denning girl went there, she married Christopher Houghton, Third; they live in New York.'

'You're crazy,' Steve said, but without heat, as one would state a fact.

'I knew you'd say that. What chance has she got in a town like this! We're nobody. Away at a good school they meet other girls, and they have brothers, and Gloria meets them and she's invited to their houses, week-ends and everything.'

'Yeah. Only maybe it would work in reverse, see. Gloria's got a brother too, you know. And maybe one of these dames would meet him, low as we are, and she might fall for him, and then you'd have nothing but a daughter-in-law on your hands instead of What's-his-name Third.'

But as it turned out they needn't have bothered. The neat white house on Wilson Street began to shake and tremble with the roar of traffic. Trucks, cars, jeeps, buses packed with workingmen and – a little later – women, all headed for the aeroplane factory that was two miles distant. Until now it had been rather a modest plant, an experimental thing, really, reached by way of another street. Now it had doubled, trebled, quadrupled in size; its hum could be heard for miles; it was served not by hundreds but by thousands, and you could hardly tell which were men and which women, for they all wore pants and shirts and the girls had their heads bound in snoods or kerchiefs. 'Like was in the Old Country, only not pants,' Anna Krupek said interestedly. She followed the news avidly; she read of the country of her birth, of the horror that had befallen it;

her kind eyes were stern. 'We've got to do something. Quick we got to do or is here in America like over in Old Country, people is killed, people is hungry, everything goes in pieces, houses, and towns and churches and schools. We got to do quick.'

Young Mart did quick. He came in at suppertime one evening with a young fellow in uniform.

'Them wings is pretty,' Anna Krupek said. 'You get a suit like that, Marty, and I make you embroidery wings on it the way this young man is got.'

They had roared at that.

'Yup, I'm getting me a suit, Gram,' Mart said. 'And I hope I'll have the wings, too. Only they come already embroidered.'

The young fellow with him was Lieutenant Gurk; the family gathered that he had been stationed in Texas, he was out at Mitchell Field on some special mission, he hoped to go overseas very soon. He was unloquacious, like Mart. He and Gloria seemed to know a number of people in common, which was strange.

'Gurk,' said Mae, pronouncing the name with considerable distaste. 'From Texas?'

'No, ma'am, I'm —'

'There were some Gurks - let me see - they had a garage and filling station - remember, Steve? We pass it near the bridge - Gurk's Garage. But of course you wouldn't be re —'

'Yes. That's me, Mike Gurk. That's my father's place.'

Mae was furious. She spoke to Mart about it later, after the young man had gone. She addressed herself not only to Mart but to her husband and to Gloria and even Anna, as one who knows herself to be right and expects the support of the family against an erring member of the group.

'I'm upset enough about your being in it and risking your life, and goodness knows aviation's the most dangerous - but at least there are wonderful boys in it of the best families, and why you have to pick one like that to bring home, a common mechanic out of a garage in greasy overalls!'

'Hi, you're getting mixed, Mom.' His tone was light, but his face was scarlet.

'You could think of your sister once in a while. There are perfectly stunning aviators. This is a wonderful chance for Gloria - and you too, for that matter - to meet the most —'

But he left the room then, to Mae's chagrined bewilderment. Gloria was about to follow him. Then she began to laugh; she laughed as you would at a vexatious but dear child. 'Look, cooky, this war wasn't arranged so that I could meet dazzling members of the Air Force, exactly.'

'But it wouldn't hurt the war if you did! And I don't need you to tell me about the war, thank you. I'm doing my share.'

Mae was serving on committees, she was busy at jobs that entailed calling people on the telephone or going to their houses. She seemed particularly occupied with the war work which necessitated canvassing the houses in the more impressive residence sections – Brooklawn, the more fashionable end of old South Park Avenue, and the tree-shaded, sizeable houses on Toilsome Hill. She would return to her own home after one of these sorties, her mood gay or sullen depending on what she had seen or heard. She would glance with new eyes at the interior of the house on Wilson Street, and even at its outside aspect.

'Well, I wouldn't have believed it. With all their money, and the place looks like a junk shop. Not even good antiques.' Or, with a baleful look around the living room, 'These curtains are dated and stuffy. They don't use that heavy material any more. Chintz, or silk with net glass curtains, or that cream kind of linen stuff, or wool. That's what's smart now. Those old things are hideous!'

Steve's job with the GE was a war job now, automatically. He worked early, he worked late, he looked tired and older, but he had the air of one who knows that his work is good and useful. Gloria said she was going to be a Wave*, she was going to join the WACs†; she applied for Red Cross Motor Service, she worked as Nurse's Aide, she gave her fresh young blood to the blood bank; she collected this and that, she was on committees, she grew thinner, her eyes were bigger, but there was a sort of bloom about her, too. She said, 'This is no damn good, this is silly, I'm not really doing anything, I wish I could be a ferry bomber pilot, I wish I could go overseas, I wish, I wish, I wish.'

Anna Krupek was not one to avoid fundamental truths. 'You wish, you wish – I know what you wish. You wish you got a husband and baby, that is what you wish.'

A look of desperation leaped into Gloria's eyes. 'They're all going away, the men. Pretty soon there won't be any to marry.'

* Women Accepted for Volunteer Emergency Service
† Women's Army Corps

Anna Krupek, standing at the stove, stirring something in a pot like a benevolent witch, said comfortably over her shoulder, 'They come back. You wait.'

'I don't want to wait.'

'Or you go where he is. Like me. I betcha I cried like anything, my folks was mad with me, but I went where Zyg was, across the ocean even I went.'

'That was different. You were different.'

'Nothing is different. On top only.'

Mae confronted Gloria one day. 'Who was that man in uniform I saw you with on Fairfield Avenue?'

Gloria flushed, but she was unable to resist paraphrasing the classic reply. 'That wasn't no man in uniform, that was my beau.'

'It looked like that Gurk.'

'It was Lieutenant Gurk.'

'How did you happen to run into him?'

'I didn't. I telephoned him.'

'I thought he was at Mitchell Field, or Texas, or – didn't he say he was going overseas?'

'He's being sent to Seattle, Washington, first. And then probably Alaska – the Aleutians – up where —' She turned her face away.

'Gloria, I hope to goodness you haven't been seeing that – that – I hope you haven't been seeing him, even with Mart.'

Gloria's voice had an even edge like cold steel. 'You couldn't call it just seeing him, exactly. I've been chasing him. I've been breaking my legs running after him.'

'You must be out of your mind!'

'You never said a truer word.'

Mae started to make a thing of it, a family to-do, with tears, reproaches, and name-calling, but then Lieutenant Gurk vanished not only physically but in all his manifestations so far as Mae was concerned, because Mart went, too; he wasn't Mart any more, he was Martin Krupek of the American Air Forces. The psychopathic dreams of a mad paperhanger had reached across thousands of miles of ocean and land and had changed the carefree boy into a purposeful man.

Each member of the family took it in his or her own way. Mae moped and cried and put up photographs of him all over the house, including rather repulsive studies taken at the age of two months. Steve looked older and more careworn than ever, but there was nothing of age or care in his voice when he spoke of him. 'My son, Martin. He's in the Air Force, you know. Aviation. Don't know yet whether he's going to be a pilot or a bombardier. Yep, aviation. That's the thing. God, if I was twenty years younger! But it's kids these days. Boys.'

Gloria said little. She was working hard in a confused and scattered effort. She was gone from morning until night. She spent her free time writing letters, and all her small change on air-mail stamps.

Anna Krupek went about her business. She was quieter. She was alone in the house now for the greater part of the day. Mae did practically nothing in the way of household work. 'My Red Cross,' she said possessively as she whisked out of the house, usually taking the car for her exclusive use. 'My Bundles Committee. My Drive Committee.'

Then a queer thing happened. The neighbours noticed that the house seemed closed almost daily for hours during the middle of the day. Anna Krupek would board a bus after the others had breakfasted and gone. She would return in mid afternoon or even later sometimes.

'Where were you, Ma? I tried to get the house on the phone and no answer.'

'Maybe out in the yard or to the store.'

The meals were prompt and good in spite of the rationing. When they complained about meat shortage she said, 'We cook *haluski* in Old Country, not meat all the time like here. Morning it would be dark yet, the men would get up and go to the farm, it was miles away, not like here in America, farmers live on the farm like Sig and Tony and Andy got it good. We would get up too, pitch-black, and make the housework and cook *haluski*, it was like little noodles, only cut with a spoon in little pieces, not like noodles with a knife. And we would put in pot hot with hot stones and we take it out to the men, miles, and they would eat it for their breakfast and it was good.'

'Sounds awful,' Mae said.

'You yell about no coffee. Maybe once a week we had coffee, it was out of barley roasted in our oven, not real coffee like you got. It tasted fine I can tell you. We had only Sunday. Meat once a month, it taste like a piece of cake, so sweet.'

'Well, thank God Mart's getting meat; steaks and things.'

'Plenty of food,' Steve said, crossly for him. 'People bellyaching. Ought to be working. Planes, that's what we need. They could use twice the help they've got. Men and women.'

'You betcha!' Anna Krupek said with enormous energy. Then again in what amounted almost to a shout, 'You betcha!'

She jumped up from the table and brought in the meat. She had managed to get a ham, juicy and tender; she served with it a hot sauce blended of homemade grape jelly and prepared mustard; it was smooth and piquant on the tongue. It was like a Sunday dinner, or a holiday.

'Gosh, you certainly did yourself proud, Ma,' Steve said. I'll bet there's no other country in the world where a family can sit down to a meal like this, middle of the week. Is it somebody's birthday or something I've forgotten?'

'No,' said Anna Krupek, and brought in a lemon chiffon pie.

There was nothing to warn them. When Mae Krupek came home next day at five her mother-in-law was not there. Gloria had just come in, the early spring day was unseasonably hot, there was no dinner in preparation, the kitchen was silent except for the taunting whir of the refrigerator.

'Well, really!' Mae snatched off her hat, ran a hand through her hair, and glared at the white enamel cabinets which gave her as good as she sent, glare for glare. 'After five! Your father'll be home and no dinner. She's probably gone to a movie or something, or running around with those everlasting points. I'm dead. Simply dead.'

Gloria, sprawled on the couch in the living room, jumped up and came into the kitchen. 'Well, let's get things started. I hope nothing's happened to Gram.'

'Never fear,' Mae retorted.

'If it weren't for Gram you'd have to get dinner every day, and breakfast too, and everything.'

'And how about yourself!'

'Oh, me too. Sure. I'd like to learn to cook.'

'Why?' snapped Mae, whirling on her.

'Well, my goodness, why not?' Gloria said, reasonably enough. 'Anyway, Gram's a kind of unpaid slavey around here.'

'She gets her room and board and everything.'

'So do you.'

'You're crazy. I happen to be your father's wife.'

'Gram's his mother.'

The heat, the annoyance, and the prospect of wrestling with the contents of the refrigerator caused Mae's taut nerves to snap. 'Oh, shut up!' she yelled, her refinement temporarily cast off like a too-tight garment. Steve Krupek, coming in at the moment, blinked mildly.

'What's the ruckus?'

'Nothing. Dinner'll be late. Your ma isn't home.'

'O.K. Too hot to eat, anyway. Wonder where Ma is.'

The three stood there in the clean, white kitchen with its gay, painted border and its polka-dotted, ruffled curtains and its geranium blooming in the window pot. Queer not to see the neat, deft figure performing expert magic with pots and pans and spoons.

Someone passed the kitchen window. Grandma Krupek always came in the back way. The kitchen door was locked. You heard her key click.

Grandma Krupek stood framed in the doorway with the new green of the backyard lawn behind her. Then she stepped into the kitchen.

They stared at her, the three of them. It is noteworthy that not one of them laughed. It was not only amazement that kept them from this; it was something in her face, a look of shyness, a look of courage, a look of resolve, a curious mixture of all three that blended to make an effect of nobility.

Then, 'Well, my God!' said Mae Krupek, and dropped a pan in the sink with a clatter and spatter.

Anna Krupek was dressed in slacks and shirt, the one blue, the other grey, and her hair was bound in a coloured kerchief. On her feet were neat, serviceable, flat-heeled shoes, in her hand was a lunch box such as workmen carry.

'Hello,' said Grandma Krupek inadequately. She put down her lunch box, went to the sink, and retrieved the pan and its contents.

Between them Steve and Mae said all the things that people say in astonishment, disapproval, and minor panic: 'What does this mean!' 'Have you lost your mind!' 'You can't do a thing like this!' 'What will people say!' 'We'll put a stop to it.' 'You're making a fool of yourself and all of us.'

Only Gloria, between tears and laughter, kissed her

grandmother and gave her a hearty smack behind and said, surveying the slim little figure in trousers and shirt, 'Sexagenarian is right!'

Anna Krupek stood her ground. Quietly, stubbornly, over and over again she said, 'I work in aeroplane factory. Is defence. Is fine. I like. I make plane for Mart. In a week only I learned so quick.'

'You can't do that kind of work. You're too old. You'll be sick.'

Anna's was a limited vocabulary, but she succeeded in making things reasonably plain.

'Say, in factory is a cinch. Easier as housework and cooking, you betcha.' Then, fearful of having hurt them, 'I cook again and make everything nice in the house after we fight the war, like always. But now I make aeroplane for Mart.' She just glanced at Gloria. 'For Mart and other boys.'

Mae drew a long breath, as though she had come up after being under water. 'We'll see about that. Steve, you've got to speak to them. You have her fired. I won't stand for it.'

'My boss is Ben Chester. I don't get fired. Years and years I work for his ma, cleaning and washing. Ben, he is crazy for me. I don't get fired. No, sir!'

Mae's lips were compressed. She was too angry for tears. 'The neighbours! And everybody laughing at us! At your age!'

Grandma Krupek wagged her head. 'Oh, is plenty old ladies working in aeroplanes.' She shot another lightning glance at Gloria. 'Old ladies and kids too. Next to me is old lady she is getting new false teeth for hundred and fifty dollar! And her hair marcel each week. I save my money, maybe I travel.'

'Travel!' echoed Mae, weakly.

But Gloria leaped the gap at last. 'Could I get a job there, do you think? Could I do it?'

'Sure thing. Two, three weeks you could travel – oh – New York or – uh – Seattle – or –' with elaborate carelessness. 'And back.'

Mae turned to Steve. 'Well, your mother won't stay here any longer, that's one sure thing. I won't have it.'

'O.K.,' said Anna Krupek, without rancour.

Steve spoke quietly. 'You're staying here, Ma. This is your home.'

Anna's face was placid but firm. 'On day shift I am through I am home five o'clock. I help you, Mae. You ain't such a bad cook;

you got to learn only. I was afraid in factory first, but I learn. Like when I cross the ocean alone to come to this country. I was afraid. But I learn.'

She looked at her two hands as she had once before, almost as though they belonged to someone else. She looked at them and turned them as she looked, palms in and then palms out, curiously, as at some rare jewels whose every facet reflected a brilliant new light.

'What you think! I make aeroplane. I sit in chair, comfortable, I put a little piece in a little hole it should fit nice, and for this I am pay fifty dollar a week.' She shook her head as though to rid it of a dream. 'Zyg, he won't believe it.'

DOROTHY PARKER

The Lovely Leave

HER husband had telephoned her by long distance to tell her about the leave. She had not expected the call, and she had no words arranged. She threw away whole seconds explaining her surprise at hearing him, and reporting that it was raining hard in New York, and asking was it terribly hot where he was. He had stopped her to say, look, he didn't have time to talk long; and he had told her quickly that his squadron was to be moved to another field the next week and on the way he would have twenty-four hours' leave. It was difficult for her to hear. Behind his voice came a jagged chorus of young male voices, all crying the syllable 'Hey!'

'Ah, don't hang up yet,' she said. 'Please. Let's talk another minute, just another—'

'Honey, I've got to go,' he said. 'The boys all want a crack at the telephone. See you a week from today, around five. 'Bye.'

Then there had been a click as his receiver went back into place. Slowly she cradled her telephone, looking at it as if all frustrations and bewilderments and separations were its fault. Over it she had heard his voice, coming from far away. All the months, she had tried not to think of the great blank distance between them; and now that far voice made her know she had thought of nothing else. And his speech had been brisk and busy. And from back of him had come gay, wild young voices, voices he heard every day and she did not, voices of those who shared his new life. And he had heeded them and not her, when she begged for another minute. She took her hand off the telephone and held it away from her with the fingers spread stiffly apart, as if it had touched something horrid.

Then she told herself to stop her nonsense. If you looked for things to make you feel hurt and wretched and unnecessary, you were certain to find them, more easily each time, so easily, soon,

that you did not even realize you had gone out searching. Women
alone often developed into experts at the practice. She must never
join their dismal league.

What was she dreary about, anyway? If he had only a little while
to talk, then he had only a little while to talk, that was all.
Certainly he had had time to tell her he was coming, to say that
they would be together soon. And there she was, sitting scowling at
the telephone, the kind, faithful telephone that had brought her the
lovely news. She would see him in a week. Only a week. She began
to feel, along her back and through her middle, little quivers of
excitement, like tiny springs uncoiling into spirals.

There must be no waste to this leave. She thought of the
preposterous shyness that had fallen upon her when he had come
home before. It was the first time she had seen him in uniform.
There he stood, in their little apartment, a dashing stranger in
strange, dashing garments. Until he had gone into the army, they
had never spent a night apart in all their marriage; and when she
saw him, she dropped her eyes and twisted her handkerchief and
could bring nothing but monosyllables from her throat. There
must be no such squandering of minutes this time. There must be
no such gangling diffidence to lop even an instant from their
twenty-four hours of perfect union. Oh, Lord, only twenty-four
hours ...

No. That was exactly the wrong thing to do; that was directly the
wrong way to think. That was the way she had spoiled it before.
Almost as soon as the shyness had left her and she felt she knew
him again, she had begun counting. She was so filled with the
desperate consciousness of the hours sliding away - only twelve
more, only five, oh, dear God, only one left - that she had no room
for gaiety and ease. She had spent the golden time in grudging its
going.

She had been so woebegone of carriage, so sad and slow of word
as the last hour went, that he, nervous under the pall, had spoken
sharply and there had been a quarrel. When he had had to leave for
his train, there were no clinging farewells, no tender words to keep.
He had gone to the door and opened it and stood with it against his
shoulder while he shook out his flight cap and put it on, adjusting
it with great care, one inch over the eye, one inch above the ear.
She stood in the middle of the living room, cool and silent, looking
at him.

When his cap was precisely as it should be, he looked at her.

'Well,' he said. He cleared his throat. 'Guess I'd better get going.'

'I'm sure you had,' she said.

He studied his watch intently. 'I'll just make it,' he said.

'I'm sure you will,' she said.

She turned, not with an actual shrug, only with the effect of one, and went to the window and looked out, as if casually remarking on the weather. She heard the door close loudly and then the grind of the elevator.

When she knew he was gone, she was cool and still no longer. She ran about the little flat, striking her breast and sobbing.

Then she had two months to ponder what had happened, to see how she had wrought the ugly small ruin. She cried in the nights.

She need not brood over it any more. She had her lesson; she could forget how she had learned it. This new leave would be the one to remember, the one he and she would have, to keep forever. She was to have a second chance, another twenty-four hours with him. After all, that is no short while, you know; that is, if you do not think of it as a thin little row of hours dropping off like beads from a broken string. Think of it as a whole long day and a whole long night, shining and sweet, and you will be all but awed by your fortune. For how many people are there who have the memory of a whole long day and a whole long night, shining and sweet, to carry with them in their hearts until they die?

To keep something, you must take care of it. More, you must understand just what sort of care it requires. You must know the rules and abide by them. She could do that. She had been doing it all the months, in the writing of her letters to him. There had been rules to be learned in that matter, and the first of them was the hardest: never say to him what you want him to say to you. Never tell him how sadly you miss him, how it grows no better, how each day without him is sharper than the day before. Set down for him the gay happenings about you, bright little anecdotes, not invented, necessarily, but attractively embellished. Do not bedevil him with the pinings of your faithful heart because he is your husband, your man, your love. For you are writing to none of these. You are writing to a soldier.

She knew those rules. She would have said that she would rather die, and she would have meant something very near the words, than send a letter of complaint or sadness or cold anger to her husband, a soldier far away, strained and weary from his work, giving all he had for the mighty cause. If in her letters she could be all he wanted her to be, how much easier to be it when they were together. Letters were difficult; every word had to be considered and chosen. When they were together again, when they could see and hear and touch each other, there would be no stiltedness. They would talk and laugh together. They would have tenderness and excitement. It would be as if they had never been separated. Perhaps they never had been. Perhaps a strange new life and strange empty miles and strange gay voices had no existence for two who were really one.

She had thought it out. She had learned the laws of what not to do. Now she could give herself up to the ecstasy of waiting his coming.

It was a fine week. She counted the time again, but now it was sweet to see it go. Two days after tomorrow, day after tomorrow, tomorrow. She lay awake in the dark, but it was a thrilling wakefulness. She went tall and straight by day, in pride in her warrior. On the street, she looked with amused pity at women who walked with men in civilian suits.

She bought a new dress; black – he liked black dresses – simple – he liked plain dresses – and so expensive that she would not think of its price. She charged it, and realized that for months to come she would tear up the bill without removing it from its envelope. All right – this was no time to think of months to come.

The day of the leave was a Saturday. She flushed with gratitude to the army for this coincidence, for after one o'clock, Saturday was her own. She went from her office without stopping for lunch, and bought perfume and toilet water and bath oil. She had a bit of each remaining in bottles on her dressing table and in her bathroom, but it made her feel desired and secure to have rich new stores of them. She bought a nightgown, a delightful thing of soft chiffon patterned with little bouquets, with innocent puffs of sleeves and a Romney neck and a blue sash. It could never withstand laundering, a French cleaner must care for it – all right. She hurried home with it, to fold it in a satin sachet.

Then she went out again and bought the materials for cocktails and whiskies-and-sodas, shuddering at their cost. She went a dozen blocks to buy the kind of salted biscuits he liked with drinks. On the way back she passed a florist's shop in the window of which were displayed potted fuchsia. She made no attempt to resist them. They were too charming, with their delicate parchment-coloured inverted cups and their graceful magenta bells. She bought six pots of them. Suppose she did without lunches the next week – all right.

When she was done with the little living-room, it looked gracious and gay. She ranged the pots of fuchsia along the window sill, she drew out a table and set it with glasses and bottles, she plumped the pillows and laid bright-covered magazines about invitingly. It was a place where someone entering eagerly would find delighted welcome.

Before she changed her dress, she telephoned downstairs to the man who tended both the switchboard and the elevator.

'Oh,' she said, when he eventually answered. 'Oh, I just want to say, when my husband, Lieutenant McVicker, comes, please send him right up.'

There was no necessity for the call. The wearied attendant would have brought up anyone to any flat without the additional stress of a telephoned announcement. But she wanted to say the words 'my husband' and she wanted to say 'lieutenant'.

She sang, when she went into the bedroom to dress. She had a sweet, uncertain little voice that made the lusty song ludicrous.

> Off we go into the wild blue yonder,
>   Climbing high into the sun, sun, sun, sun.
> Here they come: zooming to meet our thunder—
>   At 'em boys, give 'er the gun!

She kept singing, in a preoccupied way, while she gave close attention to her lips and her eyelashes. Then she was silent and held her breath as she drew on the new dress. It was good to her. There was a reason for the cost of those perfectly plain black dresses. She stood looking at herself in the mirror with deep interest, as if she watched a chic unknown, the details of whose costume she sought to memorize.

As she stood there, the bell rang. It rang three times, loud and quick. He had come.

She gasped, and her hands fluttered over the dressing table. She seized the perfume atomizer and sprayed scent violently all about her head and shoulders, some of it reaching them. She had already perfumed herself, but she wanted another minute, another moment, anything. For it had taken her again – the outrageous shyness. She could not bring herself to go to the door and open it. She stood, shaking, and squirted perfume.

The bell rang three times loud and quick again, and then an endless peal.

'Oh, *wait*, can't you?' she cried. She threw down the atomizer, looked wildly around the room as if for a hiding-place, then sternly made herself tall and sought to control the shaking of her body. The shrill noise of the bell seemed to fill the flat and crowd the air out of it.

She started for the door. Before she reached it, she stopped. There he stood in the brightly lighted little hall. All the long sad nights, and all the strong and sensible vows. And now he had come. And there she stood.

'Well, for heaven's sake!' she said. 'I had no idea there was anybody out here. Why, you were just as quiet as a little mouse.'

'Well! don't you ever open the door?' he said.

'Can't a women have time to put on her shoes?' she said.

He came in and closed the doors behind him. 'Ah, darling,' he said. He put his arms around her. She slid her cheek along his lips, touched her forehead to his shoulder, and broke away from him.

'Well!' she said. 'Nice to see you, Lieutenant. How's the war?'

'How are you?' he said. 'You look wonderful.'

'Me?' she said. 'Look at you.'

He was well worth looking at. His fine clothes complemented his fine body. The precision of his appointments was absolute, yet he seemed to have no consciousness of it. He stood straight, and he moved with grace and assurance. His face was browned. It was thin, so thin that the bones showed under the cheeks and down the jaws; but there was no look of strain in it. It was smooth and serene and confident. He was the American officer, and there was no finer sight than he.

'Well!' she said. She made herself raise her eyes to his and found suddenly that it was no longer difficult. 'Well, we can't just stand here saying "well" at each other. Come on in and sit down. We've got a long time ahead of us – oh, Steve, isn't it wonderful! Hey. Didn't you bring a bag?'

'Why, you see,' he said, and stopped. He slung his cap over onto the table among the bottles and glasses. 'I left the bag at the station. I'm afraid I've got sort of rotten news, darling.'

She kept her hands from flying to her breast.

'You - you're going overseas right away?' she said.

'Oh, Lord, no,' he said. 'Oh, no, no, no. I said this was rotten news. No. They've changed the orders, baby. They've taken back all leaves. We're to go right on to the new field. I've got to get a train at six-ten.'

She sat down on the sofa. She wanted to cry; not silently with slow crystal tears, but with wide mouth and smeared face. She wanted to throw herself stomach-down on the floor, and kick and scream, and go limp if anyone tried to lift her.

'I think that's awful,' she said. 'I think that's just filthy.'

'I know,' he said. 'But there's nothing to do about it. This is the army, Mrs Jones.'

'Couldn't you have said something?' she said. 'Couldn't you have told them you've had only one leave in six months? Couldn't you have said all the chance your wife had to see you again was just this poor little twenty-four hours? Couldn't you have explained what it meant to her? Couldn't you?'

'Come on, now, Mimi,' he said. 'There's a war on.'

'I'm sorry,' she said. 'I was sorry as soon as I'd said it. I was sorry while I was saying it. But - oh, it's so hard!'

'It's not easy for anybody,' he said. 'You don't know how the boys were looking forward to their leaves.'

'Oh, I don't give a damn about the boys!' she said.

'That's the spirit that'll win for our side,' he said. He sat down in the biggest chair, stretched his legs and crossed his ankles.

'You don't care about anything but those pilots,' she said.

'Look, Mimi,' he said. 'We haven't got time to do this. We haven't got time to get into a fight and say a lot of things we don't mean. Everything's all - all speeded up, now. There's no time left for this.'

'Oh, I know,' she said. 'Oh, Steve, don't I know!'

She went over and sat on the arm of his chair and buried her face in his shoulder.

'This is more like it,' he said. 'I've kept thinking about this.' She nodded against his blouse.

'If you knew what it was to sit in a decent chair again,' he said. She sat up. 'Oh,' she said. 'It's the chair. I'm so glad you like it.'

'They've got the worst chairs you ever saw, in the pilots' room,' he said. 'A lot of busted-down old rockers - honestly, rockers -

that big-hearted patriots contributed, to get them out of the attic. If they haven't better furniture at the new field, I'm going to do something about it, even if I have to buy the stuff myself.'

'I certainly would, if I were you,' she said. 'I'd go without food and clothing and laundry, so the boys would be happy sitting down. I wouldn't even save out enough for air mail stamps, to write to my wife once in a while.'

She rose and moved about the room.

'Mimi, what's the matter with you?' he said. 'Are you – are you jealous of the pilots?'

She counted as far as eight, to herself. Then she turned and smiled at him.

'Why – I guess I am –' she said. 'I guess that's just what I must be. Not only of the pilots. Of the whole air corps. Of the whole Army of the United States.'

'You're wonderful,' he said.

'You see,' she said with care, 'you have a whole new life – I have half an old one. Your life is so far away from mine, I don't see how they're ever going to come back together.'

'That's nonsense,' he said.

'No, please wait,' she said. 'I get strained and – and frightened, I guess, and I say things I could cut my throat for saying. But you know what I really feel about you. I'm so proud of you I can't find words for it. I know you're doing the most important thing in the world, maybe the only important thing in the world. Only – oh, Steve, I wish to heaven you didn't love doing it so much!'

'Listen,' he said.

'No,' she said. 'You mustn't interrupt a lady. It's unbecoming to an officer, like carrying packages in the street. I'm just trying to tell you a little about how I feel. I can't get used to being so completely left out. You don't wonder what I do, you don't want to find out what's in my head – why, you never even seem to ask how I am.'

'I do so!' he said. 'I asked you how you were the minute I came in.'

'That was white of you,' she said.

'Oh, for heaven's sake!' he said. 'I didn't have to ask you. I could see how you look. You look wonderful. I told you that.'

She smiled at him. 'Yes, you did, didn't you?' she said. 'And you sounded as if you meant it. Do you really like my dress?'

'Oh, yes,' he said. 'I always liked that dress on you.'

It was as if she turned to wood. 'This dress,' she said, enunciating with insulting distinctness, 'is brand new. I have never had it on before in my life. In case you are interested, I bought it especially for this occasion.'

'I'm sorry, honey,' he said. 'Oh, sure, now I see it's not the other one at all. I think it's great. I like you in black.'

'At moments like this,' she said, 'I almost wish I were in it for another reason.'

'Stop it,' he said. 'Sit down and tell me about yourself. What have you been doing?'

'Oh, nothing,' she said.

'How's the office?' he said.

'Dull,' she said. 'Dull as mud.'

'Who have you seen?' he said.

'Oh, nobody,' she said.

'Well, what do you *do*?' he said.

'In the evenings?' she said. 'Oh, I sit here and knit and read detective stories that it turns out I've read before.'

'I think that's all wrong of you,' he said. 'I think it's asinine to sit here alone, moping. That doesn't do any good to anybody. Why don't you go out more?'

'I hate to go out with just women,' she said.

'Well, why do you have to?' he said. 'Ralph's in town, isn't he? And John and Bill and Gerald. Why don't you go out with them? You're silly not to.'

'It hadn't occurred to me,' she said, 'that it was silly to keep faithful to one's husband.'

'Isn't that taking rather a jump?' he said. 'It's possible to go to dinner with a man and stay this side adultery. And don't use words like "one's". You're awful when you're elegant.'

'I know,' she said. 'I never have any luck when I try. No. You're the one that's awful, Steve. You really are. I'm trying to show you a glimpse of my heart, to tell you how it feels when you're gone, how I don't want to be with anyone if I can't be with you. And all you say is, I'm not doing any good to anybody. That'll be nice to think of when you go. You don't know what it's like for me here alone. You just don't know.'

'Yes, I do,' he said. 'I know, Mimi.' He reached for a cigarette on the little table beside him, and the bright magazine by the cigarette-box caught his eye. 'Hey, is this this week's? I haven't seen it yet.' He glanced through the early pages.

'Go ahead and read if you want to,' she said. 'Don't let me disturb you.'

'I'm not reading,' he said. He put down the magazine. 'You see, I don't know what to say, when you start talking about showing me glimpses of your heart, and all that. I know. I know you must be having a rotten time. But aren't you feeling fairly sorry for yourself?'

'If *I'm* not,' she said, 'who would be?'

'What do you want anyone to be sorry for you for?' he said. 'You'd be all right if you'd stop sitting around alone. I'd like to think of you having a good time while I'm away.'

She went over to him and kissed him on the forehead.

'Lieutenant,' she said, 'you are a far nobler character than I am. Either that,' she said, 'or there is something else at the back of this.'

'Oh, shut up,' he said. He pulled her down to him and held her there. She seemed to melt against him, and stayed there, still.

Then she felt him take his left arm from around her and felt his head raised from its place against hers. She looked up at him. He was craning over her shoulder, endeavouring to see his wrist watch.

'Oh, now, really!' she said. She put her hands against his chest and pushed herself vigorously away from him.

'It goes so quickly,' he said softly, with his eyes on his watch. 'We've - we've only a little while, darling.'

She melted again. 'Oh, Steve,' she whispered, 'dearest.'

'I do want to take a bath,' he said. Get up, will you, baby?'

She got right up. 'You're going to take a bath?' she said.

'Yes,' he said. 'You don't mind, do you?'

'Oh, not in the least,' she said. 'I'm sure you'll enjoy it. It's one of the pleasantest ways of killing time, I always think.'

'You know how you feel after a long ride on a train,' he said.

'Oh, surely,' she said.

He rose and went into the bedroom. 'I'll hurry up,' he called back to her.

'Why?' she said.

Then she had a moment to consider herself. She went into the bedroom after him, sweet with renewed resolve. He had hung his blouse and necktie neatly over a chair and he was unbuttoning his shirt. As she came in, he took it off. She looked at the beautiful brown triangle of his back. She would do anything for him, anything in the world.

'I - I'll go run your bath water,' she said. She went into the bathroom, turned on the faucets of the tub, and set the towels and mat ready. When she came back into the bedroom he was just entering the living-room, naked. In his hand he carried the bright magazine he had glanced at before. She stopped short.

'Oh,' she said. 'You're planning to read in the tub?'

'If you knew how I'd been looking forward to this!' he said. 'Boy, a hot bath in a tub! We haven't got anything but showers, and when you take a shower, there's a hundred boys waiting, yelling at you to hurry up and get out.'

'I suppose they can't bear being parted from you,' she said.

He smiled at her. 'See you in a couple of minutes,' he said, and went on into the bathroom and closed the door. She heard the slow slip and slide of water as he laid himself in the tub.

She stood just as she was. The room was lively with the perfume she had sprayed, too present, too insistent. Her eyes went to the bureau drawer where lay, wrapped in soft fragrance, the nightgown with the little bouquets and the Romney neck. She went over to the bathroom door, drew back her right foot, and kicked the base of the door so savagely that the whole frame shook.

'What, dear?' he called. 'Want something?'

'Oh, nothing,' she said. 'Nothing whatever. I've got everything any woman could possibly want, haven't I?'

'What?' he called. 'I can't hear you, honey.'

'Nothing,' she screamed.

She went into the living room. She stood, breathing heavily, her finger nails scarring her palms, as she looked at the fuchsia blossoms, with their dirty parchment-coloured cups, their vulgar magenta bells.

Her breath was quiet and her hands relaxed when he came into the living room again. He had on his trousers and shirt, and his necktie was admirably knotted. He carried his belt. She turned to him. There were things she had meant to say, but she could do nothing but smile at him, when she saw him. Her heart turned liquid in her breast.

His brow was puckered. 'Look, darling,' he said. 'Have you got any brass polish?'

'Why, no,' she said. 'We haven't even got any brass.'

'Well, have you any nail polish – the colourless kind? A lot of the boys use that.'

'I'm sure it must look adorable on them,' she said. 'No, I haven't anything but rose-coloured polish. Would that be of any use to you, heaven forbid?'

'No,' he said, and he seemed worried. 'Red wouldn't be any good at all. Hell, I don't suppose you've got a Blitz Cloth, have you? Or a Shine-O?'

'If I had the faintest idea what you were talking about,' she said, 'I might be better company for you.'

He held the belt out toward her. 'I want to shine my buckle,' he said.

'Oh ... my ... dear ... sweet ... gentle ... Lord,' she said. 'We've got about ten minutes left, and you want to shine your belt buckle.'

'I don't like to report to a new CO* with a dull belt buckle,' he said.

'It was bright enough for you to report to your wife in, wasn't it?' she said.

'Oh, stop that,' he said. 'You just won't understand, that's all.'

'It isn't that I won't understand,' she said. 'It's that I can't remember. I haven't been with a Boy Scout for so long.'

He looked at her. 'You're being great, aren't you?' he said. He looked around the room. 'There must be a cloth around somewhere – oh, this will do.' He caught up a pretty little cocktail napkin from the table of untouched bottles and glasses, sat down with his belt laid over his knees, and rubbed at the buckle.

She watched him for a moment, then rushed over to him and grasped his arm.

'Please,' she said. 'Please, I didn't mean it, Steve.'

'Please let me do this, will you?' he said. He wrenched his arm from her hand and went on with his polishing.

'You tell me I won't understand!' she cried. 'You won't understand anything about anybody else. Except those crazy pilots.'

'They're all right!' he said. 'They're fine kids. They're going to make great fighters.' He went on rubbing at his buckle.

'Oh, I know it!' she said. 'You know I know it. I don't mean it when I say things against them. How would I dare to mean it? They're risking their lives and their sight and their sanity, they're giving everything for —'

* Commanding Officer

'Don't do that kind of talk, will you?' he said. He rubbed the buckle.

'I'm not doing any kind of talk!' she said. 'I'm trying to tell you something. Just because you've got on that pretty suit, you think you should never hear anything serious, never anything sad or wretched or disagreeable. You make me sick, that's what you do! I know, I know – I'm not trying to take anything away from you. I realize what you're doing, I told you what I think of it. Don't, for heaven's sake, think I'm mean enough to grudge you any happiness and excitement you can get out of it. I know it's hard for you. But it's never lonely, that's all I mean. You have companionships no – no wife can ever give you. I suppose it's the sense of hurry, maybe, the consciousness of living on borrowed time, the – the knowledge of what you're all going into together that makes the comradeship of men in war so firm, so fast. But won't you please try to understand how I feel? Won't you understand that it comes out of bewilderment and disruption and – and being frightened, I guess? Won't you understand what makes me do what I do, when I hate myself while I'm doing it? Won't you please understand? Darling, won't you please?'

He laid down the little napkin. 'I can't go through this kind of thing, Mimi,' he said. 'Neither can you.' He looked at his watch. 'Hey, it's time for me to go.'

She stood tall and stiff. 'I'm sure it is,' she said.

'I'd better put on my blouse,' he said.

'You might as well,' she said.

He rose, wove his belt through the loops of his trousers, and went into the bedroom. She went over to the window and stood looking out, as if casually remarking the weather.

She heard him come back into the room, but she did not turn around. She heard his steps stop, knew he was standing there.

'Mimi,' he said.

She turned towards him, her shoulders back, her chin high, cool, regal. Then she saw his eyes. They were no longer bright and gay and confident. Their blue was misty and they looked troubled; they looked at her as if they pleaded with her.

'Look, Mimi,' he said, 'do you think I want to do this? Do you think I want to be away from you? Do you think that this is what I thought I'd be doing now? In the years – well, in the years when we ought to be together.'

He stopped. Then he spoke again, but with difficulty. 'I can't talk about it. I can't even think about it – because if I did I couldn't do my job. But just because I don't talk about it doesn't mean I want to be doing what I'm doing. I want to be with you, Mimi. That's where I belong. You know that, darling. Don't you?'

He held his arms open to her. She ran to them. This time, she did not slide her cheek along his lips.

When he had gone, she stood a moment by the fuchsia plants, touching delicately, tenderly, the enchanting parchment-coloured caps, the exquisite magenta bells.

The telephone rang. She answered it, to hear a friend of hers inquiring about Steve, asking how he looked and how he was, urging that he come to the telephone and say hello to her.

'He's gone,' she said. 'All their leaves were cancelled. He wasn't here an hour.'

The friend cried sympathy. It was a shame, it was simply awful, it was absolutely terrible.

'No, don't say that,' she said. 'I know it wasn't very much time. But oh, it was lovely!'

ELIZABETH BOWEN

Mysterious Kôr

FULL moonlight drenched the city and searched it; there was not a
niche left to stand in. The effect was remorseless: London looked
like the moon's capital – shallow, cratered, extinct. It was late, but
not yet midnight; now the buses had stopped the polished roads
and streets in this region sent for minutes together a ghostly
unbroken reflection up. The soaring new flats and the crouching
old shops and houses looked equally brittle under the moon, which
blazed in windows that looked its way. The futility of the black-out
became laughable: from the sky, presumably, you could see every
slate in the roofs, every whited kerb, every contour of the naked
winter flowerbeds in the park; and the lake, with its shining twists
and tree-darkened islands would be a landmark for miles, yes,
miles, overhead.

However, the sky, in whose glassiness floated no clouds but only
opaque balloons, remained glassy-silent. The Germans no longer
came by the full moon. Something more immaterial seemed to
threaten, and to be keeping people at home. This day between
days, this extra tax, was perhaps more than senses and nerves could
bear. People stayed indoors with a fervour that could be felt: the
buildings strained with battened-down human life, but not a beam,
not a voice, not a note from a radio escaped. Now and then under
streets and buildings the earth rumbled: the Underground sounded
loudest at this time.

Outside the now gateless gates of the park, the road coming
downhill from the north-west turned south and became a street,
down whose perspective the traffic lights went through their
unmeaning performance of changing colour. From the pro-
montory of pavement outside the gates you saw at once up the road
and down the street: from behind where you stood, between the

gate-posts, appeared the lesser strangeness of grass and water and trees. At this point, at this moment, three French soldiers, directed to a hostel they could not find, stopped singing to listen derisively to the waterbirds, wakened up by the moon. Next, two wardens coming off duty emerged from their post and crossed the road diagonally, each with an elbow cupped inside a slung-on tin hat. The wardens turned their faces, mauve in the moonlight, towards the Frenchmen with no expression at all. The two sets of steps died in opposite directions, and, the birds subsiding, nothing was heard or seen until, a little way down the street, a trickle of people came out of the Underground, around the anti-panic brick wall. These all disappeared quickly, in an abashed way, or as though dissolved in the street by some white acid, but for a girl and a soldier who, by their way of walking, seemed to have no destination but each other and to be not quite certain even of that. Blotted into one shadow, he tall, she little, these two proceeded towards the park. They looked in, but did not go in; they stood there debating without speaking. Then, as though a command from the street behind them had been received by their synchronized bodies, they faced round to look back the way they had come.

His look up the height of a building made his head drop back, and she saw his eyeballs glitter. She slid her hand from his sleeve, stepped to the edge of the pavement and said: 'Mysterious Kôr.'

'What is?' he said, not quite collecting himself.

'This is —

> Mysterious Kôr thy walls forsaken stand,
> Thy lonely towers beneath a lonely moon –
>
> > – this is Kôr.'

'Why,' he said, 'it's years since I've thought of that.'

She said: 'I think of it all the time –

> Not in the waste beyond the swamps and sand,
> The fever-haunted forest and lagoon,
> Mysterious Kôr thy walls —

– a completely forsaken city, as high as cliffs and as white as bones, with no history —'

'But something must once have happened: why had it been forsaken?'

'How could anyone tell you when there's nobody there?'

'Nobody there since how long?'

'Thousands of years.'

'In that case, it would have fallen down.'

'No, not Kôr,' she said with immediate authority. 'Kôr's altogether different; it's very strong; there is not a crack in it anywhere for a weed to grow in; the corners of stones and the monuments might have been cut yesterday, and the stairs and arches are built to support themselves.'

'You know all about it,' he said, looking at her.

'I know, I know all about it.'

'What, since you read that book?'

'Oh, I didn't get much from that; I just got the name. I knew that must be the right name; it's like a cry.'

'Most like the cry of a crow to me.' He reflected, then said: 'But the poem begins with "Not" – "*Not in the waste beyond the swamps and sand* —" And it goes on, as I remember, to prove Kôr's not really anywhere. When even a poem says there's no such place —'

'What it tries to say doesn't matter: I see what it makes me see. Anyhow, that was written some time ago, at that time when they thought they had got everything taped, because the whole world had been explored, even the middle of Africa. Every thing and place had been found and marked on some map; so what wasn't marked on any map couldn't be there at all. So *they* thought: that was why he wrote the poem. "*The world is disenchanted*," it goes on. That was what set me off hating civilization.'

'Well, cheer up,' he said; 'there isn't much of it left.'

'Oh, yes, I cheered up some time ago. This war shows we've by no means come to the end. If you can blow whole places out of existence, you can blow whole places into it. I don't see why not. They say we can't say what's come out since the bombing started. By the time we've come to the end, Kôr may be the one city left: the abiding city. I should laugh.'

'No, you wouldn't,' he said sharply. '*You* wouldn't – at least, I hope not. I hope you don't know what you're saying – does the moon make you funny?'

'Don't be cross about Kôr; please don't, Arthur,' she said.

'I thought girls thought about people.'

'What, these days?' she said. 'Think about people? How can anyone think about people if they've got any heart? I don't know how other girls manage: I always think about Kôr.'

'Not about me?' he said. When she did not at once answer, he turned her hand over, in anguish, inside his grasp. 'Because I'm not there when you want me - is that my fault?'

'But to think about Kôr *is* to think about you and me.'

'In that dead place?'

'No, ours - we'd be alone there.' Tightening his thumb on her palm while he thought this over, he looked behind them, around them - even up at the sky. He said finally: 'But we're alone here.'

'That was why I said "Mysterious Kôr".'

'What, you mean we're there now, that here's there, that now's then? ... *I* don't mind,' he added, letting out as a laugh the sigh he had been holding in for some time. 'You ought to know the place, and for all I could tell you we might be anywhere: I often do have it, this funny feeling, the first minute or two when I've come up out of the Underground. Well, well: join the Army and see the world.' He nodded towards the perspective of traffic lights and said, a shade craftily: 'What are those, then?'

Having caught the quickest possible breath, she replied: 'Inexhaustible gases; they bored through to them and lit them as they came up; by changing colour they show the changing of minutes; in Kôr there is no sort of other time.'

'You've got the moon, though: that can't help making months.'

'Oh, and the sun, of course; but those two could do what they liked; we should not have to calculate when they'd come or go.'

'We might not have to,' he said, 'but I bet I should.'

'I should not mind what you did, so long as you never said, "What next?" '

'I don't know about "next", but I do know what we'd do first.'

'What, Arthur?'

'Populate Kôr.'

She said: 'I suppose it would be all right if our children were to marry each other?'

But her voice faded out; she had been reminded that they were homeless on this his first night of leave. They were, that was to say, in London without any hope of any place of their own. Pepita shared a two-roomed flatlet with a girl friend, in a by-street off the Regent's Park Road, and towards this they must make their half-hearted way. Arthur was to have the sitting-room divan, usually occupied by Pepita, while she herself had half of her girl friend's bed. There was really no room for a third, and least of all for a man, in those small rooms packed with furniture and the two girls' belongings: Pepita tried to be grateful for her friend Callie's forbearance – but how could she be, when it had not occurred to Callie that she would do better to be away tonight? She was more slow-witted than narrow-minded – but Pepita felt she owed a kind of ruin to her. Callie, not yet known to be home later than ten, would be now waiting up, in her housecoat, to welcome Arthur. That would mean three-sided chat, drinking cocoa, then turning in: that would be that, and that would be all. That was London, this war – they were lucky to have a roof – London, full enough before the Americans came. Not a place: they would even grudge you sharing a grave – that was what even married couples complained. Where as in Kôr ...

In Kôr ... Like glass, the illusion shattered: a car hummed like a hornet towards them, veered, showed its scarlet tail-light, streaked away up the road. A woman edged round a front door and along the area railings timidly called her cat; meanwhile a clock near, then another set further back in the dazzling distance, set about striking midnight. Pepita, feeling Arthur release her arm with an abruptness that was the inverse of passion, shivered; whereat he asked brusquely: 'Cold? Well, which way? – we'd better be getting on.'

Callie was no longer waiting up. Hours ago she had set out the three cups and saucers, the tins of cocoa and household milk and, on the gas-ring, brought the kettle to just short of the boil. She had turned open Arthur's bed, the living-room divan, in the neat inviting way she had learnt at home – then, with a modest impulse, replaced the cover. She had, as Pepita foresaw, been wearing her cretonne housecoat, the nearest thing to a hostess gown that she had; she had already brushed her hair for the night, rebraided it, bound the braids in a coronet round her head. Both lights and the wireless had been on, to make the room both look and sound gay: all alone, she had come to that peak moment at which company should arrive – but so seldom does. From then on she felt welcome beginning to wither in her, a flower of the heart that had bloomed too early. There she had sat like an image, facing the three cold cups, on the edge of the bed to be occupied by an unknown man.

Callie's innocence and her still unsought-out state had brought her to take a proprietary pride in Arthur; this was all the stronger, perhaps, because they had not yet met. Sharing the flat with Pepita, this last year, she had been content with reflecting the heat of love. It was not, surprisingly, that Pepita seemed very happy – there were times when she was palpably on the rack, and this was not what Callie could understand. 'Surely you owe it to Arthur,' she would then say, 'to keep cheerful? So long as you love each other —' Callie's calm brow glowed – one might say that it glowed in place of her friend's; she became the guardian of that ideality which for Pepita was constantly lost to view. It was true, with the sudden prospect of Arthur's leave, things had come nearer to earth: he became a proposition, and she would have been as glad if he could have slept somewhere else. Physically shy, a brotherless virgin, Callie shrank from sharing this flat with a young man. In this flat you could hear everything: what was once a three-windowed Victorian drawing-room had been partitioned, by very thin walls, into kitchenette, living room, Callie's bedroom. The living room was in the centre; the two others opened off it. What was once the conservatory, half a flight down, was now converted into a draughty bathroom, shared with somebody else on the girls' floor. The flat, for these days, was cheap – even so, it was Callie, earning more than Pepita, who paid the greater part of the rent: it thus became up to her, more or less, to express good will as to Arthur's making a third. 'Why, it will be lovely to have him here,' Callie said. Pepita accepted the good will without much grace – but then, had she ever much grace to spare? – she was as restlessly secretive, as self-centred, as a little half-grown black cat. Next came a puzzling moment: Pepita seemed to be hinting that Callie should fix herself up somewhere else. 'But where would I go?' Callie marvelled when this was at last borne in on her. 'You know what London's like now. And, anyway,' – here she laughed, but hers was a forehead that coloured as easily as it glowed – 'it wouldn't be proper, would it, me going off and leaving just you and Arthur; I don't know what your mother would say to me. No, we may be a little squashed, but we'll make things ever so homey. I shall not mind playing gooseberry, really, dear.'

But the hominess by now was evaporating, as Pepita and Arthur still and still did not come. At half past ten, in obedience to the rule of the house, Callie was obliged to turn off the wireless, whereupon silence out of the stepless street began seeping into the slighted room. Callie recollected the fuel target and turned off her dear little table lamp, gaily painted with spots to make it look like a toadstool, thereby leaving only the hanging light. She laid her hand on the kettle, to find it gone cold again and sigh for the wasted gas if not for her wasted thought. Where are they? Cold crept up her out of the kettle; she went to bed.

Callie's bed lay along the wall under the window: she did not like sleeping so close up under glass, but the clearance that must be left for the opening of door and cupboards made this the only possible place. Now she got in and lay rigidly on the bed's inner side, under the hanging hems of the window curtains, training her limbs not to stray to what would be Pepita's half. This sharing of her bed with another body would not be the least of her sacrifice to the lovers' love; tonight would be the first night – or at least, since she was an infant – that Callie had slept with anyone. Child of a sheltered middle-class household, she had kept physical distances all her life. Already repugnance and shyness ran through her limbs; she was preyed upon by some more obscure trouble than the expectation that she might not sleep. As to *that*, Pepita was restless; her tossings on the divan, her broken-off exclamations and blurred pleas had been to be heard, most nights, through the dividing wall.

Callie knew, as though from a vision, that Arthur would sleep soundly, with assurance and majesty. Did they not all say, too, that a soldier sleeps like a log? With awe she pictured, asleep, the face that she had not yet, awake, seen – Arthur's man's eyelids, cheek-bones and set mouth turned up to the darkened ceiling. Wanting to savour darkness herself, Callie reached out and put off her bedside lamp.

At once she knew that something was happening – outdoors, in the street, the whole of London, the world. An advance, an extraordinary movement was silently taking place; blue-white beams overflowed from it, silting, dropping round the edges of the muffling black-out curtains. When, starting up, she knocked a fold of the curtain, a beam like a mouse ran across her bed. A search-light, the most powerful of all time, might have been turned full and steady upon her defended window; finding flaws in the black-out stuff, it made veins and stars. Once gained by this idea of pressure she could not lie down again; she sat tautly, drawn-up knees touching her breasts, and asked herself if there were anything she should do. She parted the curtains, opened them slowly wider, looked out – and was face to face with the moon.

Below the moon, the houses opposite her window blazed back in transparent shadow; and something – was it a coin or a ring? – glittered half-way across the chalk-white street. Light marched in past her face, and she turned to see where it went: out stood the curves and garlands of the great white marble Victorian mantelpiece of that lost drawing-room; out stood, in the photographs turned her way, the thoughts with which her parents had faced the camera, and the humble puzzlement of her two dogs at home. Of silver brocade, just faintly purpled with roses, became her housecoat hanging over the chair. And the moon did more: it exonerated and beautified the lateness of the lovers' return. No wonder, she said herself, no wonder – if this was the world they walked in, if this was whom they were with. Having drunk in the white explanation, Callie lay down again. Her half of the bed was in shadow, but she allowed one hand to lie, blanched, in what would be Pepita's place. She lay and looked at the hand until it was no longer her own.

Callie woke to the sound of Pepita's key in the latch. But no voices? What had happened? Then she heard Arthur's step. She heard his unslung equipment dropped with a weary, dull sound, and the plonk of his tin hat on a wooden chair. 'Sssh-sssh!' Pepita exclaimed, 'she *might* be asleep!'

Then at last Arthur's voice: 'But I thought you said —'

'I'm not asleep; I'm just coming!' Callie called out with rapture, leaping out from her form in shadow into the moonlight, zipping on her enchanted housecoat over her nightdress, kicking her shoes on, and pinning in place, with a trembling firmness, her plaits in their coronet round her head. Between these movements of hers she heard not another sound. Had she only dreamed they were there? Her heart beat: she stepped through the living room, shutting her door behind her.

Pepita and Arthur stood the other side of the table; they gave the impression of being lined up. Their faces, at different levels – for Pepita's rough, dark head came only an inch above Arthur's khaki shoulder – were alike in abstention from any kind of expression; as though, spiritually, they both still refused to be here. Their features looked faint, weathered – was this the work of the moon? Pepita said at once: 'I suppose we are very late?'

'I don't wonder,' Callie said, 'on this lovely night.'

Arthur had not raised his eyes; he was looking at the three cups. Pepita now suddenly jogged his elbow, saying, 'Arthur, wake up; say something; this is Callie – well, Callie, this is Arthur, of course.'

'Why, yes, of course this is Arthur,' returned Callie, whose candid eyes since she entered had not left Arthur's face. Perceiving that Arthur did not know what to do, she advanced round the table to shake hands with him. He looked up, she looked down, for the first time: she rather beheld than felt his red-brown grip on what still seemed her glove of moonlight. 'Welcome, Arthur,' she said. 'I'm so glad to meet you at last. I hope you will be comfortable in the flat.'

'It's been kind of you,' he said after consideration.

'Please do not feel that,' said Callie. 'This is Pepita's home, too, and we both hope – don't we, Pepita? – that you'll regard it as yours. Please feel free to do just as you like. I am sorry it is so small.'

'Oh, I don't know,' Arthur said, as though hypnotized; 'it seems a nice little place.'

Pepita, meanwhile, glowered and turned away.

Arthur continued to wonder, though he had once been told, how these two unalike girls had come to set up together – Pepita so small, except for her too-big head, compact of childish brusqueness and of unchildish passion, and Callie, so sedate, waxy and tall – an unlit candle. Yes, she was like one of those candles on sale outside a church; there could be something votive even in her demeanour. She was unconscious that her good manners, those of an old-fashioned country doctor's daughter, were putting the other two at a disadvantage. He found himself touched by the grave good faith with which Callie was wearing that tartish housecoat, above which her face kept the glaze of sleep; and, as she knelt to relight the gas-ring under the kettle, he marked the strong, delicate arch of one bare foot, disappearing into the arty green shoe. Pepita was now too near him ever again to be seen as he now saw Callie – in a sense, he never *had* seen Pepita for the first time: she had not been, and still sometimes was not, his type. No, he had not thought of her twice; he had not remembered her until he began to remember her with passion. You might say he had not seen Pepita coming: their love had been a collision in the dark.

Callie, determined to get this over, knelt back and said: 'Would Arthur like to wash his hands?' When they had heard him stumble down the half-flight of stairs, she said to Pepita: 'Yes, I was so glad you had the moon.'

'Why?' said Pepita. She added: 'There was too much of it.'

'You're tired. Arthur looks tired, too.'

'How would you know? He's used to marching about. But it's all this having no place to go.'

'But, Pepita, you —'

But at this point Arthur came back: from the door he noticed the wireless, and went direct to it. 'Nothing much on now, I suppose?' he doubtfully said.

'No; you see it's past midnight; we're off the air. And, anyway, in this house they don't like the wireless late. By the same token,' went on Callie, friendlily smiling, 'I'm afraid I must ask you, Arthur, to take your boots off, unless, of course, you mean to stay sitting down. The people below us —'

Pepita flung off, saying something under her breath, but Arthur remarking, 'No, I don't mind,' both sat down and began to take off his boots. Pausing, glancing to left and right at the divan's fresh cotton spread, he said: 'It's all right is it, for me to sit on this?'

'That's my bed,' said Pepita. 'You are to sleep in it.'

Callie then made the cocoa, after which they turned in. Preliminary trips to the bathroom having been worked out, Callie was first to retire, shutting the door behind her so that Pepita and Arthur might kiss each other good night. When Pepita joined her, it was without knocking: Pepita stood still in the moon and began to tug off her clothes. Glancing with hate at the bed, she asked: 'Which side?'

'I expected you'd like the outside.'

'What are you standing about for?'

'I don't really know: as I'm inside I'd better get in first.'

'Then why not get in?'

When they had settled rigidly, side by side, Callie asked: 'Do you think Arthur's got all he wants?'

Pepita jerked her head up. 'We can't sleep in all this moon.'

'Why, you don't believe the moon does things, actually?'

'Well, it couldn't hope to make some of us *much* more screwy.'

Callie closed the curtains, then said: 'What do you mean? And – didn't you hear? - I asked if Arthur's got all he wants.'

'That's what I meant - have you got a screw loose, really?'

'Pepita, I won't stay here if you're going to be like this.'

'In that case, you had better go in with Arthur.'

'What about me?' Arthur loudly said through the wall. 'I can hear practically all you girls are saying.'

They were both startled – rather that than abashed. Arthur, alone in there, had thrown off the ligatures of his social manner: his voice held the whole authority of his sex – he was impatient, sleepy, and he belonged to no one.

'Sorry,' the girls said in unison. Then Pepita laughed soundlessly, making their bed shake, till to stop herself she bit the back of her hand, and this movement made her elbow strike Callie's cheek. 'Sorry,' she had to whisper. No answer: Pepita fingered her elbow and found, yes, it was quite true, it was wet. 'Look, shut up crying, Callie: what have I done?'

Callie rolled right round, in order to press her forehead closely under the window, into the curtains, against the wall. Her weeping continued to be soundless: now and then, unable to reach her handkerchief, she staunched her eyes with a curtain, disturbing slivers of moon. Pepita gave up marvelling, and soon slept: at least there is something in being dog-tired.

A clock struck four as Callie woke up again – but something else had made her open her swollen eyelids. Arthur, stumbling about on his padded feet, could be heard next door attempting to make no noise. Inevitably, he bumped the edge of the table. Callie sat up: by her side Pepita lay like a mummy rolled half over, in forbidding, tenacious sleep. Arthur groaned. Callie caught a breath, climbed lightly over Pepita, felt for her torch on the mantelpiece, stopped to listen again. Arthur groaned again: Callie, with movements soundless as they were certain, opened the door and slipped through to the living room. 'What's the matter?' she whispered. 'Are you ill?'

'No; I just got a cigarette. Did I wake you up?'

'But you groaned.'

'I'm sorry; I'd no idea.'

'But do you often?'

'I've no idea, really, I tell you,' Arthur repeated. The air of the room was dense with his presence, overhung by tobacco. He must be sitting on the edge of his bed, wrapped up in his overcoat – she could smell the coat, and each time he pulled on the cigarette his features appeared down there, in the fleeting, dull reddish glow. 'Where are you?' he said. 'Show a light.'

Her nervous touch on her torch, like a reflex to what he said, made it flicker up for a second. 'I am just by the door; Pepita's asleep; I'd better go back to bed.'

'Listen. Do you two get on each other's nerves?'

'Not till tonight,' said Callie, watching the uncertain swoops of the cigarette as he reached across to the ashtray on the edge of the table. Shifting her bare feet patiently, she added: 'You don't see us as we usually are.'

'She's a girl who shows things in funny ways – I expect she feels bad at our putting you out like this – I know I do. But then we'd got no choice, had we?'

'It is really I who am putting you out,' said Callie.

'Well, that can't be helped either, can it? You had the right to stay in your own place. If there'd been more time, we might have gone to the country, though I still don't see where we'd have gone there. It's one harder when you're not married, unless you've got the money. Smoke?'

'No, thank you. Well, if you're all right, I'll go back to bed.'

'I'm glad she's asleep – funny the way she sleeps, isn't it? You can't help wondering where she is. You haven't got a boy, have you, just at present?'

'No. I've never had one.'

'I'm not sure in one way that you're not better off. I can see there's not so much in it for a girl these days. It makes me feel cruel the way I unsettle her: I don't know how much it's me myself or how much it's something the matter that I can't help. How are any of us to know how things could have been? They forget war's not just only war; it's years out of people's lives that they've never had before and won't have again. Do think she's fanciful?'

'Who, Pepita?'

'It's enough to make her – tonight was the pay-off. We couldn't get near any movie or any place for sitting; you had to fight into the bars, and she hates the staring in bars, and with all that milling about, every street we went, they kept on knocking her even off my arm. So then we took the tube to that park down there, but the place was as bad as daylight, let alone it was cold. We hadn't the nerve – well, that's nothing to do with you.'

'I don't mind.'

'Or else you don't understand. So we began to play – we were off in Kôr.'

'Core of what?'

'Mysterious Kôr – ghost city.'

'Where?'

'You may ask. But I could have sworn she saw it, and from the way she saw it I saw it, too. A game's a game, but what's a hallucination? You begin by laughing, then it gets in you and you can't laugh it off. I tell you, I woke up just now not knowing where I'd been; and I had to get up and feel round this table before I even knew where I was. It wasn't till then that I thought of a cigarette. Now I see why she sleeps like that, if that's where she goes.'

'But she is just as often restless; I often hear her.'

'Then she doesn't always make it. Perhaps it takes me, in some way – Well, I can't see any harm: when two people have got no place, why not want Kôr, as a start? There are no restrictions on wanting, at any rate.'

'But, oh, Arthur, can't wanting want what's human?'

He yawned. 'To be human's to be at a dead loss.' Stopping yawning, he ground out his cigarette: the china tray skidded at the edge of the table. 'Bring that light here a moment – that is, will you? I think I've messed ash all over these sheets of hers.'

Callie advanced with the torch alight, but at arm's length: now and then her thumb made the beam wobble. She watched the lit-up inside of Arthur's hand as he brushed the sheet; and once he looked up to see her white-nightgowned figure curving above and away from him, behind the arc of light. 'What's that swinging?'.

'One of my plaits of hair. Shall I open the window wider?'

'What, to let the smoke out? Go on. And how's your moon?'

'Mine?' Marvelling over this, as the first sign that Arthur remembered that she was Callie, she uncovered the window, pushed up the sash, then after a minute said: 'Not so strong.'

Indeed, the moon's power over London and the imagination had now declined. The siege of light had relaxed; the search was over; the street had a look of survival and no more. Whatever had glittered there, coin or ring, was now invisible or had gone. To Callie it seemed likely that there would never be such a moon again; and on the whole she felt this was for the best. Feeling air reach in like a tired arm round her body, she dropped the curtains against it and returned to her own room.

Back by her bed, she listened: Pepita's breathing still had the regular sound of sleep. At the other side of the wall the divan creaked as Arthur stretched himself out again. Having felt ahead of her lightly, to make sure her half was empty, Callie climbed over Pepita and got in. A certain amount of warmth had travelled between the sheets from Pepita's flank, and in this Callie extended her sword-cold body; she tried to compose her limbs; even they quivered after Arthur's words in the dark, words *to* the dark. The loss of her own mysterious expectation, of her love for love, was a small thing beside the war's total of unlived lives. Suddenly Pepita flung out one hand: its back knocked Callie lightly across the face.

Pepita had now turned over and lay with her face up. The hand that had struck Callie must have lain over the other, which grasped the pyjama collar. Her eyes, in the dark, might have been either shut or open, but nothing made her frown more or less steadily: it became certain, after another moment, that Pepita's act of justice had been unconscious. She still lay, as she had lain, in an avid dream, of which Arthur had been the source, of which Arthur was not the end. With him she looked this way, that way, down the wide, void, pure streets, between statues, pillars and shadows, through archways and colonnades. With him she went up the stairs down which nothing but moon came; with him trod the ermine dust of the endless halls, stood on terraces, mounted the extreme tower, looked down on the statued squares, the wide, void, pure streets. He was the password, but not the answer: it was to Kôr's finality that she turned.

Night Engagement

THE trouble with this shelter life (said Mrs Catchpole) is that a girl don't get a chance to make steady friends. All the regulars bringing their wives and families, nice young fellows just passing through on leave, here today and gone tomorrow, a girl that respects herself doesn't know where to turn.

Take my Doris: time and again she's come back to our corner and said, 'Mum, there's ever such a nice young fellow just been chatting to me, but he isn't a regular.'

'Bring him over,' I say, 'and let's have a look at him.' So she brings him over, and we pass a pleasant evening and then the minute the All Clear goes he says, 'It's been a great pleasure meeting you, now I'm off to Aberdeen,' and a fat lot of good that is to a girl that lives in SW1.

'Take heart, Doris,' I say, 'there's a Mr Right somewhere.'

'Not in *this* shelter,' says Doris, 'not for a girl that respects herself; I think I'll try the Tube;' so the next night, off she goes in her siren-suit with half the sandwiches and a bottle of tea.

Well, I don't see her again till next morning when I find her at home in the scullery having a wash before she goes to work.

'Well, Doris,' I say, 'how's the Tube?'

'Well, Mum,' she says, 'I really can't tell. I met ever such a nice young fellow, works in the Post Office, stood me a cup of coffee and everything, only then a Warden butted in, said I better look out he had quite a name in the shelter and no companion for a girl that respects herself; so I really can't tell.'

'Will he be there tonight?' I ask.

'Oh, yes,' says Doris, 'we made a date after the Warden cleared off.'

'Then you better take me along with you,' I say, 'and let me have a look at him.' So that night off we trek, bed and bedding, and there sure enough is Doris's new friend – ever such a nice young fellow, though not so young at that, and not what you'd call delighted to see me.

'Harry,' says Doris, 'this is Mum.'

'Pleased to meet you,' I say, 'perhaps we may offer you a sandwich?'

'Thank you very much,' says he, 'perhaps in return I may offer you a coffee?' And off he goes to fetch it, and we never see him again. Well, Doris blames me, of course, says I oughtn't to have come in my curlers, but what I say is if a fellow's put off by curlers he don't know the facts of life and you're better without him. However, Doris takes umbrage, says she thinks she'll go along to the Fire Station and see if they want a mascot.

Well, she never got there, lucky as it turned out, because they'd an Alsatian dog already, but what did happen was the blitz got something fierce, Doris popped into a cellar and down came the whole place on top of her.

Well, I know nothing about it till she doesn't turn up in the morning, and when a girl respects herself like Doris that means something, so I trot off to the Fire Station (that's when I found out about the dog), but they hadn't seen her.

So then I went round and about, and I don't mind telling you I was worried to a rind, and at last I find a whole demolition squad digging Doris out. I know it's Doris because they can hear her voice faint through the ventilator, and they let me creep in to have a chat.

'Are you all right, Doris?' I call.

'Oh, yes, Mum,' she says, 'there's ever such a nice young fellow down here with me, works on the Railway, and would you believe it, he knows Auntie Flo.'

'You bring him along,' I say, 'and let's have a word with him.' So he along he comes to the ventilator, and I call down again.

'That's my daughter, Doris,' I say, 'I'm her Mum, and when you get out I'll be very pleased to meet you.'

'Mrs Catchpole,' he says, 'that goes for me too.' So I creep out again and ask the squad how long they'll be at it. They say they can't tell, they'll be as quick as they can; so I say, if there's no danger not to hurry themselves, because it does look as though Doris is on to something at last, though I don't say that last bit aloud, perfect gentleman as the officer was; called me 'Madam' and everything.

Well, I went along and got some cigarettes and made some tea in a bottle and the lady next door very kindly let me have a tin of salmon and back I went to pass them down to Doris, who says I better go round to her office and tell them she'll have to have the day off.

The squad wasn't looking too happy and the house next door had caved in as well, but Doris says they're still quite okay, plenty of air and no gas, and her new friend had shored up the ceiling with a bedstead they found.

'Best use for it,' I think, and as I can't do anything more off I go to the office, very nice about it they were, and then on to my sister Flo.

'Do you know a fellow,' I ask, 'works on the Railway?'

'What name?' she asks.

'I don't know his name,' I say, 'but he works on the Railway and he's buried along of my Doris.'

'Well, that's either Ted Parker,' she says, 'married and three kids, or Arthur Greenway, nice young fellow lives with his Mum.'

'Well, let's hope and pray it's Arthur,' I tell her, and I think it would be a kind and neighbourly act to go and have a word with Mrs Greenway, in case she doesn't know what's happened to him. And sure enough she doesn't, worried to a rind she was, and ever so glad to hear he was safe and sound along of my Doris.

We had a cup of tea together, and I took a good look over the house, Mrs Greenway said Arthur was a teetotaller and Primitive Methodist, didn't go with the girls because he liked them steady and said that to find a girl that was steady was like getting a camel through the eye of a needle.

'Why, he ought to meet my Doris!' I say, and we both have to laugh because of course he *had* met her.

So we have a bit more pleasant chat, and I tell her about Doris, how she was a girl that always respected herself and then off we go together to where they're still digging Doris and Arthur out. A different officer, not a patch on the first, kept telling us to stand back because it was near black-out and if the blitz started there was no knowing what might happen.

'That's all very well,' I say, 'but that's my Doris down there, and this lady's Arthur, and we want to have a word with them.'

'You stand back and have a word with your Maker,' he says, really hardly polite.

Well, I don't know about Mrs Greenway, but as a matter of fact I did do a bit of praying, and it may have been that or it may not, but just as the first Jerries came over one of the men crawled in through a hole and crawled out again dragging Doris after.

Doris had a lot of plaster and such in her hair, but her siren-suit had stood up wonderful. And young Arthur too, though no beauty, had brought out a cat he found down there, which showed he had a kind nature. Well, by this time we were quite like old friends, so we thanked the squad and the officer, I also sent my best wishes to the first officer and back we went to the Greenways and had some tea.

By this time the blitz was in full swing, so I say to Doris, 'Well, Doris, is it to be the Tube or the shelter?'

'Oh, no,' says young Arthur, 'we've got an Anderson in the yard, you must stay with us.'

'That's right,' says Mrs Greenway, 'you must stay with us like Arthur says.'

'Well, if we don't intrude,' I say.

'You must come to us regular,' says Arthur, 'for I don't like to think of Miss Catchpole in a public shelter; you never know who you may meet.'

'Oh, I've never met anyone,' says Doris.

'Until last night,' says Arthur, with a meaning look; and though maybe he didn't know his fate, I and Doris and his Mum did all right, and it's lucky Mrs Greenway and me get on so well so the young people can have the place to themselves.

PAT FRANK

The Bomb

THEY had walked past the last row of bungalows skirting the village, and through the pines, and were within sight of the barbed-wire barricade enclosing the sprawling munitions factory, when they saw it first. It was very high, only a silver splinter except when the sun struck sparks from its wings.

The man squinted into the sun. 'Eight or nine thousand feet,' he estimated aloud. It was so high, and so far distant, that it seemed to crawl across the pale blue background. But Alan March knew, because he was of the Air Force and knew the deception of the sky when it is deep and measureless, that it was racing towards them at two hundred, perhaps two-fifty. Even at that height he caught the bulges of four engine nacelles, and knew it for a bomber.

'It must be one of ours,' the girl said. 'They only get here at night, so it must be one of ours.'

His right arm coiled round the girl's slender shoulders. 'I don't know, Pinky,' he said. 'I can't catch the silhouette yet. What do you think?'

'My eyes aren't good enough to make it out. It's the bad light in the factory at night. My eyes have lost their feel for daylight.'

'Let's not take a chance,' he said, his fingers tightening round her arm. 'Nothing must happen to us, not now, Pinky. Let's foot it for the factory, and duck into the shelter.' Even as he spoke he knew there wasn't time. It was a quarter of a mile to the factory gates.

'Why should there be war when people are in love?' she asked, and he felt her small, supple hands clinging to his shirt front and her warm head snuggling against the inside of his arm.

'We won't let the war bother us,' he said. 'The war will have to stop for a while.'

'The war won't stop just for us, Alan. Wars have never stopped because of love of women.'

He didn't speak, for the bomber was much closer. It would pass directly over the plant, and over them. Three tiny white clouds blossomed under the bomber, and then three more miraculously appeared above it. 'Anti-aircraft!' Alan said. 'It's theirs!' He saw the plane's belly gape open.

'Look!' the girl half-whispered. 'A bomb!'

A dot appeared below the plane, for the space of a breath seemed part of it, and then with seeming leisure disassociated itself from the larger shape above. It grew, and its nose began to slant downward. Then, like a black teardrop, it was outlined alone against the sky, and the plane had passed on, leaving only the bomb.

'Down! Down!' shouted Alan. 'Down on your face!'

Pinky was on the ground. She bent her neck, put her hands over her head, and drew up her knees until she was a small, quivering human ball.

Now I am going, she thought. I never again will bury my head in his neck, or feel the bristles on his chin, or feel his kisses on my eyes. She was an intimate of bombs. That's what they made at the factory, bombs. Five-hundred-pounders like the one diving at them. The bomb began to sing. It sang first in a low, penetrating whine. It was thus a bomb was designed to sing. Its guiding tail was fluted, so that it would whine, and shriek, and scream, and spread fear over a space of time before it killed.

For months she had helped make bombs like that. They moved along on a conveyor belt, each in its niche, each seven feet long and eighteen inches through. How they nicknamed them, and joked about them, at the factory!

'Minnie here will slap a dent in somebody's head.' That's what Helen always said, and she would pat their round, smooth aluminium-alloy surfaces. Helen worked beside her. She called all the bombs 'Minnie'.

The whine sharpened. She wanted to scramble to her feet and run, run, anywhere. She felt Alan's big arm pulling her to the ground again. 'Steady!' he commanded. 'Steady!'

Pinky wondered whether the enemy also used liquid oxygen and lignite and carbon. How delicately one must handle it! Woman's work. It took a woman's gentle hands. On the other side, some woman had fitted together this bomb calling to her. What sort of woman? Grey-haired, bent, and slow? Middle-aged, and stiff as a bayonet, and methodical? Or young, and sometimes given to dreaming, as she herself was?

Only yesterday, she thought, Mr Gordon, the assembly super-intendent, had bawled at her. He had snatched a fuse cylinder from her hands and shouted: 'What sort of a hodgepodge is this? Wires to the detonator aren't secured. What good is it? I ask you, what good is it? Young lady, keep your mind on your job!'

And Helen had snickered and said: 'She can't help it, Mr Gordon. She's in love. He's coming to see her this evening.'

Like a fire siren in the next block, the bomb was screeching now. She wanted to look up, but dared not. How long it took to fall!

The tone of the bomb grew deeper. She edged closer to Alan, and felt his arms going round her head. He is trying to save me from the blast, she thought, and then it struck.

It struck with a thick thud, as if a giant had driven a pick into the solar plexus of the earth.

Her small teeth ground together, her insides contracted, her breath was still, every muscle waited for the explosion. It did not come, but she dared not raise her eyes. She knew that if the fuse was set for penetration work it would be three or four seconds between impact and explosion – time enough to smash through ten stories of a building, or seek out the vitals of a bombproof shelter.

She found she was counting 'twelve, thirteen, fourteen' as Alan lifted her to her feet.

'Look, Pinky,' he was yelling, 'it's a dud. It didn't go off, Pinky, it's a dud!' She saw it, its snout and half its length buried in the earth between two saplings thirty yards distant. She knew it would never explode now.

'Alan,' she breathed, 'some other woman must be in love.' He did not know what she meant.

DIANA GARDNER

The Land Girl

I HAVE Jersey cream for breakfast here on the farm. It is thick enough to spread on my porridge. Unfortunately, there is not enough sugar to go with it because of the rationing, which is rather a curse. What I'd like would be oceans of brown-sugar crystals of the kind we used to have at my guardian's. As it is, I have to take it surreptitiously when Mrs Farrant goes to the kitchen for the kettle. She's very severe and down on land girls altogether. She's also against me because I'm a 'lady', or I am when compared with her. She's a hard-bitten, crusty, thin woman and I don't think she and her husband get on particularly well together. She never calls him by his name or anything else, and refers to him as 'Mr Farrant'.

They don't half work the land girls. You are expected to do a man's work right enough. Not that I mind: it's fun being out in the open all day, even if it is blasted cold. Today we fallowed a field the size of the hall at college and it took five hours. About mid-afternoon, Mr Farrant came over and gave me a cigarette. I'm not allowed to smoke at the farmhouse because of Mrs F., so I have one now and again in the fields. It's decent of him to understand. I should say he's a man of about fifty-six, tall, very thin, and his face is lined with tiny red veins. He has whitish hair and blue, amused eyes. I wish he wouldn't wear leather gaiters: they make his legs look far too thin.

'We'll make you into a farmer yet, Miss Una,' he said.

I laughed at the idea. If there weren't a war on I'd never be doing landwork. I don't believe I've got the patience. Farming is a dull game: you have to wait so long for things to grow. I like action. It was that which got me expelled from school – I used to sneak into the town to buy sweets after 'lights out'. I've also got strong feelings, with decided likes and dislikes. Which reminds me, I don't think I'm going to like Mrs F. at all.

There's a thick frost today. Miller, the cowman, says it went down to 27 degrees last night. I was late for breakfast because it was so hard getting out of bed. Mr Farrant was on the farm and Mrs F. was busy in the scullery. It was quite nice to eat alone. I didn't have to be endlessly on my best behaviour. Believe me I was in a rage when I discovered that Mrs F. had left only a teaspoonful of sugar in the bowl for both tea and porridge. Mean old pig! I thought. I'll pay you out. Before I went on the farm I upset my tea over the tablecloth.

Miller was detailed for two hours to teach me how to manage the tractor. When the weather breaks we'll be busy. Miller is a bad teacher, or I'm a dud. I expect I shall understand it in time.

Mr Farrant gave me my lesson this morning. He explains things very well. He took the whole carburettor to pieces and showed me how it worked.

The weather is still midwinter. Today I felt very bored, going up and down among the cabbages. If the war goes on much longer I shall be sick of this game. Nobody of my own age to talk to, only the farmhands and their wives, and I bet they laugh and imitate me behind my back. To tell the truth I don't feel I'm all that popular, and this makes me seem affected. Am beginning to wonder why I ever came here at all.

This morning Mr Farrant took me in his gig to market. The town looked like a Christmas card by Raphael Tuck; people were climbing the hill bent double for fear of falling on the ice, and one or two women wore red woollen caps with lipstick to match.

I enjoy going around with Mr Farrant. He's a nice old boy and treats me well. He was shy at first about taking me into the 'Drovers', because he said I was a lady. It was very hot and farmerish in there. I must say I enjoyed drinking a glass of good old brown ale with the locals. These togs, breeches and coat, etc. are very comfortable. Thank goodness I don't bulge out in the wrong places.

When we got home Mrs F. didn't seem particularly pleased to see us. She spilled my tea pouring it out, so I refused to thank her for it. When she went to lock up the fowls I am afraid I pulled a face at Mr Farrant, but he didn't seem to mind.

There has been another fall of snow. My room is in the attic and, after Mr Farrant called me to get up, I lay quite a while looking at it reflected on the ceiling.

Practically all day I was clambering about with Miller searching for a pair of ewes which have lambed too early. After we'd found them, Mrs Miller made tea for us at their cottage. It was the queerest place inside. The 'parlour' was fixed from top to bottom with pictures of the seaside and china 'gifts', mostly from Brighton. She was very pleasant and had only two teeth in the top front. I wonder what happened to the others. Miller is a robust, earnest sort of fellow, and good-looking, if you like the earthy type.

Mrs Farrant made a scene today. I have come to loathe her.

When I came in I shook off all the snow I could in the scullery before going into the sitting-room. Mr Farrant was doing accounts. I could see she was in a vile temper; her hair was screwed into a tighter knot than ever.

I sat in an armchair and took up the *Daily Mail*.

Presently she looked across.

'Why didn't you take off your boots?' she said.

Before answering I laid the paper down very deliberately, and looked her over. 'Because I've been out all day on the farm and I'm dog-tired. I shook the snow off as I came in.'

'The snow's all over the carpet, and you'll take off those boots,' she said.

She came and stood over me so menacingly that my gore rose.

'My good woman,' I said, 'I haven't taken up farming to be ordered about by you.'

'This is my house and I'll be obeyed in it.'

'No one could mistake that,' I replied curtly, and I admit I looked meaningly at Mr Farrant.

'You'll kindly leave this room,' Mrs F. said. She's certainly got a shrill voice.

'I'm going to, thanks,' I said, and I took the *Daily Mail* with me. As I climbed to my room I brushed off as much snow as I could on the stairs.

When I came down for supper I found Mrs F. had gone to bed. Mr Farrant was quiet all through the meal. I am afraid he was upset about it all.

Mrs F. is scarcely civil when I address her now. She has also taken to giving me small helpings at meals. When I object she refers to the strict rationing. I don't believe it; we live on a farm where there's plenty of food, and I tell her so.

This morning she had taken away the cream and left no milk for the porridge. She was making her bed upstairs.

I must say I wouldn't like to have a wife like Mrs F.

Last night I went to a Temperance Dance with the Millers. Mrs Miller doesn't dance, so I waggled a toe with him. It was a tiring affair. It's hard to get drunk on lemonade. When we got back to the farm after a three-mile walk through the snow, I found that damned woman had locked me out. All the doors were bolted and the place in darkness. I threw snowballs at Mr Farrant's window – they have separate rooms – and presently he came down, looking very sleepy, poor man, and let me in.

As I passed her door her room was suspiciously quiet. I am afraid I made no apology for getting him out of bed. He ought never to have married a woman like Flo Farrant.

This morning, when I accused her of locking up the house, she had the rotten taste to reply, 'Oh, I thought you'd be out all night.'

'What the hell do you mean by that?' I asked.

I think she was frightened because she did not answer.

'Come on,' I said. 'Explain yourself.'

But she wouldn't.

I'm going to get even with her for this.

I spent the whole of today carting hay for the cattle. I can't help thinking of what that bitch said yesterday.

It's open war between Mrs F. and me in this house now. I don't know how Mr Farrant can put up with it. I talk only to him. Mrs F. and I have put each other into Coventry.

I must think clearly about this evening to know what exactly happened. I admit I did it in an inexplicable, mad moment and I suppose I shall live to regret it, but I do feel Mrs F. is entirely to blame for the atmosphere which has grown up between us.

As it was Sunday she caught the early bus into town and went by train to her mother's farm.

She was gone all day.

At lunchtime Mr Farrant and I got on particularly well together. We laughed a good deal at his jokes and he seemed relieved that she was out of the way, and shy that he and I were alone, which was funny, because around the farm and all the time we are at work he treats me as if I were a sort of refined workman. In the afternoon he dozed, the newspaper over his face and his gaiters off, I was dressed in a frock for a change and feeling no longer a farm labourer.

Over tea we got on still better. I know Mr Farrant likes me quite a lot; I'm sensible and reasonably attractive. I like him in lots of ways. He's friendly and has a sense of humour.

As I poured the tea, sitting in Mrs F.'s chair, I must admit I was glad she was out of the house for once.

But not a shadow of what happened later entered my head at any time during the afternoon. I wrote some letters to one or two people I'd met at the agricultural college and amused Mr Farrant with tales about them. He thought they sounded great jokes.

When suppertime came he insisted that he should prepare it.

'After all, we're both farmers,' he said, 'so why shouldn't I get a meal for a change?'

He opened a tin of tongue and made some sandwiches. The tea was dreadfully strong. Afterwards he smoked some of my cigarettes and told me about his youth. He must have been a lad. Why on earth he had to marry Flo Farrant only the stars can tell.

As she was due on the ten o'clock bus, I decided to go to bed before she arrived. Just before nine-thirty, Mr Farrant made the fire up and went into the kitchen to make some tea. While he was gone I put the room to rights, and presently he returned with a thermos and laid it on the table.

It was then something took possession of me. The sight of the old, chipped thermos on the orange tray and his spent, thin shoulders bent over it, caused my dislike of Mrs Farrant to well up into a sudden storm of hatred. I don't remember ever having experienced such rage, and no one can accuse me of being sweet-tempered. I felt choked with hatred. As I watched the nape of his neck I gripped the back of a wooden chair so hard that my hands were bloodless. Yet despite the ferocity of this feeling I don't think it could have lasted a second. I relaxed my grip on the chair and sat down.

He looked up, alarmed.

'Are you feeling all right?'

'Yes ... th-thanks,' I stammered.

'Not ill or anything? You're so white.'

'It must be the heat of the room,' I said, and pulled myself together. I got up. 'I'm going to bed.'

'Right you are,' he said. 'I'm turning in, too.'

He went into the kitchen and I heard him stoking the 'Ideal' boiler.

Suddenly my brain began to work at a great speed. Now that I think about it I suppose my subconscious had already worked out a plan. My movements became swift and furtive. I went quickly to the door, looked to right and left in the hall and then, as softly as I could, sped up the stairs. The way I knew what to do next was quite peculiar. I went straight to Mr Farrant's bedroom and switched the light on. His bed was over in the corner. I went straight over and lay on it. I even shook off my shoes as I climbed up – a funny thing to do when I had only a few moments to spare. I could hear him moving about downstairs and I knew the bus with Mrs Farrant in it would be arriving at any minute. I lay on my back and rolled about from side to side to deepen my impression in the feather mattress. It very soon became disordered. Then I got up, took off a blue Tyrolean brooch I always wear and laid it beside his brushes on the dressing-table. Grabbing my shoes in my hand I made my way onto the landing and up the stairs to the attic.

Once in my own room I stood with my head pressed against the door, listening for the sound of his movements. I heard him lift the lid of the letter-box and let it drop. He paused by the stairs to wind the grandfather clock.

At that moment I heard the bus. It pulled up and then started off noisily. Mrs Farrant was at the gate.

He climbed the stairs softly. I don't think he heard the bus. As he came to the linoleum on the landing, his steps grew louder. He crossed to his room and went in.

Hardly breathing, I came out of mine and ran stealthily down the stairs. My eyes must have been fixed and frightening. When the front door handle turned, I gave a little gasp; nothing must prevent my plan from succeeding. If I were not wrong, Mrs Farrant would say goodnight to her husband before she drank her tea.

I slipped into his room as quickly and quietly as I could. Once inside I appeared to be in no hurry. He stood in the middle of the room in his shirt sleeves. He appeared not to have noticed the state of the bed, and was staring pensively at his feet. He looked up, surprised.

'I'm sorry,' I said, and I can't think what I must have looked like, 'but I've left a brooch on your dressing table.' I spoke slowly. 'It's a little Austrian brooch my guardian gave me years ago.'

I began to play for time.

'Stupid of me to have left it. There it is – on the little china tray' – I heard footsteps on the stairs – in a slightly higher key I said, 'On the china tray, beside your brushes.'

'Oh,' he said, vaguely, and took it up in his hands. He was stupefied and tired. 'I don't quite understand.' He looked down at it in the palm of his hand and then at me. 'How did it get there?'

But I had no need to reply. Mrs Farrant stood in the doorway, her dark clothes part of the shadow in the landing, her face compressed and challenging. She looked at her husband, at the brooch in his hand, at me, and, finally, at the disarranged bed.

I don't know what I looked like but I can remember a sensation of rising triumph as I met her eyes. He was too befuddled to know what to say and I made no effort to help him.

I waited an age for her to speak, but she said nothing. Her face became completely expressionless. She looked again at the brooch in Farrant's hand and then turned on her heel. We heard her cross the landing to her own room and close the door sharply behind her.

I must confess I didn't know what to do when he turned and looked at me in a bewildered sort of way. I snatched the brooch from his hand and rushed upstairs to my room.

This morning it is still very cold. As I lay in bed unable to sleep, a good deal of noise was going on in the house below. Eventually I got up and stared at the outbuildings of this blasted farm. Presently, Miller led the pony out and harnessed him to the gig. Almost at once Mrs Farrant piled it high with some tattered luggage. Without saying anything to Miller she climbed in and jerked the reins. The pony moved forward, through the gate and on to the highroad, his breath misty in the frozen morning air. I got cold watching her back-view until it was out of sight; the thin body and that frightful bun. That was the last I shall ever see of her, thank God.

After that I dressed and went downstairs.

As I went into the kitchen with a jauntiness I was far from feeling, Mr Farrant was making his own breakfast. He looked up with a numbed expression. I had expected reproaches: it put me off my stroke not to get any.

'She's gone,' he said, wearily. 'Nothing I could say made any difference.'

I said nothing.

Here I am waiting for the bus. It's so cold I have to run up and down beside my suitcases to keep warm. I am in my best clothes, but I do not know where I am going or what I shall do. All I am certain of is, I must get out of that house.

After all, I couldn't stay there alone with Mr Farrant. Even though he's been an awful dear to me, he's old enough to be my father. And my life has only just begun.

SYLVIA TOWNSEND WARNER

Sweethearts and Wives

SOMETIMES Justina and Midge discussed what would happen if all
their husbands came on leave together. Lettice could go to her
grandmother's – but then William would not see her, and really she
was now a nice, displayable baby. The Sheridans might find a
double bed at the farm – but that would not take away Roy and the
twins, and if Mrs Sheridan slept out, one could not expect her to be
back in time to get breakfast. Justina and Tom might have a little
honeymoon at The Griffin – but that, as Midge said, would break
up the household.

Without husbands the household consisted of three women and
four children. Justina, who liked figures, had worked out that the
average age of the party was thirteen. If one left out Mrs Sheridan,
who was over thirty, the average age fell to eight years and nine
months; but to leave out Mrs Sheridan except arithmetically was
inconceivable, for Mrs Sheridan was the king-pin and glory of the
establishment: she cooked.

Both Justina and Midge had married early in 1940. To their
respective mothers it seemed natural, since both husbands were in
the Forces, that they should stay on at home, keeping their spirits
up, poor little things, by giving a helping hand in country houses
suddenly denuded of servants and enlarged by such creative
activities as organising First-Aid Points, entertaining Polish
officers, and breeding table rabbits. When they decided to set up
house together in Badger Cottage, it seemed hopefully probable
that the poor darlings would soon tire of cooking for themselves –
the more so as Badger Cottage was such a disadvantageous
dwelling, lonely, ugly, derelict, miles from any shop, and all the
water needing to be pumped by hand. But the discovery of Mrs
Sheridan quenched this hope. Mrs Sheridan was also married to a

fighting man; he had been a circus hand, now he was in the RASC*. Mrs Sheridan, bombed out of Mitcham, had come to Suffolk to find a home for herself, her three children, her Alsatian dog, and her horse. The horse had associations. Mrs Sheridan could not bear to be parted from it. The billeting officer had washed his hands of her when a fight between the Alsatian and Justina's two poodles elicited the fact that Mrs Sheridan would do anything and everything for whoever made a kind home for her and her beautiful Shirley. Midge's baby immunized her from conscription, but the poodles could not do the same for Justina, who had been directed to replace an auctioneer's clerk in the local town. By privily dismembering her bicycle, hiding the fragments in a fox covert, and declaring it stolen, she was in a position to claim Shirley as an essential means of transport. The horse thereby received a ration, Mrs Sheridan was able to live with them and be their cook, and when the Alsatian was reconciled to the poodles the compound household worked perfectly.

Another of Mrs Sheridan's beauties was her farmer friend, Mr Cuffey. Until Shirley had become an essential means of transport he had kept her going with oats, and he still stabled her. For Mr Cuffey (though a grimly married man who had never been out of Suffolk in his life, and regularly taking the collection at a Methodist Chapel) had a romantic streak in his nature which made him the slave of Mrs Sheridan's black eyes, purple velveteen trousers, and *haute école* graces. At dusk Mr Cuffey would materialize to woo Mrs Sheridan with illegal cream and extra butter, and sometimes a nice little bit of pork, and sometimes a pheasant which had been foolish enough to get itself entangled in a rabbit snare; and having a generous circus-like outlook on windfalls Mrs Sheridan would share these courtesies with Midge and Lettice and Justina.

Arriving on the heels of his telegram, Midge's William found himself being conducted, as it were, on a tour through the Sheridans: Mrs Sheridan, Pamela, Gloria, and Roy Sheridan, Driver Sheridan (by proxy of photographs and such a wonderful likeness to the boy), the Alsatian and the horse. But unfortunately he had come on a day which was not the morrow of one of Mr Cuffey's more impassioned dusks.

'If only we had known you were coming, we could have feasted you on the wages of sin,' remarked Midge. 'As it is, it must be fish.'

* Royal Army Service Corps

'I expect William gets a lot of fish in the Navy,' said Justina. 'I expect he's sick of fish. Midge, come outside one minute.'

William heard some serious murmurings, and the sound of damp, flat objects being turned over. Then they reappeared.

'Darling, I'm afraid it won't be fish after all. You see, Justina brought back what she could get, and what she could get was one largish sole and a plaice. And we were to share the sole and Mrs Sheridan was to have the plaice. She prefers plaice. But the sole isn't big enough for three, and if we had the plaice too there would be no fish for Mrs Sheridan. So we think she had better have the sole and we'll have toasted cheese.'

Justina said: 'Fortunately there's quite a lot of cheese.'

'My only criticism is, that you don't seem to have accounted for the plaice,' said William.

'Oh, Mrs Sheridan will have it for her breakfast.'

'She likes plaice, she likes it better than sole,' Midge said. 'It would be a shame to deprive her of her plaice.'

'Especially as she will have been so obliging about the sole,' added Justina.

At breakfast (tea, toast, apple jelly, and the smell of Mrs Sheridan's plaice) and at intervals during the rest of his leave William Corby reminded himself that it is ridiculous to think much about food, that by virtue of his profession he was better fed than any civilian, that it was very handsome of Mrs Sheridan to share the wages of sin with his daughter as well as with her own children, and that it was marvellous for his Midge to have a cook. If she had not got a cook, Midge explained, she would never have time to make so much jam. Midge's jams seemed to be the mainstay of every meal; though this, as Midge also explained, was partly because if you made jam without as much sugar as the book said, it had to be eaten down immediately or it mildewed.

On Sunday, too, he got a little riding, as Mrs Sheridan lent him her horse.

'But oughtn't she to have a rest?'

'My Shirley is a professional horse. She's never missed a performance, bless her!' said Mrs Sheridan, who, as it was Saturday evening, had an agreeable odour of gin about her.

The Alsatian and the two poodles came along too, and killed and ate several rabbits. Justina's Tom, so he had heard, was a good shot. Every man, thought William, at any rate every husband, should be able to shoot; and he reproached himself that he was incapable of shooting anything except stationary bottles at fairs. One is not a good shot unless one can shoot something edible. He would like to meet Tom Debenham and have some shooting lessons. It would be fun if Tom's next leave should coincide with a leave of his own. It might mitigate, too, this disquieting impression of having four children at Badger Cottage, and two, or possibly three, wives. Yet democracy is desirable; we must all aim at a future of more equality and less formality, and the household at Badger Cottage was a step towards such a future. It was probably reactionary of him to dislike seeing so much of Mrs Sheridan's purple trousers and never feeling sure whether it was Lettice wearing Pamela's rompers or Gloria clasping Lettice's teddy bear who needed picking out of the pond. If he had spent the last three years at home instead of at sea, he would be better at recognizing his own child. Meanwhile, he was riding Mrs Sheridan's horse, and Lettice and Midge were sharing in Mr Cuffey's love-gifts, and the joint households of early Soviet days must have been more ill-assorted and infinitely hungrier.

These reflections were cut short by the necessity for galloping across a field in order to deter the two poodles from pulling down a sheep. The fact that the Alsatian had taken no part in this assault but was virtuously engaged in hunting another rabbit was a further reminder that it is the more privileged classes who have most to learn in the matter of citizenship.

Badger Cottage was going on much as usual when a parcel came for Midge containing a large tin of olives and a note from William hoping that they might come in handy. As going on much as usual meant just then that Roy and Lettice had whooping cough and that Gloria had eaten the greater part of an indelible pencil, Midge remarked that dear William must be at Gibraltar, didn't Justina think, and the tin of olives was put by in the store cupboard. Midge was too loyal to voice the wish that William had sent tinned salmon instead, Justina was too polite to say so either, and Mrs Sheridan only said: 'Well, thank God it's in a tin, anyway. Which reminds me, Midgie, my twins have got at the jam you put in the attic; at first I thought it was mice, but it's too sticky for mice.'

It might have been expected that Tom, coming on leave so soon after this, would have eaten the olives. William had allowed for it. Besides having heard that Tom was a good shot, he had heard that Tom was something of an epicure; and he had said to himself a trifle wistfully: 'To each according to his need, – being, as his father-in-law said, a damn sight too well up in all that anti-God sort of stuff. Tom did not eat the olives because, after his first meal, during which Gloria sat on his knee, toyed with his hair and addressed him with purple lips as Daddy, he announced that he was going to take Justina to London to see some shows and have her nails cleaned.

Driver Sheridan, on the other hand, entered at once into the spirit of Badger Cottage, arriving with a goose, twenty-four kippers, several tins of army stew, two bottles of whisky, four hundred cigarettes, six yellow dusters, and an invaluable collection of nails, screws, belts and washers, the property of H.M. Government. During his stay he undertook a number of repairs and improvements, mended the meat-safe, washed and clipped the poodles, lifted the main-crop potatoes several weeks too early, repainted the dog kennel and part of the front door, hung a swing for the children, fixed an aerial to the wireless, and did things to the pump. On his last evening, too, he further asserted himself as a practical man by fighting Mr Cuffey, and spent the remaining hours alternately beating and embracing Mrs Sheridan. Bruised and admiring, she passed the next day wandering among his incompleted works, saying dreamily: 'There'll be something to show for this, I shouldn't be surprised.'

The first perceptible aftermath of Driver Sheridan, however, was the cessation of cream and butter, and Mr Cuffey's inability to go on stabling Shirley; never in all his days had he known such a messy horse. It is difficult to place a full-sized horse with delicate lungs: circus life, as Mrs Sheridan explained, the draughts playing on open pores, always weakens the lungs – think of monkeys. Finally, Shirley was accommodated at the Vicarage, where the sound of the organ, said Mrs Sheridan, would be like old times for her. Justina more moodily remarked that she would now be more than a mile from her essential means of transport, and that the Transoms would henceforth expect a regular supply of prizes for their incessant Church Roof Restoration Fund whist drives – as was indeed the case.

Other tokens of Driver Sheridan's manliness were still lying around when William came on his next leave: festering heaps of wood and wire that only needed a few finishing touches to become a rabbit-hutch, rusty bolts and cog-wheels which should have been put back in the mangle, but somehow got overlooked, and several fresh neuroses in the pump.

'Come just when you're wanted,' said Mrs Sheridan warmly. 'You sailor-men are always so handy.'

If he had not been so obliteratingly in love with his wife William Corby would have remembered to arrive as a good provider. As it was, he just got into the first train with nothing more than love, lemons, silk stockings, presents for the children, and good intentions. The presents for the children were eaten in a flash, the stockings were put away, love is always impalpable, one cannot live on lemons – he did as best he could with the good intentions. There was certainly a great deal to do. It seemed to him that Badger Cottage was much dirtier and more disarrayed than the passage of six months and the transit of Driver Sheridan could justify. But then, as he told himself, he came off a ship, a childless, melancholy world of its own. Four children would no doubt make a destroyer look as tousled as Badger Cottage; and he thrust down the inward retort to this, that children on a destroyer would be kept in better order and cleaned at regular intervals.

Women, he also told himself, are less fussy than men: it is a wise, natural provision to fit them for the inevitable mess and confusion of maternity. Women, too, are braver, more adaptable, probably hardier, certainly less self-indulgent. They are more primitive and so better attuned to the primitive state of the universe when, as the scriptures so acutely remark, the earth was without form, or void, and the waters brooded on the face of the earth; which reminded him he must try to do something about the bathroom. But the brave, adaptable, hardy, self-disciplined and primitive Midge had spots on her chin, moaned in her sleep, and smoked more than was good for her. As for Justina, she had a cold in her head. It was so violent that she did not go to work, so instead Mrs Sheridan rode into town and did the shopping. Mrs Sheridan was a somewhat erratic shopper, but she always remembered the children; and it was so nice for her, Midge pointed out, to be reunited with Shirley. To give Mrs Sheridan more time to enjoy this reunion, Justina cooked. Justina had been taught cooking at a domestic college for young ladies. She knew how to make omelets, fudge, several kinds of *soufflé*, coffee, and – theoretically – soap. Unfortunately omelets and *soufflés* cannot be made without breaking real eggs, so Justina's home-lore chiefly expressed itself in coffee. For the rest there was always cheese, and Midge's jams, and the national loaf now so vitaminous that it was almost as ready to ferment as the jams. Why on earth, thought William, didn't I have at least the foresight to bring them some ships' bread? Busy himself as he might in being a man about the house, his thoughts dwelt increasingly on food. But he did not realize how enchained he was to sensual lures till the message came from Mrs Transom to say that after all she could not have them to supper as the vicar had just gone down with mumps.

'Mumps! O my God,' wailed Midge. 'None of them has had mumps! O Justina, why did we let them go to the children's service?'

(Mumps, thought William. I've had mumps. I could perfectly well have gone to that supper.)

'I expect he was in his pulpit all the time,' replied Justina. 'It isn't as if he'd been confirming them or christening them. And somebody had to go to church after they'd been so obliging about Mrs Sheridan's horse.'

Damn Mrs Sheridan, thought William.

'What's mumps?' asked Mrs Sheridan; and answered herself by adding that mumps was all in a day's work. She could afford to be philosophical, thought William: she had not lost a supper, she had been staying at home anyway to look after the children. Which, of course, was very good of her.

Justina remarked that there was still quite a lot of the beetroot soup left. Midge said she didn't wonder. William didn't wonder either.

'And there is any amount of oatmeal. Isn't there something called brose that's made of oatmeal – with cabbage in it? Didn't Robert Burns sup brose?'

Mrs Sheridan opined that there was more than that in Robbie Burns' brose.

'What a pity we gave the remains of the rabbit to the dogs!'

The word *olives* began to shape itself in William's mind, but he said nothing.

'It's the very devil,' mused Midge, 'feeding the dogs. They're much fussier than the children. Or us.'

'They don't appreciate the war, poor things,' said Mrs Sheridan. 'Do you think a jam roly-poly? That would be filling. And we must browse down that elderberry jam that wouldn't set.'

The word *olives* now thundered in William's brain. His tongue was swollen with keeping silence. Some flash of his electrical agony must have reached Justina, for suddenly her face became illumined with intellect, and she said:

'I know! I've got it! We'll open that tin of olives that William sent us.'

'O Justina, we can't! It's gone.'

'Gone? Have those blasted children ...'

'No, it's not the children this time. It's me. I gave it to the Transoms for a whist-drive prize.'

She spoke to Justina exactly as the conventional wife confesses to her husband that she has given his trousers to the jumble sale. Amid everything else that he was feeling, William was able to notice this.

'Damn! What on earth came over you? No one in this village would know what to do with an olive.'

'But you don't like them, Justina. I'm not all that fond of them, really. And Zoë doesn't like them either, for I asked her.'

'I can *eat* them,' said Mrs Sheridan. 'But that's not to say I actually enjoy it.'

Midge lit another cigarette. She was still looking like a guilty wife and spoke savagely.

'What else could I do, Justina? You know how those blackmailing Transoms hound us for their whist drives. It's all very well for you, you are out all day, you don't know much about real life. But I can assure you, what with thinking about food for the dogs, and washing for the children, and prizes for the Transoms, real life isn't worth living!'

The ensuing silence was broken by Roy Sheridan, who strolled in carrying a tin chamber-pot in which there were some baby mice. He had found the mice in Daddy's rabbit hutch, he explained. There had been lots more, but they had got away. Now could he have some cotton-wool to make a nest for them? Presently William was able to suggest that, since they could not sup at the Vicarage (where at this moment, he said to himself, those Transoms are devouring olives like quails and manna), they should walk the four miles into town and have dinner at The Griffin and try for a bottle of whisky for Justina's cold ... that is, if Mrs Sheridan would stand by her generous offer to keep an eye on the children. It was a lovely frosty night, the walk would be fun.

'We shall get up our appetites,' he concluded.

Mrs Sheridan was quite ready to stay at home, so William set out with his two wives.

The dinner and the whisky cost in all four pounds seventeen shillings. Both Midge and Justina got slightly drunk and were much improved by it. In fact, it might have been called a successful evening if it had not been riddled by a tendency to remember Mrs Sheridan and feel how unselfish she was, and what a pity it was that she had been left out of it.

ANN CHADWICK

The Sailor's Wife

THE sky lay blue between showers, giving a sharpness to the shadows in the dirty town behind her as she climbed. The water shone blue, and the little ships rode like toys on a still backwater, swinging slowly on their anchors. She climbed up past the council houses to the last street, thinking in her surface mind that these were semi-detached houses, larger than any she had tried; thinking under that that she was getting hungry; feeling under that the stares of children, the window curtains screening casual eyes: a stranger in the neighbourhood.

The woman who came to the door set her aproned front in the opening and looked out of her shut face with two small brown eyes. Yes! she said. I'm sorry to bother you, began the sailor's wife. The other woman opened her face tentatively, like a hungry clam. Not at all, she said. The sailor's wife shifted her tired feet and tried to sound conversational. I was wondering if you might know someone in this neighbourhood who lets rooms? The clam reconsidered and fixed its jaws ajar, immobile. Oh no, I'm afraid not. I can't think of a soul. Some do let, mind you – Mrs Carstairs next door – but she's all full up. Full up and booked ahead. Yes, said the sailor's wife. Pause. You'll find the town's fair packed out, said the other woman – what with the shipping and the RAF station and the torpedo factory – I can't think where you'll get in. Long pause.

Was it just for yourself? she asked. The sailor's wife smiled tightly. For myself, she said, and my husband when he's on leave. And a ten months' baby, she added. But he's out in the pram all day and I have his cot with me. He's very good. But the clam had shut like a trap. Ah well, said the woman who had come to the door. Ah well, echoed the sailor's wife. You barnacled old bitch, she thought. Sorry I can't help you, said the woman, and moved back longingly from the door. The sailor's wife smiled. Well, thank you very much, she said. She went slowly back to the pavement.

She walked stumpingly on the outside of her swollen feet. Four-thirty. Time to be starting back to the hotel. The baby would be crying and annoying people by five. I'll try two more houses in this street, she thought. That would make it up to sixteen. Then I'll take the bus back.

Cute the kid had been this morning. Kicking on the bed while she washed nappies in the hand-basin. Should be crawling by now. Thank God he wasn't. Hanging out the nappies and getting the pram ready on the green behind the hotel. Tying his toys in, and settling him. That chambermaid. Telling the chambermaid she would be back for lunch and what to do if it came on to rain. That chambermaid, laughing out of her pale face. A double coping of round curls, red and light – flashing as new farthings shaking all round her head. Hanging and brushing together silently like copper feathers on a cockerel's neck. Laughing – I never seen a like baby! Sitting there hours and never a whisht out of him – Poor wee soul. People liked babies.

Looking over her shoulder she could see the ships below her in the river. Nice to find a place up here where you could watch them in and out. Little carrier down there now. Wrong camouflage markings. Besides it had only been a week. Four or five weeks to go anyhow. There were some of the right sort of houses at the end of the row. Try this one.

She went quickly up the walk, watching the dog messes carefully, seeing the wet primroses and crocuses dismally gleaming. A large dirty brass plate under the bell said Mrs Garbutt. She rang. The milk had not been taken in yet. No one came. She rang again and turned to look out over the roofs at the slow ships moving greyly. Another shower was coming round the circle of hills. It had rained every single day so far – five days – still no place to live. She would give the baby bread and milk and the last orange. No one had come. I'll try the back door, she decided. Now that five minutes had been wasted here already – made you persistent. She went round.

Mrs Garbutt stood at her cluttered back door in an inadequate skirt and a vast, sloppy jumper belted in. She started when the sailor's wife came round the corner. Spare us! she said rhetorically, and returned to her fixed scrutiny of a pen with ducks in it that extended over most of her ruined garden. The sailor's wife looked too. There was nothing to see but filthy, stained, awkward ducks moving unceasingly in greedy circles. Mrs Garbutt said, There's been an egg missing every morning for weeks and I'm watching to see where she lays it, the besom.

A large puppy that had been under an overturned box at the corner of the house lolloped silently up behind the sailor's wife and thrust a cold wet nose up her skirts. Ah-ft! said the sailor's wife. My, my – come here you, said Mrs Garbutt absently. The puppy flung himself on his back and waved his filthy fool's paws. The sailor's wife rubbed his stomach with her foot defensively. I couldn't get an answer at the front so I came round, she said. Ah well, said Mrs Garbutt, I've been out here all the day waiting for her to lay, the tramp. This is one day I swore I'd not be fooled and neither I will. What was it you were wanting, my dear?

I was wanting to know do you know anyone around here who lets rooms, said the sailor's wife. Hm? said Mrs Garbutt, giving all her attention to the pen. The sailor's wife breathed deeply and spoke slowly and distinctly. I thought perhaps you might know someone in this neighbourhood who would let me have rooms. She fenced herself from the puppy's advances, bending over with extended hands. She wanted suddenly to cry from weariness and impatience. I hate puppies, she thought fiercely.

Well, my dear, you're asking me, said Mrs Garbutt meaninglessly. Come here you. That's a question, she added with an air of finality. I think she goes up into the hedge, the bird. Well my dear, you want what everyone in this town wants. Have you tried at the shops?

I've tried every shop in town, said the sailor's wife. They haven't even a list to give folk. She thought to herself, And you know it, or why would I be tramping the streets on the off-chance. The puppy bounced off and she straightened up. There's a fact, said Mrs Garbutt. The town's full and more than full for a fact. She knows I'm watching, the fox. She'll not lay the day. Well, my dear, and is it just yourself you want for?

My husband comes home on leave occasionally for a day or so, and we've a baby. But he's too young to run about and break things, and I've got his cot with me, said the sailor's wife. She thought – that's my family I'm talking about, brushing over. My own family – the only thing. Poor thing, you'll have a job with a baby, said Mrs Garbutt looking at her suddenly quite softly, with a morbid sympathy. No one will take you I'll allow. The sailor's wife laughed and said nothing. The last people I had fair drove me crazy with their wild ways and I'm having no more naval people, there's a fact.

The sailor's wife made the last effort of the day. You can't judge all by one, she appealed, looking as sweet as she could, what with her sore feet and thinking about the baby. Aye, but that I can, my dear, said Mrs Garbutt. She looked at the sailor's wife sharply. I don't envy your job for a fact, my dear, she said. You must expect hard hearts and robbing fingers in this town, for that's what you'll find. Where's your baby now? He's in his pram at the hotel. I'm going back to feed him now, said the sailor's wife. Left him all alone? The sailor's wife nodded. He's very good. Mrs Garbutt shook her head.

I'm glad you won't have me, thought the sailor's wife, you sloppy old duck-watcher. The puppy was gambolling back. She turned to escape. Thank you, she said loudly as she went. It was like struggling out of a swamp to leave the place. Its gloom clung to her. The smell of ducks followed sadly.

There wasn't enough time to do another house. She tried slow and fast steps alternately to ease her feet. Margot loves Alan, was written in chalk on the pavement. There was a portrait of Margot and someone else had drawn hop-scotch squares over it. The sky was clear again and the dark was already coming down.

The baby. It was almost five minutes' walk down the hill to the bus stop. She tried very long rhythmic strides and was getting on famously when right at the very bottom, what with looking to see if a bus was coming, she caught her heel on the kerb and stumbled awkwardly into the street. And there was a lorry looming along. She thought – It must have hit me – the bright colours – I've been carried quite a distance. It was as quick as that.

First of all there were just colours – sickening because they were whirled so – green, yellow, red, orange. Then darkness and that sweeping back, back, back feeling like drunkenness. Then colour again, moving slowly in sheets and planes and curtains – crimson, grey, violet. Reaching and squeezing her in. And then sounds began. Infinite ones. Whispers. Voices crowding, drowning, rising.

Well, my dear? Ah well. The besom, the bird. Sorry I can't help.
Sorry. Sorry. No babies. No naval people. No English people. No
human beings. No one. No one. Sorry. Can't help, can't help.

Margot loves Alan. This is Margot's face. As well as white chalk
can show. Margot's face loves Alan's face. Alan's face is a hop-
scotch square. Margot loves it. Margot loves. Loves.

Emergency cards? No permanent residence. Can't give you eggs
on those. Not enough for registered customers. You service wives
should stick at home. Should. Ought ... Should stick. War won't
last forever. One year. Don't marry before the peace. Wait. Don't
start babies in war-time. Wait. War-time. Four years. Don't live in
war-time. Wait. Stick. Sorry I can't help. Can't give you eggs.
Sorry, only for registered customers. Sorry no life going on in wartime. Wait ... Only four or five years.

The baby's crying. Crying? Where is he? It's dark. Where did I
leave him. He's lost, Christ he's lost. He's crying. Where? I left
him in rooms. After the liberty boat left I went back the way I had
come. But the rooms were gone. The baby is lost. Hungry and
crying in strange rooms. Lost. Oh God help me, the baby's gone.

She wept. The tears were warm and salt. People soothed her.
Pay no attention. No one cares. Just sympathies to get rid of you.
Cry like hell. Make them listen. Demand a place to stay - demand
your baby. Weep. Weep.

Can you stand up? insisted a man's heavy voice. Rough, clumsy
arms tried to support her. Don't move her - maybe she's broke
something, said a woman. She realized something had happened.
What's the matter? she demanded, resisting. Then her arm hurt
suddenly, enough to make her sick. Everyone was asking
questions. She tried to think quickly so that she could take time for
the next step. I want to go to the Bay Hotel, she said, because the
baby's there.

Then suddenly the sickness went and she saw the people round
her. First the policeman, anxious, clumsily helping her to stand,
forgetting he was a policeman. An errand boy, white, big-eyed,
silent. The loud women, frowning, exclaiming, arguing among
themselves as to what had happened, waving their fat and thin
hands. The silent staring women. The men turning to go about
their business, others still leering, others offering. These were the
people who lived in this town - thought the sailor's wife clearly.
She had their attention. Well, quick.

For a horrible moment she couldn't think of anything to say. Then because she was afraid they would all lose interest and go away, she said loudly - I did it on purpose! She started to cry again. The policeman clung to his duty. Now, my girl, he said firmly, no hysterics. I *did*, she said, I definitely did. The policeman succeeded in righting her in spite of herself. But it's against the law, he warned, and a daft thing. He gave her his handkerchief.

Crying seemed quite enjoyable. She leaned against the policeman for dizziness and tried to concentrate on what she was doing. No one will give me rooms - she sobbed as loudly as she could. The policeman was embarrassed. People were taking renewed interest. Come along quietly now, he said. I'll take you to the hotel. She looked at the beautiful sleek police car. I've nowhere for my baby to live! she wailed. And then she felt sick again and couldn't think at all.

When they got to the hotel the lorry driver had come to have a paper signed that it was the sailor's wife's own fault. He was a little worried man, thin and anxious. Then a doctor came, and prodded around until he was sure nothing was broken, and put her to bed. Then everyone threatened to go away and let her recover from the shock. Even the lorry driver wanted to go and come back tomorrow. The chambermaid was feeding the baby corn flakes. Let me see the paper I have to sign, said the sailor's wife. I must stick to the point, she thought, reading it.

Can you find me rooms in town? said the sailor's wife to the driver. He looked suspicious. The sailor's wife sighed, wishing there were more covers on the bed, wishing she could feel strong and warm and accomplish something. If you can find me rooms, I'll sign it, she said laboriously. The lorry driver smiled suddenly, pleased. O, you can stay with my sister, he said. She sometimes takes folk though it's not that she has to. Just wouldn't see a body stuck. I'll fix it. She smiled and accepting the driver's pen, signed the paper. It seemed to take a long, long time. The policeman was pretending he hadn't heard what they were saying. Now I've got a place, thought the sailor's wife. I have. I've got a place. She fell asleep half smiling.

STEVIE SMITH

Sunday at Home

IVOR was a gigantic man; forty, yellow-haired, grey of face. He had been wounded in a bomb experiment, he was a brilliant scientist.

Often he felt himself to be a lost man. Fishing the home water with his favourite fly Coronal, he would say to himself, 'I am a lost man.'

But he had an excellent sardonic wit, and in company knew very well how to present himself as a man perfectly at home in the world.

He was spending this Sunday morning sitting in his bedroom reading Colonel Wanlip's 'Can Fish Think?' letter in ANGLING. '… the fallacious theory known as Behaviourism.'

As the doodle bomb* came sailing overhead, he stepped into the airing cupboard and sighed heavily. He could hear his wife's voice from the sitting-room, a childish, unhappy voice, strained (as usual) to the point of tears.

'All I ask,' sang out Ivor, 'is a little peace and quiet; an agreeable wife, a wife who is pleasant to my friends; one who occasionally has the room swept, the breakfast prepared, and the expensive bric-a-brac of our cultivated landlord – *dusted*. I am after all a fairly easy fellow.'

'I can't go on,' roared Glory. She waved her arms in the air and paced the sitting-room table round and round.

Crump, crump, went the doodle bomb, getting nearer.

'Then why,' inquired Ivor from the cupboard (where he sat because the doodle bombs reminded him of the experiment) 'did you come back to me?'

Glory's arms at shoulder height dropped to her side. There was in this hopeless and graceful gesture something of the classic

---

* V-1 flying bombs, usually known as 'doodle bugs' or 'buzz bombs' because of the noise they made (see Footnote, page 182).

Helen, pacing the walls of Troy, high above the frozen blood and
stench of Scamander Plain. Ten years of futile war. Heavens, how
much longer.

She ran to the cupboard and beat with her fists upon the door.
'You ask that, you ... you ... you ...'

'Why yes, dear girl, I do. Indeed I do ask just that. Why did you
come back to me?'

'Yesterday in the fish queue ...' began Glory. But it was no use.
No use to tell Ivor what Friedl had said to her in the fish queue ...
before all those people ... the harsh, cruel words. No, it was no use.
The doodle bomb now cut out. Glory burst into tears and
finished lamely, 'I never thought it was going to be like this.'

Crash. Now it was down. Three streets away perhaps. There was
a clatter of glass as the gold-fish bowl fell off the mantelpiece.
Weeping bitterly Glory knelt to scoop the fish into a half-full
saucepan of water that was standing in the fender.

'They are freshwater fish,' said Ivor stepping from the
cupboard.

Glory went into the kitchen and sat down in front of the cooking
stove. How terrible it all was. Her fine brown hair fell over her eyes
and sadly the tears fell down.

She picked up the french beans and began to slice them. Now it
would have to be lunch very soon. And then some more washing
up. And Mrs Dip never turned up on Friday. And the stove was
covered with grease.

From the sitting-room came the sound of the typewriter. 'Oh
God,' cried Glory, and buried her head in her arms, 'Oh God.'

Humming a little tune to himself, Ivor worked quickly upon a
theme he was finishing. 'Soh, me, doh, soh, me. How happy, how
happy to be wrapped in science from the worst that fate and
females could do.'

'If only I had science to wrap myself up in,' said poor Glory,
and fell to thinking what she would wish, if she could wish one
thing to have it granted. 'I should wish,' she said, 'that I had
science to wrap myself up in. But I have nothing. I love Ivor, I
never see him, never have him, never talk to him, but that the
science is wrapping him round. And the educated conversation of
the clever girls. Oh God.'

Glory was not an educated girl, in the way that the Research
Persons Baba and Friedl, were educated girls. They could talk in

the informed light manner that Ivor loved (in spite of Friedl's awful accent.) But she could not. Her feelings were too much for her; indeed too much.

'I do not believe in your specialist new world, where everybody is so intelligent and everybody is so equal and everybody works and the progress goes on getting more and more progressive,' said Glory crossly to Friedl one day. She shook her head and added darkly, 'There must be sin and suffering, you'll see.'

'Good God, Glory,' said Ivor, 'you sound like the Pythoness. Sin and suffering, ottotottoi; the old bundle at the cross roads. Dreams, dreams. And now I suppose we shall have the waterworks again.'

'Too true,' said Friedl, as again Glory fled weeping.

'Sin and suffering,' she cried now to herself, counting the grease drips down the white front of the stove. 'Sin, pain, death, hell; despair and die. The brassy new world, the brassy hard-voiced young women. And underneath, the cold cold stone.'

Why only the other day, coming from her Aunt's at Tetbury, there in the carriage was a group of superior schoolgirls all of the age of about sixteen. But what sixteen-year-olds. God, what terrible children. They were talking about their exams. 'Oh, Delia darling, it was brilliant of you to think of that. Wasn't it brilliant of Delia, Lois? But then I always say Delia is the seventeenth century, if-you-see-what-I-mean. And what fun for dear old Bolt that you actually remembered to quote her own foul poem on Strafford. No, not boring a bit, darling, but sweet and clever of you – especially sweet.'

At the memory of this atrocious conversation between the false and terrible children, Glory's sobs rose to a roar, so that Ivor, at pause in his theme, heard her and came storming into the kitchen.

'You are a lazy, slovenly, uncontrolled female,' he said. 'You are a barbarian. I am going out.'

'Round to Friedl's, round to Friedl's, round to Friedl's,' sang out Glory.

'Friedl is a civilized woman. I appreciate civilized conversation.' Ivor stood over Glory and laughed. 'I shall be out to lunch.'

He took his hat and went out.

'The beans,' yelled Glory, 'all those french beans.' But it was no good, he was gone.

Glory went to the telephone and rang up Greta.

Greta was lying in bed and thinking about hell and crying and thinking that hell is the continuation of policy. She thought about the times and the wars and the 'scientific use of force' that was the enemy's practique. She thought that evil was indivisible and growing fast. She thought that every trifling evil thing she did was but another drop of sustenance for the evil to lap up and grow fat on. Oh, how fat it was growing.

'Zing,' went the telephone, and downstairs padded Greta, mopping at her nose with a chiffon scarf which by a fortunate chance was in the pocket of her dressing gown. The thought of the evil was upon her, and the thought that death itself is no escape from it.

'Oh yes, Glory, oh yes.' (She would go to lunch with Glory.)

The meat was overcooked and the beans were undercooked. The two friends brought their plates of food into the sitting-room and turned the gas fire up. Two of the asbestos props were broken, the room felt cold and damp.

'It is cold,' said Greta. 'Glory,' she said, 'I like your dressing gown with the burn down the front and the grease spots, somehow that is right, and the beastly dark room is right, and the dust upon the antique rare ornaments; the dust, and the saucepan with the goldfish in it, and the overcooked meat and the undercooked beans, it is right; it is an abandonment. It is what the world deserves.'

'Let us have some cocoa afterwards,' said Glory.

'Yes, cocoa, that is right too.'

They began to laugh. Cocoa *was* the thing.

'When you rang up,' said Greta, 'I was thinking, I said, Hell is the continuation of policy. And I was thinking that even death is not the end of it. You know, Glory, there is something frightening about the Christian idea, sometimes it is frightening.' She combed her hair through her fingers.

'I don't know,' said Glory, 'I never think about it.'

'The plodding on and on,' went on Greta, 'the de-moting and the up-grading; the marks and the punishments and the smugness.'

'Like school?' said Glory, waking up a bit to the idea.

'Yes, like school. And no freedom so that a person might stretch himself out. Never, never, never; not even in death; oh most of all not then.'

'I believe in mortality,' said Glory flippantly, 'I shall have on my tombstone, "In the confident hope of Mortality". If death is not the end,' she said, an uneasy note in her voice, 'then indeed there is nowhere to look.'

'When I was studying the Coptics,' said Greta, 'do you know what I found?'

'No, Greta, what was that?'

'It was the Angels and the Red Clay. The angels came one by one to the Red Clay and coaxed it saying that it should stand up and be Man, and that if the Red Clay would do this it should have the ups and downs, and the good fortune and bad fortune, and all falling haphazard, so that no one might say when it should be this and when that, but no matter, for this the Red Clay should stand up at once and be Man. But, No, said the Red Clay, No, it was not good enough.'

Glory's attention moved off from the Coptics and fastened again upon the problem of Ivor and herself. Oh dear, oh dear. And sadly the tears fell down.

Greta glanced at her severely. 'You should divorce Ivor,' she said.

'I've no grounds,' wailed Glory, 'not since I came back to him.'

'Then you should provoke him to strangle you,' said Greta, who wished to get on with her story. 'That should not be difficult,' she said, 'And then you can divorce him for cruelty.'

'But I love Ivor,' said Glory, 'I don't want to divorce him.'

'Well, make up your mind. As I was saying,' said Greta, '... so then came the Third Angel. "And what have you got to say for yourself?" said the Red Clay, "What have you to promise me?" "I am Death," said the Angel, "and death is the end." So at this up and jumps the Red Clay at once and becomes Man.'

'Oh Glory,' said Greta, when she had finished this recital, and paused a moment while the long tide of evil swept in again upon her, 'Oh Glory, I cannot bear the evil, and the cruelty, and the scientific use of force, and the evil.' She screwed her napkin into a twist, and wrung the hem of it, that was already torn, quite off. 'I do not feel that I can go on.'

At these grand familiar words Glory began to cry afresh, and Greta was crying too. For there lay the slop on the carpet where the goldfish had been, and there stood the saucepan with the fish resting languid upon the bottom, and there too was the dust and the dirt, and now the plates also, with the congealed mutton fat close upon them.

'Oh do put some more water in the fish pan,' sobbed Greta.

Glory picked up the pan and ran across the room with it to take it to the kitchen tap. But now the front door, that was apt to jam, opened with a burst, and Ivor fell into the room.

'They were both out,' he said. 'I suppose you have eaten all the lunch? Oh, hello Greta.'

'Listen,' said Glory, 'there's another bomb coming.'

Ivor went into the cupboard.

'Do you know Ivor,' screamed Greta through the closed door, 'I had a dream and when I woke up I was saying, "Hell is the continuation of policy".'

'You girls fill your heads with a lot of bosh.'

Glory said, 'There's some bread and cheese in the kitchen, we are keeping the cocoa hot. Greta' she said, 'was telling me about the Coptics.'

'Eh?' said Ivor.

'Oh do take those fish out and give them some more water,' said Greta.

'The story about the Angels and the Red Clay.'

'Spurious,' yelled Ivor, 'all bosh. But how on earth did you get hold of the manuscript, Greta, it's very rare.'

'I don't think there's much in it,' said Glory, 'nothing to make you cry. Come, cheer up Greta. I say Ivor, the doodle has gone off towards the town, you can come out now.'

Ivor came out looking very cheerful. 'I tell you what, Greta,' he said, 'I'll show you my new plastic bait.' He took the brightly coloured monsters out of their tin and brought them to her on a plate. 'I use these for pike,' he said.

There was now in the room a feeling of loving kindness and peace. Greta fetched the cheese and bread from the kitchen and Glory poured the hot cocoa. 'There is nothing like industry, control, affection and discipline,' said Greta.

The sun came round to the french windows and struck through the glass pane at the straw stuffing that was hanging down from the belly of the sofa.

'Oh, look,' said Glory, pointing to the patch of sunlight underneath, 'there is the button you lost.'

Silence fell upon them in the sun-spiked room. Silently, happily, they went on with their lunch. The only sound now in the room was the faint sizzle of the cocoa against the side of the jug (that was set too close to the fire and soon must crack) and the far off bark of the dog Sultan, happy with his rats.

SYLVIA TOWNSEND WARNER

Poor Mary

AT the last minute he remembered flowers. He went out and gathered some primroses from the hedgerow, hardening himself not to notice the snap of their stems. It was one of his fidgets to dislike picking flowers.

The track sloped away down hill. Here and there the leafless hedge was tufted with white where the blackthorns had come into bloom. It was like a black wave breaking into lips of foam. Down in the valley a plume of white steam rose up, its summit catching the pink light of sunset. It was still hanging there when he heard the train go on. And Mary, shouldering her pack, had handed in her ticket, and joined the nondescript civilian group waiting for the bus. The white plume thinned out, the train gathered speed, snorting on towards London. But Mary had got out at East Wickering, junction for Stoat and Saint Brewers.

I want to spend this leave at home, she had written; *unless you'd rather not. It's more than time I saw you in your hermit cell.* If it had not been for the last sentence he would have supposed she wanted to spend her leave with her family.

'Flowers for the guest-room,' he said to himself, setting down the spotted mug in the centre of the bureau. The bed, an old-fashioned double bed with brass end-rails and a white quilt, suddenly seemed a bed in which he had never slept. It looked like Wordsworth's bed, so monumentally domestic. He must contrive that she saw the camp-bed first. For the last week he had spent his spare time preparing for her, scrubbing the floors, polishing the windows, putting away his clothes, his books, his papers, so that his dwelling might offer its most impersonal face to her inspection. Now that he had remembered flowers everything seemed ready. The food on the table was covered with a napkin to keep flies off it, the kettle was in a state to boil when he wanted it to, the watercress was keeping cold in a damp cloth. He snuffed at his fingers' ends, and once more washed his hands very carefully. He had been cleaning out pigsties all the morning. Then he set off to meet his wife.

He had not seen her since 1941. A conscientious objector, he had applied for exemption from military service. The day after the tribunal had granted him exemption provided he worked on the land Mary volunteered for the ATS*. They had never agreed about war, so neither was surprised by the other.

'But as we are bound to argue,' she said, 'and people will only laugh at you if you have a military wife coming on visits, I shalln't come. Unless you are ill, of course. Then I will apply for compassionate leave.'

One of the things he had learned in four years spent as a farm labourer was an exact computation of time. So he met her where he had intended to meet her, fifty yards from where the bus had set her down. Though he knew she would be wearing uniform, it was a surprise to see that part of the uniform was a skirt. He had been similarly astonished on their wedding-day when apparently he had been assuming that she would come up the aisle wearing white satin trousers. Seeing the skirt he also saw her legs below it, and that they were fatter than they used to be.

'Hullo, Nicholas!'

'Hullo, Mary!'

She smells of metal, he thought, as much as I smell of dung. We are subdued to what we work in. He had smelled her, he had seen her legs. He did not seem to have seen her face. He took her pack, and said: 'Look! There's a hawk.'

'I suppose they do a lot of harm to the crops,' she replied.

'Wood-pigeons are worse.'

She set off, walking with quick resolute steps. Marching, in fact. So why on earth should she know about hawks? The thought prompted an enquiry about the V-2†, and they went up the track-way talking of air raids and air-raid damage. Just as there was a difference between their smells and a difference in their gait there was a difference in their manner of speech. Her voice had grown rather common and twanging, it sounded uncared for, and she jumped from one subject to another. She seemed to preface every remark with *Gosh!* and he to inaugurate every reply with *Um*.

* Auxiliary Territorial Service.

† Pilotless flying bombs. The first V-1s or 'doodle bugs' (see page 174) were launched on Britain in June 1944, and V-2s in September.

Listening to himself he thought, Do I sound more like the village schoolmaster or the village idiot?

A melancholy tenderness that was almost entirely the April dusk suffused him. Blackbirds shot across the path from hedge to hedge, scolding at them, beyond the hedges lambs bleated and rushed away at a ghostly gallop. He had been working from six in the morning, and was tired, and craved for tea. Yet each time that they paused for Mary to recover her breath he was glad to postpone the moment of reaching his house, and when the one chimney-pot reared into view above the hedge and beneath the evening star he said gloomily: 'Here's where I live.'

'It's nice. And all to yourself? Lucky bastard!'

'There are only two rooms,' he said defensively. 'The third one leaks.'

'Is it old?'

'Run up after the last war by a chicken-farming ex-serviceman. When he was ruined the farmer bought it. As he bought it very cheap, naturally he doesn't trouble to keep it in repair. So we sit in the kitchen. But I've got a chemical closet.'

It was strange to hear her feet on the floor of concrete slabs. Not strange to her, though, who had been living for four years in army constructions. The only strange thing to her would be to hear two pairs of feet instead of many. He moved the kettle forward on the range and lit the candles.

'Candles!' she said appreciatively.

'Because it's a party. Ordinarily I use an oil lamp.' His voice was still heavy with gloom.

'What queer squat candlesticks! They're clay, aren't they? Did you make them?'

'No. I bought them at a sale. They're called corpse candlesticks. The idea is that you leave them by the body all night, you see, and the rats can't knock them over.'

'I wonder you don't use them every night,' she said. 'Have you got any other cheerful curiosities?'

She had taken off her cap and unbuttoned her tunic. The candlelight softened the contest between her natural high colour and the too tawny make-up she had applied to it. If one were tracking her down in Roget's *Thesaurus*, the word would be *comely*.

Seeing that he was looking at her she said: 'Isn't it calamitous how fat I've grown? It's that army food, incessant gorges of starch. Gosh! Those puddings! Enough to make any girl look like a prize ox.'

'When I first came here I was covered with spots and boils,' he said consolingly. 'I thought I'd caught it from the pigs, till I discovered it was my well. Now I boil it.'

'I'd hate to have to do with pigs.'

'They're clean animals, really. It's just that they are overcrowded, and dirty feeders.'

'Sounds like the ATS.'

He cut more bread, reflecting that he would need to bake again on the morrow. Habit, of course, and mass-feeding, and the goaded appetite of the disciplined: though that would not account for the scatteration of egg-shell, the jam spooned on to a salted plate, the wide periphery of crumbs and cigarette ash. Nerves, he thought. Poor Mary's nerves are strained. His own strained nerves obliged him to sip his tea as though it were Napoleon brandy and frown at the iron-mould on the cloth.

'Lovely bread, Nicholas.'

'Soda bread. I bake it myself.'

'You seem to have a lot of time. Don't you ever do any work?'

'Fifty-six hours a week. Sometimes overtime. Pigs on Sunday. But it fits in somehow, and I don't dislike it. And the alternative would be to have a woman in.'

He had not meant this. She did not perceive it. Staring round her as though in a foreign country she said: 'And the polish on everything, too! You're wasted, Nicholas. You ought to be in the army.'

'Yes, sergeant.'

But more concerned than he had been over his own maladroit remarks she flushed, and refused to eat anything more, like an abashed child.

'Walk round and see the rest of it. Here's your room.'

'Pretty flowers.'

Glaring at the bed he remarked: 'I've got a bed in the third room.'

'But that's the room that leaks. You said so.'

She had turned around from the mirror, and it was as though the mirror had given back to her her former countenance, at once innocent and domineering.

'It doesn't leak in dry weather,' he said. 'I expect the cat's there now. She comes in and out by the window.'

'Cat? Why, you used to hate cats. You said they tortured birds.'

'So they do. So I do hate them. But I must needs find this animal in a gin, and dress its paw, and the damned beast has adopted me. It's a female, too.'

'Life's harder in the country, I expect,' she commented. It was for such slanting ironies that he had first loved her; for that, and for smelling of geraniums, and for the chivalrous quarrelsome disposition which had kept her at his side before his exemption was assured, saying hopefully that he might need someone to scrap with the authorities. But unseeing she went on to undo it by saying: 'You know, a lot of people are awfully interested when I tell them my husband is a CO. You'd be surprised how many feel the same way. All these murder cases, you know. Everyone's dead against the death sentence.'

'It doesn't surprise me very much,' he said. 'I was in the train the other day, I had to go to a dentist. And there was a bomber crew in the same carriage, and they were talking about a murder. They all agreed that it was wrong to take human life. I asked one of them why, and he said because you can't know what you're meddling with.'

'Exactly! I've heard dozens say the same thing. I'm beginning to think so myself. I think they ought to abolish it. I expect they will after the war.'

'They'll abolish war, my dear. Belligerents always abolish war after a war. It's harder to part with a death-sentence. And impossible to give up hunting and shooting because hunting and shooting make us what we are. Have a cigarette?'

'I don't think you've grown any pleasanter,' she said. 'Is that an owl? Let's go back to the other room.'

In the other room the clock was ticking, the kettle was boiling. Three hours earlier the bed had not seemed his own, now his living-room was not his either, but some sort of institutional waiting-room where two people had made an inordinate mess of a meal. At last, irked beyond bearing, he rose and began to clear the table and to wash up. The hot water in the bowl, the feeling of the crockery, dried and still warm as he stacked it on the dresser, the re-assumption of his ordinary evening routine began to console him. He moved to and fro more nimbly, preparing for the two breakfasts he would get in the morning, pouring the remains of the tea into the bottle he would carry to work with him – he had grown to enjoy cold tea – rinsing out the teapot and standing it on its head, throwing out the slops and bringing in the kindling for the morrow's fire, winding the clock and putting the cat's saucer down on a sheet of newspaper. Now, had he been by himself, he would have raked out the fire and gone off to read in bed. Instead, hospitality constrained him to say: 'Have you brought a hot-water-bottle?'

She did not answer. With a kettle in one hand and the wood-basket in the other he glanced at her. But she was not asleep. She was openly and directly crying.

He built up the fire and put on the kettle. This, whatever it was about, would mean more tea. Then he patted her shoulder and said: 'Poor Mary!' She put up her hand that was so plump and so demonstrably manicured, and clung to his wrist. She's going to have a baby, he thought. The cat in the gin that had clawed him to the bone, clawed and clung, had been within a few days of giving birth. He had made her a nest in the wood-house, but she had limped off to hide under a gorse-brake. The kittens had grown up and gone their wild way, and now she was pregnant again. But for poor Mary there was nothing but some sort of nursing-home.

She clung to his wrist and rubbed her head against his arm. Moulting, he thought, still clinically remembering the cat. She was going to have a baby, no doubt of it. It accounted for everything, for her nerves, for her legs, for her appetite, for her coming. Poor Mary, patriotism had not been enough, she had had no hatred in her heart for anybody, and so she was going to have a baby. The fortunes of war. Some get killed, some get maimed, some are got with child. There ought to be a pension from the War Office. And in that dreadful uniform, too, that pitiable skirt turned up. I hope to God, he thought, I shall not have to meet the father, one of those strenuous noodles, I suppose, who think badly of the death sentence. I'm damned if I will. And the next instant he was thinking, My poor Mary, I hope it wasn't a rape. Meanwhile his indifferent body was complying with the routine of his daily life, and he felt himself to be growing more and more sleepy and knew that unless he spoke he might yawn.

'If you'll let go a minute, Mary, I'll make some tea.'

She let go. The hand that had been so strong fell on her lap and crept into the other hand. Presently it moved again and pulled out a khaki handkerchief, and she began to mop her eyes and snort back her tears.

'This damned war! It's this damned war, Nicholas.'

He groaned assentingly.

'Now that it's nearly over, how I hate it!'

With an effort he refrained from pointing out that it was only in Europe that the war might be said to be nearly over.

'If they'd let me fight, as I wanted to, I might be killed by now. If we'd stayed in London and I'd driven an ambulance or a pump I might be killed by now. As it is I've never been so healthy in all my life.'

'You don't look well,' he said. 'I noticed at once that you looked tired. And you got frightfully out of breath walking up the hill.'

'Fat! My healthy army fat! When I come out of the army, Nicholas, I shall come out healthy, hideous, middle-aged, and without an interest in life. And there will be hordes and hordes of me, all in the same boat. Gosh, what a crew!'

Giving up the hypothesis of a baby he realized how much he was relinquishing. Once it was born, she would have been happy enough.

'We shall all be in that boat, dear. Besides, you're a sergeant, aren't you? That's something. You'll soon get thin, once you're out in the rough and tumble of civilian life. Once you're thin, you'll take hold, you'll get interested in something or other. Probably you'll fall in love, and make a fresh start.'

The kettle was boiling, he began to prepare for more tea.

'Fall in love? Fall in love? Not again. You see, I did it.'

He paused, kettle in hand. (Would nothing rid him of these turbulent kettles?)

'And he was killed? I'm sorry, Mary.'

'He wasn't killed. He chucked me, and now he's married to another bitch.'

'And that's all?'

'And that's all.'

He glanced towards the clock. It felt like midnight, but it was only half-past ten. If he could give her something stronger, some whisky, some rum. A little rum, now, in her tea ... But a pigeon-shooting party last week had cleaned out the Red Lion of everything except aniseed cordial.

'Sugar?' he enquired.

She looked at him.

'I'm sorry. I'm sorry! I asked you that only three hours ago, didn't I? I am an insensate clod.'

'That's all right, Nicholas. Actually, I don't take sugar. You could have had all mine, you see. Think what you've missed. Actually, why I came back was to see if you'd ever want to live with me again. Not that I thought it likely. Why should you? Anyhow, it's plain you don't. So that's over. What good tea you make.'

She drank in gulps, swallowing violently, swallowing tea and tears.

'You were always domestically inclined, weren't you? It will be a comfort to me, yes, really it will, to think of you being so happy and tidy and self-contained, with your cat and your corpse-candles and your books and your flowers. Did Robinson Crusoe have flowers on his table, as well as his old cat sitting up to it like a Christian? I can't remember. Perhaps when we are both very old I may come and spend the afternoon with you on your island. And you can make me some of your nice tea, and ask me if I take sugar with it. But of course I'll give you ample warning. I won't be a disquieting footprint. I *did* warn you this time, you know.'

She had risen, she had picked up her cap and her pack and her cigarette-case and her lighter and her lipstick and all her bits and pieces.

'I think I'll go to bed. I've got rather a headache.'

'Yes. We'll go to bed.'

Leaving the room all anyhow, he thought, staring at her submissive military back in the door-way. Whether it made things better, whether it made them worse, it was the only thing he could do, the only way he could comfort her. They would lie in the Wordsworthian bed, their smells of dung and of metal would mingle, her shoulder would feel like greengages and her hair would get in his mouth, and she would be silent. It was one of her graces that she was silent in bed. And afterwards, when she had gone to sleep, he would straighten himself and lie on his back, letting the day's fatigue run out of his limbs as the fleas run out of the body of a shot rabbit. And probably his last waking thought would be of the alarm clock, poised to wake him at five-thirty, and of the limpid innocent morning in which he would go out to his work.

DORIS LESSING

The Black Madonna

THERE are some countries in which the arts, let alone Art, cannot be said to flourish. Why this should be so it is hard to say, although of course we all have our theories about it. For sometimes it is the most barren soil that sends up gardens of those flowers which we all agree are the crown and justification of life, and it is this fact which makes it hard to say, finally, why the soil of Zambesia should produce such reluctant plants.

Zambesia is a tough, sunburnt, virile, positive country contemptuous of subtleties and sensibility: yet there have been States with these qualities which have produced art, though perhaps with the left hand. Zambesia is, to put it mildly, unsympathetic to those ideas so long taken for granted in other parts of the world, to do with liberty, fraternity and the rest. Yet there are those, and some of the finest souls among them, who maintain that art is impossible without a minority whose leisure is guaranteed by a hard-working majority. And whatever Zambesia's comfortable minority may lack, it is not leisure.

Zambesia – but enough; out of respect for ourselves and for scientific accuracy, we should refrain from jumping to conclusions. Particularly when one remembers the almost wistful respect Zambesians show when an artist does appear in their midst.

Consider, for instance, the case of Michele.

He came out of the internment camp at the time when Italy was made a sort of honorary ally, during the Second World War. It was a time of strain for the authorities, because it is one thing to be responsible for thousands of prisoners of war whom one must treat according to certain recognized standards. It is another to be faced, and from one day to the next, with these same thousands transformed by some international legerdemain into comrades in arms. Some of the thousands stayed where they were in the camps; they were fed and housed there at least. Others went as farm labourers, though not many; for while the farmers were as always short of labour, they did not know how to handle farm labourers who were also white men: such a phenomenon had never happened in Zambesia before. Some did odd jobs around the towns, keeping a sharp eye out for the trade unions, who would neither admit them as members nor agree to their working.

Hard, hard, the lot of these men, but fortunately not for long, for soon the war ended and they were able to go home.

Hard, too, the lot of the authorities, as has been pointed out; and for that reason they were doubly willing to take what advantages they could from the situation; and that Michele was such an advantage there could be no doubt.

His talents were first discovered when he was still a prisoner of war. A church was built in the camp, and Michele decorated its interior. It became a show-place, that little tin-roofed church in the prisoners' camp, with its whitewashed walls covered all over with frescoes depicting swarthy peasants gathering grapes for the vintage, beautiful Italian girls dancing, plump dark-eyed children. Amid crowded scenes of Italian life, appeared the Virgin and her Child, smiling and beneficent, happy to move familiarly among her people.

Culture-loving ladies who had bribed the authorities to be taken inside the camp would say, 'Poor thing, how homesick he must be'. And they would beg to be allowed to leave half a crown for the artist. Some were indignant. He was a prisoner, after all, captured in the very act of fighting against justice and democracy, and what right had he to protest? – for they felt these paintings as a sort of protest. What was there in Italy that we did not have right here in Westonville, which was the capital and hub of Zambesia? Were there not sunshine and mountains and fat babies and pretty girls here? Did we not grow – if not grapes, at least lemons and oranges and flowers in plenty?

People were upset – the desperation of nostalgia came from the painted white walls of that simple church, and affected everyone according to his temperament.

But when Michele was free, his talent was remembered. He was spoken of as 'that Italian artist'. As a matter of fact, he was a bricklayer. And the virtues of those frescoes might very well have been exaggerated. It is possible that they would have been overlooked altogether in a country where picture-covered walls were more common.

When one of the visiting ladies came rushing out to the camp in her own car, to ask him to paint her children, he said he was not qualified to do so. But at last he agreed. He took a room in the town and made some nice likenesses of the children. Then he painted the children of a great number of the first lady's friends. He charged ten shillings a time. Then one of the ladies wanted a portrait of herself. He asked ten pounds for it; it had taken him a month to do. She was annoyed, but paid.

And Michele went off to his room with a friend and stayed there drinking red wine from the Cape and talking about home. While the money lasted he could not be persuaded to do any more portraits.

There was a good deal of talk among the ladies about the dignity of labour, a subject in which they were well versed; and one felt they might almost go so far as to compare a white man with a kaffir, who did not understand the dignity of labour either.

He was felt to lack gratitude. One of the ladies tracked him down, found him lying on a camp-bed under a tree with a bottle of wine, and spoke to him severely about the barbarity of Mussolini and the fecklessness of the Italian temperament. Then she demanded that he should instantly paint a picture of herself in her new evening dress. He refused, and she went home very angry.

It happened that she was the wife of one of our most important citizens, a General or something of that kind, who was at that time engaged in planning a military tattoo or show for the benefit of the civilian population. The whole of Westonville had been discussing this show for weeks. We were all bored to extinction by dances, fancy-dress balls, fairs, lotteries and other charitable entertainments. It is not too much to say that while some were dying for freedom, others were dancing for it. There comes a limit to everything. Though, of course, when the end of the war actually came and the thousands of troops stationed in the country had to go home – in short, when enjoying ourselves would no longer be a duty, many were heard to exclaim that life would never be the same again.

In the meantime, the Tattoo would make a nice change for us all. The military gentlemen responsible for the idea did not think of it in these terms. They thought to improve morale by giving us some idea of what war was really like. Headlines in the newspaper were not enough. And in order to bring it all home to us, they planned to destroy a village by shell-fire before our very eyes.

First, the village had to be built.

It appears that the General and his subordinates stood around in the red dust of the parade-ground under a burning sun for the whole of one day, surrounded by building materials, while hordes of African labourers ran around with boards and nails, trying to make something that looked like a village. It became evident that they would have to build a proper village in order to destroy it; and this would cost more than was allowed for the whole entertainment. The General went home in a bad temper, and his wife said what they needed was an artist, they needed Michele. This was not because she wanted to do Michele a good turn; she could not endure the thought of him lying around singing while there was work to be done. She refused to undertake any delicate diplomatic missions when her husband said he would be damned if he would ask favours of any little Wop. She solved the problem for him in her own way: a certain Captain Stocker was sent out to fetch him.

The Captain found him on the same camp-bed under the same tree, in rolled-up trousers, and an uncollared shirt; unshaven, mildly drunk, with a bottle of wine standing beside him on the earth. He was singing an air so wild, so sad, that the Captain was uneasy. He stood at ten paces from the disreputable fellow and felt the indignities of his position. A year ago, this man had been a mortal enemy to be shot at sight. Six months ago, he had been an enemy prisoner. Now he lay with his knees up, in an untidy shirt that had certainly once been military. For the Captain, the situation crystallized in a desire that Michele should salute him.

'Piselli!' he said sharply.

Michele turned his head and looked at the Captain from the horizontal. 'Good morning,' he said affably.

'You are wanted,' said the Captain.

'Who?' said Michele. He sat up, a fattish, olive-skinned little man. His eyes were resentful.

'The authorities.'

'The war is over?'

The Captain, who was already stiff and shiny enough in his laundered khaki, jerked his head back frowning, chin out. He was a large man, blond, and wherever his flesh showed, it was brick-red. His eyes were small and blue and angry. His red hands, covered all over with fine yellow bristles, clenched by his side. Then he saw the disappointment in Michele's eyes, and the hands unclenched. 'No it is not over,' he said. 'Your assistance is required.'

'For the war?'

'For the war effort. I take it you are interested in defeating the Germans?'

Michele looked at the Captain. The little dark-eyed artisan looked at the great blond officer with his cold blue eyes, his narrow mouth, his hands like bristle-covered steaks. He looked and said: 'I am very interested in the end of the war.'

'*Well?*' said the Captain between his teeth.

'The pay?' said Michele.

'You will be paid.'

Michele stood up. He lifted the bottle against the sun, then took a gulp. He rinsed his mouth out with wine and spat. Then he poured what was left on to the red earth, where it made a bubbling purple stain.

'I am ready,' he said. He went with the Captain to the waiting lorry, where he climbed in beside the driver's seat and not, as the Captain had expected, into the back of the lorry. When they had arrived at the parade-ground the officers had left a message that the Captain would be personally responsible for Michele and for the village. Also for the hundred or so labourers who were sitting around on the grass verges waiting for orders.

The Captain explained what was wanted. Michele nodded. Then he waved his hand at the Africans. 'I do not want these,' he said.

'You will do it yourself – a village?'

'Yes.'

'With no help?'

Michele smiled for the first time. 'I will do it.'

The Captain hesitated. He disapproved on principle of white men doing heavy manual labour. He said: 'I will keep six to do the heavy work.'

Michele shrugged; and the Captain went over and dismissed all but six of the Africans. He came back with them to Michele.

'It is hot,' said Michele.

'Very,' said the Captain. They were standing in the middle of the parade-ground. Around its edge trees, grass, gulfs of shadow. Here, nothing but reddish dust, drifting and lifting in a low hot breeze.

'I am thirsty,' said Michele. He grinned. The Captain felt his stiff lips loosen unwillingly in reply. The two pairs of eyes met. It was a moment of understanding. For the Captain, the little Italian had suddenly become human. 'I will arrange it,' he said, and went off down-town. By the time he had explained the position to the right people, filled in forms and made arrangements, it was late afternoon. He returned to the parade-ground with a case of Cape brandy, to find Michele and the six black men seated together under a tree. Michele was singing an Italian song to them, and they were harmonizing with him. The sight affected the Captain like an attack of nausea. He came up, and the Africans stood to attention. Michele continued to sit.

'You said you would do the work yourself?'

'Yes, I said so.'

The Captain then dismissed the Africans. They departed, with friendly looks towards Michele, who waved at them. The Captain was beef-red with anger. 'You have not started yet?'

'How long have I?'

'Three weeks.'

'Then there is plenty of time,' said Michele, looking at the bottle of brandy in the Captain's hand. In the other were two glasses. 'It is evening,' he pointed out. The Captain stood frowning for a moment. Then he sat down on the grass, and poured out two brandies.

'Ciao,' said Michele.

'Cheers,' said the Captain. Three weeks, he was thinking. Three weeks with this damned little Itie! He drained his glass and refilled it, and set it in the grass. The grass was cool and soft. A tree was flowering somewhere close – hot waves of perfume came on the breeze.

'It is nice here,' said Michele. 'We will have a good time together. Even in a war, there are times of happiness. And of friendship. I drink to the end of the war.'

Next day the Captain did not arrive at the parade-ground until after lunch. He found Michele under the trees with a bottle. Sheets of ceiling board had been erected at one end of the parade-ground in such a way that they formed two walls and part of a third, and a slant of steep roof supported on struts.

'What's that?' said the Captain, furious.

'The church,' said Michele.

'Wha-at?'

'You will see. Later. It is very hot.' He looked at the brandy bottle that lay on its side on the ground. The Captain went to the lorry and returned with the case of brandy. They drank. Time passed. It was a long time since the Captain had sat on grass under a tree. It was a long time, for that matter, since he had drunk so much. He always drank a great deal, but it was regulated to the times and seasons. He was a disciplined man. Here, sitting on the grass beside this little man whom he still could not help thinking of as an enemy, it was not that he let his self-discipline go, but that he felt himself to be something different: he was temporarily set outside his normal behaviour. Michele did not count. He listened to Michele talking about Italy and it seemed to him he was listening to a savage speaking; as if he heard tales from the mythical South Sea islands where a man like himself might very well go just once in his life. He found himself saying he would like to make a trip to Italy after the war. Actually, he was attracted only by the North and by Northern people. He had visited Germany, under Hitler, and though it was not the time to say so, had found it very satisfactory. Then Michele sang him some Italian songs. He sang Michele some English songs. Then Michele took out photographs of his wife and children, who lived in a village in the mountains of North Italy. He asked the Captain if he were married. The Captain never spoke about his private affairs.

He had spent all his life in one or other of the African colonies as a policeman, magistrate, native commissioner, or in some other useful capacity. When the war started, military life came easily to him. But he hated city life, and had his own reasons for wishing the war over. Mostly, he had been in bush-stations with one or two other white men, or by himself, far from the rigours of civilization. He had relations with native women; and from time to time visited the city where his wife lived with her parents and the children. He was always tormented by the idea that she was unfaithful to him. Recently he had even appointed a private detective to watch her; he was convinced the detective was inefficient. Army friends coming from L— where his wife was, spoke of her at parties, enjoying herself. When the war ended, she would not find it so easy to have a good time. And why did he not simply live with her and be done

with it? The fact was, he could not. And his long exile to remote
bush-stations was because he needed the excuse not to. He could
not bear to think of his wife for too long; she was that part of his
life he had never been able, so to speak, to bring to heel.

Yet he spoke of her now to Michele, and of his favourite bush-
wife, Nadya. He told Michele the story of his life, until he realized
that the shadows from the trees they sat under had stretched right
across the parade-ground to the grandstand. He got unsteadily to
his feet, and said: 'There is work to be done. You are being paid to
work.'

'I will show you my church when the light goes.'

The sun dropped, darkness fell, and Michele made the Captain
drive his lorry to the parade-ground a couple of hundred yards
away and switch on his lights. Instantly, a white church sprang up
from the shapes and shadows of the bits of board.

'Tomorrow, some houses,' said Michele cheerfully.

At the end of a week, the space at the end of the parade-ground
had crazy gawky constructions of lath and board over it, that
looked in the sunlight like nothing on earth. Privately, it upset the
Captain: it was like a nightmare that these skeleton-like shapes
should be able to persuade him, with the illusions of light and
dark, that they were a village. At night, the Captain drove up his
lorry, switched on the lights, and there it was, the village, solid and
real against the background of full green trees. Then, in the
morning sunlight, there was nothing there, just bits of board stuck
in the sand.

'It is finished,' said Michele.

'You were engaged for three weeks,' said the Captain. He did
not want it to end, this holiday from himself.

Michele shrugged. 'The army is rich,' he said. Now, to avoid
curious eyes, they sat inside the shade of the church, with the case
of brandy between them. The Captain talked, talked endlessly,
about his wife, about women. He could not stop talking.

Michele listened. Once he said: 'When I go home – when I go
home – I shall open my arms ...' He opened them, wide. He closed
his eyes. Tears ran down his cheeks. 'I shall take my wife in my
arms, and I shall ask nothing, nothing. I do not care. It is enough
to be together. That is what the war has taught me. It is enough, it
is enough. I shall ask no questions and I shall be happy.'

The Captain stared before him, suffering. He thought how he

dreaded his wife. She was a scornful creature, gay and hard, who laughed at him. She had been laughing at him ever since they married. Since the war, she had taken to calling him names like Little Hitler, and Storm-trooper. 'Go ahead, my little Hitler,' she had cried last time they met. 'Go ahead, my Storm-trooper. If you want to waste your money on private detectives, go ahead. But don't think I don't know what *you* do when you're in the bush. I don't care what you do, but remember that I know it ...'

The Captain remembered her saying it. And there sat Michele on his packing-case, saying: 'It's a pleasure for the rich, my friend, detectives and the law. Even jealousy is a pleasure I don't want any more. Ah, my friend, to be together with my wife again, and the children, that is all I ask of life. That and wine and food and singing in the evenings.' And the tears wetted his cheeks and splashed on to his shirt.

That a man should cry, good Lord! thought the Captain. And without shame! He seized the bottle and drank.

Three days before the great occasion, some high-ranking officers came strolling through the dust, and found Michele and the Captain sitting together on the packing-case, singing. The Captain's shirt was open down the front, and there were stains on it.

The Captain stood to attention with the bottle in his hand, and Michele stood to attention too, out of sympathy with his friend. Then the officers drew the Captain aside – they were all cronies of his – and said, what the hell did he think he was doing? And why wasn't the village finished?

Then they went away.

'Tell them it is finished,' said Michele. 'Tell them I want to go.'

'No,' said the Captain, 'no, Michele, what would you do if your wife ...'

'This world is a good place. We should be happy – that is all.'

'Michele ...'

'I want to go. There is nothing to do. They paid me yesterday.'

'Sit down, Michele. Three more days, and then it's finished.'

'Then I shall paint the inside of the church as I painted the one in the camp.'

The Captain laid himself down on some boards and went to sleep. When he woke, Michele was surrounded by the pots of paint he had used on the outside of the village. Just in front of the

Captain was a picture of a black girl. She was young and plump. She wore a patterned blue dress and her shoulders came soft and bare out of it. On her back was a baby slung in a band of red stuff. Her face was turned towards the Captain and she was smiling.

'That's Nadya,' said the Captain. 'Nadya ...' He groaned loudly. He looked at the black child and shut his eyes. He opened them, and mother and child were still there. Michele was very carefully drawing thin yellow circles around the heads of the black girl and her child.

'Good God,' said the Captain, 'you can't do that.'

'Why not?'

'You can't have a black Madonna.'

'She was a peasant. This is a peasant. Black peasant Madonna for black country.'

'This is a German village,' said the Captain.

'This is my Madonna,' said Michele angrily. 'Your German village and my Madonna. I paint this picture as an offering to the Madonna. She is pleased – I feel it.'

The Captain lay down again. He was feeling ill. He went back to sleep. When he woke for the second time it was dark. Michele had brought in a flaring paraffin lamp, and by its light was working on the long wall. A bottle of brandy stood beside him. He painted until long after midnight, and the Captain lay on his side and watched, as passive as a man suffering a dream. Then they both went to sleep on the boards. The whole of the next day Michele stood painting black Madonnas, black saints, black angels. Outside, troops were practising in the sunlight, bands were blaring and motor cyclists roared up and down. But Michele painted on, drunk and oblivious. The Captain lay on his back, drinking and muttering about his wife. Then he would say 'Nadya, Nadya', and burst into sobs.

Towards nightfall the troops went away. The officers came back, and the Captain went off with them to show how the village sprang into being when the great lights at the end of the parade-ground were switched on. They all looked at the village in silence. They switched the lights off, and there were only the tall angular boards leaning like gravestones in the moonlight. On went the lights – and there was the village. They were silent, as if suspicious. Like the Captain, they seemed to feel it was not right. Uncanny it certainly was, but *that* was not it. Unfair – that was the word. It was cheating. And profoundly disturbing.

'Clever chap, that Italian of yours,' said the General.

The Captain, who had been woodenly correct until this moment, suddenly came rocking up to the General, and steadied himself by laying his hand on the august shoulder. 'Bloody Wops,' he said. 'Bloody kaffirs. Bloody ... Tell you what, though, there's one Itie that's some good. Yes, there is. I'm telling you. He's a friend of mine, actually.'

The General looked at him. Then he nodded to his underlings. The Captain was taken away for disciplinary purposes. It was decided, however, that he must be ill, nothing else could account for such behaviour. He was put to bed in his own room with a nurse to watch him.

He woke twenty-four hours later, sober for the first time in weeks. He slowly remembered what had happened. Then he sprang out of bed and rushed into his clothes. The nurse was just in time to see him run down the path and leap into his lorry.

He drove at top speed to the parade-ground, which was flooded with light in such a way that the village did not exist. Everything was in full swing. The cars were three deep around the square, with people on the running-boards and even the roofs. The grandstand was packed. Women dressed as gipsies, country girls, Elizabethan court dames, and so on, wandered about with trays of ginger beer and sausage-rolls and programmes at five shillings each in aid of the war effort. On the square, troops deployed, obsolete machine-guns were being dragged up and down, bands played, and motor cyclists roared through flames.

As the Captain parked the lorry, all this activity ceased, and the lights went out. The Captain began running around the outside of the square to reach the place where the guns were hidden in a mess of net and branches. He was sobbing with the effort. He was a big man, and unused to exercise, and sodden with brandy. He had only one idea in his mind – to stop the guns firing, to stop them at all costs.

Luckily, there seemed to be a hitch. The lights were still out. The unearthly graveyard at the end of the square glittered white in the moonlight. Then the lights briefly switched on, and the village sprang into existence for just long enough to show large red crosses all over a white building beside the church. Then moonlight flooded everything again, and the crosses vanished. 'Oh, the bloody fool!' sobbed the Captain, running, running as if for his life. He was no longer trying to reach the guns. He was cutting across a corner of the square direct to the church. He could hear some officers cursing behind him: 'Who put those red crosses there? Who? We can't fire on the Red Cross.'

The Captain reached the church as the searchlights burst on. Inside, Michele was kneeling on the earth looking at his first Madonna. 'They are going to kill my Madonna,' he said miserably.

'Come away, Michele, come away.'

'They're going to ...'

The Captain grabbed his arm and pulled. Michele wrenched himself free and grabbed a saw. He began hacking at the ceiling board. There was a dead silence outside. They heard a voice booming through the loudspeakers: 'The village that is about to be shelled is an English village, not as represented on the programme, a German village. Repeat, the village that is about to be shelled is ...'

Michele had cut through two sides of a square around the Madonna.

'Michele,' sobbed the Captain, '*get out of here.*'

Michele dropped the saw, took hold of the raw edges of the board and tugged. As he did so, the church began to quiver and lean. An irregular patch of board ripped out and Michele staggered back into the Captain's arms. There was a roar. The church seemed to dissolve around them into flame. Then they were running away from it, the Captain holding Michele tight by the right arm. 'Get down,' he shouted suddenly, and threw Michele to the earth. He flung himself down beside him. Looking from under the crook of his arm, he heard the explosion, saw a great pillar of smoke and flame, and the village disintegrated in a flying mass of debris. Michele was on his knees gazing at his Madonna in the light from the flames. She was unrecognizable, blotted out with dust. He looked horrible, quite white, and a trickle of blood soaked from his hair down one cheek.

'They shelled my Madonna,' he said.

'Oh, damn it, you can paint another one,' said the Captain. His own voice seemed to him strange, like a dream voice. He was certainly crazy, as mad as Michele himself ... He got up, pulled Michele to his feet, and marched him towards the edge of the field.

There they were met by the ambulance people. Michele was taken off to hospital, and the Captain was sent back to bed.

A week passed. The Captain was in a darkened room. That he was having some kind of a breakdown was clear, and two nurses stood guard over him. Sometimes he lay quiet. Sometimes he muttered to himself. Sometimes he sang in a thick clumsy voice bits out of opera, fragments from Italian songs, and – over and over again – There's a Long Long Trail. He was not thinking of anything at all. He shied away from the thought of Michele as if it were dangerous. When, therefore, a cheerful female voice announced that a friend had come to cheer him up, and it would do him good to have some company, and he saw a white bandage moving towards him in the gloom, he turned over on to his side, face to the wall.

'Go away,' he said. 'Go away, Michele.'

'I have come to see you,' said Michele. 'I have brought you a present.'

The Captain slowly turned over. There was Michele, a cheerful ghost in the dark room. 'You fool,' he said. 'You messed everything up. What did you paint those crosses for?'

'It was a hospital,' said Michele. 'In a village there is a hospital, and on the hospital the Red Cross, the beautiful Red Cross – no?'

'I was nearly court-martialled.'

'It was my fault,' said Michele. 'I was drunk.'

'I was responsible.'

'How could you be responsible when I did it? But it is all over. Are you better?'

'Well, I suppose those crosses saved your life.'

'I did not think,' said Michele. 'I was remembering the kindness of the Red Cross people when we were prisoners.'

'Oh shut up, shut up, shut up.'

'I have brought you a present.'

The Captain peered through the dark. Michele was holding up a picture. It was of a native woman with a baby on her back smiling sideways out of the frame.

Michele said: 'You did not like the haloes. So this time, no haloes. For the Captain – no Madonna.' He laughed. 'You like it? It is for you. I painted it for you.'

'God damn you!' said the Captain.

'You do not like it?' said Michele, very hurt.

The Captain closed his eyes. 'What are you going to do next?' he asked, tiredly.

Michele laughed again. 'Mrs Pannerhurst, the lady of the General, she wants me to paint her picture in her white dress. So I paint it.'

'You should be proud to.'

'Silly bitch. She thinks I am good. They know nothing – savages. Barbarians. Not you, Captain, you are my friend. But these people they know nothing.'

The Captain lay quiet. Fury was gathering in him. He thought of the General's wife. He disliked her, but he had known her well enough.

'These people,' said Michele. 'They do not know a good picture from a bad picture. I paint, I paint, this way, that way. There is the picture – I look at it and laugh inside myself.' Michele laughed out loud. 'They say, he is a Michelangelo, this one, and try to cheat me out of my price. Michele - Michelangelo – that is a joke, no?

The Captain said nothing.

'But for you I painted this picture to remind you of our good times with the village. You are my friend. I will always remember you.'

The Captain turned his eyes sideways in his head and stared at the black girl. Her smile at him was half innocence, half malice.

'Get out,' he said suddenly.

Michele came closer and bent to see the Captain's face. 'You wish me to go?' He sounded unhappy. 'You saved my life. I was a fool that night. But I was thinking of my offering to the Madonna – I was a fool, I say it myself. I was drunk, we are fools when we get drunk.'

'Get out of here,' said the Captain again.

For a moment the white bandage remained motionless. Then it swept downwards in a bow.

Michele turned towards the door.

'And take that bloody picture with you.'

Silence. Then, in the dim light, the Captain saw Michele reach out for the picture, his white head bowed in profound obeisance. He straightened himself and stood to attention, holding the picture with one hand, and keeping the other stiff down his side. Then he saluted the Captain.

'Yes, *sir*,' he said, and he turned and went out of the door with the picture.

The Captain lay still. He felt – what did he feel? There was a pain under his ribs. It hurt to breathe. He realized he was unhappy. Yes, a terrible unhappiness was filling him, slowly, slowly. He was unhappy because Michele had gone. Nothing had ever hurt the Captain in all his life as much as that mocking *Yes, sir*. Nothing. He turned his face to the wall and wept. But silently. Not a sound escaped him, for the fear the nurses might hear.

A. L. BARKER

The Iconoclasts

THE top step was sacred. To tread on it was not only a crime but a deliberate thumbing at fate. Of course a lot of people did – his parents, the occasional gardener, and visitors who were being shown the paved walk under the lime trees. It worried Marcus to think what a lot of trouble they were storing up for themselves, until he decided that as they were adults, they had graduated out of the power of the step. One day, he too would be beyond it, he would be able to tread there without his footstep shaking loose some dreadful animus.

Just now it was necessary to stretch his legs from the penultimate step to the square of turf beyond the top, and Marcus, small for his five years, found the reach considerable. That was as it should be, he wouldn't want it to be easy, any more than one would wish the lion one had defeated to be tame.

With the pail of earth he was carrying, the step was doubly difficult to avoid, and he had to take the secondary route up the bank and under the flowering currants. Already there was quite a beaten track there. His father didn't like him to go in under the bushes, he said Marcus must have the proclivities of a cat and would probably take to the tiles in due course. Marcus had explained, he was always explaining, that it was a matter beyond his control – the detour was as much of a nuisance to him as it was to everyone else. But they never seemed to catch the gravity of the situation, and to Marcus's father it was just a source of humour.

On the paved part at the back of the toolshed was quite a pile of earth which Marcus had carried there. He was going to make a castle, like his seaside ones, and irrigate it. That was ambitious, especially as he had only inferior materials – earth and tap water instead of sand and sea.

THE RETURN OF THE NATIVE

Rainbarrow:—
"This bossy projection of earth above its natural
level occupied the loftiest ground of the
lonliest height that the heath contained. Although
from the vale it appeared but as a wart on an
Atlantean brow, its actual bulk was great. It
formed the pole and axis of this heathery world."
It was at this remote spot that Eustacia Vye and
Wildeve held their secret rendezvous.

Nature looking
forward &
returning.

Susan xxx

HARDY'S DORSET

No. 9 in a series of 16
Rainbarrows, Duddle Heath
Ordnance Survey Sheet 194. Grid Ref. 735 920
Published by the Thomas Hardy Society Ltd.
© Kathy Still 1978

DORCHESTER
DORSET
10 30AM
14 MCH
1994

Mr & Mrs W R Rennie
30 Comiston View
Edinburgh EH10 6LP,
SCOTLAND.

16P

Marcus thought he had enough earth now, but before he started work there was a routine job to be done. Puffing and severe, he climbed to the top of the rockery and stared between the garden trees to a sloping brown field, stitched all over with green. There was a scarecrow among the furrows, a poor trashy thing of sticks, sacking and a yellow trilby. At sight of the trilby, Marcus's frown relaxed and he nodded approvingly.

Some boys had once stolen the scarecrow's hat and the farmer said jokingly that in future perhaps Marcus would keep an eye on the new one. Marcus accepted the commission in all seriousness; twice a day he made sure that the turnip head was decently covered.

He went back to the toolshed. Boddy was propped against a flower-pot, and a big beetle which had crawled out of the loose earth was advancing on him. It looked too large to squash, no doubt it would crackle and spread out on the paving. But Boddy had to be saved, and not by retreat, either. Marcus shovelled up the beetle and threw it on to the flower-bed.

When the danger was past, he said sternly to Boddy, 'You'll have to be more careful. I haven't got time to turn around today.'

Marcus turned his back then, and Boddy, whose salient feature was his big lolling head, sat meekly by, grinning his golliwog's grin. His was the function of the subordinate, the apprentice. Marcus used him without mercy and it was only because he was made of good durable leather with a head full of straw shavings and thatched with nothing more sensitive than dusty wool, that he had survived.

Marcus was much attached to him because Boddy did what no one else did, he went in awe of Marcus. That made a full circle – Marcus's father looked up to his superior at the office, Marcus's mother looked up to Marcus's father, Marcus's grandmother looked up to them both, Marcus had to look up to everybody, and Boddy looked up to Marcus.

There was a worm in the pile of earth. Marcus showed it to Boddy. 'That's a snake. It's not safe just here, you'd better tuck your legs in.'

He thought he might keep the worm and let it swim in the moat of his castle, so he put it under a flower-pot.

'This is very important,' he said, making the earth into a tight pile and cutting it with his spade. 'It's a secret.'

The new venture was now on a par with treaties and plans, the movement of armies and the sinking of oil-wells. For Marcus, frowning, absorbed, the world had very properly dwindled, it waited on his monumental mud just as it waits – for the single-minded – on diplomacy, the invention, the battle, the fortune in the making. Only Boddy, as the onlooker, could be expected to know that it never waited for anything.

As castles go, it was not a success. Marcus would not admit that it looked like a nasty chocolate pudding. He put the worm in the moat and told Boddy that it was better than any at the seaside. It was guarded by a sinister serpent and when the sun came out it would get hard as iron and no one would ever be able to knock it over. It would still be there by his next birthday – there could be no longer period of time than that. Secretly, Marcus was so disgusted with it that he couldn't stop saying what a wonderful castle it was, and pushed Boddy into the laurel bushes for not looking impressed.

After that, he gave way to baser instincts, flattened the castle, worm and all, and made some really excellent mud-pies. He chatted amiably, forgetting that Boddy was flat on his face under the ugly spotted laurels. That was the best of Boddy, whether he was there or not, he always listened.

Marcus was extremely busy when he heard his grandmother in the garden. She was calling him to lunch – that was the signal for him to double up like a jack-knife and creep through the shrubbery, away from the direction of her voice. Not because he was furtive or guilty, but simply because it was part of his policy to be elusive, not easily found – in fact, not to be found at all. He preferred to turn the tables and seek the seeker.

Coming into the shadow of the garden wall, he suddenly drew himself up, lifted one leg and began solemnly to hop. In one corner opposite him, was the husk of a summerhouse. Once it had stood on a pedestal and revolved so that anyone inside could always arrange to face the sun. That had been long before Marcus's time, and rain and frost had rotted the flimsy wood. It leaned against the wall, in the winter drenched black, in the summer whitey-grey like an old bone. When Marcus looked inside, he saw the dark glint of water that had driven in through the roof, and something with fierce red eyes set it trembling.

Marcus had skipped off quickly. Whatever it was in the

summerhouse, he believed it preferred him to hurry by and not stare too much. For dignity's sake he could not run past; he always, however sober his pace, began to skip and hop when he came in sight of the hut, thus placating its creature without loss of prestige. So the skipping and hopping became a ritual and after the manner of ritual, had a definite form. Two hops, three skips and a short jump, took Marcus on a level with the summerhouse door. He was then entitled to assert himself and his command of the ritual by a deliberate stare. Two hops, three skips and a short jump took him well out of the creature's jurisdiction again.

Marcus had this belief in ceremony. It did not constrain him, rather was it a bone in his amorphous world. True, there existed a rigid routine, imposed on him from outside, and cutting the day which should have been elastic, into sections of food, play and sleep. Yet he felt the need of something immutable and his own, and ceremony had the sure reciprocal action of a slot-machine.

Marcus crept up behind his grandmother as she stood on the lawn. She looked as if she had forgotten all about him, so he hooted in a deep, frightening voice.

'Good heavens, Marcus, must you do that? Where on earth do you get to? I can never find you.' But she wasn't really interested. She was tapping her small rounded chin and looking at the grass. 'We ought to get the lawn re-laid before next summer,' she said to herself, and nodded with the same seriousness Marcus had shown towards his castle.

During lunch, Marcus learned that Neil Farncombe was coming to spend the afternoon. He was the son of a business friend of Marcus's father and he had come to visit once before, some two years ago, when Marcus was still addicted to teddy bears and flop-eared rabbits. There had been a great deal of trouble, everyone except Marcus remembered it.

'But they'll get on better now,' said his grandmother. 'Marcus isn't such a baby.'

Neil was ten. He had a small angular face, high cheek-bones and eyes of a particular burning blue. Without waiting until they were out of hearing of the grown-ups, he said, 'What's that in aid of?' and nodded at Marcus's clothes.

Marcus looked down at his green boiler-suit with the tool pockets on the bib. 'Huh?' he said, frowning.

'Oh forget it.' Neil strolled off, casual and self-possessed in his zipped leather jacket and grey shorts. Marcus made to go in the opposite direction, but was called back by his grandmother.

'Go with Neil,' she said.

Reluctantly, Marcus trailed after the elder boy.

'No doubt,' said Marcus's grandmother, 'we shall have to buy the child a zipped leather jacket now.'

Neil mooched through the shrubbery and stopped at the bottom of the steps. He stared up at the sky from under his hand, they both heard a distant mumbling.

'Now what's that?' grunted Neil, squinting fearfully against the sunlight.

'It's an aeroplane,' said Marcus, pleased at being able to offer the information.

Neil's high cheek-bones burned scarlet. He glared at Marcus from under his shading hand. 'Don't try to be funny with me,' he said. 'Just don't try.'

Marcus was both offended and bewildered. To relieve his feelings he kicked viciously at the path.

'Blenheim,' said Neil laconically. 'It might be one of ours.'

'If it isn't, shall we go into the shelter?' Marcus was thrilled at the possibility.

Neil turned on him with the air of an officer about to rend a very raw recruit. 'What did I say that plane was?'

'Benim.'

'And a Blenheim's a British kite, isn't it? Don't you even know that? When I said it might be one of ours I meant it might have come from our field.'

'Your field?'

Neil turned away impatiently. 'Our aerodrome at Haydown.'

Marcus lost his temper. 'It's not yours! It's not your aerodrome!'

'It's as much mine as anybody else's.' Neil was still staring up from under his hand. 'I live right by it and I'm there nearly every day and I know all the men on it and all the planes. That's a Blenheim all right.'

'It's not!' shouted Marcus, red-faced and ridiculous. 'It's not! It's not!'

The visitor put his hands in his pockets, rocked to and fro on his heels and spoke with absolute authority. 'It's a twin-engined Blenheim bomber with "Mercury" engines and five machine-guns

– one in the port wing, two in the turret and two in the blister under the nose. It can carry a thousand pounds of bombs, but I expect it's on a training trip now.'

Marcus looked sulky, yet he was impressed. Under his breath he muttered, 'It's not,' just once, without conviction.

As Neil watched the plane out of sight, he looked almost homesick. He glowered at Marcus. 'Don't you know anything about planes?'

'Course I do! I've got a plane of my own!'

'What – a toy?' Neil turned away.

Marcus danced earnestly beside him. 'It flies! It flies over the house!'

Neil said nothing. He was moodily climbing the steps. Marcus, in a passion to be first, wriggled past him and went on ahead. When he stretched over the final step he almost lost his balance. Neil put his foot squarely on the sacred stone.

'No!' shrieked Marcus.

'Eh?'

'No! No!'

Neil came on to the top of the steps. 'Are you crazy?'

'You shouldn't have trod on that step!'

Neil looked at it. 'Why not?'

'Something will happen to you!'

'Eh?'

Marcus backed away, wildly mysterious. 'The awfullest thing that could happen!'

'Guff,' declared Neil and deliberately went back and jumped about on the sacred step. 'How's that?'

They stood staring at each other in the sunshine, Marcus open-mouthed, horrified; Neil with eyebrows raised, hands in pockets, feet squarely on the forbidden stone.

'It'll get you – it'll be so angry!'

'What will? The bogey under the step? Pouf!' Neil gave it a final kick and strolled on. 'There's no such thing as bogeys. Of course,' he looked grave, 'there *are* gremlins. You have to watch out for them all right.'

'What's gemlins?'

'I say!' Neil stopped to look hard at Marcus. 'Your number's still pretty wet, isn't it? You don't know anything.'

'I do! I do! I know more than you! I know more than anyone!'

But Marcus was not absolutely convinced. He catapulted fiercely to and fro across the path to hide his doubts.

'You don't either,' declared Neil crushingly. 'You don't even know what a gremlin is.'

'What is it?'

'It's a - well, it makes things go wrong.'

'Is it alive?'

'Of course it's alive. How could it upset things and get people into trouble if it was dead? It's something to be scared of, I can tell you. Not like an old step!'

'Has it got red eyes?'

'Some of them have. Some've got green eyes and horns. There're lots of them at our airfield.'

Marcus looked smug. 'I've got one!'

Neil sneered openly. 'Where? Under the step?'

'Course not! In the summrouse.'

'That's a load of guff! You only get them on airfields - anywhere where there's planes. What d'you think *you'd* have a gremlin for?'

'I've got one. In the summrouse.'

'Guff.'

Marcus danced with fury. 'I'll show you! I'll show it you then!'

'All right, I'll take a look-see.'

'You be careful! It'll bite your head off —'

Neil frowned irritably. 'Oh get on with it ! Beetle.'

'Ah?'

'Go on, show me - if you can.'

Fuming, but uneasy, Marcus led the way to the summerhouse. That dark corner of the garden was already in shadow, and to Marcus the chill in the air was sufficient warning. He hung back, pointing quite unnecessarily.

'Pouf! What a ropey old place!' Neil strolled towards it.

Marcus valiantly ran after the elder boy and dragged his arm. 'You mustn't go in! It's inside.'

Neil looked down at him, his blue eyes were suddenly fierce. 'You're scared!'

'I'm not!'

'You are! Scared stiff of a dirty old hut! Well, I'm not!'

He shook off Marcus's hand and strode up to the summerhouse. At the doorway he stopped, one foot on the threshold, and muttered, 'There is something in here.'

Marcus's green boiler-suit swelled with pride. 'It's a gemlin!' he shouted. 'Jus' you come back —' He broke off, clapping one hand over his mouth in curiously feminine consternation.

Neil had disappeared inside. Next moment the boiler-suit wilted as there sounded a dreadful uproar from the summerhouse - a stamping and shouting and a hollow clanging noise. Marcus was petrified, but when a long grey shape leapt from the hut and vanished into the shadows, he screamed at the top of his voice.

Neil, appearing at the summerhouse door, with a rusty spade in his hand, gave him one contemptuous glance. 'A gremlin says you - just a dirty old rat. I'd have flattened it if it hadn't been so dark in there.'

Marcus licked his lips and looked at Neil with new humility. He wouldn't have cared to face a rat any more than a gremlin.

Neil strolled off, looking moody and discontented. Marcus trotted at his heels. They came to the toolshed and Neil passed the mud-pies without a word. Marcus hoped he hadn't noticed them.

'What's this?'

Neil swooped into the bushes and dragged out poor forgotten Boddy. Dangling by one leg in mid-air, the limp arms flapped, the golliwog's grin and the white boot-button eyes looked frankly imbecile.

Marcus felt his cheeks burn, his eyes pricked with tears of shame as Neil swung the doll to and fro on a level with his face.

'This yours?'

'No!'

Neil's lips twisted. Tauntingly he swung the golliwog closer so that it brushed against Marcus's nose. 'Whose is it then?'

Marcus thought desperately. 'A little gurl's.'

'Yours, more likely. Got a teddy bear, too?'

'It's not! It's not! It's not!' Scarlet-faced, Marcus backed away, stamping and shouting. 'Not! Not! Not!'

Smiling thinly, Neil let the doll drop, his foot met it squarely as it fell, and poor, grinning Boddy went sailing over the shrubbery and out of sight.

'Pancaked,' said Neil obscurely, and Marcus was too deep in shame to ask what he meant.

They came out on to the lawn again. Neil threw himself down and tore up handfuls of grass. He spoke more to himself than to

Marcus. 'Why shouldn't they let me go up to the airfield instead of coming here? I asked enough times!'

'There's an aeroplane coming!' Marcus stood over him, earnestly pointing in the wrong direction. Neil rolled on his back, shaded his eyes and located the plane at once.

'It's a Benim,' declared Marcus, also squinting up from under his hand, but seeing nothing.

'It is not. It's a Bristol Beaufighter back from a recco. You don't know one kite from another.'

Marcus opened his mouth and shut it again. Even he had to admit that as an aircraft spotter he had his shortcomings.

Neil hugged his knees and chewed grass. Marcus plumped down close by, hugged his knees and chewed a gritty mouthful of grass which he had mistakenly grubbed up by the roots. The plane mumbled off into silence and the enormous province of the sun. After a while, Marcus grew bored and began to tumble laboriously about on the grass.

Neil took no notice until, in the middle of a somersault, Marcus felt a hand seize the slack of his boiler-suit and pull him upright. He swayed and blinked, Neil's fierce blue eyes, the sky and the green garden were see-sawing all together.

'The windmill —' Neil was saying, 'where is it?'

Dizzy with tumbling, Marcus could only open his mouth and say 'Ah?' very stupidly.

Neil shook him. 'The windmill! I saw it from the bus – which way is it?'

Marcus took a chance and pointed to one corner of the tipping world. Unfortunately it was in the direction of the house and Neil let go his hold on the green boiler-suit. Marcus sat down with a bump and stayed there waiting for things to sober up. Neil stood over him, scowling.

'You're the biggest dope I was ever stuck with. It's no matter, I'll find things out for myself.'

He stalked off. Marcus scrambled up and followed, conscious that once again he had cut rather a poor figure.

Neil must have had a knack of finding his way, for he went at once to the highest point in the garden – the top of the rockery – climbed it, and stared round like a sailor scanning the seas. 'There it is – about a mile away. Just right.'

He jumped from the rockery, landing lightly on all fours and springing upright almost in the same movement.

Marcus beamed. 'Are you going to the windmill?'

'Yes, I am. If anyone asks where I am, say we're playing hide-and-seek and I'm hiding. See?'

Marcus shook his head, still beaming. 'I'm coming too.'

'You're not.'

'I am!' His voice bellowed in the silence and seemed to echo against the dazzling windows of the house. Neil gripped him by the shoulder.

'Shut up! You're not coming.'

Marcus shut his mouth, but he looked mulish, and as soon as Neil moved off along the lime-walk, he trotted after, his lower lip jutting ominously. Neil knew he was being followed, but said nothing till they came to the arched door set in the garden wall. He pulled back the bolt, then turned.

'Go on back now. I'm doing this on my jack. Go on!'

'No! Won't. I'm coming too.'

Neil let the open door swing shut again. He advanced on Marcus, his long fingers twitching. 'You're asking for it! Will you go back or do I have to make you?'

Marcus was quite frightened. There was something of the pitiless stoop of a hawk in those bladed cheek-bones, the blue, burning eyes. But he could be obstinate, and even though he quailed, he planted his feet wide apart in desperation. 'If you don't let me come, I'll shout till they come and then I'll tell where you're going. I'll tell! I'll tell!'

So great was his awe of Neil that his voice grew louder and louder and he had to stamp to bolster up his courage.

Neil looked murderous, his face reddened with fury, he gathered himself as if to swoop on the yelling Marcus. And then all he did was to clap one hand over the younger boy's open mouth.

'All right! Come on – I'll settle with you later. Only shut up!'

Marcus obeyed at once and they went out into the lane. Some two or three fields and a paddock separated them from the windmill. Neil hauled Marcus bodily over the first stile and they began to tramp through the long lush grass minted with buttercups. Marcus was soon dusted in yellow pollen up to his waist, and Neil's long brown legs with the socks draggling round his ankles, glinted with rich butter gold.

It was difficult to keep up with Neil because he didn't allow for anyone else having shorter legs or less wind. Marcus dared not complain, and anyway, he was husbanding his breath in order to ask two very important questions. He seized his chance when they were clambering over the gate into the second field.

'What are we going to the windmill for?'

'Wait and see,' was all the information he got.

The next field was full of dry, bristly grass that made little knocking noises against their legs. Marcus was so fascinated by it and by the faded blue flowers growing among it, that he forgot all about his question until Neil turned and curtly told him to get a move on.

Then he said breathlessly, and with just the right degree of deference and eagerness which even Neil could not resist, 'What you going to be when you grow up?'

Neil made a sound half-laugh, half-snort. 'That's a good one! What am I going to be when I grow up? I'll be a driver, of course.'

'An engine-driver?'

Neil hooted so loudly that there came a frightened scuttling in the undergrowth.

'Engine-driver! You must be the biggest swede in the world. Don't you even know what a driver is? It's the same as a peelo. Know what a peelo is?'

Marcus took the only course open to him. He stuck his hands in the patch pockets on the front of his boiler-suit and sulked. Neil spat out the piece of grass he was chewing and strode on.

'All right – if you don't know, I'll tell you. A driver's a pilot – he takes the plane up and he's got to bring it down in one piece. Doesn't matter if it's a monoplane or a Halifax with nine machine-guns and five and a half tons of eggs – and that means bombs, not hen-fruit – the driver's the boss and what he says goes. But I'm going to be a fighter-pilot and make smoke-rings round every Messerschmitt they put up. As for Heinkels – I'll pop them off like paper bags.'

Neil was walking so fast that Marcus had to run to keep near. Suddenly he stopped and swung round.

'D'you say your prayers at night?'

Marcus nodded breathlessly.

'Then you pray for the war to go on for years – till I'm old enough to fly. If two people pray it might do more good than one.' He added threateningly: 'Will you do it?'

Marcus promised earnestly and Neil plunged on again. A

blackberry trailer snaking out from the hedge caught him squarely across his bare leg and almost tripped him. He trampled it down but Marcus was petrified at sight of the blood streaming from the lacerations of the thorns. In the sunlight, against the pale grass, it looked bright and terrible.

Neil hardly glanced at it. 'Pah! Anyone that wanted to be a pilot wouldn't bother about that!'

As they were crossing the paddock, Marcus, who had been dedicated to the trade of milkman for years, called out importantly, 'I'm going to be a pilot too!'

But Neil took no notice. He was intent on the windmill just ahead. Marcus looked at it too. Sometimes he was brought here by his mother – she would sit and try to paint. She was never pleased with what she did, she said the windmill was like an old bloated moth, it was all wrong.

Something in the grass caught Marcus's eye. He stepped aside to look, and Neil, turning to hurry him on, saw him stooping over a tiny rabbit caught in a trap. It was dead and its long ears were pressed back by the fear which had finally killed it. The small forepaws were daintily composed side by side, but the dark bubble eyes still stared – with death behind as well as before them. One hind leg, caught and smashed, had sprinkled the white scut with colour bold and incompatible among the fair grass and the faded blue flowers.

Marcus's eyes filled with tears. Gently he stroked the soft, cold fur. 'Poor rabbit, poor, poor rabbit!'

Neil's shadow fell across the grass. 'Are you coming or are you going to stay there all day?'

Marcus looked up, horrified. 'But the rabbit! The poor, poor rabbit – it's hurt!'

Neil frowned impatiently. 'Don't be daft – it's dead.'

'Dead?'

Marcus's smooth brows drew together as he pondered. He had encountered that word before. Roughtly, he understood it to mean 'gone away'. When people were dead, they went away and you didn't see them any more.

'Can't you see it's dead?' Neil made as if to nudge the rabbit with his foot, but Marcus flung out his hands in protection.

'You're not to! You're not to hurt it!'

Neil's brown pointed face darkened, and as quickly cleared

again. Shrugging, he looked down at Marcus with curling lip and chilly, remote scorn.

'You're soft,' he said, as one might to a worm. 'You're pappy. You'll never be a pilot. Go back and play with your dolls.'

He turned and strode off. Marcus looked down at the rabbit. It couldn't be dead because he could still see it, it hadn't disappeared as the kitten had last year, and old Mr Philpotts. He tried to pull the trap away and felt sick.

Neil had climbed over the gate and was out of sight. Marcus scrambled up, telling himself he would see to the rabbit on his way back. It was resting quietly, perhaps it would go to sleep until he returned.

He walked away carefully, so as not to disturb it. One or two black flies came and settled on the torn leg and crawled round the dark convex abyss of the staring eyes.

Neil was standing looking up at the windmill as Marcus came trundling across the field. It was built of wood, all bleached and bare like the walls of the summerhouse. Where the nails had given way, slats hung down so that you could see right through into the mill, and if you walked round, you caught twinkles of light where the holes linked up with other holes on the far side. The great sails had only their bones left, even these were snapped and shredded like the flimsiest cane – they lay back against the mill building with the exhaustion of broken mechanical things. Time had stripped off every vestige of use, rotted the last grain, blacked into cobwebs the honest crust of flour; the marks of labour were all lost in dissolution and decay.

Neil glanced at Marcus but hardly seemed to see him. He had eyes only for the windmill, he stared at it, and his queer blue eyes blazed above his high Slav cheek-bones. Marcus couldn't see what there was to be so excited about, but he was excited all the same. He trotted behind Neil, chattering and undismayed when the other boy never said a word.

Neil ignored Marcus until he wanted to go inside the mill. Then he said, 'Wait here,' and his tone was such that Marcus never thought of disobeying. Neil vanished silently into the blackness of the mill.

He was a long time gone. Marcus hopped first on one leg then on the other to occupy himself. He found a grasshopper and lost it immediately. He did somersaults until the mill took to dancing sombrely in the background. Marcus preferred it still, so he sat on the grass and listened.

There was no sound of Neil moving about inside. Marcus shouted, but no one answered. He decided that Neil was doing this on purpose to see how quickly he would get frightened. Then he would jump out and say that Marcus could never be a pilot.

That thought kept the green boiler-suit very still for a while. He sat bolt upright, chewing a stalk of grass as Neil had done. The slow, leathery flapping of a great black bird was the only sound in the afternoon quiet. If he had not been so excited, he might have gone to sleep.

And then Neil came suddenly out of the mill. Marcus ran up to him, chattering and effusive after his enforced silence. Neil took no notice of what Marcus said. He was whistling softly and looking at the mill-sails. His leather jacket was grey with dust, and the scummy fabric of a cobweb clung to his sleeve. Across the back of one hand was a long, important scratch. Marcus observed it with envy.

Neil flung himself down on the grass. 'See that sail – the top one on this side? I'm going to get out through a hole in the boards and hang on it and make it swing round. When it's pointing down at the ground, I'll let go and make a four-point landing.'

Marcus didn't understand just what Neil meant to do, but it sounded reckless and exciting beyond his dreams of adventure. He was completely carried away by the prospect of danger.

'Me too!' He stooped over Neil. 'I'll make a point landing too!'

'You will not.' Neil stood up and calmly stripped off his jacket. 'You can stay here and mind this and watch what I do.'

'I'm going to do it too!'

Marcus was jumping up and down in a frenzy. Neil gripped and held him. 'You fool! You can't do what I do. It's a test, don't you understand – I have to test my nerve. I'm going to be a fighter-pilot, I've got to have nerve, I've got to be tough and take risks and keep cool. I might not be good enough. I've got to find out, I've got to keep testing myself!'

Marcus was too young to know what fanaticism was, or he might have seen in Neil's face the fatal unity, feral and precipitate, and no more amenable than flame. The clear, freckled brow, gathered and jutting over those oddly empty blue eyes, the firm, intolerant mouth, were dominated by an ardour so extreme, so pitiless that it chilled and almost repelled.

Marcus was sobered by it. He wriggled free of Neil's grasp and drew away, wary as an animal at another's oddity.

'All right.' Neil brushed aside Marcus and his change of heart like a bothersome gnat. He stood there rolling up the sleeves of his grey flannel shirt. Marcus watched, frowning. He felt unsure of himself. He did not properly understand what Neil meant to do, and the desire to emulate fought with his natural caution. It would be as well, perhaps, to see just what the feat might be before doing it himself. Besides, once Neil was busy with it, he wouldn't be so free to stop Marcus from doing as he wanted. So Marcus reasoned, scowling under the weight of his own cunning.

Neil nodded towards the windmill. 'It's not such a wonderful test at that. I guess anyone could do it.' All at once he looked quite miserable; driving his hands deep into his trousers pockets, he went off without another word.

Marcus waited until he had vanished inside the mill, then, carrying Neil's jacket, he found a point of vantage and settled himself with all the fuss of an audience in a theatre.

For a long while nothing happened. Marcus sat gravely attentive for a few moments, and then as there was nothing to attend to, began to swivel round and round on his seat – to the detriment of the boiler-suit. When that amusement palled, he wandered over to the hedge and pulled up armfuls of rank grass in a search for frogs. Soon his fingers were stained green. He smelt them curiously and in a spirit of strict empiricism, sucked his thumb. It tasted bitter and he began to feel irritable and thirsty and the corners of his mouth turned down in a sudden mood of discontent.

He would have gone on to the next stage of intoning wearily, over and over again, his need to go home, and from there proceeded to a restricted but persistent grizzle, had not a slight sound made him look towards the windmill.

In relation to the mill itself, the sails stood at the angle of an 'X'. Neil had emerged – miraculously as it seemed to Marcus, although in fact he had crept through a gap in the boarding which was hidden from below – and was now braced in the angle between the two right-hand sails. The lower sail looked fairly sound, but the upper one had been slashed by the winds until it was twisted and hung askew.

Marcus's mouth opened slowly. Weariness forgotten, he scrambled out of his ditch and ran back to the mill for a closer view of this performance. Neil had his back to Marcus, but he was manoeuvring to turn sideways, his left shoulder outwards, and his right to the mill. Chips of dry, rotten wood flaked from under his feet and dropped softly to the grass. He glanced down once and called, 'It's a piece of cake!' and Marcus's mouth watered. He hoped Neil would save him some because he wasn't so sure, now, that he wanted to go and do what Neil was doing, even for a piece of cake.

The sails did not move, they hadn't changed their position since the boys came; but then there was no wind, so it was silly to expect them to turn. Neil moved out from the angle of the sails as far as he could, until the lower one sloped too much for him to reach it. Then he took a firm grip on the under edge of the upper sail; swinging up his feet, he caught and held with his hands so that he was strung along it, monkey-wise. In this position, he began to work his way up to the tilted tip of the sail. He was about ninety feet from the ground, Marcus could not have been more impressed if he had been a thousand feet up. From being merely a subject of imitation, with contagious habits and rare knowledge, Neil had become a hero. Blinking upwards, Marcus surrendered his own considerable ego to unquestioning devotion. He did not suppose now that he could do what Neil did. He would have to wait years before he was so tall and strong, before he would be able to test his nerve like this.

Marcus looked distastefully at his plump arm. It hadn't got any bronze hairs on it like Neil's had, and he hadn't any hairs on his legs, either. He pulled up one leg of the boiler-suit and looked hopefully, but his knee was smooth as ivory, and the whole leg still had its generous baby curves. Frowning, Marcus blinked up again at the mill.

He forgot all about his unsatisfactory self at once; Neil had almost reached his objective. He was now over a hundred feet from the ground, at the highest point of the sail, still moving easily. Marcus almost forgot to breathe in his excitement.

The feat looked spectacular, yet it would have been straight-forward enough for an agile boy with no fear of heights, had it not been for something which meant nothing to Marcus, but wherein lay the real unobtrusive danger.

The sails were rotten. They hardly supported their own weight; time and the winds had wilted them like sad feathers. The top right-hand sail juddered under Neil's weight, now and then chips of grey wood came away in his hands. Neil knew all about it, he regarded it as the saving danger which made this test of his nerve worth the while. When he reached the tip of the sail, he rested for a moment.

Marcus felt his heart beating so hard against his chest that he had to fold his arms to keep it quiet. He thought that Neil, with his pilot's magic, meant to jump from where he was and thus make the mysterious 'four-point' landing.

What Neil had planned was that his weight on the end of the sail would cause it to swing downwards and he would be taken within jumping distance of the ground. But he had reckoned without the axle being jammed and out of true, he had not thought of the years of binding rust. The sails would never turn again, they were splayed and fixed at the mercy of every gale. Neil thought only that they must be made to move, and he thought that he could do it. He did not care for the alternative of going back the way he had come. Besides, that would be an admission of defeat.

Marcus blinked as Neil let his feet drop and hung by his hands. He swung a little at first, then steadied himself. It was a sight Marcus could recall ever afterwards – the gaunt mill with the daylight in its broken sails, and that remote, impersonal figure dangling in the blue air.

Neil began to try to shift the sail. He could not bear that any obstacle should impede and change the course of his test. He believed that his weight would alter the balance, would drag his sail down according to plan. He had not understood the greater art of adapting plans to the speed of changing circumstance.

Again and again he tried to break down the rigidity of the sail and set it swinging. He drew himself up by his hands and then let himself drop, in the hope that the sudden jerk would disengage the cogs so that at least one half turn might be accomplished. That was all he needed – one half turn.

But the sails were fixed and the muscles of his arms already ached unbearably from his climb. He thought he might not be able to hold on much longer, he had strength enough for only one more effort. In a sort of bitter frenzy, his sight blurred by tears of pain and impotence, he drew himself up until his waist was on a level with his hands. His teeth bit deeply into his lip, the sweat shone on his pale forehead. The sail was an enemy which he must subdue or be subdued by it. When he could draw himself no higher, he hung there poised for a second to gather his strength and reinforce his grip. Then, savagely, he threw himself down from his hands.

Marcus was puzzled because Neil had not jumped and made his four-point landing. So, when after his last jerk, Neil parted company with the sail and came hurtling down, Marcus thought he was at last carrying out his plan, and in his opinion, the shrill cracking sounds which accompanied the fall greatly improved it as a spectacle.

And in fact, Neil seemed intent on making the performance as exciting as possible. He did not come straight to the ground. Instead, he fell on the lower right hand sail, lay across it for a second or so as if to prove his mastery, and then, almost languidly, tipped over and continued his journey to the ground.

He landed on his back. The ground shook him once, flinging up his arms and legs like a doll's, then he lay still. Marcus ran over to him shouting, 'I saw the point landing! I saw it! I saw it!'

Delightedly he capered round Neil, fulfilling the desire and purpose of the celebrant who marks a victory and honours a hero.

Neil did not move. He was so still that Marcus checked his dance with sudden misgivings. The performance might not be finished, or worse – he might have offended against the etiquette of the four-point landing. He had to admit that it was a far more impressive adventure than any of his own, it might well have a certain form which Neil would presently demonstrate.

So he waited patiently. It was quite silent now, the big black bird had flapped away; the sunlight, like a bright empty gas under a glass bowl, had dissolved all motion, even the crepitant motion of the beetles.

Neil said nothing. He did not even look at Marcus. His head was tilted back so that from where Marcus stood, only the under part of his chin and his brown throat were visible. Legs and arms were flung out just as Marcus had seen Boddy's arms and legs spread wide when he was thrown on the floor.

It was odd. On tiptoe, stretching his neck as if to peer over a fence, Marcus moved closer to Neil. He looked down at his face. The elder boy's eyes were closed and his skin, which had been brown and warm, was a cold creamy colour. A grey shadow seemed to be creeping over his jaw, changing his face. His lips were pale and dry like paper, his wide nostrils pinched.

Marcus stooped down, hands on his knees, deferential.

'Neil.'

No movement, no sign that he had even heard.

'Neil!' Marcus stooped lower, frowning. 'Neil – what you doing?'

Only one of the grasses by Neil's ear moved under Marcus's breath. Disapprovingly, he sat back on his heels, noting fragments of dry wood still gripped between the pale fingers. It was obvious then what had happened. Neil had gone to sleep, forgetting about everything, even forgetting to put down the bits of wood he had brought back.

Neil's head rolled a little to one side, his eyelids moved, lifted unwillingly; he looked out from under them like someone in a blessedly dark room looking out at the blaring daylight.

'You mustn't go to sleep,' said Marcus reprovingly. 'It's not night.'

Neil's eyes opened wider. It seemed as if he had to force himself to see Marcus, although he was only such a little way away. Marcus obligingly bent closer and touched his hand.

The touch troubled the elder boy. His whole body shuddered. He drew his arms slowly in to his sides and tried to raise himself. His head lifted slightly from the ground, then fell back. He did not move again, only the grey shadow deepened across his mouth.

'Aren't you going to get up?'

Neil licked his lips, looking at Marcus almost furtively. 'No, I – think I'll stay here a bit.'

'I saw you do the point landing!'

Neil closed his eyes and began to mutter. 'I came a crumper. The sail was stuck. I couldn't get it to turn like I wanted – I wanted it to turn—'

He moved his head restlessly from side to side. Marcus couldn't think why he didn't get up.

'Let's go home now.'

'I don't want to go home.' Neil felt around with his hand, picked a stalk of grass and stuck it in the side of his mouth. His lips closed on it, pressed together so tightly that his chin wrinkled. He did not chew the grass, he made it a gesture of defiance, and once it was made, seemed unable to carry it to any conclusion. The stalk just stayed there, straight and still, in the corner of his mouth.

Marcus wandered about, moodily kicking the ground with his heels. He could not understand this turn of events, it made him irritable that there was neither point nor pleasure in it.

'I want to go home now!' He shouted from a little way off and stamped.

Neil looked at him with hatred. But he spat out the grass, put his arms flat against the ground and pressed on them. His head lifted, his lower lip drew in under his teeth and even the grey shadow was dredged from his face. It was as if he had no flesh, only bone.

A sound came from deep in his throat, and with it, his rigidity collapsed. He fell back, gasping. Suddenly his eyes were dark and fierce with terror, they shone like the rabbit's eyes, rounded and brittle as a bubble. His fingers unclenched and let fall the chips of dry wood from the mill sail.

Marcus was deeply puzzled. He picked up the wood and examined it politely. It wasn't at all unusual – only out of deference to Neil he stowed two pieces away in the pocket of his boiler-suit. After that, he sat down and waited patiently for orders.

But Neil gave no orders. He lay there staring at Marcus, and now the shadow had come back. He had a grey cloth face. He never looked away, and the terror in his eyes was so violent and so inexplicable that Marcus was frightened too. He glanced round about; there was only the bland empty sunshine and the stooping mill. There was nothing to be afraid of – that made Marcus more frightened than ever. He began to whimper.

'I want to go home.'

The other boy moved his lips and Marcus stopped grizzling to listen hopefully. A rustle, as of some slight insect slipping through the dry grasses, was the only sound Neil made.

At that Marcus lost patience.

'I want to go home!' He seized Neil's arm to try to pull him up.

Neil seemed to flatten himself to the ground, his lips drew back, baring his teeth in another extreme of fear, both savage and agonized.

Marcus stepped back. Quite obviously Neil didn't want to get up. He had no intention of going home, he meant to stay here and sleep. Marcus's lower lip jutted. Never had home and tea seemed so important. Neil was trying to stop him, just because he wanted to go to sleep in the daytime.

He glared at the still figure on the ground – then caught sight of the wilting sails of the mill and remembered the four-point landing, how Neil had even paused in his descent to balance casually on the lower sail. Humility and deference returned immediately.

Pondering, he decided that this wish to sleep at a time so inappropriate, might be the habit of heroes. Perhaps it was a ritual to lie down on the ground and shut your eyes after an adventure. Marcus wondered if he ought to do the same. He thought not. He was too hungry and besides, it hadn't been his adventure. Instead, he would prove to Neil that he wasn't so soft and go home by himself, leaving Neil to follow when he was ready.

'I'm going home now,' he said and beamed with self-sufficiency. He would have turned and marched off, had not Neil reached out to hold him by the ankle. Marcus skipped back, frowning. An odd qualm chilled him as he looked into Neil's face.

There was something wrong with his eyes. They had been blue before, Marcus could remember just how blue and fierce they had been. Now they were dark and they shone into the full glare of the sun without blinking or once looking away from Marcus. Yet he had a cold feeling that the darkness in the eyes was also outside them, so that Neil couldn't see properly. He kept moving his lips, they moved all the time as if he were speaking, but didn't say anything. He didn't even whisper.

Marcus backed away. Neil's hand, flung out on the ground towards him, opened and shut like a crab. It puzzled Marcus that the look on Neil's face was of fear, and the dark, unblinking eyes were never turned away from him as if Neil dreaded being left alone.

But that could not be, Neil was never frightened, and there was nothing to be frightened of here. Besides – Marcus turned stoutly on his heel – Neil hadn't asked him to stay. He could have said if that was what he wanted.

At the gate into the paddock he stopped to look back. Neil had not moved. His body was spilled negligently on the grass, one arm still stretched towards Marcus, his face blurred by distance but turned the way Marcus had gone. The mill drooped behind him, the shadow would soon lie across him and he would be out of the sun.

There was something else on the grass near the mill. It was Neil's leather jacket. Marcus wrinkled his nose. He still thought it a funny time and place to go to sleep. Perhaps Neil would like his jacket as a pillow. He hesitated, on the verge of going back. But then he had a vision of Neil's scorn, his 'You're soft! You'll never be a pilot!' Neil would be contemptuous, and rightly so, if he went back for such a womanish gesture. Fighter pilots probably never used pillows but just stretched out on the hard ground. Marcus was impressed by this Spartan routine, he knew he would find it very difficult to keep as still as Neil had for such a long time.

He waved to Neil and scrambled under the gate. Very soon he came to the place where the rabbit lay. He stalked past, head averted. Neil had said it was soft to worry about the rabbit, Neil had shown how to be tough and daring. He was going to be like Neil and some day test his nerve by doing a four-point landing.

It was the first time he had been out for a walk by himself, he felt grown-up and independent. He walked through the field of knocking grasses and his legs struck them stoutly aside.

In the last field he stopped, lifting his pink damp face to the sky. A far-off bumbling, filling the air, filling every nook and cranny, every mouse-hole, every fold in every shrivelled leaf – and there were three shapes, tiny against the blue – Oriental, precise.

'Benims,' said Marcus, and stood looking from under his hand, paying them due reverence until they were out of sight.

MALACHI WHITAKER

The Mandoline

THE morning was still, bright yet ethereal, and an elderly sun had warmed the dead bracken on the hillside so that already it glowed golden brown. For a few days there had been fog and a blanketing silence and drops of moisture hanging stagnant from the leafless twigs, so that now in the sunlight, although it was only November, spring seemed to be poised, motionless but sure, over the far hills.

Two figures were approaching the long, low, stone farmhouse which stood in the middle of the common, one of them wearing nankeen trousers banded against the mud, an earth-coloured jerkin and a newish dark blue cap. He had a broken nose and friendly brown eyes and gesticulated with hands and arms as he walked.

His companion was a very pale, thin youth with an almost expressionless face, his eyes partially enlarged by thick-lensed glasses. His features were small and delicate, his teeth regular but yellowish. He wore the grey-green uniform of a German prisoner, a loose-brimmed cap, the crown of which fitted tightly, and large, heavy boots which seemed to drag along behind him.

The first man, who was a kind of foreman-guard, opened the iron gate of the farmyard, and walking up to the door, knocked in a light, hesitant way. The prisoner stood behind him, looking like some tall, stupid bird. He had not spoken except to say yes or no.

In the low, dark farmhouse kitchen, which opened straight on to the yard, an elderly man and his wife were working, the woman washing cans and the man carefully mending a cracked pipe stem with thin string. They looked an old couple, bent and grey-haired, but neither of them had yet reached sixty years of age. As they heard the low knocking, they turned and went to the door together, being full of curiosity about the two men, one of whom they knew well, the other not at all.

A new road, which ran a lane's-length from the farm, was being built by German prisoners, still retained though the war was long over, and from eight in the morning until dusk there was the sound of continuous noisy activity about the moorland farm, as the grey-green figures broke up the stones which were brought in by lorries from the neighbouring stone quarries. The old people, who were called William and Mary Illingworth, had often seen the prisoners, but had not yet spoken to one of them.

The woman dried her hands and opened the door, looking out past the men into the still autumn morning. The foreman, Sam Proudle, smiled and moved his arms about uncertainly.

'Good morning, Mrs Illingworth. I've come to ask you a favour,' he said, 'but I don't know if you'll grant it.'

'What is it?' asked the woman quickly. In some way, she was afraid. She could not think what a prisoner could require of her, and searched her mind timorously.

'Well, it's a funny request,' went on the foreman slowly, 'I don't know whether I ought to ask you. But I know you've got a mandoline, and this gentleman' – he waved a couple of fingers at the prisoner – 'wants to know if he can borrow it for one of his kamerads for the camp concert. For Sunday, he wants it, for next Sunday, and a few days to practise in.'

The farmer stood with his hands on the table, looking mildly at the pair.

'Can you play it?' the woman asked the prisoner.

He stood up more straightly, opened his mouth once or twice, and said, 'No, no.'

The foreman explained hurriedly, 'This gentleman plays the piano. It's one of his kamerads that plays the mandoline. VERY GOOD,' he suddenly shouted at the prisoner. He had evidently grown so used to shouting simple English words at the prisoners that for the moment he had forgotten something. In a much lower tone he continued, 'This is our interpreter. I'll leave him with you to explain.' And he went away.

The couple stared dumbly at the tall youth, who looked back at them, his eyes very wide behind his army spectacles.

'Come in,' the woman said suddenly; and to her husband she said: 'He wants to borrow our Godfrey's mandoline.'

The boy stepped over the threshold and stood motionless upon a stone flag of the floor. The old man had retreated behind the kitchen table and remained there without speaking, only looking at the young German with calm eyes. The thin string slowly unwound itself from the pipe in his hand. The woman began bustling about and talking in a high-pitched voice, and outside, in the walled garden which was a continuation of the yard, the sun searched the wet, brown, withered bushes, the dying Michaelmas daisies, and the two heaps of garden refuse beneath the aged pear tree.

'I have been in hospital,' said the boy suddenly, 'for a long time.'

'Sit down,' said the woman, motioning towards a wooden chair.

He sat abruptly, looking at his muddy boots, the marks from which remained where he had stood. His hands lay lax on his knees. He had not removed his cap. He did not notice the flickering fire, the red grandfather clock in one corner of the room, the two brass candlesticks on the high, narrow mantel-shelf.

'What do you do? In Germany?' the farmer asked in a very loud, careful voice.

'I am a schoolmaster.'

'My son is – was – going to be a teacher.'

'The one who played the mandoline,' the woman broke in. 'Our Godfrey. He played the mandoline.'

The boy looked round, but could not see the mandoline. It was not in the kitchen. He looked towards the farmer.

'Your son?' he asked, searching for words with some difficulty, apologizing, 'I only know English these few months, since I kom heer. Your son, does he not wish to lend the mandoline to my kamerad?'

'My son was killed,' said the farmer harshly. 'In Germany.'

'Oh!' said the prisoner. A pale flush ran slowly over his paler face, and drained away. There was a long silence.

The woman broke it. 'Come into the parlour,' she said. 'We have a piano. Come and play it.'

'The parlour?' asked the boy. He did not understand.

'Come and play the piano,' said the woman, bright-eyed with nervous haste. 'Come with me.'

The boy followed her out of the kitchen, over the flagged hall to a small sitting-room. The sunlight showed crude colour-patches in a faded carpet. Across one corner of the room stood a shiny, walnut-veneered piano, with pleats of green silk showing under an ornamental lattice at the front. The piano was open, and upon the stand lay a cheap copy of some music on which was printed Gem No.79, Strauss Waltz Medley.

The woman pointed to it. 'Play that,' she said.

The boy peered at the simple music, and sitting down on the piano stool, put his muddy boots on the pedals. His cap was still upon his head.

'It is a long time since I played the piano,' he said.

'Go on. Go on. Play it,' said the farmer who had come through from the kitchen and was now sitting stiffly in a corner, still holding in his hand the half-mended pipe with its dangling string.

There were many pages of music, and the boy played steadily through them. Here and there he struck a false note, and said 'Oh!' in quick shame. The woman had gone back into the kitchen, where she drew down from a high shelf in the cupboard an old coffee-grinding machine. There were a few beans in the brass cup. She ground them, and making one cup of coffee with milk from a jug on the table, took it into the parlour. The boy was still playing.

She put down the coffee on a small table beside him.

'Here,' she said gently, 'drink this.'

At her words, the boy stopped playing in the middle of a bar, and turning, thanked her. The old man had left his chair and could be heard moving in the bedroom above the parlour.

'You will take care of Godfrey's mandoline?' asked the woman anxiously. 'Yes, yes,' answered the boy, drinking his coffee.

'Godfrey played the mandoline. He played the piano, too. We bought the piano for him.' She smiled slightly at her own work-worn hands. 'But now he is dead. The war.' She looked full at the boy.

Again the pale flush broke over his thin face.

After a little while, 'I have had a letter from home,' he said. 'The first in a year. All is well.'

'All is well,' she repeated after him.

'All is well,' he said. And there was again silence until the old man came slowly downstairs, carrying the mandoline in a shiny black case.

He handed the case to the boy, who stood abruptly. Some of the mud on his boots had dried, and fell off in small clumps, silently, as he moved his feet.

'What do they call you?' asked the farmer in the same loud, careful voice he had used before. 'What is your name?'

'My name is Adolf,' said the boy, 'Adolf Klein.'

And for the third time his face flushed.

'Klein. That, in German, means little, I think.' He smiled, as if it were a joke being called little, who was so tall. But Klein was only a foreign word to the farmer and his wife, and meant nothing.

'Now I shall have to go. They might miss me. Thank you very much for the coffee, and for the piano, and for the mandoline.'

They moved awkwardly to let him pass through to the kitchen and out of the door.

'Come again and play the piano,' said the woman. She touched his sleeve gently, wonderingly, as he crossed the flagged passage again. And as he walked through the house, the boy looked around at everything, at the grandfather clock ticking away the years, at the brass candlesticks polished to a rounded fineness. He seemed to be looking for a picture of Godfrey. But there was no picture, no sign of his death anywhere. Godfrey seemed to be alive in the kitchen, in the parlour, at the piano playing the Strauss Waltz Medley, even carrying the mandoline.

'Yes, come again,' said the old man in his strange, loud voice.

He walked across the yard to the iron gate and opened it, to let the prisoner through, and then looked across the common to the bracken-brown hill, lying drenched in yellow light. His wife joined him, and they stood together in the silence until the tall boy carrying the mandoline was out of sight.

INEZ HOLDEN

According to the Directive

THE day the Information Officer brought a journalist to the camp a lorry was waiting in the yard to take some of the Displaced Persons away.

Those who were leaving stood shoulder to shoulder in the back of the lorry clasping the packets of chocolates and cigarettes which they had been given for the journey. Some of them also carried bunches of flowers which they held, like Victorian posies, closely to their chests.

Some wooden steps had been placed against the back of the lorry. The last man to walk wearily upwards wore a long grey overcoat, a peaked cap and dark blue civilian trousers, he carried a cheap cardboard suitcase and he smiled as the others moved to make room for him beside them.

A man in uniform stood by with a list; when the last Displaced Person had answered, and had his name checked against the list, the steps were taken away. A little group waited in the yard to wave goodbye to their friends as they drove out of the camp.

Lisa Wilson asked where the people were going. 'Are they all on the way home?' she said.

'On the way home,' Edward Syler repeated. 'No, I don't think so. The lorry's on the way to Hanover, maybe there's a convoy going from there and perhaps a few will be repatriated, but I reckon the majority are just planning to link up with friends in other camps. No doubt they've all got permission to visit relatives in some distant DP Assembly Centre, but of course you can't believe everything they say.'

'No, I suppose not.'

Edward Syler, the Information Officer, wore pince-nez but they were strong pince-nez, bridged together with a tough piece of metal. His shirt had been washed so often and so earnestly that it had lost its original khaki and become almost cream coloured, he wore a faded field-jacket and he had a shouting manner as if he was forever lecturing to a group of deaf foreigners.

'Well now, Miss Wilson, you've come here to write a feature on DP's,' he said. 'So you just go ahead and ask me any questions you like.'

'What about the last man in the lorry,' Lisa said. 'Wasn't that a Wehrmacht coat he was wearing?'

'Yes, I guess so. As I told you I used to be in this Camp myself as a Welfare Officer. That Italian guy was already here when I arrived, I remember he had some story about being forced into the German Army – anyhow, he went on wearing his Wehrmacht overcoat on cold days because he didn't have any other coat – of course he must have been an ex-enemy alien when he first came into the camp and according to the directive he wouldn't have been entitled to DP status – we used to get all sorts here you know, Poles, Balts, Turks and one or two types claiming British or American citizenship. Why we even had Menonites.'

'Menonites, what are they?'

'Oh, they're an agricultural community, they mostly came from Russia, they'd been driven right across two continents and finally landed up here. They don't believe in war.'

'How do you mean they don't believe in war? They must have noticed that something of the sort was going on around them.'

'Oh, sure, they noticed that there was some shooting, many of them were killed, but they don't take an active part in war themselves. Their religion forbids it.'

As Syler and Lisa walked slowly across the courtyard Syler said, 'I thought we'd go across to the Sick Bay, you might get a story there.' He rattled through some statistics and then he said, 'Well, I reckon you're familiar with the overall DP situation in Germany right now.'

Lisa wondered where Syler came from. 'Are you an American?' she asked him.

'An American? Hell no,' he said. 'I was born in Tokyo and educated in Heidelberg, but both my parents were of British nationality though I've spent a number of years in the United States. My second wife came from Florida. I've never regretted marrying an American.'

'Is your wife in Europe now?'

'I dunno,' Syler said. 'We were divorced some while back. Well, here's the Camp Sick Bay, but of course there are only convalescents here. We have a directive to send all serious cases straight to the hospital in the town.'

There were sixteen beds in the Sick Bay but only four of them were occupied. One man was sitting on the edge of his bed, he wore a check shirt and grey flannel trousers. His black hair was parted in the middle, his eyes were dark with a melancholy expression, but he smiled all the time as if to show that he knew, more than anyone else, what was going on around him.

'Another Italian?' Lisa asked.

'No, a Frenchman,' Syler said.

At the far end of the room a man with a blackened face and close-cropped hair leant back against the coarse cotton of his pillow reading in a low tone from a book which he held in both hands as if afraid that someone might try to take it from him. He did not look up as Edward and Lisa came in but continued to read, his lips moving rapidly and his eyes, which were red-rimmed and distressingly bloodshot, staying open all the time.

On the other side of the room a fair-haired boy, propped up by two pillows, lay back with both his eyes closed.

Near the entrance, and opposite the check-shirted Frenchman, an old man, with frail transparent hands and a long thin face, was sitting up in bed. Edward Syler walked over to him.

'Well, Monsieur Dumaine,' Syler said. 'How are you getting on?'

Dumaine inclined his head graciously and answered in French. He said that he was not getting the right diet. 'Some of the food I eat now is not at all good for me in my enfeebled state.'

The check-shirted convalescent on the bed opposite gave a contemptuous smile.

The old man went into elaborate explanations of the kind of diet which, he believed, would suit him best. 'Diet,' he said, 'is a very subtle and important thing. We live by what we eat, and, in fact, it affects all our thoughts. But I shall recover quickly when I have all I need. On Monday I take the train to Paris.'

'But it is not certain that you will be able to go to France,' Syler told him.

'Why not?' Dumaine asked sharply.

Syler looked round the room as if seeking some help from the convalescents, but the man with the blackened face still muttered on at the same speed and in the same tone, the fair-haired boy kept his eyes closed and the man in the check shirt did not give up his sneering smile.

'Well, Monsieur Dumaine,' Syler said. 'You had better see the French liaison officer, he will explain all the circumstances.'

'Circumstances,' Dumaine said. 'I have no need to be told anything about them. I know my own circumstances only too well – who better?' But after these words the old man's thoughts seemed to wander away from the camp and the convalescents' room. He began to talk about his farm in France. 'We had plenty of cheese there,' he said. 'Cheese and butter,' and with one thin hand he made a swirling movement round and round as if he was churning butter in a bowl. 'And when I am there again I shall make more cheese and butter and look after animals and so become a farmer as before.'

The check-shirted convalescent on the bed opposite laughed softly.

The fair-haired boy had opened his eyes and he was leaning on his elbow staring. Syler walked over to him. 'Well, Harry,' he said. 'How's the rheumatism?'

'It's better, thank you,' the boy answered. 'But I sleep a lot.'

'Ah, that's what you want,' Syler said in his shouting manner. 'Plenty of rest and you'll soon be all right. Now here is Miss Wilson, a journalist from London, to see you.'

'I'm from London, too,' said the boy. 'I was born there in Castle Street.' He was silent for a few moments nervously touching the covers of a book lying on the bed.

'What have you been reading there?' Syler asked.

'World History,' the boy told him. 'But in the Red Cross Club last month I was reading an illustrated paper. There were some pictures of cadets training. It shows that they do accept boys of my age as soldiers. I should like to join the British Army now.'

'He's been reading about Sandhurst,' Syler explained. 'It's true, isn't it, Harry, that you walked here all the way from Danzig?'

'From Danzig. Yes.'

'Without food or water?'

'No,' the boy said. 'I had some water to drink on the way.'

'How many days did it take?'

'It took ten days,' Harry answered.

'A long journey.'

'Yes, it was a long journey.'

The camp doctor came in. The check-shirted man stood up. Dumaine, looking forward to further conversations about his diet, waved his hand in greeting, but the man with the blackened face went on reading aloud.

'Come on,' Syler said. 'Let's get out of here.'

As they walked across the courtyard Syler said, 'I keep asking them questions. Maybe you can pick up a story from some of their talk.'

'Yes,' Lisa said. 'Maybe I can. Will the boy Harry be able to go back to England soon?'

'No, I don't think so. You see,' Syler said, 'his father was killed in the Wehrmacht, his mother died during an air raid on Hamburg, the boy says he was born in Castle Street, London, but there's no trace of him in that district at all. The British haven't accepted him for citizenship, he has no relatives, no friends, no proof of how his early life was spent, so he must wait in the camp till all these questions have been cleared up.'

'How old is he?'

'It is believed that he has just passed his fourteenth birthday.'

'Oh, I see. Too young to decide his own future.'

'It's not so much a question of age as of nationality. You see, he's the son of a German father, and, as far as we know, of a German mother, he speaks perfect English and he wants to be British, but that doesn't make him British. If there was no definite ruling on this sort of thing we'd be snowed under with Germans claiming to be British. You'd be surprised how many Germans want to be British, nowadays.'

'I daresay. What about Dumaine? He seems to think he'll be going back to France on Monday.'

'Yes, he thinks so, but he won't be going. You see, according to an USFET* directive, all Western Nationals must return to their homes before the fifteenth of this month. That's next Monday. Their alternative is to join the German economy with its certainty of lower rations and likelihood of unemployment.'

'It sounds harsh.'

'Yeah, but it isn't. It only applies to a few hudred DPs, French, Dutch, Belgians, and so on. They can't have any reason for staying here unless they've been collaborators.'

* United States Forces European Theatre.

'Then why can't Dumaine go back?'

'Because he's a collaborator. In any case there's some uncertainty about his nationality, it's being investigated right now. He speaks French and German equally well. Mostly he speaks a mixture of both. He may be German. Of course it's true what he says about his farm in France. But I don't suppose he'll ever see it again.'

'But surely a feeble old man of eighty years old wouldn't be likely to start a Fascist revival wherever he went?'

'No, but you see Dumaine's war work rules him right out. He was employed by the Todt Organization. He's quite frank about it himself, he says, "I needed a job so I offered my services to the Germans as an interpreter." Well, the Todt Organization was a Nazi set-up so Dumaine couldn't be accepted in France now.'

'No, I see that. What will happen to him?'

'If it's proved that he's a German he will be moved to the German refugee hospital about a quarter of a mile from here. Wherever Dumaine goes he'll be the hell of a nuisance. I remember when he came into the camp. He refused, at first, to go through the usual de-lousing process and he wanted a room of his own and all that sort of thing.'

The winter was over and the sun was shining through the black boughs of three slender trees which had survived the bombardment, grass was already struggling up through the uneven ground giving the edge of the courtyard a green and hopeful look.

'Well, what do you think of the DP Camp?' Syler said. 'Can you get a story out of it?'

'I don't know yet,' Lisa answered. 'I was still thinking about the convalescents' room. What about the man in the end bed?'

'Oh, you mean the Bible reader? No one knows who he is. He arrived in the camp with a completely burnt and blackened face and red-rimmed eyes. He still looks the same way, but he was much worse then. He had a brown paper parcel with him and he could only say, "I was in the centre of an explosion." He said it over and over again, in perfect Polish without any accent. The brown paper parcel contained some clean underclothes and a Bible in German – nothing else. So that guy just lies there all day reading the holy scriptures in German, but we think he may be Polish.'

'Will he be sent back to Poland then?'

'Well, according to the directive nationals can return to the country of their origin but we don't know anything of this man's origin – neither does he. A Pole must prove he's a Pole before he can go to Poland. We haven't been able to find anyone who knows the Bible reader and it's doubtful if they could recognize him the way he is now and, of course we can't expect any help from him, his memory's gone. He is, in fact, now mad.'

'He's a bit beyond the reach of directives then?'

Syler seemed to feel affronted as if he was a man of honour whose sister had just been insulted in public. 'Nothing's beyond the reach of directives,' he said. 'The directives are O.K. They've all been planned on a high level.'

As they made their way towards the Assembly Room they passed a long wooden corridor which connected the sick bay with the main building. The corridor had been divided into a series of small offices and in the centre there was a larger room with wide windows.

'See that room?' Syler said. 'I was responsible for that when I was here. I had it made into a little library.'

There were only two people in the wide windowed room, a young man wearing a Norfolk jacket, and the boots and breeches of the continental refugee, and a girl with long straight hair who held a book in her hand but did not appear to be reading.

'Of course, there's nobody much there now,' Syler said. 'The rest are working outside, or in the administration of the camp, but that little library has been a big success. The DP Committee said it was a grand idea. I fixed for the bookshelves to be six foot along the back and eight foot four along the side walls. We painted them white.'

'Who's the girl in there?' Lisa asked.

'The girl? – Oh, she's Polish, she used to belong to a large family. She told me how they all used to go to a country house each summer – all the aunts, uncles, nephews, nieces, cousins and grandparents – they were thirty-seven in all. What d'you know about that? Thirty-seven in one family. But now none are left – all killed or lost, deported by the Russians, killed in air raids or in the Warsaw Rising. 'Course the majority were murdered by the S.S. The girl and her sister were liberated from Auschwitz by the Allies but the sister committed suicide a few weeks later. This girl won't go back to Warsaw, she says she'd be willing to go to the United States but there's no one to sponsor her. I guess she'll have to wait for mass emigration.'

'What about the man – the other DP in there?'

'Oh, he's not a DP, he's an Infiltree. He was in this camp as a DP but he was repatriated to Poland, then he came back here. Maybe he's holding out for Palestine.' Edward Syler peered into the library room. 'Some of the paint's got scratched,' he said sadly. ''Course we were very short of paint in this camp; and that's how it is that some of the Germans' slogans are still up in the passages. This place used to be one of Ley's Labour Ministries you know.'

When Syler took Lisa into the Assembly Room she saw that there was a frieze round the wall of square-shouldered German workers painted in pastel colours, some with hammers or spanners, some with pick-axes and others with spades.

Lisa stared at the large-limbed lifeless figures. 'A bit depressing, aren't they?'

'Sure they're depressing, but we'd need the hell of a lot of paint to paint them out.'

At the end of the room there was a notice board. 'Reminds me of school,' Lisa said.

'Oh, the notice board. There's all kinds of notices up there, the concerts the DPs organize for themselves, the elections for the DP Commandant, the classes in the DP school, and now this census they're planning to take on how many of those who come from Russian occupied territory are willing to go back there.'

Lisa looked at the notice and saw that someone had scribbled on it in pencil. 'No. Don't want to go back because they take away your food card, and also they hang you.'

Syler stared closely at the notice board through his pince-nez. 'They're very confused right now,' he said. 'We may as well leave this camp if we want to get to the other camp in good time. It's mainly a Transit Camp.'

As they walked towards Syler's car Lisa said, 'What about that dark man in the convalescents' room. I mean the Frenchman – is he going back to France on Monday?'

'Oh, yeah. The guy in the check shirt. Sure he's going, but he doesn't want to. He says he served five years in the French navy and he's been in the French police force too, but the authorities in France sent for him – that was during the occupation, of course – there was some doubt about his activities and they informed him that he wasn't a Frenchman – it seems his mother was Italian.

When he told me this story he said, "I can stand a good deal, but when they told me I wasn't a Frenchman that was another matter – I didn't hesitate an instant, I thought if they say I'm an Italian all right I'll be an Italian, and I came voluntarily into Germany." Of course none of this was official – off the record you know – don't quote me. As a matter of fact I wasn't very clear about what had happened to him and nothing he told me made much sense.'

'It looks as if he was as much a collaborator as Dumaine.'

'Oh, no, he comes into the category of "forced worker". There's no evidence that he collaborated with the Germans, he's not a political type at all. He belongs to the criminal class really. You can't believe much he says, he's an experienced liar and very bitter because his nationality was called into question.'

As they entered the yard two men were coming back into the camp from work in the fields, they both wore military mackintosh capes which did not fit them very well and gave them a comic air.

'See those two men?' Syler said.

'Yes.'

'Menonites. Don't believe in war. See?'

When they had been driving for a little while and the camp was out of sight Syler stopped the car and said that he had two bottles of cognac with him. 'Wouldn't go on a trip without liquor,' he said. 'I've brought a glass for you.' He opened the bottle and poured some out for Lisa, but he himself drank out of the bottle, throwing his head back as if he was a GI drinking Coca Cola.

'The mortality rate amongst the Anglo-American personnel in Berlin is very high just now,' he said.

'What do they die of?'

'Oh, "mortality rate" – that's just a figure of speech. I mean the guys that get sent home with DTs.'

After Syler had drunk some more he began to talk, in a soft voice, about a woman he was planning to meet in Berlin. 'You ought to meet my girl friend,' he said. 'You'd like her, you know, she's sympathetic, that's what she is, sympathetic. To tell you the truth, I aim to marry her.'

'Another American?' Lisa asked.

'No, she's German. Most of her relatives are interned or something, so she's all alone now. She hasn't got anyone but me.' Syler sighed deeply. 'Still, she'll be all right when we're married.'

'Have you got permission already?' Lisa asked.

BERYL BAINBRIDGE

Bread and Butter Smith

WHENEVER the Christmas season approaches I always think of the good times we had, my wife and I, at the Adelphi Hotel just after the war. When I say 'times' I wouldn't like to give the impression that we were regular visitors to the hostelry at the foot of Mount Pleasant – that would be misleading. As a matter of fact we only stayed there twice. Before and in between those occasions we put up at the Exchange Hotel in Stanley Street, next door to the station.

Though born and brought up in Liverpool, I had crossed the water and gone to live on the Wirral at the earliest opportunity – you did if you came from Anfield – but I was in the habit of popping over on the ferry each Christmas to carve the turkey, on Boxing Day, for my sister Constance. She was, apart from my wife, my only surviving relative. Leaving aside the matter of Mr Brownlow, Constance's house in Belmont Road wasn't a suitable place to stay – to be accurate, it was one up and one down with the WC in the back-yard – and as the wife and I found it more convenient to occupy separate bedrooms I always booked into an hotel. I could afford it. I was in scrap metal, which was a good line of business to be in if you didn't mind being called a racketeer, which I didn't. The wife minded, but as I often tell her, where would she be today if I hadn't been. She'd soon buck up her ideas if she found herself languishing in the public ward of a National Health hospital.

If it hadn't been for Smith, we'd have stuck with the Exchange and not gone on switching hotels the way we did. Not that it achieved anything; he always ferreted us out. I fully believe that if we had changed venues altogether and given Blackpool or Hastings a whirl he'd have turned up in the grill room on the night before

Christmas Eve, wearing that same crumpled blue suit, as though drawn by a magnet. I don't want to malign the poor devil, and don't think I'm being wise after the event, but I always found him a bit of a strain, not to mention an aggravation, right from the moment we met him, which was that first year we stayed at the Exchange.

We'd had our dinner, thank God, main course, pudding and so forth, and the waiter had just brought us a bowl of fruit. No bananas or tangerines, of course – too soon after the end of hostilities – but there was half a peach and a few damsons and some apples nicely polished.

'Shall I have the peach?' my wife said.

'Have what you like,' I told her. I've never been enamoured of fruit.

It was then that this fellow at the next table, who seemed to have nothing in front of him but a plate of bread and butter, leaned forward and said to me: 'The waiter is doing what King Alcinous may have done to the storm-beaten Greeks.'

That's exactly what he said, give or take a few words. You meet a lot of loopy individuals among the educated classes, and at the time I mistook him for one of those. Loopy, that is.

I ignored him, but the wife said: 'It's a thought, isn't it?' She was nervy that far back. Once she'd been foolish enough to respond, we couldn't get shot of him. I'm an abrupt sort of person. I don't do things I don't want to do – never have – whereas the wife, long before her present unfortunate state manifested itself, is the sort of person who apologizes when some uncouth lout sends her reeling into the gutter. Don't get me wrong, Smith was never a scrounger. He paid his whack at the bar, and if he ever ate with us it was hardly an imposition because he never seemed to order anything but bread and butter. Even on Christmas Day all he had was a few cuts of the breast and his regular four slices. He wasn't thin either. He had more of a belly on him than me, and he looked well into his fifties, which I put down to his war experiences. He was in the desert, or so he told the wife, and once saw Rommel through field glasses.

All along, I made no bones about my feelings for Smith. That first night, when he intruded over the fruit, I turned my face away. Later on, whenever he began pestering us about the Maginot line, or the Wife of Andros, or his daft theory that the unknown soldier was very probably a woman who had been scurrying along the hedgerows looking for hens' eggs when a shell had blown her to pieces at Ypres, I just got to my feet and walked away. My wife brought it on herself. She shouldn't have sat like patience on a monument, listening to the fool, her left eyelid twitching the way it does when she's out of her depth. His conversation was right over her head.

Not that he seemed to notice; he couldn't get enough of us. When we said we wouldn't be available on Boxing Day, he even hinted that we might take him along to Belmont Road. I was almost tempted to take him up on it. Mr Brownlow was argumentative and had a weak bladder. Constance had picked him up outside the Co-op in 1931. It would have served Smith right to have had to sit for six hours in Constance's front parlour, two lumps of coal in the grate, one glass of port and lemon to last the night, and nothing by the way of entertainment beyond escorting Mr Brownlow down the freezing back-yard to the WC.

The following year, to avoid the possibility of bumping into Smith, we went to the Adelphi. And damn me, he was there. There was a dance on Christmas Eve in the main lounge, and I'll never forget how he and the wife began in a melancholy and abstracted manner to circle the floor, her black dress rustling as she moved, and he almost on tiptoe because he was shorter than her. Every time he fox-trotted the wife in my direction he gave an exaggerated little start of surprise, as though I was the last person he expected to see. When he fetched her back to the table, he said, 'I do hope you have no objection to my dancing with your lady wife. I wouldn't like to give offence.'

'No offence taken,' I said. I've never seen the point of dancing. 'Do as you please.'

'We shall, we shall,' the wife said, laughing in that way she has.

We had to play cards with the blighter on Christmas Day. On Boxing Day it was almost a relief, which was saying something, to travel out on the tram to Anfield for the festivities with Constance and Mr Brownlow.

The next year we tried the Exchange again, never thinking that lightning would strike twice, or three times for that matter but, blow me, it did. Smith turned up an hour after we arrived. I did briefly begin to wonder who was avoiding who, but it was obvious that he was as pleased as punch to see us.

'My word,' he cried out. 'This is nice. My word, it is.'

I sensed he was different. There was nothing I could put my finger on; his suit was the same and he still blinked a lot, but something had changed in him. I mentioned as much to the wife. 'He's different, don't you think?' I said.

'Different?' she said.

'Cocky,' I said. 'If you know what I mean?'

'I don't,' she said.

'Something in the eye,' I insisted.

But she wouldn't have it.

All the same, I was right. Why, he even had the blithering nerve to give me a present, wrapped up in coloured paper with one of those damn soft bows on the top. It was a book on golf, which was a lucky choice, inspired almost, as I'd only taken up the game a few months before. I didn't run amok showing my gratitude, nor did I scamper upstairs and parcel up one of the handkerchiefs the wife had given to me. To be frank, I didn't even say thank you.

I didn't need acquaintances, then. As long as I had the wife sitting there, reading a library book and smoking one of her Craven A cigarettes, I didn't have to go to the bother of being pleasant. Not that Smith noticed my lack of enthusiasm for his company. It appeared to me that no matter where I was, whether in the corridor minding my own business, or coming out of the lift, or having a quiet drink in the Steve Donoghue Bar, he was forever bobbing up alongside me, or behind me – and always a mine of useful information. 'Are you aware,' he'd ask, eyeing the beer pitching in my glass as a train rumbled out of the station below, 'that the first locomotive was so heavy that it broke the track beneath it?'

He didn't seem to know anybody in the city, but a couple of times I saw him going down in the lift very late at night with his hat and coat on. God knows where he was off to. Once, I saw him in the deserted booking-hall of the station. I was on the fourth floor of the hotel, in the small hours, looking out of the back windows at the arched roof beneath, estimating what price, per ton, the cast-iron ribs would fetch on the scrap market. It was raining and Smith was perambulating up and down, hatless, holding an umbrella in a cock-eyed way, followed by a flock of pigeons. While I was watching, Smith suddenly spun round and flourished his brolly at the pigeons. I took it that he was drunk. The birds flapped upwards in alarm. There wasn't a pane of glass left intact in the roof – it had all been blasted to smithereens during the Blitz. One of the pigeons in attempting to escape through the ribs must have severed a wing on the shards of glass. It sort of staggered in mid-air and then dropped like a lump of mud to the granite floor of the booking-hall. I couldn't hear the noise it made, flopping down like that, but it obviously gave Smith quite a turn. He froze, his gamp held out to one side like some railway guard waiting to lower his flag for a train to depart. I couldn't see his face because I was looking down on him, but I could tell by the stance of the man, one foot turned inwards, one arm stuck outwards, that he was frightened. Then he took a running kick at the thing on the ground and sent it skidding against the base of the tobacco kiosk. After a moment he went over to the kiosk and squatted down. He stayed like that for some time, rocking backwards and forwards on his haunches. Then he took out his handkerchief, laid it over the pigeon, and walked away. He was definitely drunk.

That final year, 1949, I switched back to the Adelphi. You've never clapped eyes on anything like that hotel. It's built like a Cunarder. Whenever I lurched through the revolving doors into the lobby, I never thought I'd disembark until I'd crossed the Atlantic. The lounge is the size of a dry dock; there are little balconettes running the entire length of it, fronted by ornamental grilles. Sometimes, if the staff dropped a nickel-plated teapot in the small kitchen behind the rostrum, I imagined we'd struck an iceberg. I never used to think like that until Smith put his oar in. It was he who said that all big hotels were designed to resemble ocean liners. On another occasion – because he was a contrary beggar – he said that the balconettes were modelled after confessionals in churches. I never sat in them after that.

We arrived at four o'clock on the 23rd December and went immediately into the lounge for tea and cakes. I had just told the wife to sit up straight – there's nothing worse than a slouching woman, particularly if she's got a silver fox fur slung round her shoulders – when I thought I saw, reflected in the mirrors behind the balconettes, the unmistakable figure of Smith. I slopped tea into my saucer.

'What's up?' asked my wife.

'I could swear I just saw that blighter Smith,' I said. 'Could I have been mistaken, do you think?'

'What?' she said. 'You? Surely not.' She was lifting up her veil and tucking it back over the brim of her hat, and you could tell how put out she was; both her cheeks were red with annoyance.

The odd thing was that he never came into the grill room that night. 'Perhaps it wasn't him,' I said. 'Perhaps it was a trick of the light.'

'Some trick,' she said.

'If he has the effrontery to present me with another little seasonal offering,' I warned her, 'I'll throw it back in his face.'

After we had finished our pudding my wife said she was off to her bed.

'You can't go up now,' I said. 'I've paid good money to be here.'

'If I'm to live through the excitement of visiting Constance and Mr Brownlow,' she said, 'I'll need all the rest I can get.' She fairly ran out of the grill room; she never had any staying power.

I had a drink in the bar and asked the fellow behind the counter if he'd seen Smith, but he didn't seem to know who I was talking about. That's the trouble with shifting from one hotel to another – none of the staff know you from Adam. I looked into the smoking-room about ten o'clock and he wasn't there either. I could have done with Smith. The hotel was crowded with guests, some in uniform, full of the Christmas spirit and anxious that everyone should join in. Several times I was almost drawn into one of those conversations about what branch of the services I'd been in during the hostilities. I'll say that much for Smith; he never asked me what I'd done in the war. At a quarter past ten I went into the lounge and ordered myself another drink. There weren't too many people in there. A dance was in progress in the French room; I could hear the band playing some number made popular by Carmen Miranda. The waiter had just set my glass down in front of me when the doors burst open at the side and a line of revellers spilled into the lounge and began doing the conga down the length of the pink carpet towards the Christmas tree at the far end. They wound in and out of the sofas and the tables, clasping each other at the waist and kicking up the devil of a noise. Mercifully, having snaked once round the tree, showering the carpet with pine-needles, they headed back for the dance floor. And suddenly, for a split second, before he disappeared behind the tree, I thought I saw Smith near the end of the line, clutching hold of a stout individual who was wearing a paper hat. The fat man appeared again, but I was mistaken about Smith. Oddly enoough, he must have been on my mind because for the rest of the evening I fancied I caught glimpses of him - coming out of the gents, going into the lift, standing at the top of the stairs looking down into the lounge - but it was never him.

Shortly after midnight I went upstairs to unpack my belongings. My room was on the first floor and overlooked Lewis's department store. I'd changed into my pyjamas – such as they were – and was putting my Sunday suit on a hanger when I realized that my wife had forgotten to include my grey spotted tie among the rest of my things. It wasn't that I gave a tinker's cuss about that particular tie, it was just that Mr Brownlow had bought it for me the previous Christmas and my not wearing it on Boxing Day would undoubtedly cause an uproar.

I went out into the corridor, determined to ask the wife what she meant by it. It wasn't as if she had a lot on her mind. Unfortunately, I forgot that the door was self-locking and it shut behind me. I rapped on my wife's door for what seemed like hours. I've never seen the point of chucking money away on pyjamas; the draw-string had gone from the trousers and there wasn't one button left on the jacket. When my wife finally deigned to open up, she too stepped over the threshold, and in an instant her door had slammed shut as well. I admit I lost my head. I ran up and down, swearing, trying to find a broom cupboard to hide in; any moment those blighters from the French room could have come prancing along the corridor.

'Fetch a porter,' advised my wife.

'Not like this,' I shouted. 'I'm not fit.'

'Here,' she said, and she took off her dressing-gown - it had white fur round the sleeves - and handed it to me.

I had crept half-way down the stairs when I heard carol singing one floor below. I just couldn't face anyone, not wearing that damn-fool dressing-gown and my trousers at half mast. I hopped back upstairs and at that moment the wife called out to me from the doorway of her room; apparently her door hadn't been locked after all.

I spent an uncomfortable night in the wife's bed – I don't sleep well – and when I switched on the light to see if I could find anything to read, there was only the Bible. The room was a pig-sty; she hadn't emptied her suitcase or hung anything up, and there was a slice of buttered bread on top of her fox fur. I woke her and asked if she had a library book handy.

'For God's sake,' she said. 'I'm worn out.'

I was having afternoon tea the following day, on my own – the wife had gone window-shopping in Bold Street – when Smith arrived at the hotel. He said a relative had been taken ill and he'd had to visit them in hospital. Being Smith, he couldn't leave it at that. He had to give me a lecture on some damn-fool theory of his that we thought ourselves into illnesses. Our minds, he said, controlled our bodies. Some blasted Greek or other had known it centuries ago.

Faced with him, and realizing that he'd be dogging my footsteps for the next forty-eight hours, I grew irritated. Don't forget, I hadn't had much sleep, and there was some sort of expression on his face, some sort of light in his eyes that annoyed me. I don't know how to explain it; he looked foolish, almost happy and it rubbed me up the wrong way. I wanted to get rid of him once and for all. It was no use insulting the man; I had done that often enough and it was like water off a duck's back. Then an idea came to me. I had recognized right from the beginning that he was a prudish sort of fellow. I knew that he had never married, and I had never seen him strike up a conversation with an unescorted woman, apart from the wife. He preferred the company of married couples, providing they were respectable.

'Blow me down,' I said. 'I've been getting pains in my legs for the past eight years. Now I know why.'

'Why?' he asked.

'On account of the wife,' I said.

'Your wife?' he said, tugging at his little ginger moustache.

I implied that the wife had led me something of a dance. She was under the doctor for it, of course. It had gone on for years. She couldn't be blamed, not exactly. That's why I was forced to keep changing hotels ... there had been various incidents of a somewhat scandalous nature with various men. As I spoke I stumbled over the words – I knew he wasn't a complete fool. I expressed the hope that he wouldn't betray my confidences. I didn't feel bad telling lies about my wife. It wouldn't get back. There was no danger of Smith repeating it to somebody he knew, who might repeat it to somebody we knew, because none of us knew anybody. It shut him up all right. The light went out of his eyes.

At seven o'clock that evening, according to the waiter on duty, Smith came into the smoking-room and ordered a pot of tea. The waiter noticed that he kept clattering the ash-tray up and down on the table. When the tea was brought to him, he said, 'Oh, and I'll need some bread and butter if it's all the same to you.' While the waiter was gone Smith took out his service revolver and shot himself in the head. He died almost at once. He must have been more upset about his relative being ill than he let on.

We never went back to the Adelphi, or to the Exchange for that matter. Not because of anything to do with Smith, but because less than a year later the wife began to show signs of instability; in any case the following August Constance passed on and there was certainly no call to clap eyes on Mr Brownlow ever again.

One could say that my wife has passed on too, only in her case it's more that she's wandered out of reach. As Bread and Butter Smith might have put it: 'All the world's against her, so that Crete (alias Rainhill Mental Institution) is her only refuge.'

JEAN STAFFORD

The Maiden

'I BOUGHT the pair of them in Berlin for forty marks,' Mrs
Andreas was saying to Dr Reinmuth, who had admired the twin
decanters on her dinner table. 'It sickens me, the way they must let
their treasures go for nothing. I can take no pride in having got a
bargain when I feel like a pirate.' Evan Leckie, an American
journalist who was the extra man at the party, turned away from
the woman on his right to glance at his hostess to see if her face
revealed the hypocrisy he had heard, ever so faintly, in her voice,
but he could read nothing in her bland eyes, nor could he discover
the reaction of her interlocutor, who slightly inclined his head in
acknowledgement of her sympathy for his mortified compatriots
but said nothing and resumed his affectionate scrutiny of the
decanters as Mrs Andreas went on to enumerate other instances of
the victor's gains through the Germans' losses. Evan, just
transferred to Heidelberg from the squalor and perdition of
Nuremberg, joined in the German's contemplation of these relics
of more handsome times. One of the bottles was filled with red
wine, which gleamed darkly through the lustrous, sculptured glass,
chased with silver, and the other with pale, sunny Chablis. The
candlelight invested the wines with a property beyond taste and
fluidity, a subtile grace belonging to a world almost imaginary in
its elegance, and for a moment Evan warmed towards Mrs
Andreas, who had tried to resuscitate this charming world for her
guests by putting the decanters in the becoming company of heavy,
florid silverware and Dresden fruit plates and a bowl of
immaculate white roses, and by dressing herself, a plump and
unexceptional person, in an opulent frock of gold brocade and a
little queenly crown of amethysts for her curly, greying hair.

The double doors to the garden were open to admit the

moonlight and the summer breeze, and now and again, in the course of the meal, Evan had glanced out and had seen luminous nicotiana and delphiniums growing profusely beside a high stone wall. Here, in the hilly section of the city, it was as quiet as in the country, there was not a sound of jeeps or drunken GIs to disturb the light and general conversation of Americans breaking bread with Germans. Only by implication and indirection were the war and the Occupation spoken of, and in this abandonment of the contemporary, the vanquished, these charming Reinmuths, save by their dress and their speech, could not be distinguished from the conquerors. If chivalry, thought Evan, were ever to return to the world, peace would come with it, but evenings like this were isolated, were all but lost in the vast, arid wastes of the present hour within the present decade. And the pity that Mrs Andreas bestowed upon her German guests would not return to them the decanters they had forfeited, nor would her hospitality obliterate from their hearts the knowledge of their immense dilemma. Paradoxically, it was only upon the highest possible level that Germans and Americans these days could communicate with one another; only a past that was now irretrievable could bring them into harmony.

For the past month in Nuremburg, ever since Evan's wife, Virginia, had left him – left him, as she had put it in a shout, 'to stew in his own juice – Evan had spent his evenings in the bar of his hotel, drinking by himself and listening, in a trance of boredom, to the conversations of the Americans about him. The mirrored walls and mirrored ceilings had cast back the manifold reflections of able-bodied WACs in summer uniforms, who talked of their baseball teams (once he had seen a phalanx of them in the lobby, armed with bats and catchers' mitts, looking no less manly than the Brooklyn Dodgers) and of posts where they had been stationed and of itineraries, past and future. 'Where were you in '45?' he had heard one of them cry. 'New Caledonia! My God! So was I. Isn't it a riot to think we were both in New Caledonia in '45 and now are here in the Theatre?' Things had come to a pretty pass, thought Evan, when *this* was the theatre of a young girl's dreams. They did not talk like women and they did not look like women but like a modern mutation, a revision, perhaps more efficient and sturdier, of an old model. Half hypnotized by the signs of the times, he had come almost to believe that the days of men and women were over and that the world had moved into a new era dominated by a neuter body called Personnel, whose only concerns were to make history and to snub the history that had already been made. Miss Sally Dean, who sat across from him tonight, had pleased him at first glance with her bright-blonde hair and her alabaster shoulders and the fine length of her legs, but over the cocktails his delight departed when, in the accents of West Los Angeles, she had said she wished General MacArthur were in Germany, since he was, in her opinion, a 'real glamour puss'. The woman on his right, Mrs Crowell, the wife of a judge from Ohio in the judiciary of the Occupation, was obsessively loquacious; for a very long time she had been delivering to him a self-sustaining monologue on the effronteries of German servants, announcing once, with all the authority of an anthropologist, that 'the Baden mind is *consecrated* to dishonesty'. He could not put his finger on it, but, in spite of her familiar housewife's complaints, she did not sound at all like his mother and his aunts in Charlottesville, whose lives, spun out in loving domesticity, would lose their pungency if cooks kept civil tongues in their heads and if upstairs maids were not light-fingered. Mrs Crowell brought to her housekeeping problems a modern and impersonal intellect. 'The Baden mind', 'the Franconian mind', 'the German character' were phrases that came forth irrefutably. And the blue-stocking wife of a Captain McNaughton, who sat on Evan's left and who taught library science to the wives of other Army officers, had all evening lectured Dr Reinmuth on the faults (remediable, in her opinion) of his generation that had forced the world into war. Dr Reinmuth was a lawyer. She was herself a warrior; she argued hotly, although the German did not oppose her, and sometimes she threatened him with her spoon.

It was the German woman, Frau Reinmuth, who, although her grey dress was modest and although she wore no jewels and little rouge, captivated Evan with her ineffable femininity: she, of all the women there, had been challenged by violence and she had ignored it, had firmly and with great poise set it aside. To look at her, no one would know that the slightest alteration had taken place in the dignified *modus vivendi* she must have known all her life. The serenity she emanated touched him so warmly and so deeply that he almost loved her, and upon the recognition of his feeling he was seized with loneliness and with a sort of homesickness that he felt

sure she would understand – a longing, it was, for the places that
she would remember. Suddenly it occurred to him that the only
other time he had been in Heidelberg, he had been here with his
wife, two years before, and they had gone one afternoon by trolley
to Schwetzingen to see the palace gardens. Virginia had always
hated history and that day she had looked at a cool Louis Quatorze
summerhouse, designed for witty persiflage and premeditated
kisses, and had said, 'It's so chichi it makes me sick.' And she had
meant it. How she had prided herself on despising everything that
had been made before 1920, the year of her birth! Staring at the
wines aglow in their fine vessels, Evan recaptured exactly the
feeling he had had that day in Schwetzingen when, very abruptly,
he had realized that he was only technically bound for life to this
fretful iconoclast; for a short while, there beside the playing
fountains, he had made her vanish and in her place there stood a
quiet woman, rich in meditations and in fancies. If he had known
Frau Reinmuth then, she might have been the one he thought of.

Evan watched Dr Reinmuth as he poured the gold and garnet
liquids, first one and then the other, into the glasses before his
plate. The little lawyer closely attended the surge of colour behind
the radiant crystal and he murmured, in a soft Bavarian voice,
'Lovely, lovely. Look, Liselotte, how beautiful Mrs Andreas'
Karaffen are!' Frau Reinmuth, wide-faced, twice his size, turned
from her talk of the Salzburg Festival with Mr Andreas and
cherished both her husband and the decanters with her broad grey
eyes, in whose depths love lay limitlessly. When she praised the
design of the cut glass, and the etching of the silver, and the shape
of the stoppers, like enormous diamonds, she managed somehow,
through the timbre of her voice or its cadences or through the way
she looked at him, to proclaim that she loved her husband and that
the beauty of the bottles was rivalled and surpassed by the nature
of this little man of hers, who, still fascinated, moved his
handsome head this way and that, the better to see the prismatic
green and violet beams that burst from the shelves and crannies of
the glass. His movements were quick and delicately articulated,
like a small animal's, and his slender fingers touched and traced
the glass as if he were playing a musical instrument that only his
ears could hear. He must have been in his middle forties, but he
looked like a nervous, gifted boy not twenty yet, he was so slight,
his hair was so black and curly, his brown face was so lineless, and

there was such candour and curiosity in his dark eyes. He seemed now to want to carry his visual and tactile encounter with the decanters to a further point, to a completion, to bliss. And Evan, arrested by the man's absorption (if it was not that of a child, it was that of an artist bent on abstracting meanings from all the data presented to his senses), found it hard to imagine him arguing in a court of law, where the materials, no matter how one elevated and embellished justice, were not poetry. Equally difficult was it to see him as he had been during the war, in his role of interpreter for the German Army in Italy. Like every German one met in a polite American house. Dr Reinmuth had been an enemy of the Third Reich: he had escaped concentration camp only because his languages were useful to the Nazis. While Evan, for the most part, was suspicious of these self-named martyrs who seemed always to have fetched up in gentlemanly jobs where their lives were not in the least imperilled, he did believe in Dr Reinmuth, and was certain that a belligerent ideology could noᵗ ⁻nlist the tender creature so unaffectedly playing with Mrs Andreas' toys, so obviously well beloved by his benevolent wife. Everyone, even Mrs Crowell, paused a second to look from the man to the woman and to esteem their concord.

Frau Reinmuth then returned to Mr Andreas, but it was plain to see that her mind was only half with him. She said, 'I envy you to hear Flagstad. Our pain is that there is no music now', and in a lower voice she added, 'I have seen August bite his lip for sorrow when he goes past the opera house in Mannheim. It's nothing now, you know, but a ruin, like everything.' Glancing at her, Evan wondered whether she were older than her husband or if this marriage had been entered upon late, and he concluded that perhaps the second was true, for they were childless – the downright Mrs McNaughton had determined that before the canapés were passed – and Frau Reinmuth looked born to motherhood. But even more telling was the honeymoon inflection in her voice, as if she were still marvelling now to say the name 'August' as easily as she said 'I' and to be able to bestow these limnings of her dearest possession generously on the members of a dinner party. It was not that she spoke of him as if he were a child, as some women do who marry late or marry men younger than themselves, but as if he were a paragon with whom she had the remarkable honour to be associated. She, in her boundless patience, could endure being deprived of music and it was not for herself that she complained, but she could not bear to see August's grief over the hush that lay upon their singing country; she lived not only for, she lived *in*, him. She wore her yellow hair in Germanic braids that coiled around her head, sitting too low to be smart; her hands were soft and large, honestly meriting the wide wedding band on the right one. She was as completely a woman as Virginia, in spite of a kind of ravening femaleness and piquant good looks, had never been one. He shuddered to think how she must be maligning him in Nevada to the other angry petitioners, and then he tried to imagine how Frau Reinmuth would behave under similar circumstances. But it was unthinkable that she should ever be a divorcée; no matter what sort of man she married, this wifely woman would somehow, he was sure, quell all disorder. Again he felt a wave of affection for her; he fancied drinking tea with her in a little crowded drawing-room at the end of one of these warm days, and he saw himself walking with both the Reinmuths up through the hills behind the Philosophenweg, proving to the world by their compassionate amity that there was no longer a state of war between their country and his.

But he was prevented from spinning out his fantasy of a friendship with the Reinmuths because Mrs Crowell was demanding his attention. Her present servant, she told him, was an aristocrat ('as aristocratic as a German can be', she said *sotto voce*, 'which isn't saying much') and might therefore be expected not to steal the spoons; now, having brought him up to date on her below-stairs problems, she changed the subject and drew him into the orbit of her bright-eyed, pervasive bustling. She understood that he had just come from Nuremberg, where she and the judge had lived for two years. 'Isn't it too profoundly *triste*?' she cried. 'Where did they billet you, poor thing?'

'At the Grand Hotel,' said Evan, recollecting the WACs with their moustaches and their soldierly patois.

'Oh no!' protested Mrs Crowell. 'But it's simply *overrun* with awful Army children! Not children – brats. Brats, I'm sorry to say, is the only word for them. They actually roller-skate through the lobby, you know, to say nothing of the *ghastly* noise they make. I used to go to the hairdresser there and finally had to give up because of the hullabaloo.'

At the mention of Nuremberg, Dr Reinmuth had pivoted around

towards them and now, speaking across Mrs McNaughton, he said dreamily, 'Once it was a lovely town. We lived there, my wife and I, all our lives until the war. I understand there is now a French orchestra in the opera house that plays calypso for your soldiers.' There sounded in his voice the same note of wonder that he had used when he acclaimed the decanters that he could not own; neither could he again possess the beauties of his birthplace. And Evan Leckie, to whom the genesis of war had always been incomprehensible, looked with astonishment at these two pacific Germans and pondered how the whole hideous mistake had come about, what Eumenides had driven this pair to hardship, humiliation, and exile. Whatever else they were, however alien their values might be, these enemies were *sub specie aeternitatis*, of incalculable worth if for no other reason than that, in an unloving world, they loved.

Mrs Andreas, tactfully refusing Dr Reinmuth's gambit, since she knew that the deterioration of the Nuremberg Opera House into a night club must be a painful subject to him, manoeuvred her guests until the talk at the table became general. They all continued the exchange that had begun with Frau Reinmuth and Mr Andreas on the Salzburg Festival; they went on to speak of Edinburgh, of the *Salome* that someone had heard at La Scala, of a coloratura who had delighted the Reinmuths in Weimar. Dr Reinmuth then told the story of his having once defended a pianist who had been sued for slander by a violinist; the defendant had been accused of saying publicly that the plaintiff played Mozart as if the music had been written for the barrel organ and that the only thing missing was a monkey to take up a collection. This anecdote, coinciding with the arrival of the dessert, diverted the stream of talk, and Judge Crowell, whose interest in music was perfunctory and social, revived and took the floor. He told of a murder case he had tried the week before in Frankfurt and of a rape case on the docket in Stuttgart. Dr Reinmuth countered with cases he was pleading; they matched their legal wits, made Latin puns, and so enjoyed their game that the others laughed, although they barely understood the meanings of the words.

Dr Reinmuth, who was again fondling the decanters, said, 'I suppose every lawyer is fond of telling the story of his first case. May I tell mine?' He besought his hostess with an endearing smile, and his wife, forever at his side, pleaded for him, 'Oh, do!' and she explained, 'It's such an extraordinary story of a young lawyer's first case.'

He poured himself a little more Chablis and smiled and began. When he was twenty-three, in Nuremberg, just down from Bonn, with no practice at all, he had one day been called upon by the state to defend a man who had confessed to murdering an old woman and robbing her of sixty pfennig. The defence, of course, was purely a convention, and the man was immediately sentenced to death, since there was no question of his guilt or of the enormity of his crime. Some few days after the trial, Dr Reinmuth had received an elaborate engraved invitation to the execution by guillotine, which was to be carried out in the courtyard of the Justizpalast one morning a day or so later, punctually at seven o'clock. He was instructed, in an accompanying letter, to wear a Prince Albert and a top hat.

Mr Andreas was shocked. 'Guillotine? Did you *have* to go?'

Dr Reinmuth smiled and bowed to her. 'No, I was not required. It was, you see, my *right* to go, as the advocate of the prisoner.'

Judge Crowell laughed deeply. 'Your first case, eh, Reinmuth ?' And Dr Reinmuth spread out his hands in a mock gesture of deprecation.

'My fellow-spectators were three judges from the bench,' he continued, 'who were dressed, like myself, in Prince Alberts and cylinders. We were a little early when we got to the courtyard, so that we saw the last-minute preparations of the stage before the play began. Near the guillotine, with its great knife - that blade, my God in Heaven! - there stood a man in uniform with a drum, ready to drown out the sound if my client should yell.'

The dimmest of frowns had gathered on Judge Crowell's forehead. 'All this pomp and circumstance for sixty pfennigs?' he said.

'Right you are, sir,' replied Dr Reinmuth. 'That is the irony of my story.' He paused to eat a strawberry and to take a sip of wine. 'Next we watched them test the machine to make sure it was in proper - shall I say decapitating? - condition. When they released it, the cleaver came down with such stupendous force that the earth beneath our feet vibrated and my brains buzzed like a bee.

'As the bells began to ring for seven, Herr Murderer was led out by two executioners, dressed as we were dressed. Their white gloves were spotless! It was a glorious morning in May. The flowers were out, the birds were singing, the sky had not a cloud. To have your head cut off on such a day!'

'For sixty pfennigs!' persisted the judge from Ohio. And Miss Dean, paling, stopped eating her dessert.

'Mein Herr had been confessed and anointed. You could fairly see the holy oil on his forehead as his keepers led him across the paving to the guillotine. The drummer was ready. As the fourth note of the seven struck in the church towers, they persuaded him to take the position necessary to the success of Dr Guillotin's invention. One, he was horizontal! Two, the blade descended! Three, the head was off the carcass and the blood shot out from the neck like a volcano, a geyser, the flame from an explosion. No sight I saw in the war was worse. The last stroke of seven sounded. There had been no need for the drum.'

'Great Scott!' said Mr Andreas, and flushed.

Captain McNaughton stared at Dr Reinmuth and said, 'You chaps don't do things by halves, do you?'

Mrs Andreas, frantic at the dangerous note that had sounded, menacing her party, put her hand lightly on the lawyer's and said, 'I know that then you must have fainted.'

Dr Reinmuth tilted back his head and smiled at the ceiling. 'No. No, I did not faint. You remember that this was a beautiful day in spring? And that I was a young man, all dressed up at seven in the morning?' He lowered his head and gave his smile to the whole company. 'Faint! Dear lady, no! I took the tram back to Fürth and I called my sweetheart on the telephone.' He gazed at his wife. 'Liselotte was surprised, considering the hour. "What are you thinking of? It's not eight o'clock," she said. I flustered her then. I said, "I know it's an unusual time of day to call, but I have something unusual to say. Will you marry me?" '

He clasped his hands together and exchanged with his wife a look as exuberant and shy as if they were in the first rapture of their romance, and, bewitched, she said, 'Twenty years ago next May.'

A silence settled on the room. Whether Evan Leckie was the more dumbfounded by Dr Reinmuth's story of a majestic penalty to fit a sordid crime or by his ostentatious hinting at his connubial delights, he did not know. Evan sought the stunned faces of his countrymen and could not tell in them, either, what feeling was the uppermost. The party suddenly was no longer a whole; it consisted of two parts, the Americans and the Germans, and while the former outnumbered them, the Germans, in a deeper sense, had triumphed. They had joyfully danced a *Totentanz*, had implied all the details of their sixty-pfennig marriage, and they were still, even now, smiling at each other as if there had never been anything untoward in their lives.

'I could take a wife then, you see,' said Dr Reinmuth, by way of a dénouement, 'since I was a full-fledged lawyer. And she could not resist me in that finery, which, as a matter of fact, I had had to hire for the occasion.'

Judge Crowell lit a cigarette, and, snatching at the externals of the tale, he said, 'Didn't know you fellows used the guillotine as late as that. I've never seen one except that one they've got in the antiquarian place in Edinburgh. They call it the Maiden.'

Dr Reinmuth poured the very last of the Chablis into his glass, and turning to Mrs Andreas, he said, 'It was nectar and I've drunk it all. *Sic transit gloria mundi.*'

Gravement Endommagé

THE car devoured the road, but the lines of poplars were without end. The shadow of sagging telegraph wires scalloped the middle of the road, the vaguer shadows of the pretty telegraph posts pleased Louise. They were essentially French, she thought – like, perhaps, lilies of the valley: spare, neatly budded.

The poplars dwindled at intervals and gave place to ruined buildings and pock-marked walls; a landscape of broken stone, faded Dubonnet advertisements. Afterwards, the trees began again.

When they came to a town, the cobblestones, laid fan-wise, slowed up the driving. Outside cafés, the chairs were all empty. Plane-trees in the squares half-hid the flaking walls of houses with crooked jalousies and frail balconies, like twisted bird-cages. All had slipped, subsided.

'But it is so *dead*!' Louise complained, wanting to get to Paris, to take out from her cases her crumpled frocks, shake them out, hang them up. She dreamed of that; she had clung to the idea across the Channel. Because she was sick before the boat moved, Richard thought she was sick deliberately, as a form of revenge. But seasickness ran in her family. Her mother had always been prostrated immediately – as soon (as she so often had said) as her foot touched the deck. It would have seemed an insult to her mother's memory for Louise not to have worked herself up into a queasy panic at the very beginning. Richard, seeing walls sliding past port-holes and then sky, finished his drink quickly and went up on deck. Hardier women than Louise leaned over the rails, their scarves flapping, watching the coast of France come up. The strong air had made him hungry, but when they had driven away from the harbour and had stopped for luncheon, Louise would only sip brandy, looking away from his plate.

'But we can never get to Paris by dinner-time,' he said, when they were in the car again. 'Especially driving on the wrong side of the road all the way.'

'There is nowhere between here and there,' she said with authority. 'And I want to *settle*.'

He knew her 'settling'. Photographs of the children spread about, champagne sent up, maids running down corridors with her frocks on their arms, powder spilt everywhere, the bathroom full of bottles and jars. He would have to sit down to telephone a list of names. Her friends would come in for drinks. They would have done better, so far as he could see, to have stayed in London.

'But if we are pushed for time ... Why kill ourselves? ... After all, this is a holiday ... I do remember ... There is a place I stayed at that time ... When I first knew you ...' Only parts of what he said reached her. The rest was blown away.

'You are deliberately going slow,' she said.

'I think more of my car than to drive it fast along these roads.'

'You think more of your car than of your wife.'

He had no answer. He could not say that at least his car never betrayed him, let him down, embarrassed him, because it constantly did and might at any moment.

'You planned this delay without consulting me. You planned to spend this night in some god-forsaken place and sink into your private nostalgia while my frocks crease and crease ...' Her voice mounted up like a wave, trembled, broke.

The holiday was really to set things to rights between them. Lately, trivial bickering had hardened into direct animosity. Relatives put this down to, on his part, overwork, and, on hers, fatigue from the war, during which she had lived, after their London house was bombed, in a remote village with the children. She had nothing to say of those years but that they were not funny. She clung to the children and they to her. He was not, as he said – at first indulgently but more lately with irritation – in the picture. She knit them closer and closer to her, and he was quite excluded. He tried to understand that there must be, after the war, much that was new in her, after so long a gap, one that she would not fill up for him, or discuss. A new quirk was her preoccupation with fashion. To her, it was a race in which she must be first, so she looked *outré* always, never normal. If any of her friends struck a new note before her, she by-passed and cancelled out that particular foible. Men never liked her clothes, and women only admired them. She did not dress for men. Years of almost exclusively feminine society had set up cold antagonisms. Yes, hardship had made her superficial, icily frivolous. For one thing, she now must never be alone. She drank too much. In the night, he knew, she turned and turned, sighing in her sleep, dreaming bad dreams, wherein she could no longer choose her company. When he made love to her, she recoiled in astonishment, as if she could not believe such things could happen.

He had once thought she would be so happy to leave the village, that by comparison her life in London after the war would seem wonderful. But boredom had made her carping, fidgety. Instead of being thankful for what she had, she complained at the slightest discomfort. She raised her standards above what they had ever been; drove maids, who needed little driving, to give notice; was harried, piteous, unrelaxed. Although she was known as a wonderful hostess, guests wonderfully enjoying themselves felt – they could not say why – wary, and listened, as if for a creaking of ice beneath their gaiety.

Her doctor, advising the holiday, was only conventional in his optimism. If anyone were benefited by it, it would be the children, stopping at home with their grandmother – for a while, out of the arena. What Richard needed was a holiday away from Louise, and what Louise needed was a holiday from herself, from the very thing she must always take along, the dull carapace of her own dissatisfaction, her chronic unsunniness.

The drive seemed endless, because it was so monotonous. War had exhaled a vapour of despair over all the scene. Grass grew over grief, trying to hide collapse, to cover some of the wounds. One generation hoped to contend with the failure of another.

Late in the afternoon, they came to a town he remembered. The small cathedral stood like torn lacework against the sky. Birds settled in rows on the empty windows. Nettles grew in the aisle, and stone figures, impaled on rusty spikes of wire, were crumbling away.

But it looks too old a piece of wreckage, he thought. That must be the war before last. Two generations, ruined, lay side by side. Among them, people went on bicycles, to and fro, between the impoverished shops and scarred dwellings.

'After wars, when there is so little time for patching up before the next explosion, what hope is there?' he began.

She didn't answer, stared out of the window, the car jolting so that her teeth chattered.

When Richard was alone in the hotel bedroom, he tried, by spreading about some of Louise's belongings, to make the place seem less temporary. He felt guilty at having had his own way, at keeping her from Paris until the next day and delaying her in this dismal place. It was destined to be, so far as they were concerned, one of those provincial backgrounds, fleeting, meaningless, that travellers erase from experience – the different hotel rooms run together to form one room, this room, any room.

When he had put the pink jars and bottles out in a row above the hand basin, he became dubious. She would perhaps sweep them all back into her case, saying, 'Why unpack before we reach Paris?' and he would find that he had worsened the situation, after all, as he so often did, meaning to better it.

His one piece of selfishness – this halt on the way – she had stubbornly resisted, and now she had gone off to buy picture-postcards for the children, as if no one would think of them if she did not.

Because he often wondered how she looked when he was not there, if her face ever smoothed, he went to the window, hoping to see her coming down the little street. He wanted to catch in advance, to be prepared for, her mood. But she was not moody nowadays. A dreadful consistency discoloured her behaviour.

He pulled the shutters apart and was faced with a waste of fallen masonry, worse now that it was seen from above, and unrecognisable. The humped-up, dark cathedral stood in an untidy space, as if the little shops and cafés he remembered had receded in awe. Dust flowed along the streets, spilling from ruined walls across pavements. Rusty grasses covered debris and everywhere the air was unclean with grit.

Dust, he thought, leaning on the iron rail above window-boxes full of shepherd's-purse – dust has the connotation of despair. In the end, shall we go up in a great swirl of it? He imagined something like the moon's surface, pock-marked, cratered, dry, deserted. When he was young, he had not despaired. Then, autumn leaves, not dust, had blown about these streets; chimes dropped like water, uneven, inconsequential, over rooftops; and the lime-trees yellowed along neat boulevards. Yet, in the entrancement of nostalgia, he remembered, at best, an imperfect happiness and, for the most part, an agony of conjecture and expectancy. Crossing the vestibule of this very hotel, he had turned; his eyes had always sought the letter-rack. The Channel lay between him and his love, who with her timid smile, her mild grimace, had moaned that she could not put pen to paper, was illiterate, never had news; though loving him inordinately, could not spell, never had postage stamps; her ink dried as it approached the page; her parents interrupted. Yes, she had loved him to excess but had seldom written, and now went off in the dust and squalor for picture-postcards for their children.

At the window, waiting for her to appear, he felt that the dust and destruction had pinned down his courage. Day after day had left its residue, sifting down through him – cynicism and despair. He wondered what damage he had wreaked upon her.

Across the street, which once had been narrow and now was open to the sky, a nun went slowly, carrying bread under her arm. The wind plucked her veil. A thin cat followed her. They picked their way across the rubble. The cat stopped once and lifted a paw, licked it carefully, and put it back into the grit. The faint sound of trowel on stone rang out, desultory, hopeless, a frail weapon against so convincing a destruction. That piteous tap, tap turned him away from the window. He could not bear the futility of the sound, or the thought of the monstrous task ahead, and now feared, more than all he could imagine, the sight of his wife hurrying back down the street, frowning, the picture-postcards in her hand.

Louise was late. Richard sat drinking Pernod at a table in the bar where he could see her come into the hotel. There was only the barman to talk to. Rather clouded with drink, Richard leaned on his elbow, describing the town as it had been. The barman, who was Australian, knew only too well. After the '14–'18 war, he had put his savings into a small café across the road. 'I knew it,' Richard said eagerly, forgetting the lacuna in both years and buildings, the gap over which the nun, the cat had picked their way.

'I'll get the compensation some day,' the Australian said, wiping the bar. 'Start again. Something different.'

When a waiter came for drinks, the barman spoke in slow but confident French, probably different from an Englishman's French, Richard thought, though he could not be sure; a Frenchman would know.

'She gets later and later,' he said solemnly.

'Well, if she doesn't come, that's what she's bound to do,' the barman agreed.

'It was a shock to me, the damage of this town.'

'Twelve months ago, you ought to have seen it,' the barman said.

'That's the human characteristic – patience, building up.'

'You might say the same of ants.'

'Making from something nothing,' Richard said. 'I'll take another Pernod.'

The ringing sound of the trowel was in his ears. He saw plodding humanity piling up the bricks again, hanging sacking over the empty windows, temporizing, camping-out in the shadow of even greater disaster, raking ashes, the vision lost. He felt terribly sorry for humanity, as if he did not belong to it. The Pernod shifted him away and made him solitary. Then he thought of Louise and that he must go to look for her. Sometimes she punished him by staying away unaccountably, but knowing that did not lessen his anxiety. He wished that they were at peace together, that the war between them might be over for ever, for if he did not have her, he did not have all he had yearned for; steadied himself with, fighting in the jungle; holding fast, for her, to life; disavowing (with terrible concentration) any danger to her.

He wondered, watching the barman's placid polishing of another man's glasses, if they could begin again, he and Louise, with nothing, from scratch, abandoning the past.

'First I must find her,' he thought. His drinking would double her fury if she had been lingering to punish him, punishing herself with enforced idling in those unfestive streets; a little scared, he imagined; hesitantly casual.

She came as he was putting a foot unsteadily to the floor. She stood at the door with an unexpectant look. When he smiled and greeted her, she tried to give two different smiles at once – one for the barman to see (controlled, marital), the other less a smile than a negation of it ('I see nothing to smile about').

'Darling, what will you have?'

She surveyed the row of bottles hesitantly, but her hesitation was for the barman's benefit. Richard knew her pause meant an unwillingness to drink in such company, in such a mood, and that in a minute she would say 'A dry Martini,' because once he had told her she should not drink gin abroad. She sat down beside him in silence.

'A nice dry Martini?' he suddenly asked, thinking of the man with the trowel, the nun with the bread, the battered cathedral, everybody's poor start. Again she tried to convey two meanings; to the barman that she was casual about her Martini, to her husband that she was casual about him.

Richard's head was swimming. He patted his wife's knee.

'Did you get the postcards all right?'

'Of course.' Her glance brushed his hand off her knee. 'Cheers!' she held her glass at half-mast very briefly, spoke in the most annulling way, drank. Those deep lines from her nose to her mouth met the glass.

'Cheers, my darling!' he said, watching her. Her annoyance froze the silence.

Oh, from the most unpromising material, he thought, but he did seem to see some glimmer ahead, if only of his own patience, his own perseverance, which appeared, in this frame of mind, in this place, a small demand upon him.

Notes on the Authors

BERYL BAINBRIDGE was born in Liverpool in the 1930s and spent her early working years there as an actress in repertory. She took up writing after leaving the theatre to have a baby. Several of her macabre and often wildly funny novels, including *The Dressmaker* and *A Quiet Life*, are set against an unobtrusive but impeccably realised wartime or post-war background. 'Bread and Butter Smith' appeared in *Mum and Mrs Armitage* (1985). *The Dressmaker* and *The Bottle Factory Outing* were both runners-up for the Booker Prize, and *Injury Time* won the 1977 Whitbread award. She also writes for television.

A. L. BARKER has been writing since the age of nine. She worked in a City office after leaving school, and spent six months in the Land Army and three years working for the National Fire Service during the war before joining the BBC. *Innocents*, her first book of stories including 'The Iconoclasts', was published in 1947. She has since written three more collections, including *Life Stories*, in which stories are juxtaposed with fragments of autobiography as they shaped her writing. She has also written eight novels, the latest of which, *The Gooseboy*, was published in 1987. She is a brilliant and much under-rated short-story writer who can compact a shocking intensity into deceptively unassuming prose.

ELIZABETH BOWEN (1899–1973), one of this century's finest novelists and short-story writers, was born in Dublin but brought up in England; *Bowen's Court* (1942) recounts the history of her family and their home in County Cork. Her first book of short stories, *Encounters*, was published in 1923, the year of her marriage. The war years could justifiably be called the peak of her life; she was at the height of her writing powers, identified closely with England in crisis, and she was also deeply in love. She stayed on in London throughout the Blitz, working as an air-raid warden in between journalistic assignments and her 'Activities' for the Ministry of Information, which involved reporting on

Irish attitudes to the war. Her novel *The Heat of the Day* (1949), and collection of stories, *The Demon Lover* (1945), both written and set in wartime, are among the most memorable British fiction from this era. Her many other works include *The Death of the Heart* (1938) and *Look at All Those Roses* (stories, 1941).

KAY BOYLE (1902-) was born in Minnesota, and travelled to Europe in 1922. In Paris she became friends with a group of expatriate artists and began writing for avant-garde magazines. Her first novel *Plagued by the Nightingale* was published in 1930; since then she has written, edited and translated more than 30 books, including short stories, poetry and essays. In 1941 she left occupied France to return to America, but was back in Paris as correspondent for the *New Yorker* in 1945. She was awarded the 1941 O. Henry Memorial Prize for her story 'Defeat'.

ANN CHADWICK's story 'The Sailor's Wife' was published in *English Story* VI, edited by Woodrow Wyatt, in 1945.

EDNA FERBER (1887-1968), American novelist and playwright, a vivid and powerful storyteller in the traditional mould. The daughter of a Hungarian storekeeper, she started out as a journalist and went on to write a string of bestselling novels including *Showboat*, *Cimarron* and *Giant*, all later made into films, and several plays. Her central characters are strong pioneer women, dedicated to their families and the land; there is often an underlying anti-racial theme. 'Grandma Isn't Playing' was written in 1942 in response to the war, whose aftermath left her deeply disillusioned. She introduced the story as follows in her collection *One Basket*: 'Only during World War I and World War II have I ever written according to plan or theme ordered or suggested by someone else ... In "Grandma Isn't Playing", one can detect ... the somewhat heavy tool of propaganda. A necessary and an important wartime weapon, but often unwieldy in unaccustomed hands.'

PAT FRANK's story 'The Bomb' appeared in the *Strand Magazine*, 1941.

DIANA GARDNER (1913-) was the youngest of three, with two brothers; her mother died when she was nine. She became a dedicated short-story writer from the age of 11, and her work appeared in nearly every literary review, including *Horizon*, during the Second World War. In 1947 Tambimuttu of Poetry London Editions published a collection of her stories *Halfway Down the Cliff*, and her novel *The Indian Woman*, based on one of her stories, was published in 1953. She also studied art, and has given six one-person shows of her water-colours in London and four out of town.

INEZ HOLDEN, journalist and writer, was a contributor to various periodicals during and after the war. She was a Special Correspondent in Germany just after the war, covered the Nuremberg Trials, the Slanksy Tribunal and other events, and wrote two books about her experiences during the war in an aircraft factory and a Royal Ordnance Factory. Perhaps her best-known novel is *The Owner* (1952). She was a close friend of Stevie Smith, and each based fictional characters on the other – Inez appears as Lopez in Stevie Smith's third novel *The Holiday* and 'The Story of a Story' (see under Stevie Smith), while Inez Holden's character Felicity strongly resembles Stevie Smith in the fictionalised diary *It Was Different at the Time*.

ANNA KAVAN (1901–68), née Helen Ferguson, was born of English parents in France; she wrote several conventional novels under this name in the 1920s and 30s. She took the name of Anna Kavan by deed poll, and after a breakdown and treatment in a mental hospital wrote the remarkable series of sketches *Asylum Piece* (1940). During the war she worked on *Horizon*, and 'Face of My People' is one of several stories in *I Am Lazarus* (1945) which first appeared in the magazine. The rich, strange, visionary qualities of her writing – notably in *Ice*, a novel, and *Julia and the Bazooka*, posthumously published stories – have given her a cult following. She was a heroin addict for over 30 years, and died in London holding her 'bazooka' – a plastic syringe.

MOLLY LEFEBURE was born in London; her studies at London University were interrupted by war, and she became a reporter in East London and the first regular woman police-court reporter. She was then taken on as secretary to Home Office pathologist Keith Simpson and spent most of the war working with him in public mortuaries (another first, if not an enviable one, for a woman); she wrote an account of this work in *Evidence For the Crown* (1954). She married at the end of the war, and had two children. After working for 15 years with the GLC youth service she took to full-time writing; her books include lives of Samuel Taylor Coleridge and Sara Coleridge. Her new war novel *Blitz!* (1988) is based on 'Night in the Front Line'.

ROSAMOND LEHMANN (1901–), novelist and short-story writer, was born in Buckinghamshire and studied at Girton, Cambridge. Her first novel *Dusty Answer* caused a sensation when it was first published in 1927; it was followed by *A Note in Music*, then by *Invitation to the Waltz* and its sequel *The Weather in the Streets*, all written during the thirties, which established her as a leading novelist of her generation. Her finest achievement, *The Echoing Grove*, appeared in 1953. She is a writer of great subtlety and sensitivity, outstandingly perceptive on the pains of women in love. During the war her brother, John Lehmann, persuaded her to write stories for *Penguin New Writing*, which he edited; 'When the Waters Came' was among them. They were collected in *The Gipsy's Baby* (1946).

DORIS LESSING (1919–) was born of British parents in Iran; the family emigrated to a farm in Rhodesia when she was five. She came to England in 1949 with the manuscript of her first novel, *The Grass Is Singing*; it was published in 1950, and became an international success. It was followed by a succession of novels and stories, the former including the five-volume *Children of Violence* series, *The Golden Notebook, Memoirs of a Survivor* and recently a series of five futuristic novels, *Canopus in Argos: Archives* (1979–83) *The Good Terrorist* (1986) and *The Fifth Child* (1988). Her stories about Africa are collected in *This Was the Old Chief's Country* and *The Sun Beneath Their Feet;* other collections include *To Room 19* and *The Temptation of Jack Orkney*. The earlier writing is fuelled by her political commitment; moral conviction and an almost ruthless honesty and directness characterise all her work.

ROSE MACAULAY (1881–1958) lived in Italy for seven years as a child and never lost her thirst for travel. She studied history at Oxford and subsequently produced a steady flow of novels, poetry and non-fiction which won her high literary standing, although her prevailing dry, satirical tone is less popular today. Among her best novels are the historical *They Were Defeated* (1932), and *The World My Wilderness* (1950), set in post-war London and France. She was created a Dame Commander of the British Empire in 1958, shortly before her death. The war years were deeply troubled for her personally. In 1939 her married lover was seriously injured in a car crash while she was driving. 'Miss Anstruther's Letters' was written when he was dying of cancer in 1942, shortly after her flat and all her possessions were destroyed in an air raid. She wrote few short stories; this outstanding exception, which she described as 'unoriginal, but veracious (mainly)', was written at the request of Storm Jameson for *London Calling*, an anthology of British writing for American publication after the US entered the war.

OLIVIA MANNING (1908–80) was the daughter of a naval officer and an Irish mother; born in Portsmouth, she came to London in her early twenties after an art-school training. Her first novel, *The Wind Changes*, was published in 1937. The war years were the subject of much of her later fiction, including her two best-known works, the *Balkan Trilogy* and *Levant Trilogy*. Just before war was declared she married R. D. Smith, a British Council lecturer (her friend Stevie Smith was a bridesmaid) and went with him to Bucharest; they went on to Greece, to

be evacuated to Egypt as the Nazis moved in. From 1941-5 she worked in
Jerusalem at the Public Information Office and for the British Council.
The death of her brother at sea in 1941 was a source of lasting grief.
After the war she moved back to London. As well as twelve novels she
wrote two collections of short stories, *Growing Up* (1948) from which 'A
Journey' is taken, and *A Romantic Hero* (1967). 'A Journey' is
characteristic of her comment that 'My subject is simply life as I have
experienced it, and I am happiest when I am writing of things I know.'

ROSAMOND OPPERSDORFF was an American by birth who until the
war lived most of her life in Paris. Her husband was Polish, and after
leaving France in 1940 she worked in a Polish military hospital in
Scotland. 'I was Too Ignorant' was published in *New Writing and
Daylight*, edited by John Lehmann, in 1942.

MOLLIE PANTER-DOWNES (1906-), Anglo-Irish writer whose first
novel was published when she was 18. She wrote four more, but refers to
One Fine Day (1947) as 'her only novel'. Certainly it is a fine achievement: a subtly evocative picture of an ordinary middle-class household
coming to terms with post-war life made shabbier, harder, yet imbued
with quiet optimism. She describes herself first and foremost as a
reporter; she was the London correspondent for the *New Yorker* for
some 40 years from 1939, and her wartime 'Letters from London',
collected in *Letters from England* for American publication, enjoyed a
success similar to Jan Struther's *Mrs Miniver*. 'Goodbye, My Love'
appeared in the *New Yorker* in 1941.

DOROTHY PARKER (1893-1967): born Dorothy Rothschild in West
End, New Jersey. Her bittersweet verse and stories, collected in *The
Portable Dorothy Parker* in 1944, evoked the bright, brittle,
wisecracking pre-war era which had brought her fame as a contributor to
Vogue, Vanity Fair and the *New Yorker* and as a central figure of the
celebrated Algonquin Hotel Round Table. 'The Lovely Leave' was one
of the last stories she wrote; it appeared in 1943, and is cruelly apposite in
the light of her own experience. Her first husband, Edwin Parker, was
posted overseas in the First World War and they divorced after years of
separation; her second marriage to Alan Campbell was also a war
casualty (though they remarried in 1950).

BARBARA PYM (1913-80) was born in Oswestry, Shropshire and
educated at St Hilda's, Oxford. During the war she served in the WRNS
in Britain and Naples. Her first novel, *Some Tame Gazelle*, was
published in 1950, followed by four others within the next decade. After
her publishers turned down her seventh novel she had nothing published

for 16 years, until the *Times Literary Supplement* asked selected critics to nominate the most underrated writer of the past 75 years. She was the only author to be mentioned twice – notably by Philip Larkin. A new book, *Quartet in Autumn*, was accepted for publication; she took up writing again, and two more novels followed, the last published posthumously. 'Goodbye Balkan Capital' first appeared in 1988.

JEAN RHYS (1894–1979) was born Gwendolyn Williams, in Dominica. She was sent to England at 16, and ran away from drama school to join the chorus line in a touring theatre production. Her first book of stories, *The Left Bank* (1927), written in Paris after the break-up of her first marriage, was followed by four novels in the next decade, all with a similar tough-talking yet intensely vulnerable heroine. Their passivity is old-fashioned, but the cool, laconic treatment is entirely modern. The Second World War, for her, 'smashed everything'; she had lost touch with her daughter in Holland, and her second husband had joined the air force, leaving her alone. 'I Spy a Stranger' is one of several stories from this time describing nervous breakdown. With the failure of *Good Morning, Midnight* (1939) her work went out of print and it was only after nearly 20 reclusive years that she was 'rediscovered' and her last, best-known novel, *Wide Sargasso Sea*, published. A third book of stories, *Sleep It Off Lady*, was published in 1976.

MARGERY SHARP (1905–), English novelist, playwright and short-story writer, popular in 1930s Britain and America for her light comedies with ingenious plots. After the success of *The Nutmeg Tree* (1937), her cheerfully loose-living heroine Julia Packett enjoyed further adventures in the *Saturday Evening Post*. 'Night Engagement' was written for the wartime magazine *Lilliput* (1941).

STEVIE SMITH (1902–71) was born in Hull; when she was three her mother brought her and her sister to live with her aunt in Palmer's Green, North London, where she stayed for the rest of her life. She wrote three novels: *Novel on Yellow Paper* (1936), *Over the Frontier* (1938) and *The Holiday* (1949), and nine volumes of poetry – all imbued with her idiosyncratic blend of graveyard humour, pathos and childlike directness. By the 1950s she was much in demand for live performances, reading and singing her poems to her own music. 'Sunday at Home' caused a permanent breach between Stevie (who appears in the story as 'Greta') and the married friends on whom she based the main characters, even after she changed the title from its original and more pointed 'Enemy Action'. It was broadcast on radio in 1949. After the falling-out she wrote an account of the difficulties of making 'these transcripts from life' in 'The Story of a Story'.

JEAN STAFFORD (1916–79) was brought up in Colorado, the daughter of a Western writer and a nurse. In 1936 she won a travelling scholarship to Heidelberg, and on her return to America settled on the East Coast. In 1940 she married the poet Robert Lowell, against the wishes of his patrician Boston family; the theme of the misfit in urbane establishment society recurs in her fiction. Her first novel, *Boston Adventure*, was published in 1944, and became a bestseller; at the same time her marriage became a disastrous private battleground, and she and Lowell were divorced in 1950. She married twice more, the third time to the journalist and critic A.J. Liebling. Her later novels, *The Mountain Lion* and *The Catherine Wheel*, were less popular than the first and she switched to writing her stylish, elaborately crafted short stories many of which, including 'The Maiden', first appeared in the *New Yorker*. Her *Collected Stories* won the Pulitzer Prize in 1970.

JAN STRUTHER (1901–53), pen-name of Joyce Anstruther, later Joyce Maxtone Graham – she took the pseudonym because both her mother and mother-in-law were writers. In the 1930s her mainly humorous articles and light verse were published in *Punch, The Spectator* and other magazines. The *Mrs Miniver* sketches based on her own family life first appeared weekly in *The Times* in 1938–9, and the book became a bestseller. Mrs Miniver's patriotic sentiments notwithstanding, Jan Struther was criticised in Britain for her departure to America with her two younger children soon after war was declared; she stayed there for the duration.

ELIZABETH TAYLOR (1912–75): her subtle and delicate craft, and the small worlds she chose to portray, belie the work of a major artist. She was born Elizabeth Coles in Reading, Berkshire; the daughter of an insurance inspector, she worked as a governess and in a library before marrying at 24. She wrote her first novel, *At Mrs Lippincote's* (1945), while her husband was in the air force during the war; eleven more novels followed, the last published posthumously. Her stories appeared in leading magazines including the *New Yorker* and the *Saturday Evening Post*, and were collected in four volumes: *Hester Lilly and Other Stories* (1954) (from which 'Gravemont Endommagé' is taken), *The Blush and Other Stories* 1958), *A Dedicated Man and Other Stories* (1965) and *The Devastating Boys* (1972).

SYLVIA TOWNSEND WARNER (1893–1978) had no formal education, though she was the daughter of a housemaster at Harrow school. After working in a munitions factory in the First World War she spent ten years as an editor on a ten-volume project, *Tudor Church Music*, for Oxford University Press. The success of her first novel *Lolly Willowes*

(1926) encouraged her to take up full-time writing. During the 1930s she became active in politics in response to events in Spain and Nazi Germany, and in 1937 she worked briefly for the Red Cross Bureau in Barcelona. Her writing was by then known in the United States as well as Britain, and many of her stories first appeared in the *New Yorker*. She was in New York for a writers' conference when war was declared, but returned to England soon afterwards. After the war she added an acclaimed biography of T. H. White to her novels, stories, journalism and poetry. Two of her eight short story collections, *A Garland of Straw* (1943) and *The Museum of Cheats* (1947), are full of witty, compassionate glimpses into wartime life.

MALACHI WHITAKER (1895–1975) – 'the Bradford Chekhov', as one critic called her – made her name with four books of stories, all published before the Second World War, and then declared herself 'written out'. Born Marjorie Olive Taylor, she left school early to work in her father's bookbinding business, and married a Yorkshire businessman. She was a self-taught writer, and wrote prolifically as a child, throwing everything away. Under the pen-name of Malachi Whitaker she sent a story to Middleton Murry at the *Adelphi*, a magazine she had admired in the public library. He printed her stories, and her first collection was published to literary acclaim in 1929. The vivid, spare, unsentimental stories are perfectly matched to her first subject, the people and landscapes of her native Yorkshire.